★ GO-for-GOLD ★
GYMNASTS

Book One
Winning Team

Book Two
Balancing Act

by **DOMINIQUE MOCEANU**
and **ALICIA THOMPSON**

Disney • HYPERION
Los Angeles   New York

Winning Team and *Balancing Act* copyright © 2012 by Dominique Moceanu and Alicia Thompson
Introduction copyright © 2016 by Simone Biles

Printed in the United States of America

Winning Team and *Balancing Act* First Paperback Editions, April 2012

First Bind-Up Edition, June 2016

10 9 8 7 6 5 4 3 2 1

FAC-025438-16072

Library of Congress Control Number for *Winning Team*: 2011023718

Library of Congress Control Number for *Balancing Act*: 2011023747

Designed by Tyler Nevins
Text is set in 13-point Minion Pro.
ISBN 978-1-4847-7178-5
Visit www.DisneyBooks.com

Introduction

Dominique **Moceanu** has always been one of my biggest role models, and over the past few years we've become friends. She's a really great mentor, always texting me before competitions, and it's amazing to know that I have her support since she has been through the same things I have. She's like my gym mom, so I was really excited to be asked to participate in her Go-for-Gold Gymnasts series!

As you read these books, you'll see Brittany, Noelle, Christina, and Jessie beginning their Elite careers. They go through many things that I can relate to, like moving to a new gym, transitioning to a higher level, and dealing with big expectations. Since I know many of you readers might be gymnasts yourselves, or fans of the sport, I thought I'd share a little bit about how I've handled these same hurdles during my time in gymnastics.

During my first year as a National Team member, I became the World All-Around Champion! But when my coach decided to leave the gym I had grown up in, I knew I needed to follow her. Like it is for Brittany, going to a new gym was challenging. Leaving my teammates was especially heartbreaking since my gym was like a family, but over time things got better. Meeting new teammates and training in new places can be intimidating, but I grew to look at these experiences as fun and positive new challenges. Though adjusting to unfamiliar surroundings can be hard, a new coach can provide the opportunity for a fresh perspective, and new teammates give you a bigger gym family. What's better than that?

I've been able to enjoy an amazing gymnastics career so far, and I'm so thankful for all that my family has done. They always make sure I have everything I need to compete at my best. When you read Noelle's story, you will see how much pressure she feels since she knows her family makes sacrifices for her gymnastics. I always tell people to try not to stress too much, even though that's hard to do! Competing should be fun—no matter the outcome. To me, doing my best at competitions is a way to give back to my family and fans for all they've done for me. Your family and friends might make sacrifices to support you, but they love watching you perform, so go out there and enjoy it!

This is advice that I think Dominique would second. I can be so hard on myself, but she always reminds me that gymnastics isn't everything; there will be other things I care about in my future—so try to embrace the moment! I hope you enjoy reading about Brittany, Noelle, and the other Texas Twisters as much as I did as they celebrate their own time in the spotlight.

—Simone Biles
Three-Time World All-Around Champion

★ GO-for-GOLD ★
GYMNASTS

Book One
Winning Team

Gymnastics fans past, present, and future,
I dedicate this book to you. Your devotion is
the most essential part of our sport. I have
only the greatest affection for you.
—D.M.

For my sister, Brittany Lee, who inspires me
—A.T.

One

It was late, and my parents and I had been driving through the same state for four hours. I just wanted to go home—well, to my *new* home, which I'd only seen in pictures—but my mom insisted on driving past the gym first.

"After all," she said, turning toward the backseat to smile at me, "it'll practically be your home away from home, right?"

"I guess."

"Aren't you excited? This is such a wonderful opportunity for you." I realized she was waiting for me to smile in return, and so I did, figuring that her neck would probably hurt if she kept her head in that position for too long. Satisfied, she beamed at me and turned back to face the front.

When my parents told me we were moving to Austin, Texas, so I could train with an Elite team, "excited" was certainly not what I felt. It was like everything happened in slow motion—first I heard *moving*, and I thought about everyone I would have to leave behind and my bedroom with the window facing my neighbor's birdbath and the fact that next year for my birthday we were going to play paintball, and I felt sad. Then I heard *Texas*, and I remembered this boy at my gym who used to wear a shirt that said, DON'T MESS WITH TEXAS! in huge letters, and I was scared at the idea of moving to a state that seemed to be all about picking fights for no apparent reason. Ohio doesn't care if you mess with it or not. I mean, obviously it would prefer that you didn't, but if you do, no big deal.

Team, though—that was a little exciting. I used to wish for a teammate. My best friend at my old gym, Dionne, was good, but it would be at least a couple of years before she qualified as Elite, and in the meantime we were split up when it came time to work on specific moves in our routines. With teammates, however, everything would be different. We'd get together in the locker room and say, *Hey, what was up with Coach today? Mood swings much?* At competitions, we'd wear matching French braids and make up silly cheers to spur each other on. During practice, we'd push each other to be better than we'd ever thought possible. I could see it all, running through my head like credits for a sitcom on the Disney Channel as we chalked up the bars for each other and playfully wiped some of the chalk on each other's nose.

When we finally pulled up to the gym, though, it didn't look like the place I'd imagined. For one thing, it was totally deserted. That made sense, considering there aren't too many gymnasts who train at eleven o'clock at night, but it still gave it this really creepy vibe, like it was a ghost town.

"Wow, it's big, huh? Can you believe you'll be training here?" my mom said as my dad parked the truck by the curb. "Come on, let's just take a peek inside."

It wasn't just big. It was *gigantic.* From the outside, it looked like an airplane hangar, or the world's largest indoor flea market or something. Weird, when you think that most of the people who trained there were probably under five feet tall. And when we pressed our faces up against the glass and peered inside, it looked as if it stretched on forever, a wide-open desert with shadows of beams and bars instead of cactuses.

Behind us, I could hear the truck idling as my dad waited for us inside.

I traced the raised letters of the sign on the front door with my fingers: TEXAS TWISTERS: HOME OF STATE BEAM CHAMPION NOELLE ONESTI!

Back in Ohio, my gym had been attached to the Aquatic Center. People would walk into the reception area and go, "Wait a sec, those are *leotards,* not bathing suits. . . ." and then the receptionist would explain that, yeah, the big building wasn't just an indoor pool, it actually had a whole separate gymnastics facility as well. When I made the Elite team, months ago, they put a congratulations message up on the marquee outside for two days, but then they took it down to make room to wish Mrs. G. a happy seventeenth anniversary as office manager.

"Well?" my mom said now. "What do you think?"

All I could think was that it was way cooler to announce a state beam champion than someone who'd just made the team, and how raised letters seemed pretty permanent, while the crappy plastic ones they put on the marquee at my old gym kept falling off so it read CONGRA S instead of CONGRATS. Rather than French-braiding each other's hair, we'd be competing for titles and medals, and it looked like the girls here were way ahead of me on that score.

Yeah, all of a sudden, the whole team thing didn't seem so exciting.

My mom was smiling at me again, and I forced myself to smile back. "It's awesome," I said. "When do I start?"

I started a couple of days later, once we'd had the chance to settle into our new house, which was one story high and smelled a little of stale smoke, although my mom said it was nothing a little Lysol wouldn't take care of. So now, it smells like stale smoke and Lysol.

"Oh, sugar," she said to me as we pulled up to the gym, this time in daylight. It wasn't said as an endearment, since my mom's not big on those. It was simply what she said when she wanted to say something else, but had to watch her language.

"What?" I asked.

"No, nothing," she said, giving me a hasty smile. "It's just that I forgot I was supposed to go in early this morning to meet the furniture delivery guys— we're getting a couple new rockers for the infant room. And there was a mom who wanted to talk to me about moving her son to the three-year-old group. I keep telling her we can't do that until he can use the big-boy potty, but you know how moms can be."

"Oh." I knew how *my* mom could be. She managed a day care center, and her job was the most important thing in the world to her. She had been wheeling and dealing on her cell phone the whole car ride down, and even though we've been in the South for less than seventy-two hours, she'd already spent a lot of them at the day care, making sure the transition was smooth.

"So . . . I take it you're not going to stay for the whole practice," I said.

She gave me another stressed-out smile. "Sorry, Britt. Maybe once I'm settled in at the day care, I can come watch you. You ready to go inside?"

"I guess," I said.

In the gym, everything was very white, and with

the harsh sunlight coming through the windows, it all looked bigger than it had in the shadows. The ceiling was high enough in this gym that there was no danger of the rhythmic girls throwing their hoops in the air and hitting it. That used to happen all the time at my old gym. The little kids couldn't throw their hoops hard enough for it to matter, but the competitive rhythmic girls would have to chase after the hoop when it bounced off the ceiling and went flying across the gym.

Rhythmic gymnasts used props like balls and ribbons and clubs as part of their routines, which consisted of more dancing and leaping and fewer tumbling skills. Of course, the brochure that I had found on my mom's nightstand said that this place didn't offer rhythmic classes. So all that extra ceiling height was a total waste.

The brochure also had biographies of the coaches, a couple who had emigrated from China, and featured a glossy picture of a very beautiful girl standing on one tanned leg, the other curved behind her until her toes almost brushed her dark ponytail. Was that the famous beam champion Noelle? Or was it just a model hired to look like a gymnast?

My mom headed straight for the front desk, which was over by the pro shop. At least this was familiar. Gyms *always* have pro shops, and they're inevitably right by the front desk, so that while parents are filling out boring paperwork, kids can roam around and decide which things they want to put on their gift wish lists. If I weren't so distracted right now, I could probably convince my mom to get me a three-pack of sparkly scrunchies.

There were three pillars dividing the front area from the gym, where I could see girls practicing on the beams (there were *twelve* beams—totally excessive!). I wanted to check the girls out, but my mom was beckoning to me.

"I'm Mrs. Morgan, and this is my daughter, Brittany," she said to the woman at the desk, placing her arm around me to draw me closer. "I believe we spoke on the phone? I faxed over the final enrollment paperwork yesterday."

The woman's name tag said MELANIE, and she was all business. "Level?" she asked, looking at me over the rims of her glasses.

She probably thought I was a Level Seven or something, since I'm so short. I'm twelve years old, but I look nine. You know you've got serious issues when you're a gymnast and you're *still* considered tiny. "I'm a Junior Elite," I said quickly.

"I see," she said. "Well, your group is just finishing up on the beam. You'll have to do some stretches first, of course, but would you like to join them now?"

I shrugged. "Sure, why not?"

"Mrs. Morgan, you're welcome to stay. We have a comfortable viewing area for the parents, and a full concession stand with snacks and drinks available."

I glanced at my mom, looking for some sign that she was at least *tempted*. That she was considering watching me practice, even for a second. It wasn't that she was a bad mother. She made sure I ate breakfast every morning, and on the weekends sometimes we would do something fun, like go to the aquarium or the mall. It's just, you know how little kids are always calling out to their moms when they're in the pool, or on top of the jungle gym? *Look at me! Mom, look!* I saw her glance at her watch, obviously worried about getting back to Ben and the big-boy potty, and wondered when she had stopped *looking*. She used to cheer when I did somersaults in the living room, but she hadn't even come to my last competition, because it was Parents' Night Out at the day care.

"Don't worry," I said to her before she could answer. "I'll be fine. And if I fall and break my neck, they have your info, right? So they'll call you."

"Britt, don't even joke about something like that," my mom said, giving a little laugh like, *Kids say the darnedest things, don't they?* "But I do have to get going. You behave yourself, okay? I'll be back to pick you up after practice."

"On time," I said. My mom had a habit of being late to *everything*. Her autobiography could have been titled *I'm on My Way: The Pamela Morgan Story*, because she's always saying she's "on the way" when in fact she's just about to jump into the shower, or she's still putting on her makeup.

"I'll do my best. But if I'm not here by then—" She dug through her purse, which was this huge lumpy designer thing that was like an abyss for receipts, credit cards, and cell phones. Finally, she pulled out a ten-dollar bill and handed it to me. "Just buy yourself a snack, all right?"

"Fine."

She tugged on my short blond ponytail and gave me a smile. She thinks it's the greatest thing that I'm a natural blonde, because she's not—she goes to the salon once a month to get her color touched up. She says by the time I'm her age, my hair will have turned a light brown, too, and that I'll be "pleased as punch" if and when I have a blond daughter who'll match my dye job and make it look natural. I'm not even kidding—she actually thinks about things like that.

Once she was gone, Melanie stood up to lead me toward the Excessive Beams. She nodded at my duffel bag, which had the name of my old gym, Loveland Gymnastics, emblazoned across the side. "Do you have a leo in there, or . . ."

I unzipped my hoodie, showing a shiny blue leotard underneath. "A girl's always gotta be prepared, right?"

She laughed. Now that my mom was gone, she didn't seem so uptight. "Very true. And your name is Brittany?"

"You can call me Britt," I said.

There were three girls practicing on the beams, and as we walked up, one of them did a perfect punch front tuck, landing squarely on the four-inch-wide balance beam. I do a back tuck in my routine, but it's not nearly as hard-core—you can see the beam as you come down, so it's easier to land. The punch front has a completely blind landing.

There was the Chinese woman I recognized from the brochure—the head coach, Mo Li—directing another girl, who was practicing full turns. "Keep your eyes focused ahead," Mo kept saying. "Look at one spot on wall. Are you looking at one spot?"

Full Turn Girl spun around once more and wobbled slightly. "I'm trying," she mumbled. I don't know if the coach heard her, but I did.

Maybe later, I thought, I could start up a conversation with Full Turn Girl. "Hey," I would say casually while we were at the fountain filling up our water bottles. "I totally feel you on the full-turn thing. I mean, 'do a complete three-sixty but keep your eyes on one spot?' How is that even possible?"

It was a start, but I'd have to make it funnier. "Did you ever see that movie where the girl gets possessed or whatever? My mom wouldn't let me watch it, but once I came downstairs to get a Coke and I saw the girl's head spinning all the way around. I bet you *she* could do that full turn, no problem!"

It would really have helped if I'd remembered the name of that movie, or if I'd seen more of it.

Maybe I'd just pretend I had seen the whole thing. Then Full Turn Girl wouldn't think I was a baby.

On the third beam, a tall girl with a long, curly ponytail executed a flawless full turn. I recognized her instantly: Brochure Girl. She was even more gorgeous than she'd looked in the picture, and I was suddenly very conscious of my small, pale legs and the way my too-short ponytail jutted out from my head instead of cascading down my back.

"Mo," Melanie said, trying to get the coach's attention, "this is Britt. She's the Junior Elite from Ohio."

Mo looked me over with sharp eyes, from my flip-flops with my bright pink toenails peeping out to the top of my white-blond head. "No gum," she said.

I'd played this scene in my head several times on the drive over and imagined many two-word introductions. *Hello, Britt,* maybe, or *Oh, fantastic!* or even *You're just the gymnast we've been waiting for!*—which is more than two words, but still. I hadn't really considered the idea that the first words my new coach would say to me might be *No gum.*

But I wanted to show her that I was serious, so I

swallowed it whole, making an exaggerated gulping sound, then smiled. "No gum," I agreed.

From her position high up on one of the beams, Brochure Girl rolled her eyes.

"I introduce you," Mo said. "Britt, these are your new teammates: Jessie, Noelle, and Christina."

Noelle was the one with the awesome punch front, so it made sense that she was the state beam champion. She had the perfect body for a gymnast, too—she was small and compact, like me, but *she* didn't look nine. Although she smiled at me when I looked at her, her brown eyes were very serious, and I knew she was going to be competition.

That's okay, though. I like a challenge.

Brochure Girl was Christina. She was slim, and supertall—for a gymnast, anyway. It'd be a while before I could even *dream* of being five feet tall, so anyone who came close seemed like a giant to me. She also didn't look very friendly. Maybe her ponytail was too tight.

The girl who'd been struggling with the full turn was Jessie. She gave me a little wave, and I waved back. Suddenly the friendly conversation I'd imagined with her by the water fountain didn't seem so impossible.

I wriggled out of my pants, shoving them into my bag with my hoodie, and started to climb up onto one of the beams, but Mo shook her head. "We move to floor, but stretch first."

Mo quickly listed the succession of stretches she wanted us to do before walking over to talk to someone at the front desk. I didn't catch the exact order, but I figured I could just follow what everyone else was doing. Jessie took a spot on the floor next to me, and Noelle and Christina faced us, stretching out into a straddle position. This was my first chance to speak to them, and I tried to think of something to say. Something clever, preferably. Something that would make them think, Man, that new girl's all right.

"So," I said. "Is it all work and no play here, or what?"

Christina snorted. "It's an *Elite* gym," she said. "What did you expect? For us to take turns jumping on the trampoline?"

"No, that's not—" I tried to think of a better way to phrase it. "I mean, I was training Elite back in Ohio, too. I just meant . . ."

"Lay off, Christina," Jessie said, her voice muffled as she reached to touch her toes. She lifted her head, looking at me. "How long have you been in gymnastics?"

"I started when I was three," I said. "My mom says I was always doing somersaults and rolling off the couch, and she started to worry about me cracking my head open."

"That would explain a lot," Christina muttered.

I was kind of stunned by Christina's open animosity, and I couldn't formulate a decent comeback. I was grateful when Mo finally called us to line up at the corners of the forty square feet of blue carpet we called "the floor."

"Tumbling passes!" she said. "Warm up."

For several minutes, we took turns flipping across the floor. They weren't the passes we were actually going to do in competition or anything, just easy stuff, like handsprings and layouts, which are basically just flips with or without hands. No twists, no extra flips, nothing fancy. It got us ready for our big moves, and for me, it had the added benefit of getting me used to the floor.

Every floor mat is slightly different. This is weird, because they're regulation size and made out of the same materials, but each one has a different feeling under your feet. Like, the one at my old gym was a little spongier than this one, somehow. Even though I knew that the carpet was probably bought from the exact same place, the one at my old gym used to feel like you could sink your toes in it if you pressed down hard enough. This new floor felt nothing like that. It was like linoleum—flat and hard, but with springs underneath it, of course.

"Okay," Mo said, after telling me my legs had come apart as I did back handsprings. (This was not the first time I'd heard that, believe me. So far, the only solution I could think of was to superglue my ankles together. For this year's state competition, maybe I would try it.) "Jessie, you stay on floor to do combo pass. Other girls, to the pit."

The pit is the reason I am in love with gymnastics. Seriously, I want to marry it. The pit is where you get to do crazy tricks and land on an eight-inch-thick foam mat, and you don't have to worry as much about hurting yourself. If you're trying something really new, you get to do it and land in a pit filled with loose foam, which is like flipping into marshmallows, only less sticky. My old coach used to spot me on a triple tucked somersault in the loose foam pit, even though I probably never would've been able to do it on the actual floor. I hoped Mo was that cool.

I lined up behind Noelle and Jessie at the pit and glanced at Mo. "What should I do?" I asked.

"What *can* you do?"

I shrugged.

"Show me," Mo said.

Noelle did a back double pike into the pit, her body folded in half and rotating two complete times in the air. Then Christina turned out a double twist that was pretty good, I had to admit (when I did twists, I had a tendency to overdo them; at one competition back in Ohio, I just kept spinning like a cyclone, even when my feet had already hit the mat. I lost a few tenths of a point for stepping out of bounds on that one).

Then it came to me. All the other girls were lined up by the mirror on the wall, and they stared straight at me as I took a deep breath and prepared for my pass. I could feel Mo's eyes on me, too, and I knew this was big. I had to impress her. I had to impress *them*.

Technically, I hadn't done gymnastics in a week—I mean, other than some aerials in our brand-new front yard (which had a huge cactus in the middle of it—*not* good if your flipping gets a little wonky, like mine does sometimes), and I walked around the house on my hands until my mom told me to quit, but that was all. I knew I probably should play it safe on this first pass, and ease myself into it.

But that just wasn't my style. Instead, I ran as fast as I could, my arms pumping as my instincts took over, and then I was leaping into a round-off to a back handspring. I could feel the momentum in my body, and I knew I would pull it through before my feet even left the ground: a full-twisting double somersault.

I could've piked it to make it a little harder; it would've been the same move that Noelle had done, but with a twist added to make it interesting. But instead, I tucked my legs up close to my chest, just to be sure I could make it all the way around. I landed in the pit with room to spare, so I knew I would've rocked it if we'd been on the actual floor. As I sank into the soft foam, I threw my hands up in a salute, even though this wasn't a competition and there were no judges.

At least, not the kind who give you scores. I

heard light applause from Mo's direction. "Not bad," she said.

Just then, Christina burst into tears and ran for the locker room. Noelle shot me a look before heading after her.

I glanced at Jessie over on the floor.

"What?" I asked. "What'd I do?"

Jessie bit her lip, and her green eyes looked worried. "Christina's been trying to do that move for months," she said. "She can do it with a spot, but without one . . . she wipes out every time."

Later, I came up with about fifteen appropriate responses to that, like: *Oh, I'm sorry to hear that* and *Maybe I can help her.* But for some reason, my channel-surfing brain garbled the message, and I ended up blurting out a snarky line from one of the reality shows my mom liked to watch when she came home from work. "If you can't stand the heat," I said, "get out of the kitchen."

When the head chef on the reality show declared that exact same thing, all the contestants had laughed. But Jessie wasn't laughing, and I wondered how I was supposed to land on my feet when I always had one firmly planted in my mouth?

Two

Mo gave us a five-minute break, and Jessie joined the other girls in the locker room. Mo said it would be a good time for me to claim a locker and put my stuff away.

I really didn't want to go in there. I mean, I *wanted* to say something to Christina, but what? I barely understood what I'd done, much less how to fix it.

Then again, I felt kind of stupid hanging out all by myself. I inched over to the water fountain, but there was only so long I could pretend to gulp down the frigid water. I didn't *really* want to drink a lot, because then it would have sloshed around in my stomach for the rest of practice, and I hated that.

I thought about working on my leaps on the floor; my last coach had always been telling me I could use some serious improvement in that area. Don't get me wrong, I could jump super high, and getting at least a 180-degree split was absolutely no problem. But it was the whole too-much-energy thing again. Sometimes, I had trouble controlling my leaps and connecting them to other dance elements, which meant I lost valuable bonus points from my score.

But then I started imagining all the things they might be saying in there behind my back, and so I crossed over to the locker room and pushed the door open. Like the rest of the gym, it was state-of-the-art, with lockers that actually looked as if they'd been painted in this century. At Loveland, my old gym, I'd chipped almost all the orange paint off the front of my locker. If I'd stayed there for another month or two, I probably could've gotten the whole thing down to the metal.

"—big deal," Noelle was saying. "She's just a kid."

So, they *had* been talking about me. "Hey, guys," I said.

You know that phrase *If looks could kill*? Yeah, so did Christina, apparently. She was glaring at me with her dark eyes, her expression intensified by the sheen of tears.

Noelle and Jessie just looked uncomfortable. I decided to try to make amends. "Look, Christina, I'm sorry if—"

"How *old* are you, anyway?" Christina asked.

"I'm twelve," I said. At least that would make it better, right? That I wasn't some kind of wonder kid?

Although I did kind of like the idea of being a wonder kid.

"You're *twelve*?" Noelle said. "So am I. When will you be thirteen?"

"Next February." My birthday had just passed, so I hadn't been twelve for very long.

"I'll be thirteen in December," Noelle said.

"Cool," I said, turning to Christina and Jessie. "How old are you guys?"

"I'm fourteen," Jessie said, cautiously adding, "Christina is thirteen."

Christina just rolled her eyes.

I wondered if I should try to apologize again. "Hey," I said. "I'm really sorry that I upset you, with my full-in, I mean."

Sometimes gymnastics can be kind of confusing. If you do a double flip with a full twist on the first flip, you call it a full-in. If it's on the second flip, it's a full-out. And if you split the twist evenly between both flips, it's a half-in, half-out.

Maybe that explained why I was so good at math—even doing a floor routine could be like a word problem.

Christina stood up, and I remembered how much taller than me she was—I only came up to her chest.

Noelle picked at some dry skin on her hand (one of the many side effects of being a gymnast, unfortunately—all that chalk that we use makes our hands like parchment), acting as if she didn't even notice the tension between Christina and me. But Jessie's eyes darted between the two of us.

"Come on, Christina," Jessie said. "You know she didn't mean anything by it. So she can do a move that you can't; big deal. Maybe she could teach it to you, ever think of that? Then you could finally make the Elite team."

"Wait," I said. "You're not an Elite yet?"

Christina put her hands on her hips. "I practically am," she insisted. "I train with the Elite squad, don't I? I just haven't gotten the scores at a competition to make it official yet. So, please, spare me. Like I need *you* to teach me anything."

Um, excuse me. I wasn't the one who'd brought it up in the first place. It'd be like teaching a rattlesnake the etiquette of formal tea—totally impossible. Right then, I couldn't think of anything *less* appealing. Maybe beam reps. That was it.

"Hey," I said, holding up my hands defensively. "Don't take your failure out on me."

In my head, that hadn't sounded so harsh, but for a second, Christina looked seriously stung. I started to apologize for the second time. "Okay," I said. "It's like this. I—"

Just then, Mo came through the door. "Pity party over," she said, clapping her hands. "Yes?"

"Yes, ma'am," Christina said, her eyes lowered.

"Sometimes practice is hard," Mo said. "That makes you stronger. But we do not run out. This will not happen again."

"No, ma'am," Christina said, although it hadn't been a question, but more a command.

Mo looked at all of us. "Good," she said. "Now, back to work. Get your grips—we go to bars."

Once she'd left, I thought about trying one more time to fix things with Christina. But then she looked up, and I saw a new gleam in her eyes that made any words I'd been about to say stick in my throat. She'd been crying, but she wasn't hurt anymore. Now she was just mad.

I was beginning to somewhat get that T-shirt that said: DON'T MESS WITH TEXAS. 'Cause I had the feeling I had just messed with it, at least a little, and it didn't look pretty.

After bars practice with Cheng (Mo's husband and also the quietest man in the *universe*), we took a fifteen-minute snack break. I used my money to buy some apple slices and a Gatorade, and I was trying to find a place to eat by myself when Jessie gestured to me to come over.

"Hey," she said when I reached her table. "Come on, sit with me."

"Won't Christina and Noelle be mad?" I asked.

"Nah," she said. "They usually eat their snacks up front, by the pro shop. Christina's mom sometimes fills in at the front desk, since she practically lives here. Christina's dad is some big-shot cardiologist, so her mom doesn't need a job. Other than Christina and her gymnastics, at least."

I tried to remember who'd been sitting in the parents' viewing section. "Was she the woman with the long, wavy black hair?"

"Yup."

I noticed that Jessie didn't have anything in front of her, even though it was our snack break. I asked her if she needed to borrow some money, but she just shook her head.

"Oh, no," she said. "I'm not really hungry."

I was always starving after a workout, especially after doing something like floor, which required a lot of energy. But whatever. To each her own, I guess.

"So," I said, crunching on an apple slice. "Is Christina just mean, or does she not like me?"

Jessie hesitated.

"It's okay," I said. "You can tell me if it's me."

"Christina can be really sweet once you get to know her," Jessie said. "But I think she's just intimidated by you. I mean, you're only twelve, but you can do stuff that she can't *and* you're already Elite."

"Are you an Elite?"

Jessie made a face. "No," she said. "I have to compete at this Elite qualifier, too. Only Noelle is already Elite, but Christina and I are almost there."

When I became an Elite, I had been so excited. No more compulsory routines like in some of the lower levels, where you all have to do the exact same thing to the exact same mind-numbingly irritating music. And even after I'd gotten to do my own routines, the competitions were always held in some tiny gym with a handful of parents in the bleachers. But now, I'd hit the big time.

Elite is the absolute top level in gymnastics. Once you turn a certain age, you can become a Senior Elite instead of a Junior Elite, but that's it. Only Senior Elites can qualify for the Olympics, and there are tons of gymnasts who are awesome when they're juniors and then choke when they're seniors.

"Well," I said. "I hope you guys both make it. And I hope Christina gets over herself soon. I don't want to have to practice with her glaring at me."

"She'll come around," Jessie said. "We've been training together for three years, so it's just weird to have someone new in the mix. And Noelle's really nice—she's Christina's best friend, so she goes along with her a lot. Get her by herself and you'll probably end up being friends."

"Great," I said. "I'm glad that the girl who happens to *hate* me has so much influence. That's really encouraging."

Just then, Christina and her mom passed by, and I hurriedly popped an apple slice into my mouth, hoping it looked like I'd been chewing the whole time. I wondered if she'd heard me.

"You're not *trying* hard enough," Christina's mom was saying. She was just as beautiful as Christina, I noticed, with the same coloring and dark curly hair. "You have to put in a little effort."

"Mom, I'm working my butt off," Christina said. I raised my eyebrows and looked at Jessie.

"Obviously, it's not good enough," Christina's mom continued. "You think they give out medals for trying your best?"

"I know, I know."

"And now with that new girl, you're going to have to try harder."

Before I could look away, Christina glanced at me, and I knew from the look in her eyes that Jessie was wrong. She was *not* going to change her mind any time soon.

"She really doesn't like me," I said to Jessie.

"Well, I like you," Jessie said. "I'm glad you moved here. It was getting kind of old being third wheel to Christina and Noelle all the time."

I grinned at her. "Well, that's one thing you definitely don't have to worry about with me. Right now, you're the only wheel I've got."

For once, I was kind of grateful that the coaches had a strict no-talking rule during the final team conditioning and stretching exercises of the day. As much as it sucked having to sit in a split or straddle position until my legs were numb, it would've been way worse if I'd had to listen to the other girls whisper and snicker through the whole thing.

I was the first one packed up and out of there, even though I *knew* my mom still wouldn't be there to pick me up. I sat on the sidewalk in front of the entrance to the gym to wait for her. The early spring air was a little too cool to take my hoodie off, and my butt was like an icicle as the cold pavement cut through my thin workout pants. I tried to use the Jedi mind trick to make my mom hurry.

The door opened, and the other girls stepped out. They were giggling and talking, but they didn't see me. The way I knew this was that they kept laughing, instead of stopping to shoot me various dirty looks. I tried to seem nonchalant, so that if they did glance my way, they wouldn't think I'd been waiting for them. Because I hadn't.

"My mom said the sleepover is totally on," Christina was saying. It was weird to hear her talk in a normal tone that wasn't all snotty. "I got Rock Band, so I was thinking maybe we could make it a rock 'n' roll theme? What do you guys think? Oh, and of *course* we'll play Truth or Dare."

"Sounds like fun," Jessie said. "My stepdad won't let me go unless I clean my room, though. So I guess I'd better get on it."

"Clean *your* room? Don't you need to call in disaster relief for that?" Noelle said, and the girls giggled. See, if I'd said something like that, I would've gotten a huge eye-roll from Christina. Life is so unfair.

"Maybe cleaning Jessie's room should be a dare," Christina said. "It's the only way it'll get done."

"Hey," Jessie said. "I didn't ask *you* for a truth right now, okay? So leave me alone about my room."

"Whatever," Christina said. "This is going to be so fun! Way better than last year's, not that we didn't have an awesome time then, too. But we didn't even really *know* about Truth or Dare, and I didn't—"

Just then, Christina spotted me. I tried to paste on my nicest smile.

"*What*?" Christina demanded.

Supposedly, smiles are the universal language, but if that's true, Christina wasn't fluent. "Nothing," I said. "Your party sounds cool. I had a rock 'n' roll–themed party when I was ten, and we did karaoke. It was a blast."

"If you think it's so juvenile, I'd like to hear you come up with something better," she snapped.

"No, I—" Why did she seem to take everything as sarcasm? "I didn't mean it like that. I really do think it sounds cool."

"Well, I guess you'll never know," Christina said, "since I already sent the invites out before you got here. Sorry."

I knew that that had to be a lie. Who sent invitations to only two people? Like, what, Christina actually went out and bought one of those packets of ten or twenty invitations, took out two, and then handed them to Noelle and Jessie? Yeah, right.

"Christina—" Jessie began; I cut her off.

"That's a relief," I said, dragging my hand across

my forehead in an exaggerated *whew* gesture. "Saves me the awkwardness of having to turn you down."

Christina's mouth tightened.

"Sorry," Noelle said, shooting a glance at Christina. At least she looked a little apologetic. "We always have this big sleepover at Christina's over spring break. We've done it for the last couple of years—it's kind of a tradition. Maybe next year?"

Just then, the door opened again, and Christina's mom stepped out. Whereas my mom couldn't stay for five minutes to watch me land a move, Christina's mom had watched our entire practice from the bleachers. And from the way she chatted with parents bringing their toddlers in for tumbling class, and with the staff at the front desk, I could tell she was there a lot.

"Let's go, Christina," she said, putting her arm around Christina. "'Bye, girls!"

"'Bye, Mrs. Flores," Noelle and Jessie said in unison. But Mrs. Flores didn't reply—she was too busy leading Christina toward a shiny red SUV. Christina climbed in, but as the passenger-side door swung closed, I heard: "What was going on with your vaulting today? Hasn't Cheng told you—"

The door slammed shut.

"I'd better go, too," Noelle said. She was talking to Jessie, but she glanced at me at one point, as if she wasn't sure whether or not she should include me. Without her little boss Christina around, I guess she couldn't make decisions for herself. Well, I'd make it for her. I ignored her, pretending that the stripe down the side of my workout pants required my full and complete attention.

Noelle unchained a bike from a rack on the other side of the sidewalk, and I watched with some envy as she rode away. I wished I could just ride a bike home. Then I wouldn't have had to sit out here like a big dork waiting for my mom.

A car pulled up to the curb; Jessie started to open the passenger door before it stopped. "Um, do you need a ride?" she asked, leaning out.

"No," I said, a little more harsh than I'd meant to. I was really angry with my mother right now. Why did she always put me in this position?

Jessie just stared at me for a few moments, as if she was trying to figure me out. "Christina's not so bad," she said. "I know you didn't hit it off today, but don't worry about her."

"Thanks," I said. I decided to push my luck.

"Who knows, maybe she'll invite me to her sleepover."

Jessie smiled. "I don't know," she said. "Christina makes this sleepover into a really big deal. It's not like I haven't gone over to her house and played Rock Band before. But she plans this thing out like it's her wedding or something."

"If she wants help planning a *real* party, she should talk to me," I said. "My friend Dionne and I went paintballing once back home, and it was so much fun."

"That sounds fun," Jessie said. "Anyway, see you around."

Jessie got into her car, and as she rode away, I scanned the entrance to the parking lot for my mom's red Toyota. I knew I would probably be waiting for a while, but that was okay, now that I was alone again. And it gave me more time to daydream about how I was going to make the Texas Twisters see what I could bring to the table. I'd show Mo and Cheng my power and strength and flexibility, and I'd liven up practices and show the girls I could make them laugh. In a couple of weeks, they'd be thinking, How did we ever survive without Brittany Lee Morgan?

But as I sat there waiting, I thought of all the times I'd done this same thing back in Ohio. My mom would be running late, and I'd sit and wait at one of the picnic tables outside the gym. In April, Ohio was still chilly, and sometimes Dionne would wait with me, both of us shivering in our jackets more than was really necessary, in a silent contest to see who was colder. Occasionally, we would convince the concession stand at the aquatic center to spot us a hot chocolate, which we would split; then we'd beg our parents for the money to pay the concession back.

Now I felt the warmth of the sun on my face as I glanced left and right, taking in the low, flat buildings and the brown grass. My mother had said that I'd be feeling at home in no time, but right now I couldn't conceive of feeling that way about the Texas Twisters, much less this vast, lonely state.

Three

"So, you liked your new gym?" my mom asked as she dished mixed vegetables out onto my plate. I hate mixed vegetables. Unless it's a packet of Skittles, there shouldn't be so many colors in one meal.

"It was okay," I said. We'd already been over this in the car, but it was like my mom was a reporter on one of those morning talk shows, and she only had so many index cards with questions on them. *How was school? How was gym? What are you watching?* Once she rattled through them, she just started back at the beginning.

Of course, my dad wasn't at dinner. This was

what happened when your mom ran a day care center and your dad was the head chef at a restaurant: your mom raised other people's kids, and your dad cooked other people's dinners. I knew lots of kids back in Ohio who'd probably have killed to have parents as completely uninvolved as mine. I mean, it *was* kind of a bonus that I got to do whatever I wanted, including have my run of the remote control when they weren't around. But sometimes it got lonely having a house all to yourself.

"Well, it's a *lot* more money than Loveland, that's for sure," my mom said. "So I hope it's better than okay."

The doorbell rang, and I sprang from my seat. "I've got it!" I yelled, even though there was no need. My mom had barely taken the napkin off her lap.

I knew who it was before I opened the door, but I still screamed when I saw her. "Grandma!"

"Miss Brittany Lee," she said, hugging me tightly to her. "How's my favorite little acrobat?"

"I'm fine. How's my favorite art historian?"

A corner of her mouth lifted. "I'm doing well, thank you. The weather is nicer here than in Ohio— but wait until the summer!"

I didn't really want to think that far ahead. It was still depressing me that I was here right now, so why get all sulky thinking about my long future in Austin?

"Do we have to start school again on Monday?" I asked. "Lots of the kids have spring break right now."

"Are the other girls in your gym on spring break?" my mom asked, coming out into the living room and butting in on our conversation. "Hello, Asta."

My parents were all about my grandmother living with us, but she said that she was just too "stuck in her ways." I don't know exactly what she meant by that, since, after all, she uprooted herself to move all the way out here. But she *is* stuck in her ways when it comes to that gross toothpaste that tastes like minted chalk, and the way she always reads the arts section of the paper first, followed by the editorials, and then finishes up with the crossword.

Both my mom and my grandmother were staring at me, and I remembered that I was supposed to be answering a question. "Oh, um," I said, "I don't know, actually."

Christina's sleepover was for the weekend

before spring break started, so I figured it must be coming up.

"Well, do they go to public or private, or are they homeschooled?"

"I . . . don't know."

My grandmother laughed. "And you're the one who wants to take a break from school? Seems like there's a lot you don't know."

As if there was a whole class I was missing out on, called Introduction to What Everyone Else in the Gym Is Up To. Without studying, I already had a pretty good idea—Christina was probably busy watching *Mean Girls* to figure out how to act, Noelle was following in her footsteps, and Jessie . . . well, at least Jessie seemed nice.

"Have you started reading *To Kill a Mockingbird* yet?"

The problem with being homeschooled by your grandmother was that she could hassle you about homework pretty much any time of any day.

"I can't find my copy," I said truthfully. "It might still be in a box somewhere."

My mom frowned at me. "You'd better find it," she said, "since I bought you that nice hardcover edition for your birthday."

The other problem with being homeschooled. I'd gotten some cool things for my birthday, including a metallic-looking leotard with straps that crisscrossed in the back, but I always received at least a couple of books for school. One Christmas, when my grandmother had wanted me to use a particularly expensive math workbook, it had been wrapped up and put under the tree. I'd almost rather have gotten socks.

From what I'd read on the back of the book, *To Kill a Mockingbird* seemed like a downer. It was all about the "pains of growing up," according to one reviewer. Why did I need to read about that? I was practically living it.

Later that night, after I heard the sounds of my mother and grandmother talking in the living room die down, I grabbed the portable phone from the hall and took it into my closet.

Even though every kid I know has a cell phone, my mom says children under the age of thirteen should not be dependent upon new technology. Whatever that means. But my friend Dionne has a cell phone, and I quickly dialed her number, hoping that she had her ringer turned down so her parents wouldn't go ballistic over the lateness of the call.

After a few rings, she finally answered.

"Hey," I whispered.

"Hey," Dionne whispered back. "How's the new life?"

"Sucky," I said. "How's the old one?"

"You know. Nothing's changed, it's all the same old thing."

We were quiet for a few moments. I don't know what Dionne was thinking about, but I was remembering the time that we tied fishing wire to one of the rhythmic girls' hoops, and, when she tried to reach for it, kept pulling it away from her. It was the funniest thing.

Now, my new gym doesn't even *have* rhythmic gymnasts, and I doubted the others would be able to appreciate a good prank like that.

"How's your new gym?" Dionne asked, as though reading my mind. Best friends are good at that.

"Tough," I said. "Everyone's so serious. And the girls are total snobs."

"Really?"

"Yeah," I said. "Like this girl Christina—she had

a complete meltdown because I could do a full-in and she couldn't. I'm surprised she didn't slap my face with a glove when we were in the locker room together."

There was some miniseries on TV all the time, starring a guy in a top hat and these really tight pants tucked into boots, who smacked another guy's face with a glove after an insult about a woman. I don't think I'm ready for a boy to feel that strongly about me, but when I am, I guess that'd be a nice way for him to show he cares.

"That's dumb," Dionne said. "Like it's your fault you're awesome."

"Plus, she's really good on the bars," I said. "And the beam. Like, *really* good. She looks like a professional ballerina or something, the way she points her toes and spins so perfectly."

"So maybe she's just full of herself."

"She's not getting any gold medal for congeniality, that's for sure," I said. "And then there's this other girl, Noelle. She seems all right, but she's, like, Christina's sidekick. As long as Christina decides to give me the stink-eye, Noelle will hate me, too."

"Is there anyone worth hanging out with?"

I thought about Jessie. Not only did she seem a little more laid back than the other girls, but she'd actually been nice to me today. But for some reason, I didn't want to mention her—just in case she turned out to be a snob-in-nice-girl's clothing. I'd have hated to look pathetic, talking her up now only to find out she was just like the rest of them. "Maybe," I said. "We'll see."

"You're probably getting up insanely early to train, huh?"

"Yeah," I said.

At Loveland, I didn't start training until eight o'clock, since I was homeschooled and also the only Elite girl there. So I'd gotten a lot more one-on-one time with the coach, while all the other gymnasts were at school. At Texas Twisters, training started at six thirty sharp, and all the Elite girls were expected to be there. They also didn't do a whole lot of private sessions with only one gymnast, because apparently they thought that "an atmosphere of cooperation and competitiveness pushes gymnasts to be their very best." Believe me, if they had done one-on-ones, I'd be all over it by now.

"Hey," Dionne said. "I have an idea that will help you make friends there. Try a prank."

I rolled my eyes, even though Dionne couldn't see me. "It's not really that kind of gym, Dee."

"Only because they haven't experienced the true genius of one of Brittany Morgan's practical jokes. Remember that time you switched the sugar with the salt, and Coach had to gulp down that whole Gatorade just to wash out the taste of salty coffee?"

I smiled at the memory. It had been truly classic, but I still couldn't see Mo or Cheng having a good laugh about a joke at their own expense. They'd probably just make me do a hundred push-ups and run around the gym a billion times.

"Just think about it," Dionne said. "It could break the ice."

"Okay," I promised. "If a good opportunity presents itself, I'll consider it."

"Well, I have to get going—as cool as my mom is, she'd ground me from my cell phone if she caught me talking on it after ten at night."

"It's only nine fifteen," I said, glancing at my alarm clock.

"Man, it's true what they say about home-schooled kids, huh?" Dionne said. "You go on field trips to museums and spend hours talking about philosophy, but when it comes to time zones, you're clueless. You know how TV shows always say 'eight, seven central'? You're in central now."

Of course. How perfect that Dionne had already moved on, while I was stuck in the past.

Four

If I had to rank the four gymnastics events in order of real-world practicality, it would have to go like this: floor, vault, bars, beam. Floor makes the most sense, considering it's basically another version of what humans walk on all the time. Sure, ours has springs under it and a white line all around that you're not supposed to step past, but otherwise it's the same. We just do more flips on ours.

Vault is pretty logical, too. What if you had to jump over a fence? Not because you were a criminal or anything, but maybe because you were running from a criminal. Or a mean dog. Vaulting teaches me to run superfast and jump over something, but also how to twist and turn in the air so I look cool while I do it. That's clearly helpful.

Bars are more of a stretch, but I can still see *some* sort of point to them. If I ever had to hang from a tree limb for a really long time—like if I was climbing out of a burning building or something—I could totally do it. My hands are all calloused and ripped up from swinging on the bars, so the rough bark probably wouldn't even hurt that much. And with my upper body strength, I could pull myself up on the branch to wait out the fire if I needed to. Although I hope the tree's not *too* close to the burning house in this scenario, considering that wood is highly flammable and all.

But beam? I just don't get it. It's like: here, balance on this four-inch-wide surface, and while you're at it, throw out crazy tricks that are bound to make you wobble or fall. And then, of course, you'll lose massive points from your score if you *do* fall, even though only a moron would've tried to do a full twist on that narrow a surface anyway.

So, of course I was thrilled to find out that beam was our first morning event after warm-ups.

"This is cruel and unusual punishment," I

muttered as I rummaged through my gym bag for my beam shoes. I tried to say it low enough that Mo wouldn't hear me and so that it would seem as if I was just talking to myself, but at the same time loud enough that one of the girls would hear.

Okay, if I were being honest, I kind of hoped they would hear. After all, if there's one thing any gymnast can bond over, it's how much morning practice really sucks. Especially on beam.

But if Jessie and Noelle heard me, they didn't acknowledge it. Instead, they climbed up on two of the beams and started their tiptoe walks from one end to the other. It's an exercise that's supposed to help with balance, but it also bears a striking resemblance to torture.

Christina heard me, though. Just my luck. "If you don't like it," she said, "don't do it."

She climbed onto a beam, leaving me alone on the floor, clutching my beam shoes. A lot of the girls at my old gym had used them, but now I saw that I was the only one here who did—the three other girls were barefoot. I wondered if they thought beam shoes were babyish.

Whatever. If any of them tried to say something about my shoes, I decided I would just point out the stuffed Dalmatian I had seen poking out of Noelle's bag. I mean, if *that* was okay, then beam shoes, by comparison, were the height of sophistication.

I glanced around the gym, but Mo was over by the front desk, talking to someone who was hidden by one of the pillars. *Try a prank.* That's what Dionne had told me. *It'll break the ice.*

Before thinking it through, I swiped Noelle's stuffed dog and shoved it into my bag. Later, when the girls weren't watching, I'd find something really hilarious to do with it, like putting it in the middle of the vaulting table or setting it up to look like it was manning the front desk. It'd be classic.

"What's so funny?" Jessie whispered to me once I'd climbed up on the beam next to her. But Mo was coming, and anyway, I really wanted to see the look of surprise at my comic genius on everyone's face. So I just shook my head, stretching my arms straight out from my body as I began my tiptoe walk down the length of the beam.

The other girls stopped and turned to look at something, but I just concentrated on keeping my balance, feeling every muscle in my calves pulling as I reached the other end of the beam.

"Uh-oh," Christina said out of the corner of her mouth. "Noelle's future husband is here."

Noelle hushed her, although I did notice that Noelle's face turned abnormally red, and it couldn't have been from exertion, because, in spite of the fact that I personally hated these pointless beam exercises, they were far from being the most strenuous things we did.

"Don't try to hide it," Jessie teased. "There's nothing to be ashamed of. He's cute!"

Mo arrived just in time to catch us talking and gave us a sharp look. One thing I'd learned in the few practices I'd had so far: Mo and Cheng took gymnastics very seriously. Our leotards might as well have been those orange vests people wore when they picked up trash on the side of the road— the second we put them on, it was time to work. I missed the atmosphere back at Loveland, where Dionne and I had been able to scheme and giggle all through practice.

I executed my half turn at the end of the beam, sneaking a peek to see this guy the girls were talking about. Personally, I didn't see anything special about him. He was wearing a faded gray shirt with BIRCHBARK HIGH SCHOOL emblazoned across the front of it, and a pair of those baggy shorts that basketball players wear. His dark hair was way too curly (in my opinion), and he had a little bump on his nose. But the way the girls were drooling over him, you'd think that he'd stepped right off the cover of a teen magazine and started doing chin-ups on the high bar.

Of course, I wasn't about to mention that I thought he looked like a dork. Not when I was only a prank away from getting them all to see that practice could be fun—that *I* could be fun.

Because Mo was watching, Noelle tried to look as if she was working on her dance series instead of sneaking peeks at the boy. But it was so obvious it was kind of funny.

"Posture, Noelle," Mo said. She must've noticed Noelle's distraction, too, because there didn't appear to be anything wrong with her posture—other than the fact that she was craning her neck to scope out the cute guy.

"Jessie, I need to see at least one hundred eighty degrees on leaps," Mo added.

This woman did not play around.

The cute guy was now doing handstand push-ups on the parallel bars. Apparently, he didn't play around, either. Although I didn't really see his appeal, I did have to admit that that was pretty impressive to watch. I could probably have done five of those before getting tired or bored, but he was still going.

"You have all seen Scott train before," Mo said, exasperated; I whipped my head around so she wouldn't think I was one of his admirers. "He is training for the college team this fall. In some years, maybe you will get scholarship like him. But it won't happen if you don't *practice*. So I want to see your series—Christina, go."

As though Mo had whistled loudly or clapped her hands, Christina took her position at the end of the beam, looking taller than ever as she stretched both arms above her head. One minute she was facing backward, clenching the fingers of one hand with the other, and then all of a sudden she was flipping. She did a flawless Onodi to twist herself into a forward-facing position, and then executed two elegant front aerial flips in a row.

Front flips with no hands are *tough*.

"Good," Mo said. "But do not pause so much after first element. Square your body, and go right into second. They should flow, yes?"

As far as I was concerned, Christina had been flowing so much she was practically Niagara Falls. But what did I know?

"Jessie, go," Mo said, and Jessie launched into two back handsprings and a layout that got high above the beam, finally landing on both feet. Which, on a four-inch beam, is not exactly a cakewalk. Most moves on the beam have you landing one foot in front of the other, to make it easier.

Mo grunted. "Britt, go."

I'd been working on a tucked full twist back at my old gym, but didn't quite have it down yet. Still, I figured, why not give it a whirl? I took a deep breath and did my round-off, but as soon as my feet hit the beam, I knew my center was off. I could feel my body leaning one way, trying to twist before I actually got into the air. Rather than crash and burn, I balked, stopping in the middle of the move and jumping off the beam.

Mo just nodded. "Your series will be round-off to layout with two-foot landing," she said. "You need to refine before you add twist."

Okay, so obviously I was still struggling with my full twist. But how was I supposed to learn it if I didn't even get to practice it?

I barely heard Mo signal Noelle to go, but all of a sudden, she was flipping across the beam. And then her foot must've slipped or something, because her third layout lacked a lot of height. She missed her landing on the beam and ended up with both feet on the mat, a startled expression on her face.

"Again," Mo said. I saw Noelle glance at Scott over on the parallel bars, but I doubted he was even paying attention to her. Why would a high school guy care about a twelve-year-old gymnast practicing her beam routine?

We were all supposed to continue working on our dance series, but none of us could take our eyes off Noelle as she climbed back onto the beam. I'm sure Christina and Jessie were thinking exactly what I was: Come on, come on. You can do this.

Noelle took a long time setting up for her pass, making sure that her feet were in a straight line on the beam and her arms up by her ears. Finally, she launched into the series—one, two, three, and then, *bam*! She split the beam on her way down and found herself belly-flopping onto the mat, her face hitting the blue vinyl with a sickening smack.

Even though I barely knew Noelle, and still had no clue how she felt about me, I almost jumped down to make sure that she was okay. But neither Christina nor Jessie made a move, so I just stood there, unsure of what to do. Was there some rule about comforting fallen gymnasts? Was it like a war zone? Each girl for herself, with no time to go back for anyone left behind?

Noelle barely flinched, though. Her expression was stoical as she got to her feet, placing her hands on the beam like she was going to go again.

Mo stopped her. "Okay," she said. "Get a drink of water. Girls, I need to see your dance series. Let's go!"

Considering we all had our own water bottles, I figured that sending Noelle to the water fountain was just a way to make her take a break for a second. This time, when she walked by the area where Scott was training, she kept her eyes straight ahead.

"We need to choreograph new beam routine," Mo said, watching me as I did a series of mincing dance steps and struck a small pose. "This one is choppy."

It's not that I disagreed with her. My beam routine involved a lot of quick, jarring motions with my hands, where I whipped them up above my head and then back down again. It made me look like a toy that had been wound up too tightly.

But still. This was the routine that my old coach had worked with me on, the routine that had gotten me Elite status. This was the routine that was *supposed* to include a tucked full twist, instead of some lame back layout.

"Where's Sparky?" Noelle asked, holding her open gym bag, which held a neatly folded workout suit and extra leotard, but no stuffed Dalmation.

Mo was watching Jessie do a scale and barely glanced up. "Hmm?" she said.

"Where's my stuffed dog? Where's Sparky?" Noelle demanded, and now her voice sounded really strained, as if she'd been crying or was about to be.

Oh, crap. My eyes immediately went to my gym bag, which was zipped up, thank goodness. I could make out the vague outline of a stuffed animal in there, but surely it was just because I knew what to look for. Right? No one else would be able to tell that the dog was in there.

"Someone took Sparky," Noelle said, and now she was definitely crying. Her face was splotchy and red, and she was frenziedly emptying her gym bag. "No wonder I can't stay on the beam. Sparky hasn't left my gym bag for three years. Who would take a stuffed animal?"

Mo was paying attention now. Everyone was, including Scott, who'd stopped doing press handstands and was looking in our direction.

What had I done? Noelle wasn't supposed to know that her dog was gone until I'd had the chance to think of something funny to do with it. By then, everyone would have been laughing, and there'd have been no way she could get mad.

But nobody was laughing, least of all Noelle. Just my luck: the first prank I tried to pull involved Noelle's special charm. But how was I supposed to have known that?

"Are you sure you had Sparky today?" Mo asked calmly.

"I told you, that dog *never* leaves my gym bag. Aren't you listening?"

Christina and Jessie exchanged a shocked look. I hadn't heard Noelle snap at anyone like that before, much less the coach.

"Maybe we should look in the locker room," I said. If only I'd had a second alone I could have taken the stuffed animal out of my bag and put him somewhere else, like in one of the younger gymnasts' cubbies or something. Noelle might have thought it a little weird, but at least she wouldn't have thought I'd purposely stolen her good-luck charm.

Just then, Scott walked over. Up close, I guess he looked a little cuter than I'd previously thought. He had really blue eyes, for one thing. But I still didn't see anything to swoon over.

"What's up?" he asked. "Is there anything I can do to help?"

Noelle just put her head in her hands, emitting a weird muffled noise when Christina patted her on the back.

Mo shook her head. "Cheng will be here soon to work with you on tumbling," she said to Scott. "We need to get back to practice, too."

"I can't practice without Sparky!" Noelle wailed, lifting her head. "You saw what happened. I almost killed myself!"

"Where did you last see Sparky?" Scott asked. I had to give him credit. He somehow made it sound like a legitimate question, instead of letting it seem as if he was asking, *What's your problem, psycho?* Which is the way it would've sounded coming out of my mouth.

"Right here, this morning," Noelle said. "He was in my gym bag when I got ready. Then I went to grab my water bottle to fill it up, and he was gone."

Her voice broke on the last word, and I considered coming clean. I could just say it was an accident. But what, like someone else's stuffed animal just *fell* into my gym bag? Everyone would think I was a thief.

I considered explaining the prank idea, but when I actually imagined saying it out loud, it sounded really dumb. And also like a flimsy excuse that I'd made up on the spot, to hide the fact that I was a thief.

The only way to do it would be to find a way to distract everyone again, and then make the switch when no one was looking. Maybe I could think of another prank to redirect their attention. If only I'd known how to throw my voice.

"Well, why don't we start here?" Scott said. "Everyone, empty your gym bags, and if he's not in any of them, we can check the lost-and-found."

I take it back—Scott was *not* cute. He was obnoxious. "I think I see Cheng waiting for you," I said.

"Britt," Mo said warningly, but Scott just smiled.

"I know what it's like to depend on a good-luck charm," he said, winking at Noelle. "On the morning of big meets, I always put on the same pair of socks. They're full of holes, now, but I won't trade them for anything."

That sounded kind of gross.

Jessie and Christina were already down from their beams and had unzipped their bags and turned them inside out. I started to seriously sweat. Would the gym kick me out for stealing?

"Why don't you look in your bag?" Mo said, cocking her head toward me.

"But why would it be in there?" I asked. I could feel this terrible itch on the bridge of my nose, but I'd watched a whole TV program about how little tics like scratching a nose or pulling at an ear were dead giveaways of liars. "It's probably sitting on her dresser at home or something, and we're just wasting time."

"Perhaps so," she said. "But Noelle will not feel comfortable unless we look."

"Fair enough," I said. I tried to make it sound breezy, but I think it came off as more wheezy instead. "I'll check out the locker room. That would make the most sense."

Mo's gaze grew sharp. "Why don't you just open your bag?" she said. "Noelle will feel better once every possibility has been eliminated."

I could feel my face turning red as I leaned down to unzip my gym bag, immediately revealing a patch of black-and-white spotted fur inside.

Noelle gasped. "Sparky!" She reached into my bag and snatched the dog, clutching it to her chest as if it was her most prized possession. If you asked me, she was just hamming it up.

"I was going to give it back," I said, but it sounded weak even to my ears. Why did I have to make the truth sound like a lie? I *had* planned to return the dumb dog. "It was just going to be a little joke. I was going to do something funny, like put it on the vaulting table or . . . whatever."

Mo looked at me with an expression that made my throat tighten. It wasn't even like she was angry. It was more like she'd just found out that I was a completely different person from who she thought I was. "We don't touch other people's personal property," she said. "Ever. Not even for joke. Understand?"

"Yes," I said, raising my chin. Noelle was staring at me as if I was the devil, Christina looked ready to punch me, and Jessie was shaking her head. At least stupid Scott and his stupid nose that he liked to stick into other people's business had walked away. As if I needed one more member of this jury, which had all decided I was totally guilty.

I would *not* cry.

"Are we ready to go on?" Mo asked, her tone letting us know that there was only one answer. "We've lost enough time."

"Yes," the other girls answered in unison.

Mo looked at me.

"I'm ready," I whispered.

As I passed by Noelle to climb up on my beam, I wanted to tell her I was sorry. But she wouldn't meet my gaze, and I didn't know how to say it. So instead I just went back to working on my choppy hand movements.

It was a badly choreographed routine, but at least I'd done it a million times before. So when my eyes got too watery to see the beam, it didn't really matter.

Five

At Texas Twisters, it was a tradition every Friday after practice for the Elite girls to go get frozen yogurt. It was supposed to build team spirit or something.

Technically, if you really wanted to get down to it, we were not all Elite. Noelle and I both were, but neither Jessie nor Christina had qualified yet. In fact, that was why Christina was so determined to get that tucked full-in on floor—Mo told her she had to upgrade her level of difficulty if she expected to make the Elite team.

Ever since the incident with Sparky, Christina had been shooting me death glares in practice, Noelle had been ignoring me, and Jessie just lifted her shoulders in a helpless gesture, like, *It'll get better*.

How can you have team spirit when you're part of a team that doesn't completely exist, and where nobody trusts you?

Jessie and Noelle rode with Christina and her mom, since she came to every practice. They didn't invite me to join them, but whatever. Mrs. Flores must have driven one of those newfangled SUVs with only four seat belts. Right.

Mo drove me to the yogurt place. Cheng was back at the gym, since, as Jessie said, "If it doesn't directly deal with gymnastics, he's like a fish out of water." Apparently, once he'd had to attend a banquet, when Noelle made the Elite team, and he had just sat there shredding his napkin until Mo told him to go on home.

At first, it was superquiet—Mo didn't even play music in the car, which struck me as the weirdest thing ever. She didn't seem to be in the mood for conversation, either, but I decided to start one up anyway.

"So," I said, "I can totally do a full twist on beam, you know. I just messed it up before. But you should really think about putting it back in my routine, because that's the move that's going to get me to the Olympics someday."

Okay, so the last part might have been an exaggeration, but that move would definitely have gotten me there faster than a stupid layout, that's for sure.

"You want to go to the Olympics?" Mo asked.

Duh. Doesn't everyone? Mo's voice hadn't lost its calm, even tone, so I wasn't sure how she meant the question. Was she surprised because she didn't think I could make it? Was she just curious? Was she bitterly reflecting on her own missed opportunity? I'd read in my mom's brochure that Mo had been all set to make the Chinese Olympic team when she was eighteen, but that they'd replaced her with a vault specialist at the last minute, and that by the time the next Olympics rolled around, she had been past her prime.

"Um, yeah," I said.

"Toe point get you to Olympics," Mo said. "Clean lines. Consistency. Hard work. Those get you to Olympics."

"Right," I said. "I know. All of those things, and awesome moves, like a full twist on beam. It qualified me as Elite, didn't it?"

"I saw that competition," Mo said. "Full twist was good, but not good enough. You not ready."

"What do you mean, you saw that competition?"

This time when she glanced at me, there was a slight sparkle in her eyes. "You think I sign just anyone for my gym?"

This was the first I'd heard about there having been any sort of audition. Had she seen me compete and approached my parents? Or had they sent her a tape, and had she then invited me to come? I had so many questions, but when I opened my mouth to speak, Mo just shook her head.

"You know what else get you to Olympics?" she said. "No talking. Just doing."

That seemed to be the Li family motto, because Cheng hadn't spoken more than ten sentences to me during the last week I'd been training. And Mo didn't say another word until we reached the yogurt place.

To be honest, I'm more of a straight-up ice-cream girl. But welcome to the world of Elite gymnastics, I guess—from here on out, it was all about the frozen yogurt.

Jessie's mom was waiting for us, having headed over directly from her job. She'd brought a couple of bags of chips—"After a long day at work, I need something more substantial than yogurt," she said—and she offered Jessie the sour-cream-and-onion ones, but Jessie refused.

"I thought they were your favorite," Jessie's mom said.

"They *were*," Jessie mumbled. "They're just not anymore."

It was the first time I'd met Jessie's mom, so I introduced myself, and when she offered me the bag of chips, I wasn't about to turn them down. Jessie might not have wanted that sour-cream-and-onion goodness, but I loved it. I'd go straight for the ones at the bottom, that had the most seasoning on them, and then I'd lick it off my fingers. Yum.

Jessie got a cup of 99 percent fat-free white chocolate mousse; Christina got a parfait; and Noelle ordered mango sorbet. Finally, it was my turn, and I chose root beer–flavored yogurt. At least it would be interesting.

Mrs. Flores also ordered mango sorbet, winking at Noelle. "If you're going to be good, then I will, too," she said. "Christina, I can get you an extra cup and you can split my sorbet, if you want."

"No, Mom," Christina said, rolling her eyes. It was good to know I wasn't the only one who inspired that response. "I always get the parfait."

"I know that," Mrs. Flores said. "But yogurt still has milk in it. Sorbet is just fruit."

"It still has, like, a million pounds of sugar," Christina said, but she gave in, canceling her order and asking the attendant for another Styrofoam cup for her half of the sorbet.

I wouldn't have changed my order, but I still didn't get why Christina seemed to be so dismissive of her mom. Mrs. Flores actually cared about the skills Christina was learning and how she was doing in practice. And she dressed like a magazine model, with fancy alligator shoes and really heavy eyeliner.

When our orders were up, Mo and the two moms took theirs to one table, and Jessie, Noelle, and Christina sat at another. For a minute I almost considered sitting with the adults, but that was just too lame. So instead, I took a deep breath and joined my teammates.

"Hey," I said brightly, pretending I didn't see them glaring at me. "Gotta love frozen yogurt, huh?"

The girls just licked their spoons, like I wasn't even talking.

"I think frozen yogurt can tell you a lot about a person," I said. "It's like a Magic 8 Ball. Want to know what your choices say?"

"What does root beer–flavored yogurt mean?" Christina sneered. "You're immature?"

I blinked at her. "How is root beer immature?" I asked. "I've seen adults drink it. My dad loves root beer. And it has the word *beer* in it, which is definitely grown-up, since kids aren't allowed to have beer."

Christina went back to licking mango sorbet from her spoon, but this time I could tell it was because she couldn't think of anything to say. Point for me.

"Anyway," I said, "if you want to know what *my* choice means, it's that I'm fun. I don't pick something superboring, like sorbet. I'm not afraid to try something new."

"Like a full twist on beam?" Christina snickered.

"Like a full-in on floor," I countered.

Point two for me.

"What does mango sorbet say?" Noelle asked finally. It seemed as if she'd calmed down since the Sparky incident. She wouldn't look me in the eye, but because she was now sitting next to me, she didn't really have to. So it was easier to pretend that she wasn't still mad at me.

"Hmm." I let a spoonful of root beer yogurt

melt on my tongue while I thought about it. "Mango sorbet says that you're refreshing. You're simple, but not in a bad way. It's more like you don't believe in hiding behind a lot of crap. And the color of mango sorbet is bright and cheerful, so you're an optimist."

"I don't know about that last part," Noelle said, letting out a little laugh.

"But I got sorbet, too," Christina said. "How can it mean the same thing for both of us?"

"It doesn't," I said, trying not to sound as if I were just talking off the top of my head. Which, of course, I totally was. "Noelle got sorbet because she wanted it, so it reflects her true personality. Your mom thought it was healthier, so all that shows me is that she cares about her appearance. And you got it because your mom made you, so that makes you kind of a pushover."

"You know," Christina said, dropping her spoon into her cup of sorbet so hard that drops of orange splattered on the table. "I used to look forward to this."

I don't know how I manage to mess *everything* up, but somehow I do. "Sorry," I said. "I was trying to make conversation, that's all. No big deal. Let's just eat our yogurt."

For a moment it seemed as if I'd accidentally said, "Let's whittle the tips of our plastic spoons into points and stab each other in the eye," because that's totally what Christina looked like she was going to do. But she just sighed.

"Whatever," she said.

For the next few minutes, we lived up to the Li family motto that silence is golden. The only sound was that of Jessie, slurping slightly on her spoonful of yogurt. I think it was the same one she'd started with, and she still hadn't eaten it all.

"Noelle," I said, because I can always be counted on to break up an awkward moment. Or to create one. "Is there any story to your name? I was just wondering, because I think it's really cool."

"Oh," Noelle said. It was obvious that she was struggling with her natural politeness and her simultaneous desire never to talk to me again; the politeness won out. "Um, actually, my first name is Nicoleta. My parents made my middle name Noelle, because I was born on Christmas. So that's just what I go by."

"Nicoleta?" I repeated. "Wow, that's even cooler. What is that, French or something?"

"Romanian," Noelle said, and for the first time

she met my gaze. "My mom was an Elite gymnast back in Romania. My parents defected to the States just a year before I was born."

"No wonder you're so awesome at gymnastics," I said. Now that she mentioned it, she looked Romanian, too. I'd seen some footage of Nadia Comaneci on the internet, and that was what Noelle looked like—straight brown hair pulled back in a ponytail, serious brown eyes. "What's your last name?"

"Onesti."

I had to ask her to spell it, which was good, because it was completely different from what I would've guessed. Based on the pronunciation, I probably would've spelled it Ohnesht.

After that, I asked both Jessie and Christina for their full names. I think names also tell you a lot about a person, possibly more than dessert choices do. Jessie mentioned that her name was Jessica Marie Ivy, which fit her. Her eyes were the color of ivy, so the last name would be easy to remember.

I could tell Christina didn't want to answer, but that she knew it would seem too rude not to, after the other girls had. So she told me her name was Aurelia Christina Flores. How's that for a crazy cool name?

"How come you two go by your middle names?" I asked.

Noelle shrugged. "My parents just started calling me Noelle," she said, "and I guess it stuck."

"It's very common in Mexican culture to go by your middle name," Christina said, almost belligerently, as if I was stupid for not knowing that. "Aurelia's my grandmother's name, but I'm called Christina so we don't get confused."

"Neat," I said.

Nobody asked me about my name, but I didn't care. At least they were talking to me a little bit.

"So . . . are you still having that sleepover?"

Christina made a face, twisting a long strand of her black hair around her finger. "No, it's totally off."

"Wow, that was quick," I said. "Well, maybe we can have one at my house instead. When is your spring break again?"

I knew Christina elbowed Jessie in the ribs, because I saw Jessie wince. "Of course it's not *off*," Christina said. "I was being sarcastic. It's next weekend, and it's going to be an absolute *blast*. Sorry—it was kind of planned before you came here."

"Otherwise I'd be invited for sure," I said, finishing her sentence for her. "Right, I got it. It can be hard to work in—what, *one* more person?—on such short notice."

"Well, it's kind of a Texas Twisters party," Christina said. "You know, our last really big thing before the competition season starts and we have to get more serious."

It was hard to imagine them becoming *more* serious. Although my mom had put me in some tumbling classes at the local YMCA, I hadn't really considered doing gymnastics as a sport until a friend of mine had her fifth birthday party at a gym. We got to play around on the equipment, just walking the length of the beam or swinging from the lower bar, and ever since then, that's what gymnastics was for me. Playing. Having fun.

"I'm a Texas Twister now," I said, even though I'd meant to drop it, not wanting Christina to think I was begging to go to her stupid party.

"Yeah," Christina said, wrinkling her nose. "But, you know. Not really."

"I'm an Elite, aren't I?" I shot back. "Whereas *you*—"

"Hey," Noelle cut in, glancing anxiously back and forth between Christina and me, "you never told Jessie what her yogurt flavor says about her."

"Oh," I said. "Well . . . she picked white chocolate mousse, so that tells me that she's very decadent."

"Decadent?" Jessie asked, pausing in midbite.

My grandma uses that word all the time when she takes me to museums, to describe baroque artwork, so I forget that not everyone my age knows it. "Yeah, decadent. You enjoy nice things. You don't have a problem treating yourself to something really rich and, um . . . decadent."

Jessie slowly lowered her spoon back to her cup. All of a sudden, her face looked as white as her yogurt. "Excuse me," she said, and then she pushed her chair back and headed for the restroom. Jessie's mom reached out to stop her, then shrugged at Mo as Jessie brushed past.

I just stared at the spoon, which had a small pat of yogurt in it that was now turning into a puddle. "That was weird."

"Not really," Christina said. "So far, you've made Noelle and me cry, so why not Jessie, too?"

That stung. I hadn't *meant* to make anyone cry; why did I seem to upset every single person I spoke to? Especially Jessie, who was the only one who'd been semi-nice to me. "I don't get it," I said. "What'd I say?"

Christina shrugged. "With Jessie, who knows? She can be sensitive sometimes."

You mean, a girl who sobs because of a stupid gymnastics move, or a girl who makes a fool out of herself because of a stuffed animal? I wanted to say that, but I didn't. Instead I just got up, tossing my empty cup into a nearby trash can. "Well, I'm going to go see what's up," I said.

I knocked on the outer bathroom door, even though I knew it was the kind that had a bunch of stalls and I could have just walked right in. I didn't want Jessie to feel as if I was crowding her.

"Jess?" I said, stepping inside. Okay, so she'd never told me I could shorten her name even more than it already was, but that's just how I rolled. I made someone cry for completely random reasons, and then I overstepped the bounds by using a nickname. I liked to think it was part of my charm.

"Jess?" I said again, leaning down to look under the stall doors. In the handicapped stall, I saw the yellow flip-flops that Jessie'd been wearing, but they weren't flat on the floor. Instead, it looked as if she was on her knees. "Jess? You okay?"

There was a quick flush, and then the stall door opened. Just to be sure I hadn't imagined it, I glanced at her knees. They were red and had lines imprinted on them from the tiles.

"Everything all right?" I asked. "Sorry if I made you upset. I don't know what I am saying half the time."

She crossed over to the sink and splashed cold water on her face. When she lifted her head, our eyes met in the mirror. "It's cool," she said. "Don't worry about it. It was nothing you said."

"Are you sure?" I asked. "Because all of a sudden you just got up and left . . ."

"I'm fine," she said, smiling. Her face was ruddy, and it almost looked as if she'd been sweating. But of course, she'd just splashed water on her face. So that must have been it. "I just didn't feel well. It was probably the yogurt—I usually don't eat that much."

"You barely ate any."

"Because I wasn't feeling well," Jessie said slowly, as if she was talking to an idiot. "Come on. Let's get back out there."

"Okay," I said. "If you're sure that we're cool. Honestly, you're the only one who's actually been nice to me, so I'd hate to think I'd screwed that up somehow."

"You haven't," Jessie said, putting her arm

around me. "But, look, let's not talk to Christina and Noelle about this whole thing, okay? I don't want to gross them out with my illness while they're trying to enjoy their dessert—especially Noelle; she's got such a sweet tooth. It would suck if I ruined the one treat she enjoys every week."

"Totally," I said. It just felt really good to have *someone* on my side, finally. "I won't tell."

"Promise?"

It seemed like a weird thing to promise. I don't know why, but for some reason I remembered a girl at Loveland, Kim, who'd tried to tell Dionne and me about these laxatives she'd bought from the pharmacy, and how great they worked to help take the weight off. Dionne and I both thought that was pretty gross, and then Kim begged us not to say anything to our coach. As if we'd want to talk about bowel movements in any form, especially premeditated diarrhea, which seemed awful.

So I didn't know why I would want to talk about Jessie's puking in the first place, but I would've said just about anything at that moment to keep her almost-friendship. "Promise."

Six

"Okay, girls," Mo said after we'd finished our morning stretches. "Line up at edge of floor. Tallest to smallest."

We'd gotten the day before off—our one free day of the week, but now it was Monday and time to work again. Even that one day off was enough to make me feel extra achy and a little out of it. Sometimes, with gymnastics, the best thing to do is power through it. You'll hurt *somewhere* every day, but at least you won't have time to stop and think about it.

In a way, it had been nice to have a day away from the drama at the gym, but Dionne hadn't been around any of the times I'd called, and my mom had had to go in to the day care for some inventory thing. The day went by really slowly, and by the end of it I found myself craving interaction of any kind, even if it meant hanging around people like Christina, who hated me. I must be nuts.

Now, luckily, I was as far from Christina as possible, since she was the tallest of the four of us and I was the shortest, so I didn't have to intercept her dagger glares. Having to line up in order of height made no sense to me, but I fell into line anyway. I swear it was just a way to bring attention to the fact that I was still a good three inches shorter than Noelle, who was the second smallest after me. Whatever.

For a few moments, Mo just looked at all of us, her eyes sliding from one girl to the next. When she got to me, I resisted the urge to stick out my tongue.

"Elite qualifier is in one month," Mo said. Cheng came to stand next to her, his eyes on the blue floor mat as he nodded. This must have been important, because the only time we usually saw Cheng was during bars and vault practice, or when we ran through tumbling passes on the floor. I got the impression he did a lot more behind-the-scenes stuff than Mo did and was busier.

"Britt and Noelle, you do not have to qualify," Mo continued. "But you need to get ready for the Classic and Nationals, which are coming up in next few months. So I want half routines, with increased numbers. Understand?"

I said that I didn't, for once not because I was trying to be funny or clever. I really didn't understand. At my old gym, we'd trained competitively, of course, but I'd never been given this kind of structure.

Mo explained what Noelle and I were supposed to do. She wanted ten flawless first halves for our beam routines, followed by ten flawless second halves. Then we would be expected to stick three beam dismounts and to do five first and second halves on bars, both perfectly, with three stuck bars dismounts. On floor, we were to do one routine focusing on our dance, with simple layouts for our tumbling passes, except for our big last pass, which would be practiced in the pit. Then we'd do one full routine with connection passes on floor and our big final pass in the pit. As if that wasn't enough, we were also supposed to do twenty competitive vaults.

That would be our practice schedule for the next four weeks.

"We will be giving more attention to Jessie and Christina," Mo said, "but that does not mean that you can rest."

No kidding. The only thing that kept this place from being a sweatshop was that we didn't make anything. But if nasty rips on our palms and sore hamstrings could somehow be packaged and sold, we'd have been in trouble.

"Jessie and Christina, you will also do twenty competitive vaults," Mo said. "But instead of half routines, you do full. Five on bars and beam and two on floor."

This time, it seemed like she looked at all of us at once. I don't know how that's possible, with us spread out the way we were, Christina on one end and me on the other, but she did it. It felt like there was no escaping those intense black eyes.

"No falls," she said. "Only perfection counts."

"Yes, Coach Mo," all the girls said in unison. I must have missed the memo about when to reply and when to keep my mouth shut.

Mo reminded the other girls about the extra ballet classes they were supposed to be taking once a week to hone their dance skills. My mother was all over me to sign up, too, but I just couldn't see the point of mincing around in a little skirt and waving my arms in the air. Who needed grace when you had raw power?

"We also need to be more careful with eating," Mo said. "Eat healthy, but do not starve yourselves. You need energy. Understand?"

Out of the corner of my eye, I glanced at Jessie, on the other side of Noelle. I don't know what I expected—a flicker or a nervous tick, *something* to show how she felt about the subject of food—but she just faced forward, saying, "Yes, Coach Mo," with the rest of the girls.

"Britt?"

I turned my eyes back to Mo. "Yeah?"

"Do you understand?"

Why was I being singled out? "Yes, Coach Mo," I said.

She nodded curtly. "Good. You and Noelle, go to vault with Cheng. Jessie and Christina, you come with me to beam."

It was the first time we'd been split up, and it was a little weird. I mean, not that I was complaining. Having to deal with only one girl was way better than having to deal with three of them. But still. Jessie was my only real friend on the team.

Without saying a word (of course), Cheng crossed over to stand by the vaulting table. Noelle and I went to the chalk bowl and started rubbing the dry white powder on our hands and feet. You could always tell where gymnasts had started on the runway by the white circle they left behind.

When I was five years old and too young to need the chalk, I used to think it was the coolest part of gymnastics. Before my grandmother started teaching me at home, I used to go to school and run my fingers along the rim of the blackboard, applying the chalk dust carefully to my hands. My teachers hated when I did that.

Of course, our chalk is totally different—it's this powdery magnesium stuff, instead of the hard chalk that used to scratch against the blackboard. And it serves its purpose. Without it, my hands would be slick from sweat and would slide right off the bars or vault or beam. It would be superdangerous. But it also completely dries out my hands, making my skin peel off like layers of an onion.

"So . . ." I said, trying to think of something to say. I once saw a commercial where all these people working in an office are trying to make awkward conversation over the water cooler, but it just isn't happening. The chalk bowl is like the water cooler of the gymnastics world.

It was pointless, anyway. Noelle was staring at Scott, who was practicing a front handspring to three front layouts on the floor.

"That's easy," I said, following her gaze. "I could do that in my sleep. I thought he was practically a college gymnast."

She flushed, as though I'd just insulted *her*. "Maybe he's just warming up," she said. "Ever think of that?"

"Well, if he's going to warm up front handsprings, he could at least do them right. His knees are bent."

"You're one to talk," Noelle muttered.

"What?" I asked, even though I'd totally heard her.

"Nothing," she said. Just as I'd thought. Noelle was a coward. Without her ringleader, Christina, around, she didn't know what to say or do. In my book, that was way worse than a sloppy front handspring.

I decided to try to make amends, though. It

wasn't like I needed any more enemies at the gym, and I still felt bad about the stuffed-animal incident with Noelle. I searched for some small talk that might make her open up. "So, he competes for his high school team?"

Noelle nodded, a dreamy expression on her face. "Did you know that he's already been accepted to Conner University with a full gymnastics scholarship?"

I remembered Mo's mentioning something like that, but since I hadn't gotten my copy of Scottie-the-Hottie Trivia, I hadn't known the name of the college. "Cool," I said. "Where's Conner?"

Noelle reddened. "It's only in Houston," she pointed out. "It's not that far away."

I was about to point out that I'd never said it was when I realized that Noelle was just supersensitive about the idea of never seeing Scott again. It seemed to me that she already had a long-distance relationship with him when he was practicing twenty feet away. How do you measure the distance of *not going to happen*?

Down by the vaulting table, Cheng stuck his fingers in his mouth and whistled. It was startling, not just because, hello, it was a piercing whistle, but because Cheng had actually made a sound. Would wonders never cease?

"You go first," Noelle said uncharitably.

"Fine," I said. I took my place about sixty feet down the runway. A lot of gymnasts like to start farther back—the runway is just around eighty feet long—but I don't need that much room. My legs are so short that those extra twenty feet make me feel like I'm running a marathon.

Well, that might be exaggerating. But I get a little bored running.

I sprinted down the runway, hurdling into a round-off onto the springboard. I propelled myself backward onto the vaulting table, my hands hitting squarely as I performed a single layout into a pit just like the one we used for floor. Vault timers, we call these. They're just for warm-up.

Cheng nodded, so I guessed it was okay. I started walking back to my place at the end of the runway, Noelle whooshing past me as she ran toward the vault. I didn't bother to glance back to see how she did. Of course, it was going to be perfect. Noelle's vaults always were.

After a few more vault timers each, Noelle and I were ready to work on our competitive vaults. We were both doing a Yurchenko one-and-a-half twist for our first vault, so basically, we just had to add the twists to the layout. Easy, right?

I couldn't even imagine what kinds of vaults people had done before Natalia Yurchenko came up with pretty much the coolest one ever. Now almost everyone does Yurchenko vaults. The move consists of a round-off onto a springboard, so that when you hit the vault table, you're facing backward. It totally revolutionized vaulting, and it all happened way back before I was born, which means I've never known a world without such an awesome skill.

On my first vault, I completely sat down. It felt as if I'd landed on the very edge of my heels, and my feet slipped right out from underneath me, until I was sitting on the mat. The worst part of it was that I couldn't count it toward my twenty vaults. I'd probably still be vaulting ten years after all the other girls were done.

As Noelle did her vault (stuck landing, what else?), I watched Jessie and Christina on the beam. Christina was already working on the second half of her beam routine, flowing through the leaps and acrobatic skills like she was on a beam four feet wide instead of four inches. Jessie was still on the first half, jumping down from the beam after a wobbly sheep jump, her landing totally blind as she kicked both legs up behind her until her toes touched the bottom of her red ponytail. She'd have to start over.

Jessie got back up on the beam, but she leaned too far forward and ended up having to jump to the mat on the other side. She blew her bangs out of her eyes, muttering something to herself as she climbed back up. I saw her check her balance one more time before continuing her routine. What was with her?

"Hey," I said as Noelle joined me at the end of the runway.

"What?" Noelle asked, but her eyes were on Scott, who was doing a scale at the corner of the floor mat.

I wanted to ask her if she thought Jessie was okay. I wanted to ask her if she'd noticed anything weird, like the way that Jessie picked at her food during snack or skipped it entirely, or the way that she disappeared sometimes into the bathroom. But I didn't know how to ask without her having some questions of her own, like what I was talking about or why I cared. And besides, I'd promised not to tell.

"Nothing," I said. "Don't worry about it."

When I got home, my grandmother was waiting, ready to discuss the part of *To Kill a Mockingbird* that I was supposed to read, where Jem and Scout mess with this weirdo who lives across the street, Boo Radley. They come up with this awesome game where they playact what they imagine he'd be like, making him crazier and crazier in every incarnation.

My grandmother gestured for me to take a seat, and I plopped down at the kitchen table, dropping my gym bag at my feet.

"Why do you think Atticus isn't happy about Jem and Scout's game?" she asked.

Because he was an adult, and adults never like seeing kids have fun. I wanted to say that, but I knew my grandmother would just ask me to elaborate, and then I'd have to defend it, when really I just liked to complain sometimes for no reason. So I decided to take the question at face value and respond to it the way I knew she wanted me to.

"Because they shouldn't be making fun of

Boo Radley," I said. "He hasn't done anything to them."

My grandmother beamed her approval, making some notation in her copy of the book. She encouraged me to write in mine, too, but that seemed like a horrible way to treat a nice hardcover book. *Engage the text*, she would say, but I don't go scribbling all over clothes my mother buys me, either, so it seemed like a wasteful thing to do.

"How could they turn their playacting into something more positive?"

My grandmother loved to do this, tie fictional characters up in knots and ask you how you would untie them. I always wanted to say, like, *I don't know, they're not real people. So they can't do anything.*

This time, though, I really didn't know what my grandmother wanted me to say. I shrugged. "They could join the school drama club?" I offered. "I don't know."

She considered that answer, pursing her lips and tilting her head first to one side, then the other, as though weighing whether it were right or wrong. "Interesting," she said. "I'm not sure their school would have a drama club. But what I meant was that they could imagine how Boo Radley might *feel*—

being an outcast—instead of vilifying him further. Does that make sense?"

Of course it did. I found myself wishing that the other girls at the gym would imagine how I might feel, being a new girl in a highly competitive gym, with no way to make friends at school or anywhere else. But then again, I also sympathized with the kids in the book, who were just trying to have fun with their little games. It was kind of like the way I had wanted to liven things up with my prank on Noelle, but instead wound up doing something that made everyone jump down my throat.

So the question wasn't whether I understood the stupid book or not. The question was whether, in comparison with the characters, I was the one trying to have fun but getting shut down or I was the misfit. Was I the Boo Radley of the Texas Twisters?

Seven

My mom called the gym to say she was running late that day after practice. I was surprised when Jessie invited me over to her house. "Your mom can pick you up from there," she said. "Come on, it'll be fun."

Jessie's house was in a gated community where all the houses had big columns in front and were painted in variations on the same three yellows, pinks, and beiges. Compared to my small brown ranch house with its huge prickly hedges in front, it looked like a palace.

Jessie led me through the front foyer and the

stuffy-looking living room ("We never use this; it's just for when my grandparents come.") to a large kitchen. A teenage girl with long blond hair was chatting on a cell phone.

"I know, right?" the girl was saying. "You get it; I don't know why Jake doesn't. He is *such* a jerk. Do you know that he—"

She spun around and saw Jessie and me staring at her, then rolled her eyes. "Sorry," she said to the person on the other end of the line as she disappeared behind a door into a bedroom, "I can never get any *privacy* here."

"My stepsister, Tiffany," Jessie explained. "She thinks the world revolves around lip gloss. Come on, I'll show you my room."

Jessie's room had to be as big as the rest of the house, and it was a masterpiece of messiness. I saw what the other girls had been teasing her about on my first day at gym. She had more clothes than I'd ever owned in my life, strewn about every surface of the room, and there was just *stuff* everywhere. As I crossed over to her bed, I stepped on a Minnie Mouse Pez dispenser, nearly slipped on a piece of notebook paper with doodles all over it, and had to move a Scrabble board over to clear a place to sit.

"So," I said, "what do you want to do?" I was very aware that Jessie was my only quasi friend in Texas so far, and I was afraid to mess everything up by suggesting something babyish like painting each other's nails. Not that nail polish was allowed at Texas Twisters—at least, other than the clear kind, and, if it's not a color, what's the point?

"I have a bunch of old gymnastics competitions saved on my DVR. Want to watch those?"

She was already selecting last year's American Invitational from her list, so I figured she didn't need me to reply.

The first few minutes were filled with all that stupid commentating the announcers do—here's the girl to beat, blah blah blah, but look out for young hopeful so-and-so, the ultimate rivalry, and all that—and so I pushed the rest of the stuff off Jessie's bed to stretch out, propping my chin in my hands. "Do you have any other brothers or sisters?"

"Just Tiffany, who's fifteen, and Josh, my seventeen-year-old stepbrother."

"I always wanted to have a sister," I said. "Or a brother. You know, someone to hang around with when my parents weren't home."

Jessie laughed. "Count yourself lucky. I used to have it sweet when it was only me, but then Mom married Rick, and they came with the deal. I barely hang around with Rick's kids at all."

I guess it's not the same when they're not related to you, because then there's no rule saying they have to love you no matter what.

"I am so jealous of her," Jessie sighed; for a second I thought she was talking about Tiffany. But then I saw the gymnast on the screen, dancing around the floor mat on the balls of her feet as if she had all the energy in the world.

"Yeah, she's good. She ends up winning, right?"

"Of course," Jessie said. "She always wins. You can tell just by looking at her."

There was a close-up of the gymnast's face, and I squinted, trying to see whatever elusive superiority might exist in her features. Her nose was kind of pointy, her eyebrows were way too plucked, and her hair was pulled back so tightly it gave me a headache just to look at it. "She does look kind of smug," I agreed.

Jessie had turned her desk chair around and was straddling it with her arms resting on the back. She shook her head. "She looks smug because she wins. But she wins because she's thin."

Something about the way Jessie said it sent shivers down my spine. It was almost like she'd said it many times before, even if never out loud.

"I wish I was taller, like you," I said, "and had more muscle. That's what's really important—imagine if your arms looked like twigs. They'd snap in half if you tried to do a back handspring!"

I expected her to laugh, but she simply kept watching as the gymnast on television flipped her way through her last tumbling pass. "It's just scientific," she said.

"Right. Science says twigs and gymnastics are not a good combination. It *is* scientific."

The score flashed on the screen. With a high difficulty level and nearly perfect execution, it was hard to deny that she was the best.

"See, it pays to be little," Jessie went on. "Like you—your routines are harder than mine, and yet you barely break a sweat. If I tried the same thing, I'd have to work twice as hard just to get my body to rotate all the way around."

"I'm also shorter," I said. "Christina is tall and skinny, and she can't do all the hard stuff, either."

"That's because she doesn't want to."

When Christina had been crying over her failure to do a full-in, it had seemed as if she wanted to pretty badly, although now that Jessie mentioned it, I did wonder what motivated her. The other girls had more obvious reasons for being involved in such a demanding sport. Noelle's mom had been a gymnast, so maybe Noelle wanted to follow in her footsteps. Jessie had told me that after her parents got divorced and her mom remarried, she'd latched on to gymnastics as something to make her special, to help her stand out in a house that was filling up with other people. I didn't love the strict regime of workouts, but it was all worth it for that feeling I got as I was flying over the bars, or propelling my body through the air with a single push against the vaulting table. Christina was an only child; I doubted that her mother, with her perfect hair, had ever been an athlete, and Christina didn't seem to relish the adrenaline rush of gymnastics the way I did. So, what was her story?

Another gymnast on the screen slipped off the bars and belly-flopped onto the mat below. It was obvious she wasn't really a contender, though, since they didn't bother to show any of her other routines, just the one where she face-planted it. That's why I planned to be the best gymnast ever by the time I made it to a televised meet. At least if I messed up one routine, I'd still have the other three to show my grandkids someday.

There was a knock at the door, and Jessie's mom poked her head into the room. Her carrot-red hair was pulled back in a French braid, and her cheeks puffed out a little like a chipmunk's when she smiled.

"I'm Britt," I reminded her. "I'm new at the gym."

"Of course, I met you at the team yogurt outing. And Jessie's told me all about you." She chipmunk beamed at me. I wondered what Jessie had told her. "Jess, honey, have you finished your homework?"

"Most of it," Jessie mumbled.

"I'm sorry?"

"I said I'm doing it," Jessie replied in a louder voice; her mom raised her eyebrows as she shut the door.

"Want me to rewind?" Jessie asked after her mom had left. I shook my head, since we'd only missed a routine that hadn't looked very interesting anyway. I mean, it was the American Invitational, and this girl was doing a side somi on the beam, which basically looked like an aerial cartwheel with ugly tucked legs and flexed feet. Why didn't she just yank some other moves from her compulsory Level Five routine and throw those in while she was at it?

I shared my opinion with Jessie, but she said that the side somi was "acrobatic" and part of the "presentation." It was so nice to chat about gymnastics without its being about weight that I immediately reversed my opinion, and we rewound the tape so we could analyze the way simple skills could add elegance to a routine.

"What do you have to do for homework?" I asked. "Maybe I could help."

"Nah, it's eighth grade stuff. Algebra."

"I can do that. My grandma taught me."

It wasn't like homework was my favorite thing in the world, either. But I was determined to make Jessie see how awesome a friend I could be, and this seemed as good a way to do it as any.

At first, Jessie looked at me as if I'd just suggested doing a balance-beam routine over an ocean filled with piranhas, but eventually she reached into her backpack and pulled out a glossy orange textbook. I turned it over in my hands.

"So this is what it's like being in public school, huh?" I said. "I do a lot of stuff out of workbooks and from stuff my grandma gets online."

There were a whole bunch of names written on the inside cover of the book, ending with Jessie's name, written in big, bubbly handwriting with a purple pen. I flipped through the book and saw at least one obscene word that was not written in purple pen, so I figured Jessie wasn't the vandal. My money was on the kid two names above hers, Justinn Myers. I'd act out, too, if my parents had saddled me with a random extra letter at the end of my name.

"We all go to the public school," Jessie said. "Our parents agreed we should have normal lives outside of gymnastics, even though we take the first period off to practice and eat grilled-chicken salads for lunch instead of pizza like everyone else. But I guess it's better than being totally isolated." She glanced at me. "No offense."

"Well . . ." I didn't know what to say. Being homeschooled could feel very lonely, considering that it was just me and my grandmother, so I couldn't seriously be offended by Jessie's comment.

And yet it still kind of stung. "So let's see what chapter you're on," I said instead.

One of the homework problems was to illustrate the equation $2x - 10 = x + 1$ with a real-life problem. "All you really have to do is figure out what you want x to stand for," I said, "and then fill in the blanks."

"Okay," Jessie said. "I weigh twice as much as I want to, and so I'll lose ten pounds. Whereas you weigh exactly as much as you want to, and you could gain one. Does that work?"

It didn't on so many levels, but where would I even begin? "If that were really true, your ideal weight would be, like, fifty pounds or something," I said. "That's just sick."

Jessie scowled, snatching the textbook back from me. "Obviously, I'm not being *literal*," she said. "I thought the point was just to come up with stuff for the numbers to stand for. You never told me it had to actually make any sense."

I didn't want to pick a fight, so instead I just focused on the part of her equation that didn't work, the part that could be better explained.

"We can't be the same variable," I said. "The x can't stand for both you and me."

But in some ways, wouldn't it have been easier if it could've? If I could somehow have been Jessie, and known the secret to earning Christina's and Noelle's friendship, and had a mother who cared enough to come to the gym at least *sometimes*? And then Jessie could have been me, and known what it was like to be scared—terrified that I'd never fit in, and worried that the only friend I had was dealing with something much bigger than I could ever handle.

That night, when I got home after my mom finally picked me up, I locked myself in the bathroom. I stood on the edge of the bathtub so I could see all of my body reflected in the mirror.

Everything looked familiar. My blond hair with its wisps around my face, that wouldn't be restrained by any clips. My eyes that I had used to wish were blue-green, but that were just blue. My strong shoulders, my arms that looked normal under a T-shirt but that I knew were made of muscle and sinew and could spin me around the high bar in twenty giant swings in a row. My narrow hips, my short legs, my feet that were always too dry from all the chalk I used, so they didn't look cute in flip-flops.

I stared at the girl staring back at me, until the image started to warp and become the reflection of a stranger. I wondered if that was what Jessie saw when she looked at herself in the mirror—although maybe she didn't have to try so hard to see it.

Eight

We were split up again at the next morning's practice, so I didn't really get to talk to Jessie. Noelle and I spent the whole time on vault. And then, when it was over, the other girls retreated to the locker room to shower before school. Since my grandmother was coming later to pick me up and take me home for my own schooling, I didn't need to worry about it. So what if I felt isolated sometimes? I also got to take a shower in the middle of history if I wanted to. I reminded myself to tell Jessie this, the next time she talked about homeschooling.

But I hated to be left out, so I joined the girls in

the locker room anyway. I just packed and unpacked my gym bag, trying to sccm busy as I listened to the conversations behind the shower curtains.

"Sucks to be you, Noelle," Christina said, from stall number one. "Vault is the *worst*."

"I think it's kind of fun," I said, both because I liked to argue with Christina and because I wanted to make my presence known. It wasn't clear if Christina had been addressing Noelle in order to make a point of ignoring me (a total possibility) or because she thought I'd already left (also a possibility). Normally, I might've waited her out, interested in hearing whatever she might say behind my back. This time, I didn't feel up to that.

"*You* would," Christina said, as if having an affinity for vault were right up there with wanting to harm small animals.

Noelle's voice was barely audible over the sound of water streaming slowly but steadily from the faucets. "I don't mind vault."

"You don't mind anything," Christina said, and somehow she made that, too, sound right up there with serial murder. "That's your problem."

"Speaking of problems," I said, "how's that tucked full-in coming along?"

I tried to make my tone as friendly as possible, but I wasn't surprised when Christina peeked out from behind the shower curtain. Her face was dripping wet, and her black hair was plastered to her head. Her less than perfect look took a little of the steam out of her angry glare.

"Shut up," she said.

"Fine," I said. "Don't listen to me. But I'm telling you, it's all in your back handspring."

Christina made a face at me. "I've been doing back handsprings practically since I could walk. I sincerely *doubt* it has anything to do with that."

"Okay," I said in my best bored voice. This was the same voice I used on my mom a lot when she would talk about the arts and crafts she did with the four-year-olds. Like, who cares? It was either Popsicle sticks and glue or cotton balls and glue. Sometimes, it was Popsicle sticks, cotton balls, *and* glue. That was when it got semi-interesting.

"All right, Coach Brittany," Christina said, disappearing behind the curtain again. "Let's hear it. What's wrong with my handspring?"

"Nothing," I said, "for a double twist or a double tuck or whatever. But a tucked full-in is a double flip *with* a twist. It needs more power. You have to get stronger right from your round-off and snap your feet under your body. Right now, your feet are too far behind, and you don't get the height."

"Well, thanks for the insight," Christina said, "but I'll go ahead and wait for what the *real* coaches have to say, if it's all the same to you."

"You do that," I said, shrugging, even though she couldn't see me, "and continue to wipe out. It *is* all the same to me."

I saw Jessie's hand groping for the towel that was hanging on a hook just outside the shower, and I reached over to hand it to her. "Thanks," she said when she finally emerged, the towel wrapped around her like a strapless dress.

"How was practice today?" I asked. "I hate it when they split us up."

She shrugged. "Fine. Same as usual."

"Do you think you'll be ready for the qualifier?"

"Hmm?" Jessie brushed out her red hair, and I repeated the question. "Oh," she said. "Yeah, I'm sure it'll be fine."

She packed up her bag and retreated into one of the stalls to get changed. Noelle and Christina had already put on their sports bras in the main area and were now sliding shirts over their heads.

I wanted to ask Christina if anything had happened during practice to make Jessie so distracted, but I knew she'd just roll her eyes and tell me to mind my own business. I wanted to ask Noelle if she was aware of anything, but she'd been with me the whole morning.

"We'd better head out if we want to make third period," Noelle said.

"Hey, Jessie, are you riding with us?" Christina called through the stall door.

It swung open, and Jessie stepped out. "Of course," she said, and then she glanced at me. "Oh— Thanks for the help with my algebra homework, Britt. See you!"

And then somehow I was alone in the locker room, clammy with steam from other people's showers. It occurred to me that in the future I should take a shower, too, even though I could totally take one in the comfort of my own home, with the new showerhead my dad had put in that was supposed to make it feel like rain, and with my mom's fruity-smelling shampoo. Right now, the fact that I was the only one who didn't shower there just made one more way I was different from everyone else in this new gym. I wore beam shoes;

I was homeschooled; I wasn't invited to sleepovers. I was Boo Radley.

Normally, I wasn't the kind of person who wanted to be like everyone else. In fact, I liked being a little quirky. Dionne had always said that the thing she liked best about me was the way I could make her laugh, and that she never knew what I would say or do next.

So far, though, Texas didn't seem to like quirky.

"What do you think that means?"

It was probably the third time my grandmother had asked, but I wasn't listening. Instead of following along with her discussion of *To Kill a Mockingbird*, I was doodling stick figures flipping on a beam I had drawn along the edge of my notebook page. For now, they were just doing simple layouts. It turned out that drawing a full twist was just as hard as doing one.

"You know," I said, "Jessie told me that they don't read *To Kill a Mockingbird* until ninth grade."

I knew Grandma must have been getting impatient, but she didn't let on. That was one of the best things about her. "Is that right?"

"Uh-huh," I said. "She's in eighth grade. She

said that it's on the reading list for next year, when she gets to high school. She said it was crazy that I was learning it now."

"Do *you* think it's crazy?"

I should've anticipated that question. Another of my grandmother's not-so-secret weapons is turning a question around so that you're forced to actually think about something. It can get really annoying.

"I don't know," I said. "It's just that there's a lot of other stuff going on right now. If I have to try to understand this supertough book, too, my head may explode."

"That's unfortunate," Grandma said, but she just tilted her book to let me see the part she'd underlined. "It's in the third chapter," she said. "Atticus tells Scout that you can never fully understand someone until you climb into his skin and walk around in it. What does that mean to you?"

"I don't know," I said. "Sounds kind of gross, walking around in someone's skin. Like Buffalo Bill in that really creepy movie about the serial killer. You know, the one who makes dresses out of people's skin?"

Grandma closed her book in exasperation.

"How in the world did you even see that kind of thing?"

I shrugged. "Late-night television."

"So, you're telling me that if I showed you the movie *To Kill a Mockingbird*, maybe you'd pay attention?"

Just the mention of a movie made me perk up a bit. "So there is one? Sweet. Let's order it."

"Settle down, Miss Brittany Lee," Grandma said. My voice had been rising, and since my dad was sleeping upstairs after a late-night shift at the restaurant, I had to keep my voice low. "There's no serial killer in the movie, either. Let's focus on the book for now. Remember what we talked about last time. What do you think Atticus means when he tells Scout that you have to walk in someone's skin to understand them?"

"I guess, just that . . ." I colored in the heads of my stick figures until they were completely filled with blue ink. "Like, you have to see where people are coming from."

"Good," Grandma said. "Can you give me an example?"

"Well, at gym, my friend Jessie . . ." I stopped, glancing at my grandmother.

"Go on."

By now, I'd punched a hole in the head of one of my figures with my ballpoint pen. It looked as if some stick person had lost her head in mid-handspring. "I don't know," I said. "It's weird. She thinks she's fat or something, and she always obsesses about food and losing weight."

"And what do you think?"

"I think she looks like one of these people," I said, holding up my stick-figure drawings. But I couldn't keep a straight face, and I broke into a grin. "Not really, that would be scary. But she's totally fine. I mean, maybe she could eat healthier or whatever, but I think she shouldn't worry about it so much."

"Try to put yourself in her place," Grandma said, "the way Atticus says to do. What do you think she might be feeling?"

My grandmother is a huge fan of these assignments, where you learn something from a book but you also learn something about yourself. "Um, she's scared?"

"Scared," Grandma repeated, but not as if she was questioning it—more like she wanted to turn it over in her mind a little bit. "That's an interesting choice of words. Why do you think she's scared?"

"Because," I said, "she hasn't made it to Elite yet, and Noelle and I have. Christina's definitely got what it takes, if she can just up her difficulty. But Jessie's different. Things come slower for her."

"So, why do you think that would make her scared about her weight?"

"Well, I mean, it's true that less weight makes you flip faster and jump higher. Noelle is on the shorter side, like me, and we're both pretty tiny. Christina is the tallest, but she's naturally really skinny. Jessie's just got more muscle, that's all."

My grandmother nodded. One major benefit to being homeschooled is that I can bring up gymnastics examples all I want, and I'm never shut down or mocked by classmates. Dionne told me once that she felt like a freak show being in public school, where people treated her as if she was from a completely different universe. Sometimes I wanted to go to regular school, just to see what it would be like, but I also liked the fact that I could say whatever I wanted to with my grandmother. She doesn't mind that I live on Planet Gymnastics all the time.

"Putting yourself in Jessie's skin, what do you think she needs right now?"

Personally, I thought she could use a big, juicy

hamburger, but I knew that wasn't the answer my grandmother was looking for. I was about to respond when I heard the front door slam and the slap of my mom's work flats on the tiled floor.

"Hello, Pamela," Grandma said. "You're home early."

It was kind of weird, actually. At two thirty in the afternoon, my mom should definitely have been watching the rug rats at her day care center; it was prime time, when all the younger kids were waking up from their postlunch naps and all the older kids were starting to trickle in from school.

"Yeah," I said. "Why are you here?"

"Ah, just the way a mother likes to be greeted," my mother said ruefully, pressing a kiss on the top of my head. "Hello, Asta. Good lesson today?"

"We were just discussing *To Kill a Mockingbird*," my grandmother said, glancing at me, "and the importance of empathy."

I didn't remember that word being thrown around, but I nodded anyway. "So, what's up?"

It was only then that I realized my mother was seriously glowing. Like, she was practically *radiating* all over me. I'd never seen her that happy.

"Well," she said, the words coming out in a rush,

"Debbie—you know, the woman who owns the center?—is looking to sell. I told her I'd definitely be interested, so we were talking about drawing up some documents to have the licenses transferred this week. Isn't that exciting?"

Owning a business consisting of a bunch of screaming kids? Wow, someone needed to work on her definition of "exciting."

"Yeah," I said. "Totally."

"That's great, Pamela," Grandma said, and obviously she'd drunk the Kool-Aid, because she seemed to mean it. "It's what you've always wanted."

"I know!" my mom said. "It's going to be great. I just came home for a few minutes to pick up some of the financial stuff we need to go over after work, but then I'm heading back in time for an after-school snack. So I'll be out of your hair!"

I rolled my eyes. Like *that* was my problem.

"That's fine," Grandma said. "Congratulations again."

My mom turned to me. "I was hoping to repaint the classrooms at some point. Maybe one Sunday, when you girls are off practice. What do you think? Would you all like to come out and have a paint-and-pizza party?"

It was weird the way she said "girls." Like we were all such close friends and she saw the four of us as inseparable, when nothing could have been further from the truth. "Mom, we're not supposed to have pizza," I said. "Remember? Our bodies are our temples and all that?"

"Well, when your father finally gets a night off, I'm sure he can make us something *healthy* for a celebratory dinner. I know it'll be tough to arrange, with all of our schedules."

And about to get tougher still, if my guess was right. But I didn't want to seem like a total brat, so I forced a smile. "Yeah," I said. "Sounds awesome."

My mother let out one last strange, giddy laugh before disappearing into her bedroom. If I ever get that jazzed about owning a place where you basically change dirty diapers all day, someone shoot me.

"Well, that's exciting," Grandma said.

That was the buzzword of the day, apparently. "Yeah."

She looked at me for a moment; the skin around her eyes didn't crinkle like it usually did. "Where were we?" she asked quietly.

It wasn't as if I had short-term memory loss.

I knew *exactly* where we'd left off. I just didn't feel like pursuing it, in case Grandma wanted me to project myself into my mother's skin or something.

"I don't know," I said. "But I have to go to gym in, like, half an hour. Can't we move on to social studies?"

I half expected her to protest, but she nodded. "Fine," she said. "Open your American History book where we left off, about the industrial revolution."

I did as she told me, sliding *To Kill a Mockingbird* under the coffee table. If she'd insisted, I could definitely have answered her question before my mom came home. *What do you think Jessie needs right now?*

I thought Jessie needed a friend like Atticus Finch, someone who could be strong and do what was right, no matter what the consequences. But then I remembered the promise I'd made to Jessie, and the one glaring thing I'd neglected to tell my grandmother. I wondered if I was up to the task.

Nine

That afternoon at practice, I tried to find a way to bring up the painting, but I couldn't seem to find a good time. It didn't help that I was still conflicted about the answer I was hoping for. I dreaded their saying yes; I also feared their saying no.

As it turned out, Christina approached me first, at the water fountain during a break. "Look," she said. "I'm not happy about this, so I'm just going to say it."

I waited, too stunned to speak.

She rolled her eyes. "WillyoucometomysleepoverSaturday?"

"What?"

I saw her clench her jaw. She obviously thought I was just being difficult. "Will. You. Come. To. My. Sleepover. Saturday."

"Oh," I said. "I'd love to."

I was pretty impressed with how cool I'd been about the whole thing. I leaned down to get a sip of water, but Christina's hand shot out to cover the water fountain button.

"You know that my mom is making me ask you, right? It was supposed to be just me, Noelle, and Jessie."

"I know," I said.

"But—" Christina shook her head. "Then why would you agree to come? Wouldn't you just feel . . . unwelcome?"

"I know you'll try to make me feel unwelcome," I said, "but the sleepover sounds like fun, and I'm happy to be invited. So, thank you. Yes, I'll be there."

She continued to stare at me until I gently reached under her hand to depress the button, sending a clear stream of water shooting toward my mouth. It tasted more refreshing than any water I remembered drinking.

"So, Saturday night," I said, when I'd filled my

water bottle and was heading back to the floor, "should be fun. And Sunday, my mom asked if we could help her paint her new day care, so this will be perfect—we can all just head over there together."

"Sounds . . . perfect," Christina said. She looked as if she'd hit her head on the balance beam.

"Oh, yeah," I said. "We'll have a blast."

Of course, that night I had to call Dionne and try to hash out what I should wear and what I should bring and how I should act. I was asking her whether I should bring my Twister game when Dionne cleared her throat.

"What?" I asked, aware that she'd been silent for a while.

"It's just that . . . Do you remember when we played Twister at my birthday party last year?"

"Uh, yeah." That was why I was thinking about bringing it this time. Nothing got more competitive or more hilarious than a group of gymnasts in contortions trying to touch right hands to green and left legs to yellow. It had been the hit of Dionne's party.

"Well, I shouldn't say 'we.'" Dionne paused, as though she was carefully considering before deciding to go ahead. "*I* didn't really participate. In fact, I spent most of the night reading a book on my bed while you guys played."

I remembered now. I had thought it was really weird that Dionne would be so antisocial when it was her party. If she hadn't felt like playing Twister for any reason, she could always have offered to operate the spinner to see what configuration we'd have to get into next.

"So, what's your point?"

"You still don't know?" Dionne said. "Britt, it was *my* party. I wanted to watch movies and paint each other's nails and talk. Instead, you totally took it over with your game, turning it into this crazy competition."

I was stung by her words, especially because they were completely unfair. Dionne's party had been a dud. If I hadn't saved it with Twister, everyone would've watched some dumb movie about girls who were also mermaids or something and gone to bed by nine. Instead, I got it rocking. Everyone had been laughing and having a great time, gathered around the Twister board, while Dionne had pouted over in the corner. Now, she was saying it was because I somehow "took over" her party, although that was absolutely ridiculous. I'd just given it a much-needed makeover.

"What's your point?" I asked again, my voice tight.

Dionne sighed into the phone. "Look, that was a while ago," she said. "I'm not still mad. I'm just trying to say that you should watch yourself. Remember that this party is *not* the Brittany Show."

"The *Brittany Show*?"

"It's not—you know what I mean."

"Yeah," I said. "I guess I do." And then I pressed TALK on the phone to end the call, my finger pounding the spongy button with more force than was really necessary.

Dionne was the one who'd suggested I try a prank in the first place, and look at how that had turned out. Now she wanted me to play it safe? All because of something I'd done a year ago that had annoyed her and that she hadn't even told me about at the time?

It wasn't as if I made everything about me. It was just that some situations needed to be livened up, and that was kind of my specialty. And if there had ever been a group of girls that could have used my brand of fun, it was the Texas Twisters.

But then I had a brief flash of Jessie in that bathroom, her knees red from kneeling on the tile, and I wondered if "fun" would be enough. And I wondered if it could be too much, if it could mask something else that was going on—such as the fact that I'd never even noticed that Dionne was mad at her party, or that Jessie might starve herself until she was so thin that she could just slip through the cracks—all because we were too busy having fun to notice.

Ten

Christina's house had a curvy orange roof and white stucco walls. My mom called it Spanish-style.

"But Christina's from Mexico, not Spain," I said.

She laughed. "Oh, honey, it's just a style of architecture. Do you have everything? Your bathing suit?"

I had probably overpacked, but I wouldn't have put it past Christina to "forget" to tell me key details of the night, like that you were supposed to bring your own sleeping bag, or that you should have brought a swimsuit, since she had a pool. I didn't know if she had a pool, but I wasn't taking any chances. I didn't want to be sitting on a lounge chair talking to Mrs. Flores while everyone else played Marco Polo.

I gave my mom a kiss good-bye. She tugged at my sleeve before I got out of the car. "You did ask them about painting tomorrow, right? It's just that I really need to do it on a weekend when none of the little kids are there, and I'd like it to be sooner rather than later."

"Yeah, I told Christina. She said it sounded perfect." It was totally true. I hadn't *asked* Christina. I had told her, and that was exactly what she'd said. The only part I left out was that she was so shell-shocked when I said I was actually going to come to her sleepover that I doubted she'd even heard me.

"Great!" My mom smiled. "Well, have fun."

My duffel bag was so heavy I had to drag it up to the front door. Before I could ring the bell, it swung open to reveal Mrs. Flores, wearing a huge smile and an apron right out of a Betty Crocker commercial. Still, she managed to look stylish.

"Brittany! Come in, come in." She made a move to grab the duffel bag, but as soon as she tried to lift it and felt how heavy it was, she withdrew her hand.

"I would have driven you from gym, you know," she said as she led me into the kitchen. "All the other girls have been here for a couple of hours."

I'd thought about pushing my luck with that, but there were some last-minute things I'd needed to pack, anyway, like a comic book (in case I got bored), several extra changes of clothes (in case whatever I was wearing wasn't appropriate or got ruined because of some horrible prank), and a bottle of air freshener. I'd been purposely avoiding beans or anything else fart-producing for the past few days, but I didn't want to take any chances that there'd be some smell I'd want to cover up.

I'd left Twister at home. Not because I actually put any stock in what Dionne had said, but, you know, just in case.

As soon as I walked into Christina's room, everyone got silent. Christina was sitting on a huge, canopy bed with a frilly purple comforter on it, Noelle was at her feet with a forkful of speared shrimp suspended near her mouth, and Jessie sat on an uncomfortable-looking white stool in front of a vanity. I'd never actually seen a vanity in a real-life room before, only in catalogs and on TV. I definitely got the name—when a piece of furniture is basically one gigantic mirror, it's pretty obvious that its only purpose is to let people stare at themselves and think about how beautiful they are. Perfect for Christina.

It was hard to believe that in the last week I'd been in both Jessie's room and Christina's. I dragged my duffel bag over to a corner and plopped down on the floor next to it.

"So," I said, "what's up?"

Christina went back to flipping through an issue of *International Gymnast*, and Noelle chewed slowly, as though she preferred turning the same bite over in her mouth again and again to responding to me. Sometimes I thought Noelle was worse than Christina. Christina actively hated me, but it was hard to tell with Noelle—it seemed as though she was more interested in staying on Christina's good side than in actually speaking up for herself.

"Christina was about to start up Rock Band," Jessie said.

"Cool," I said. "I can be the drummer. My grandma thinks music is part of any well-rounded education, so I know all about different time signatures and stuff. My grandma says I can keep a mean beat."

"Did your grandma sew your outfit?" Christina asked, her gaze flicking up from the magazine.

I looked down at my capri pants and my T-shirt with sparkly turquoise polka dots on it. When I'd chosen these clothes to wear, I had thought they seemed cool—effortlessly casual, as if I couldn't have cared less what I wore but had somehow managed to pull it together anyway. But suddenly it felt like the stupidest outfit ever.

"My grandmother is an art historian," I said. "She doesn't make art, she just critiques it."

I thought that was a fitting response, but Christina's comeback was swift.

"Who called *that* art?"

The room was silent for a few moments. Surprisingly, it was Noelle who spoke up. "Can we not do this tonight?" she said. "Please? I'm all achy from practice, and I just want to chill out."

"I'm pretty sore, too," I said, seizing on that as a neutral conversation starter. Who doesn't like to compare scars? "Check out my hands. They're all ripped up."

I held out my palms for everyone to see. Weeks of constant friction against the bars and rubbing dry chalk into every crease made them look like

130

parchment. I had a blister on one palm that refused to go away no matter how much cream I put on it.

Christina shrugged. "That's what you get for not wearing grips," she said.

Grips help support your wrists and have strips of leather that cover the palms of your hands. Some gymnasts use them; some gymnasts don't. Personally, I like to feel the full contact of the bar beneath my hands, even if it means I pay for it later.

"I don't wear grips," Noelle pointed out. "Neither do the Chinese gymnasts, who are some of the best bar workers in the world."

Christina was silent.

"Come on, let's play Rock Band," Jessie said.

Once we got into the game, it was surprisingly fun. Even Christina seemed to forget that she thought I was the scum of the earth, and we both laughed at Noelle's singing. As soon as Noelle realized you could get extra points by diva-ing out some parts of the song, she started yodeling and trilling all kinds of weird noises into the microphone. Every time *GREAT JOB!* flashed across the screen, I just about died.

"I'm still hungry," Christina said. "Who wants a Popsicle?"

Noelle and I both chimed in to say yes. Jessie just shook her head. "I'm okay," she said.

After Noelle and Christina left to get the Popsicles from the fridge, I glanced at Jessie. "There aren't many calories in Popsicles, you know," I said, trying to keep my voice casual. "It's basically flavored water."

"Oh, it's not that," she said. "I just don't really feel like it."

Christina brought back cherry for her, orange for Noelle, and grape for me. I tried to read some significance into the choice of flavors, but I couldn't. I liked grape, so who cared if somehow it was meant as a slight?

"I'm sick of Rock Band," Christina said. "Let's play something else instead."

Noelle stuck her tongue out and caught a drip of orange juice running down her Popsicle stick. "Can we play Super Mario Brothers?" she asked. "We could just take turns."

Christina smiled, her eyes sparkling devilishly. "I had something else in mind," she said. "What about Truth or Dare?"

I had heard about Truth or Dare before. Dionne said that mostly it was just people asking who you liked or daring you to tell someone's older brother you liked him. To me, that didn't sound as fun as Super Mario Brothers or even Twister, but I wasn't about to say so and look lame.

"I'm up for it," I said. "How do we start?"

"Well, since you seem to want to play so badly, why don't we start with you?" Christina said. She still had that look in her eyes that made me distrust her.

"Okay," I said. "Dare."

"Wait, we're not even doing it right," Noelle said. "We should all be sitting in a circle on the floor. And, Christina, you should put on some music so that your mom can't hear."

"Like she has nothing better to do than listen at my door," Christina said.

Noelle looked at her with raised eyebrows. "What about the time that you said you hated gymnastics and always had, and she burst out crying, until you had to tell her you were just joking?"

Christina flushed. "God, Noelle, save it for the game, why don't you?" But she got up and plugged her iPod in to the speakers on her nightstand, turning the volume down until I could just barely make out the sounds of the latest Miley Cyrus single.

Once we were all sitting cross-legged in a circle, Christina turned to me. "Okay, Britt, so, truth or dare?"

"Dare," I repeated.

"You can't do that," Christina said.

"What?"

"You can't pick dare this early on. Nobody picks dare. You have to do a few truths first."

That was the dumbest rule I'd ever heard. "Then why call it Truth or Dare? Why not call it Mostly Truth but a Little Dare Toward the End?"

Noelle giggled.

"It's not a *rule*," Jessie said. "Britt can pick dare if she wants to."

"Whatever. Fine. Let me just think of something."

The circle got quiet as they decided my fate. I listened to Miley's twang over some pulsing electronic beat and realized I'd probably have the song stuck in my head for days.

"Okay, I've got it." Christina squinted at me. "I dare Britt to . . . lick the toilet seat."

Jessie made a gagging noise. "Gross! Isn't it supposed to be a dare that you would do yourself?"

"Who says I wouldn't?"

"*Would* you?" Noelle asked.

Christina threw up her hands. "All right, you suggest something, then. This is already no fun."

I guessed that it wasn't the time to say that I would totally have licked the toilet seat if that were my dare. I mean, sure, it was disgusting, but I was okay with that. It was a *dare*. It was supposed to be horrible. And it wasn't like I couldn't wash my mouth out right afterward.

But at the same time, if I could get out of it, why not?

"What about a toilet-paper shirt?" Jessie said. "Britt has to wrap herself in toilet paper and wear the shirt for the rest of the game."

Everyone agreed that that was a way better idea, so we trooped into the bathroom to begin the process of making a toilet-paper shirt. Basically, it consisted of wrapping my torso up like a mummy and then winding the toilet paper around my arms. It was scary how good the shirt ended up looking. That's what you get with four girls who probably learned how to wrap an Ace bandage at the age of five.

Christina grabbed her digital camera and snapped some pictures of me as I hammed it up, standing with a hand on my hip and striking a diva pose, then sitting, with my chin resting on my fist, looking pensive. She laughed, but for once it didn't feel as if it was at me, so I didn't mind.

When we were back in the circle, Christina said it was my turn to ask the person next to me a question. Noelle picked truth, and I thought for a few moments, trying to figure out a good one.

"Why do you like Scott so much?" I asked finally.

I saw that the tips of Noelle's ears were turning bright red.

She picked at some fuzz on the carpet before looking up. "I don't know," she said. "I mean, he's cute."

Christina and Jessie laughed.

"Is that all?" I asked. "I mean, it can't be just those blue eyes, right?"

Noelle blushed even more, if that were possible. "No," she said, her voice low. "It's not just that. It's . . . everything. He's so nice, and mature. Not like the boys at school, who are always trying to snap girls' bras and stuff. And he's a serious gymnast. It's totally possible that he'll go to the next Olympics, and I'll be seventeen then. . . ."

She broke off, as though she'd said too much. "Of course, I would never dream of letting a relationship stand in the way of Olympic gold," she said stiffly.

I now knew my next question for Noelle: *If your only chance to be with Scott was during the Olympics, would you take it?* I already knew her answer—none of us would risk something as huge as an Olympic medal, no matter how cute the guy. But I was betting she'd hesitate for just a second, and that would be enough to tease her about later.

Not that the women's gymnastics team got to interact much with the men's team during the Olympics. The men often stayed in the Olympic Village, while the women's team had stayed off-site for the past three or four games. I guess the coaches didn't want people getting any ideas.

Jessie picked truth, too, and Noelle asked her what famous person she'd want to have lunch with. Boring!

"Nadia Comaneci," Jessie replied. "So I could ask her how she did it. Or maybe that cute guy from the cell phone commercial."

"So you could ask him what?" Christina asked snidely.

"How about asking him why he doesn't stop texting that girl with the braces and go out with one of us?" I put in.

"How about because he probably lives in California and has a supermodel girlfriend?" Christina returned, but with less venom. As if she wouldn't totally have dated that guy. Even I had to admit he was adorable, with a dimple in his cheek that showed every time he smiled down at his phone in the commercial.

After Christina had picked truth when it was her turn, Jessie glanced around the circle. Her eyes landed on me for just a second, and then she asked, "Christina, why don't you like Britt?"

I felt my pulse start racing, as though I was running laps around the floor mat. This was going to be interesting.

Christina looked at me for a long time, and I wondered if she was trying to figure out a nice way to phrase her reply or if she was trying to figure out the nastiest thing she could possibly say. But nothing could have prepared me for what she said when she did finally speak.

"Because she's better than me," she said.

I stared at her.

"Oh, come on," she said. "You know it. I know it. You're younger and shorter and way more obnoxious, but you have absolutely no fear. You can flip your body through the air and not worry about what's going to happen when you hit the ground. I'm not like that. I'm always a little scared."

"But that's not Britt's fault," Jessie pointed out.

"I know that," Christina snapped. "I answered the question, didn't I? No one can say I wasn't honest."

In a way, it was just as fearless of Christina to tell the truth as it was for me to do the tucked full-in on floor. I thought about saying so, but figured she would think I was teasing her.

Christina tossed her head impatiently. "So I get to ask the next question, right? Let's get to the juicy stuff. Britt, truth or dare?"

My dare last time hadn't actually been too bad, but I knew I had to pay my dues. "Truth," I said.

Christina leaned in as though it were only the two of us. "What's your biggest secret right now?" she asked.

I ran through all the possibilities in my head. Whenever my mom took me to the grocery store, I would grab a caramel from the candy bin and eat it while we shopped, even though I know you're supposed to put it one of the baggies and pay for it. Sometimes, if I was over at someone else's house and I had a booger, I wiped it under the table or on the wall. I worried that my mother didn't love me as much as she loved those kids at her day care.

And then, for some reason, I thought about *To Kill a Mockingbird*. And I thought about staring at myself in the mirror and trying to see what Jessie might see. And I thought about how the only thing lonelier than moving to a new place with no friends was carrying around a secret that was as big as the state of Texas.

I glanced at Jessie. Her eyes were wide and panicked, and I heard the words coming out of my mouth before I had a chance to think about them, or to will them back.

"I think Jessie might have an eating disorder," I said.

Eleven

Noelle spoke first. "Why would you say that?"

"It's just—" I stopped when Jessie stood up and rushed out of the room, slamming the door behind her. "Don't you notice how she barely eats? And she goes to the bathroom all the time?"

I didn't tell them about the time I'd caught her in the bathroom at the yogurt place. Even though I was almost positive she'd been lying about not feeling well, I figured there was no point in revealing that part.

"That's a big accusation," Noelle said.

"It's a big deal," I said. "I know. That's why

it's been so hard to carry this secret inside me."

"It's not even really a secret, is it?" Christina asked. "It's more like speculation. You just didn't want to have to spill one of your own secrets."

I don't know what reaction I'd been expecting. Maybe that was the problem—I hadn't stopped to think about the various ways this could have blown up in my face. But still, I felt tears sting my eyes, and I tried to blink them away before the other girls noticed.

"I said I *think*. I *think* she has an eating disorder. You guys don't see that something is up? Seriously? I could tell she was acting weird from the second I got here, and I've only been training with you guys for a few weeks. You've trained with her for years. You didn't see anything wrong?"

"There's a difference between dieting and a disorder," Noelle said. "I know you came from a smaller gym, Britt, but at the Elite level it's very common to watch your weight. You have to. It's just part of the training."

Maybe I'd gone to a less competitive gym before, but I'd seen behavior like Jessie's. At Loveland, Kim had started using those disgusting laxatives when the regionals were coming up, because she thought they would help her. Instead, they had ended up making her so weak she'd had to withdraw from the meet.

"Don't you get it?" My voice was becoming squeaky; I tried to calm myself down. "That's why she can get away with it. That's why nobody does anything. She says she wants to lose weight for the qualifier, and everyone gives her a pat on the back. Nobody stops to think about how she's doing it!"

Christina's eyes were jet black, and I could tell I'd lost any ground I might have gained with her during that one hour when we all played Rock Band together like friends, or at least like a team. I had more than lost it—I had gone miles in the other direction. "I forgot to add the other reason why I don't like you," she said. "You get into everybody's business. You're here for two seconds and you start giving me advice on my gymnastics, going through Noelle's stuff, and spreading nasty rumors about Jessie. *It's not all about you.*"

I tried to blink back the tears that I felt gathering. Her words stung, because I'd heard them just hours before—from Dionne, when she'd called me out for monopolizing her party. Maybe I would have been a lot better off if I'd kept my head down and worried only about my gymnastics. But in this case, I *knew* I was right. Why did nobody else see it?

"I'm going to check on Jessie," Noelle said. She hesitated, then gave me an apologetic look. "It might be best if you aren't here when she comes back, Britt."

"You want me to go home?" Tears were streaming down my face now, and I hiccupped on the last word. "I can't call my mother and tell her to come get me. She'd want to know why, and I don't—"

I don't want to admit to her that I'm universally hated at the fancy new gym where I'm training. I don't want her to know that her daughter is a pariah.

"Just sleep in the den," Christina said. "I'll tell my mom you weren't feeling well."

It wasn't so far from the truth, at that point. I felt like I could've thrown up. Silently, I dragged my duffel bag out of Christina's room. I hadn't ended up needing the bathing suit, the change of clothes, or the air freshener. The only thing that stank around here was me.

Jessie was sitting on the couch when I arrived in the family room, and for several moments we just stared at each other.

"Look," I said, "I'm sorry—"

"You promised."

I could tell she'd been crying, but her voice wasn't quavering now.

"I know, but I'm worried about you. I only want to help you, Jessie. Please believe me."

Noelle appeared in the doorway and looked nervously from Jessie's face to mine. "I was looking for you," she said to Jessie. "Come on, we're going to watch a movie in Christina's room."

As she passed me, Jessie deliberately turned so our shoulders didn't touch. When she was just beyond me, she paused. "It wasn't your secret to tell," she said in a low voice.

How could I explain to her that it had been starting to feel like my secret? That I lay in bed at night worrying that my only friend in Texas was destroying herself, and I had no idea how to stop it?

"It wasn't your secret," she said again, so quietly that I doubted Noelle could hear her. And then she and Noelle were gone, leaving me alone in the family room. I sat on the uncomfortable leather couch listening to the ceiling fan whoosh in the otherwise quiet house and cried.

* * *

I didn't sleep well that night, but somehow I dozed off around three in the morning, and when I woke up, my head throbbed and my mouth felt like cotton. From the kitchen, I could hear laughter and the sound of plates clacking against the table and pans being moved around the stove. Judging by the smell, Mrs. Flores was making eggs. The glowing numbers on the cable box said that it was already eleven o'clock.

I was still wearing my shirt and capris from the night before, and I knew my hair was all matted on one side, but I didn't bother about my appearance as I headed into the kitchen. What did I care? If they were going to hate me, let them. I was done trying to impress them.

As expected, the girls grew silent when I stepped into the room, as though my presence formed a vacuum, sucking a room dry of any happy noise. Then Christina started giggling, as though she had been reminded of some hilarious joke at my expense.

Whatever. I sat down at the table and ignored them. "Are there any more eggs?" I asked.

"Britt, I'm sorry," Mrs. Flores said. "Christina said you weren't feeling well, so we didn't save you any."

I glanced around the kitchen and saw that all the dishes had been put in the sink. Everyone was obviously done eating.

"Would you like some cereal?" Mrs. Flores asked. "I think we have some oat crunch."

That stuff tasted like squirrel food, but I nodded as though it were my favorite meal in the whole world. Mrs. Flores poured me a bowl. I'd taken only one bite when the doorbell rang.

"Oh, Mrs. Morgan!" I heard Mrs. Flores say. The sound of my chewing seemed deafening.

"Please, call me Pamela," my mom said; she seemed breathless. I was trying to figure out why she sounded so . . . happy. And then I remembered. The painting.

Crap. There was no way that the other girls were going to agree to help out now.

"Hi, honey," my mom said, entering the kitchen and stopping to press a kiss on my forehead. "Good thing you wore an old shirt you can paint in. Girls, do you want to change before we head over?"

The shirt was *not* old. I loved that shirt. Why did everyone seem to think that it was something off *What Not to Wear*? Okay, so most of the sparkles had fallen off, and the hem was a little stretched out.

"Head over where?" Noelle asked.

My mom glanced at me, then at Mrs. Flores. "Didn't Brittany mention the painting party?"

I closed my eyes.

"I'm opening my own day care," my mom explained. "And I need to paint the classrooms today. I was hoping to recruit the girls with the promise of some pizza. . . . I thought Britt had already asked everyone."

"We can't have pizza," Christina said. "It'll interfere with our training."

"It's very common for gymnasts to watch what they eat," Jessie added, giving me a pointed look.

My mom nodded enthusiastically, as though pleased that the choice of food was the only impediment to her plan. "That's right, I remember Britt mentioning that. . . . Well, we could get something else instead. Mrs. Flores, would it be all right with you if I borrowed the girls for a couple of hours?"

"Oh . . ." Mrs. Flores seemed to feel put on the spot, but eventually she gave a wide, fake smile. "Sure, I don't see why not. Jessie, your mom wasn't going to pick you up until three, and Noelle was going to stay over here to do homework with Christina anyway."

Three pairs of eyes were glaring at me, but I just took a spoonful of my cereal so large that milk oozed out of the corners of my mouth. Why should I let a little bit of old-fashioned hatred ruin my appetite?

If my mom noticed that everyone at the day care was more strained than smiling, she didn't mention it. She was her usual too-chipper self, handing out brushes and painter's tape.

"I chose bright colors because I wanted the rooms to look cheerful," she said. "Don't you think that's important for kids? To have happy colors?"

"Super important," I mumbled.

She sighed with satisfaction. "This is going to be a whole new era, Britt. Just you wait and see."

She gave me one of the smaller brushes to do the edges with. It was like she didn't know me at all. There were some people who had very fine hand-eye coordination. I was not one of them. I could flip backward and manage to catch the beam with my hands, but ask me to play a game of Operation and I was zapping myself all over the place trying to get the stupid organ pieces out of the guy's body.

I made up for it by painting very slowly. At least, that's what I told myself. But I also took my time because I didn't really feel like doing it, and I figured that this way I could paint as little as possible.

Christina and Jessie were on the other side of the room, using rollers to cover the entire wall with yellow paint. They were laughing and trying to paint over each other's strokes as though they were competing for territory. I wished that I could've had that job.

Noelle also had a little brush, but she had soon done twice the area I had covered in the same time. When I actually looked at it, there were no drips or smears, either. Was there *anything* she wasn't good at?

Even my mother noticed. "Nice job, Noelle," she said, coming to stand behind her. "You're a natural. Have you painted before?"

Noelle stepped back to survey her work. "I helped my parents paint their store," she said. "I like to paint. It's relaxing."

"Well, you're a hard worker! Any time you'd like to help out around the day care, I'm sure I could find something for you." My mom crossed over to where I was standing on a stepladder, slathering paint onto the corner by a doorway.

"Britt, you have to be more careful!" She took

the brush from my hand and turned it so that the bristles were angled correctly for the tight space. "You see how I'm making it as small as possible, so I can get a neat line of paint in there? If you do it your way, we'll have to repaint the entire door!"

She handed me back the brush, but not before making a clucking sound and bending down to wipe away a drop of paint on the doorjamb. She licked her thumb and rubbed at it, but a very light tint of color still remained.

As she headed back into the other classroom, which she was painting a vibrant orange, she touched Noelle's shoulder. "Keep up the good work," she said.

I know that my mother probably justified having Elite gymnasts paint her day care by pretending that this was somehow a team-building exercise. I watched Noelle charm my mother while Jessie and Christina laughed over in the corner, and I guessed that the whole experience might be bringing them closer together.

Me, I'd never felt less part of anything in my life.

Twelve

At practice on Monday, I tried really hard to pretend I didn't care when Christina shot me dirty looks, or when Noelle ignored me, or when Jessie's eyes accused me of breaking my promise. I did my half routines, focusing on making each one perfect so I could move on to the next set. Out of the corner of my eye, I could see Jessie and Christina over with Cheng, working on their vaults. Jessie was opening up too early, and she looked tired. But of course, I had no right to tell her those things anymore. We weren't friends.

When I finally talked to Noelle, I kept my voice

light, just so she wouldn't think I was like a dog with its tail between its legs or something. "I bet you I can land my full twist on the beam three times in a row," I said.

Noelle glanced nervously toward the front of the gym. Mo had disappeared into the office for a second to take a phone call. "We're not supposed to be practicing our acrobatic series without supervision," Noelle said. "We're just doing the leaps and dance elements right now."

"How much do you want to bet?"

"How much do I want to bet that you'll get into *huge* trouble?" Noelle said. "Nothing, because I already know the outcome. You *will* get into huge trouble, and I don't want to be dragged into it with you."

"I'll bet you Sparky," I said, my gaze flicking over her gym bag, where I knew the stuffed dog was safely stored. I was goading her on purpose, and I didn't care. If Boo Radley had known that all the neighborhood kids were making fun of him, he probably would've gotten them right back. Even a freak who locks himself in his house knows that sometimes the best defense is a good offense.

Noelle turned white. "Don't be ridiculous."

"Keep count," I said, and set myself up for the first in the series. I crouched down before throwing my arms back for momentum, propelling myself backward, my body already twisting. When my feet hit the beam, they were totally flat, my toes curling around the edges of the apparatus to maintain my balance.

I took a deep breath. "One."

Noelle didn't even pretend she was still working on her pirouette. "Britt, *please*," she said, glancing toward the office.

"Your wish is my command," I said, and executed a second flawless standing full twist. I was on fire! I almost wished Mo could see this. She'd have let me put it back in my routine for sure.

"You've made your point," Noelle hissed. "Can we get back to work now? Please?"

"This *is* work," I said. "This is me working on the skill that's going to make me national champion one day." I saw Mo emerge from the office, but a woman stopped her to chat. "Watch this. Third time's a charm."

I knew from the moment my feet left the beam that I didn't have the height. My timing had been a little off, my movements too jerky, and I hadn't been able to fling my body backward with as much momentum as I usually did. It seemed like I was suspended in the air forever.

My head hit the beam squarely, and I scraped my cheek as I slid down the side of it and crumpled to the floor.

"Britt!" Noelle jumped down from her beam and knelt beside me. "Britt, say something!"

But I couldn't speak. I had the words in my head: *I'm okay,* or even, *What goes up must come down, right?* But they wouldn't come out of my mouth.

And then I saw Mo's face looming over me. She told Noelle to move aside. Her hands were light as they skimmed over my body, my shoulders, my neck, asking me what hurt and what I could move. Once she was certain I didn't have a broken neck or back, she helped me to my feet. She walked with me, supporting my weight so gently I barely registered that we had already crossed the whole gym and were in her office.

Then she sat me down, and her eyes were not gentle.

"Very dangerous, what you did," she said.

"I'm okay," I said. I really did feel fine. I must've

been a little dazed earlier, but other than a slight headache, I was ready to go back out there and continue practice. But when I suggested that to Mo, she shook her head.

"You go home," she said. "No more practice for you."

"For today? Or ever?" I asked the question, but I didn't actually fear the answer. Of course it would just be for today. I'd taken a little fall, but that was it. There was no reason for it to derail my whole future in this sport.

But Mo's face told a different story. "I have to think about," she said. "You took risk."

"I thought that's what made me a good gymnast," I said. "I take risks. I did a full twist at the competition where you saw my tape, and I did two standing back fulls in a row today. Perfectly! You should have seen them."

"Two standing back fulls mean nothing if you paralyzed," Mo said.

"I'm not." I waved my arms and held up my foot, rotating the ankle. "See? I was just a little shocked before. But I'm fine."

Mo steepled her fingers and paused, as though she had something difficult to say and was trying to think of the best way to put it. That was when I started to get really scared.

"You don't listen," she said finally. "You don't follow rule. A gymnast is worthless to me if she don't listen."

I started to protest, but Mo picked up the phone. "I call your mother," she said. "She come get you."

The car ride home was silent; when I tried to talk to my mother, she said that she had a lot to think about. As soon as we got home, she said she was going to her room to do some of that thinking and suggested I do the same.

I wanted to call Dionne, but we hadn't talked since the time I had hung up on her. She'd actually called me, but I'd told my mother to tell her I was out. It wasn't that I didn't want to talk to Dionne. Once I had gotten over my initial shock that she was apparently still mad at me for something that had happened almost a year ago, I had felt bad. I *had* kind of monopolized her party, and I knew that sometimes I could be a little self-centered. I realized that all those times I'd turned things into the Britt Show, as she called it, I'd made people want to stop tuning in, and that was one of the reasons I felt so alone now. I wanted to apologize to her. I wanted my friend back.

But with everything that was going on with Jessie and at the gym, I hadn't felt as if I could handle anything else. Now I missed her, but I worried that every day that passed without us talking made it that much harder for us to make up.

When my mom finally called me down to dinner, I was surprised to see my dad there, too. He usually worked until late at night, which meant he came home after I was in bed and slept most of the day while I was being homeschooled by Grandma. It was rare to see him at dinner, since that was the meal he was always cooking for other people.

"Hi, Dad," I said, trying to act like I didn't already know the reason he was home. He kissed my cheek but looked at me as though he had a big presentation later that night and people were going to expect him to report on everything he had observed about me.

Dinner was homemade macaroni and cheese, the kind with six different cheeses, which my dad could whip up in no time. Although I'd never have told him this, a part of me preferred the processed version made with orange powder. His macaroni and cheese had won awards and everything, but I guess I was just used to having the instant version, from all the nights we'd made dinner without him. There's something comforting about the way the orange sauce congeals on top of the macaroni.

I'd finished most of the food on my plate when my father finally turned to me. "Do you know why we made the move to Texas?"

"Gary—"

He held up his hand. "Pam, she needs to hear this. Do you know why?"

I wanted to say, *Because it's warmer?* But I sensed that this was not the time for jokes. "No."

"We moved here so that you could go to Texas Twisters. We didn't come here and then find the gym. We came here *because* of the gym. Do you know what that means?"

My grandmother had taught me about rhetorical questions last year. She'd said they were questions that you weren't supposed to respond to. I'd asked her what the point was of a question with no answer, and she'd said that it often meant that both parties knew what the answer should be. According to her, if you actually tried to answer the question, it would just seem rude. Apparently you're supposed to let the person just ramble on and make the point both of you know he's trying to make, without interruption.

I didn't think this question was rhetorical, though, because I still didn't completely know what it meant that my parents had moved here for my gym. The full implications of it were just starting to sink in. Still, I didn't say anything.

"That means that we drove for two days for you. We sold our house in Ohio, left our friends, left our jobs . . . all for you."

"Gary," my mom said quietly, "don't make her feel guilty."

"She should feel a little guilty," he said. "She should feel guilty that we've made sacrifices and she's throwing it all away because she can't stop goofing off. Do you like gymnastics?"

It took me a minute to realize he'd shifted from talking about me to talking to me. I wasn't sure how he wanted me to respond, so I just stared at him. I wished my grandmother were there, but there was an exhibit at the museum she'd wanted to see. She'd probably made herself scarce on purpose, because she was smart like that.

"Do you?" he repeated. "Answer the question."

"Sorry," I said. "I thought it was rhetorical."

My mom tried to suppress a smile, but my dad wasn't having it. "It's not rhetorical," he said. "It's an actual question, and one which you shouldn't have to think about too hard. Do you like gymnastics?"

It was true—I didn't have to think about it too hard. Even though I hated the tedium of drills sometimes, even though I hated all the stretches they made you do, even though I complained about beam and resisted ballet training to improve my floor work, I really loved every second of it. It was the one place where I felt truly free.

"Yes," I said.

"Do you want to be a champion?"

"Yes. More than anything else in the whole world."

His face softened, and he looked more like the dad I remembered: the scruffy face, crinkly smile, and twinkling blue eyes of someone I could joke with and tell things to. I realized I'd missed him since we'd moved to Texas.

"We don't want to force you into anything," he said. "You know that, right, monkey? But we want you to have the opportunity to achieve your dream, and we thought this would be the best place for that. I'd just hate to see you throw it away."

"I won't," I whispered.

Maybe I hadn't kept my promise to Jessie. Maybe it wasn't one I was meant to keep. But this was a promise I would see through.

All of this had to be worth it, right? Moving to a new city; leaving the safety and comfort of Loveland behind; saying good-bye to Dionne, my best friend since I was eight; alienating the only three girls I'd met so far, who happened to also be my teammates; failing to prove myself to my coach, who obviously thought I was reckless and immature.

My grandmother wanted me to put myself in other people's shoes, the way Atticus told Scout to do in *To Kill a Mockingbird*. But sometimes it was hard enough to wear my own shoes, when I couldn't tell if they were getting me anywhere.

Thirteen

First thing next morning, I marched into Mo's office.

"I'm sorry about yesterday," I said. "It won't happen again. I'm listening. Please just tell me what to do."

She looked at me as if weighing my words. "Get out there and run laps around the floor until girls get here. Then you can stretch with them."

I'd be lying if I said I didn't balk a little bit in my mind at that. I'd dragged myself out of bed thirty minutes earlier than usual to get to practice before anybody else and talk to Mo, and the idea of running circles around the blue mat sounded like the biggest waste of time. But I didn't say any of that to Mo, as I might have just the day before. Instead, I nodded and headed out to the floor.

I don't know if it was something about the monotonous pounding of my feet or the constant left turns, but as I jogged I started to think. I thought about what my dad had said the night before, about my whole family uprooting itself so that I could train at one of the best gyms in the country. I thought about my mother's opening the day care, and how excited she'd been to change the colors of a couple of rooms to put her personal touch on them. Mostly, I thought about Jessie.

It was possible that I was being a drama queen. Maybe everyone else was right. Jessie had one of the biggest meets of her life coming up, and of course she'd be looking for anything that might help her performance. It was true that gymnasts at the highest levels had to watch what they ate and keep to a strict diet in order to ensure that their bodies were in peak condition. Wasn't that what being an athlete was about?

But then I remembered again the way her knees had looked, red and scraped from kneeling on that bathroom floor in the yogurt place. She hadn't been sick that day; I felt it in my gut. I remembered the way she admired other gymnasts' thinness on television and made comments about gymnasts who she thought could stand to lose a few pounds. I remembered all the times I'd seen her during snack break, or at the frozen yogurt place, or at her house, or at Christina's house, not eating, not eating . . . always not eating. Maybe it was just a diet. But it had gone too far.

The question was what to do about it. Obviously, bringing it up during a game of Truth or Dare had not been the brightest idea. I had to talk to someone who would actually listen, someone who could help Jessie. But who?

I saw Mo in the office, her head bent over something at her desk. Before I could have second thoughts, I ran over to her door. I stood there, panting, as she looked up.

"If this how you listen—" she said, but I cut her off.

"I know I'm supposed to be doing laps," I said. "And I will. I'll do as many laps as you want me to. I'm even ready to start those ballet classes you mentioned. But I have something I need to talk about with you first. Is that okay?"

She inclined her head, and I pulled up a chair. "It's about Jessie. . . ."

And then I told her everything. I told her about Jessie never eating during snack time, Jessie throwing up at the yogurt place, Jessie commenting on how thin the gymnasts at the American Invitational were. I tried to stick to just the facts, not coloring them with my perceptions. Mo had dealt with gymnasts for longer than I'd been alive. If she didn't think that Jessie's behavior sounded problematic, then obviously I *was* in the wrong. I just didn't think so.

Mo let me talk without interrupting, and when I was done, she asked only one thing. "Have you talked to Jessie?"

I nodded. "And the other—" I almost mentioned that the other girls didn't seem to think she had a problem, either. But I didn't want them to find out and think I'd thrown them under the bus. This was about Jessie. "I just have a really strong feeling about this."

Mo put her hand on my shoulder. "You have good instinct," she said. "You need to listen to it more."

I snorted. I couldn't help myself. Wasn't that

my problem? That I went with my gut instead of listening to authority? It seemed like that was what had gotten me into a lot of these messes in the first place.

"Yeah, right," I said to Mo. "Like my instinct to show off on the beam, until I fell and could've hurt myself. Or my instinct to show off in front of Christina, until I made her hate me."

Mo smiled. "Perhaps you see pattern not to show off," she said. "Sometime it not about power. Yes?"

I still believed that a full twist on the balance beam was the biggest, coolest move I could do, but I understood that Mo was talking about more than gymnastics. Even in competitions, you couldn't just do trick after trick if you wanted a high score. You had to use those little connecting moves to help tell a story to the judges. Those little moves could seem pointless, but without them, your whole routine would fall apart.

Mo's eyes turned thoughtful. "Deep down, you know what to do. But then you second-guess yourself and get in trouble. If you follow what's in here"—she gestured toward my heart—"you be just fine."

It was the most obvious advice in the world. It had probably been written on a thousand Hallmark cards. And yet this time it felt like an epiphany, like something was changing inside me that I couldn't change back—as if I'd ever want to.

In the middle of practice, Mo called Jessie into the office. Jessie came out a little later, crying. Mo hadn't thought it would be a good idea for me to sit in on the meeting, and I was kind of relieved. But of course, Jessie knew who had talked to Mo.

I followed Jessie into the locker room. "Just listen to me," I said. "Please."

She turned around, not bothering to hide her red-rimmed eyes and quivering chin. "Haven't you done enough talking? God, as if it's not bad enough that you told Christina and Noelle. At least they weren't stupid enough to believe you. But then you have to go and tell Mo? That's really low, Britt."

"I knew you'd be mad at me," I said. "I knew you'd probably hate me forever. But I'd rather you hate me forever than do this to yourself. Did I ever tell you about Kim, back at my old gym?"

Jessie chewed her left thumbnail, her *no*

so quiet and sullen that I almost thought I'd imagined it.

"Well, she had a problem, and you really remind me of her. One time, my friend Dionne and I caught her in the bathroom with these laxatives she was using to lose weight, and—"

"I've never used laxatives in my life," Jessie said. "That's disgusting."

"Maybe not, but you and I both know that you're obsessed with your weight, just like Kim was. I don't think you see yourself in the mirror anymore."

"I'm ugly," she cried. "Why would I want to see myself?"

"You're not ugly. That image you're making up is ugly. I don't want to be friends with that girl."

"Well, she doesn't want to be friends with you!"

I shrugged. "I can't help that. But I can help you, or at least try."

"Some help," Jessie snorted. "Thanks to you, I'm probably not going to the qualifier, not after Mo meets with my parents. Can you believe that? I'm going to have to wait even longer to become an Elite. Christina will make it, and I'll be the last person still training as a stupid Level Ten."

"Maybe it's for the best," I said, but it sounded

weak even to my ears. I hadn't known that Jessie would be left out of the qualifier. If the pressure to compete was part of her stress, then it made sense that Jessie's parents and Mo might want her to take it easy and help her focus on getting better. But I was getting better at imagining myself in someone else's shoes, and I knew I'd have been devastated if I lost the chance to move up to Elite-level competition.

The chances that I'd completely wrecked my friendship with Jessie were high. But at the same time, I couldn't regret what I'd done. I might have been the least-liked member of the Texas Twisters team, but I was beginning to realize that teamwork wasn't always just about getting along. It was about looking out for one another, even if it meant making hard decisions. And this had been the hardest decision I'd ever made in my life.

It was easy to keep my head down and just concentrate on gymnastics during practice. Jessie had been sent home, and the other girls wouldn't even meet my gaze. After I did five perfect first halves of my beam routine, Mo stopped me. "I think we add full twist," she said.

I knew better than to get my hopes up, but I still felt my adrenaline surge. "Really? A standing back full?"

She flicked her wrist dismissively. "You not ready for that. But you could do a round-off to full twist for your acrobatic series. I think you can handle."

I would've jumped up and down, but that wasn't the best idea when standing on a surface that was only four inches wide. Obviously, Mo could see that I was really ready to change. Otherwise, why would she have finally decided to trust me?

Apparently, Mo was wary of letting me get too excited. "For now, you do only on practice beam. Is that clear?"

"Yes," I said. Kind of a bummer, but still way better than not being able to try the move at all. The practice beam was shorter and had mats stacked up on either side so you never fell too far. When I was younger, I used to love the practice beam, because it meant I was doing something cooler than anything they'd allow me to do on a regular beam. But now, it felt a little bit like being told you have to sit in a flight simulator when you've already orbited the moon.

Still, I wasn't going to complain. The New Britt would never complain.

I was smiling as I started working on the second half of my beam routine. Noelle gave me a weird look. She was probably wondering what I could possibly have been happy about, given everything that was going on.

It did give me a pang when I glanced over at the other side of the gym and saw Christina and Cheng at the bars. Jessie should have been there, working on her transitions from low bar to high bar and trying to stick her dismount. But she wasn't, and it was all my fault.

"Why would you do it?" Noelle asked, her voice low. She was still standing on her beam, hands on her hips, looking at me. Mo had been pulled aside by a parent; I glanced over to see if there was any chance she might catch us talking. She moved slightly to her right, and I saw that the parent was Jessie's mom.

I wanted to tell Noelle that I'd had to, but when I opened my mouth, no words came out. Had I really? What if I'd waited until after the qualifier, at least, so Jessie could've had her chance to compete? Should I have thought it through?

"You don't know any of us," Noelle said. "You think you do, but you've only been here a few weeks."

It was weird how it felt like so much longer. I tried to remember messing around in the pit with Dionne, pretending that we were competing in the X Games as we spun like cyclones into the soft foam. Had I really been doing that only a few months ago? It was hard even to picture that Britt now—the one who just had fun without worrying about the consequences, the one who hadn't known what it was like to compete for a team. There had been Dionne, and there had been me, and we had been friends without really worrying about how we might get in each other's way in the gym. Maybe that was the way to do it.

"If you think this will get to Christina and stop her from qualifying, you're wrong," Noelle said.

Honestly, it hadn't even occurred to me to worry about Christina. This wasn't about my beef with her; I didn't really even *have* a beef. Christina was the one who seemed to have it in for *me*. This had nothing to do with Christina, and I told Noelle that.

"What about Jessie?" I asked. I hated the idea

that anything I'd done would damage Jessie, and I needed reassurance that she'd be okay. I knew Christina was tough, but Jessie was different.

Noelle looked down at the beam, smoothing a line of chalk with her toe. "Just give her time," she said. "She'll be okay."

Did Noelle mean that Jessie would return to her training without any problems? Was Noelle acknowledging the fact that Jessie *wasn't* okay now, that she did have some issues? Or did she mean that Jessie would eventually forgive me?

From my vantage point up on the beam, I watched Mo and Jessie's mother talk, and I tried to figure out what was happening. Mo's back was to me, but I could see Jessie's mom's face, the way her forehead was all crinkled up so that her freckles looked like little raisins. She was nodding at whatever Mo was saying, pressing her hand to her chest as though taking responsibility for something.

Noelle went back to her drills, and I watched her execute an absolutely perfect full turn with her leg held up the whole time. She looked like one of those ballerinas in a music box, spinning on the toes of one foot without even a wobble.

Maybe it wouldn't hurt to take those extra

ballet lessons that Mo kept telling my mother I should have. I knew that both Christina and Noelle did them once a week, and they were two of the best dancers I'd ever seen. Especially Christina, who—as much as I hated to admit it—looked like she could have starred in *Swan Lake* if she'd wanted to. Well, if *Swan Lake* had also included some back walkovers and ring leaps, which, although I'd never actually seen it, I kind of doubted. My mom took me to see *The Nutcracker* one year for Christmas, and I'd sat through most of the show trying to figure out how the nutcracker guy got into that crazy costume. If all they were going to do was twirl around the stage a bunch, what was the point? Why not throw in some backflips?

We did our stretches at the end of practice as usual, and my mom was actually on time to pick me up. After the long day I'd had and the added stress of the whole Jessie situation, I was relieved to see her red car pull up near the parking lot.

"Hi," I said, climbing into the passenger side. I sighed as soon as my head hit the seat.

My mom gave me a sideways glance. "Did your chat with Mo go well?" she asked.

How to explain to my mom the completely

complicated situation our talk had created? For the moment, I chose to forget about the whole Jessie part and just tell my mom what I knew she was waiting to hear. "Yeah. Mo even said I could put the full twist back into my beam routine."

"That's great, honey!"

I felt myself get excited all over again. "It was totally cool. I mean, I'll be on the practice beam for a little while, but that's not so bad. As long as I get to rock it in competition. Can you imagine me on TV someday, Mom? Landing a full twist on two feet perfectly, without bobbling or anything?"

"Mm-hmm," she murmured, but I could tell she was distracted by having to merge lanes; she put on her turn signal and started glancing over her shoulder.

"I know I won't be on TV for a while," I said. "But someday, when I'm a Senior Elite, I bet I could be. Imagine if I went to the American Invitational. Or the Olympics!"

"Noelle—she's the state beam champ, right?" my mom asked, obviously just putting Noelle's name together with the gigantic sign that hung on the outside of the gym. I could still remember the first time I'd ever seen Texas Twisters, driving by it at night in our U-Haul and peering through the windows.

"Yeah. She's really good."

"She's such a hard worker," my mom said. "And seems like a sweet girl. You should ask her for any help you need with your beam routine. I bet you could learn a lot from her."

I doubted anyone would ever have thought to call me a hard worker. Grandma used to give me assignments that she said she wasn't going to look at but that were for my own "personal edification," whatever that meant. Then she realized that as soon as she said that, I would just doodle all over my paper, or sometimes write the same nonsense sentence over and over to make it look as if I was writing. It wasn't that I didn't know how to do the work—I just didn't really want to. Grandma said if I spent half as much energy actually doing what people asked of me as I did trying to get *out* of doing what people asked of me, I'd have been a force to be reckoned with.

But that was the Old Britt. The New Britt would run a hundred laps around the gym if that was what Mo wanted, or write twenty pages on the themes of *To Kill a Mockingbird*. The New Britt could be just as hard a worker as Noelle was.

Still, I doubted that anyone would ever have called me sweet. I wasn't bitter or anything, but I wasn't the kind of person who would break off half of my candy bar to give to a starving orphan, either.

But that was also the Old Britt. The New Britt was going to be pleasant to everyone, even Christina and Noelle, who didn't seem to want to return the favor. I hoped my mom could see how hard I was trying.

Fourteen

As soon as we got home, my mom disappeared into her bedroom like she usually did. I stood in the living room for a second before knocking on her door. Although I didn't hear her tell me to, I went in anyway.

She already had the TV tuned to some show about supernannies, where these women with British accents were always telling parents it was "all about boundaries." I reached over and switched the TV off.

"Britt! I was watching that."

"Could I talk to you for a minute?" I asked. "It's really important."

Maybe it was because I was feeling energized, as the New Britt, maybe it was because I'd already braved two huge confrontations that day, with Mo and with Jessie, although those hadn't been very successful. But all I knew was that I didn't want things to be the same as before.

"I'm sorry that you and Dad had to move all the way here for me," I said. "I know you liked it in Ohio."

"Oh, honey." My mom patted a spot next to her on the bed, and I plopped down to join her. "He shouldn't have said that."

"I'm glad he did," I said. "I had no idea how much I was messing everything up."

"You need to know that we take your gymnastics seriously. So you should, too."

"I know." It was the next part that was the hardest for me to say. The part that, no matter how many times I rehearsed it in my head, I didn't know quite how to phrase; finally I figured I would just ask it straight out and not care how stupid it sounded. "You love me, right, Mom?"

She laughed. "What kind of a question is that? Of course I love you."

"You don't wish that I was smarter, or better,

or . . . more like Noelle?" From what I knew of Noelle's parents, who were Romanian immigrants, it didn't seem like they had a single bit of trouble from Noelle. She would never put glue in the water fountain (it was *supposed* to be a fun prank, but Dionne and I had to clean the glue out, and then it wasn't so fun) or talk back to her grandmother about the absolute uselessness of converting decimals to fractions using arithmetic (that's what a calculator is for, after all).

"Of course not." Her brows drew together as she studied my face. "Why are you asking all of these questions? Where is this coming from?"

"It's just that you spend a lot of time at the day care." The words came out in a rush, as though I was worried they'd get stale if they stayed inside me too long. "Sometimes I think other people's kids get to see you more than I do. And that sucks, because I don't have another mother to go home to like they do. I have you, but you're always busy. And then you say that Noelle is so great, and it seems like maybe you'd spend more time with me if I was like her."

"Oh, Brittany." She pulled me close to her, stroking my cheek and burying her face in my hair.

"I didn't know you felt that way. I know I haven't been around a lot lately—"

"Well, you're starting your own day care," I said. "It's your dream, I know, like I spend all my time at gym, because my dream is to go to the Olympics. I guess I just miss you. And Dad."

"We both love you very much. You. Not Noelle or the kids at the day care, but my spunky, smart little Britt. Don't forget that. And we'll figure out a way to spend more time together, I promise."

Twelve's a little old for this kind of warm and fuzzy sitcom moment, probably, but it felt good to curl up on the bed with my mom and find an old movie on TV. After all, a lot had changed since I'd moved to the second-biggest state in the country. I'd left behind a friend who got my sense of humor and understood that, while I could be thoughtless sometimes, I was never malicious. I'd given up a spot at a gym where, even if they didn't produce Olympic champions, they knew that having fun was just as important as winning medals.

I couldn't stand the thought that I might've hurt my parents, too, so it was good to know that they were on my side. The New Britt might have been more mature than the Old Britt, but one thing hadn't changed—at the end of the day, I still needed my mom.

After dinner, I picked up the phone and dialed Dionne's number. Her mom answered.

"Um, hi," I said, suddenly nervous. I hadn't expected Dionne's mother to pick up her cell phone. What if Dionne had told her what a bad friend I was? What if she'd already told her to screen any call from me with some lame excuse about being in the shower or out with friends?

Or what if she really *was* out? Dionne had had other friends besides me, and they'd probably gotten superclose after I left. Dionne might even have been wondering why she'd wasted so much time with me when she could have been hanging out with them all along.

Meanwhile, I had no friends here. Worse, I had mortal enemies.

"Is Dionne home?"

"Sure, just one second." Dionne must have deleted me from her contacts. Obviously, her mother didn't recognize my voice, or else she wouldn't have been so cavalier about handing her daughter the phone.

"Hello?"

"Hi, Dionne. It's me, Britt."

"I know." So obviously she hadn't deleted me from her address book. Maybe she wasn't mad at me after all. "What's up?"

"Not much," I said. "Is this still your number? Or is it your mom's now?"

"It's mine. The phone was just on the counter, so she picked it up. I hate it when she does that."

"At least you have a cell phone." It was a familiar discussion, and I felt myself relax a little bit. "I'd rather have a cell phone with a thousand restrictions than no cell phone at all."

"True. So what's up? I called you a couple times."

Where did I even begin? I explained to Dionne the whole situation with Jessie, the way the other girls treated me, the truth about why my parents moved here, and the conversation I'd had with my mom.

"Wow," she said when I was done. "You've been busy. I was going to tell you about how I invented a new cereal by combining Rice Krispies with Cocoa Puffs, but now it doesn't seem so important."

"You were right," I blurted out. "I should've

stopped to think about your feelings at your birthday party. I'm sorry."

"Don't worry about it," she said. "You wouldn't be Britt without being totally crazy."

"Great. Just what I want to be known for."

Dionne laughed. "You're not," she said. "Well, okay, sometimes. But you dive right into something headfirst and worry about the consequences later, and that can be a really cool way to be."

"Yeah," I said. "If you don't end up with brain damage."

We chatted for an hour. I laughed at all of her stories about people at our old gym, and she tried to figure out a time when she could come down to visit. We were cool, just like we'd always been. It felt good to have a friend.

This time, it was my mother who told us to get off the phone. "I gotta go," I said. "I'm about to play Battleship with my mom, and I've got a strategy that's going to help me win big, I just know it."

"Is it your thing where you put all your ships on one side of the board? Everyone sees right through that."

Crap. That had been exactly my plan.

* * *

I didn't have a strategy for talking to Jessie after the incident the week before, except that I knew I had to do it. I told my mom that I thought I'd left something over at Jessie's, so she stopped by the sprawling suburban house on our way from the gym to the grocery store.

"You'll be only a second, though, right?" she said, glancing at her watch. "You know the frozen lasagna will take two hours to cook once we get it in the oven."

"I'll be quick," I assured her. It was probably not a lie. Worst-case scenario: Jessie would see me through the peephole and unleash her hounds (she didn't have dogs before, but she would have them now, to protect herself against me), and it only took them a few moments to tear me to shreds. Of course, best-case scenario was that Jessie and I would totally make up, and then I would run back and tell my mom to count me out for dinner, because I was going to spend the night with my new best friend.

Like that would happen.

Tiffany opened the door when I rang the bell. She stared at me as if I'd come from an entirely different planet. I was still in my leotard, with my shorts pulled over it, while she was wearing a baby T and low-rise jeans and looked as if she should have been on the cover of a teen magazine, so I guess I might as well have been an alien.

"Hi!" I smiled to let her know that I came in peace. "I'm, uh, one of Jessie's friends. Is she here?"

Tiffany's eyes flicked over me again. "Come in," she said grudgingly. "Jess is in her room."

She led me through the kitchen toward the closed door of Jessie's room. I smiled again at her, trying to tell her with my eyes that everything was cool and she could leave me alone now, but she just stood there.

"Go ahead," she said. "Knock. She's in there."

My hands were trembling a little, but I wanted to look confident, so I ended up rapping on the door way harder than I meant to. It sounded as if I was the police coming to break up a party or something. "Jess?"

There was silence for a moment. Then, through the door: "Who is it?"

At that point, I could have told her Adolf Hitler and she'd probably have been more likely to open the door. "Um, it's Britt. From gym."

I don't know why I felt the need to add that

last part. I'm sure she knew exactly who I was.

The response was swift. "Go away!"

Tiffany raised her eyebrows. "I don't think she wants to see you," she said.

Thank you, Captain Obvious.

"Jess, please," I said. "Open the door. I need to talk to you."

"Go. Away."

I glanced at Tiffany, who still showed no sign of moving. I'd seen Mo talking with Jessie's mom that day at the gym, but I didn't know how much Tiffany was in the loop about the situation, and it would only have upset Jessie more if I'd started blabbing everything in front of the stepsister who barely tolerated her.

"I know you're mad at me," I said. "You think I told Mo about your, uh, balance problems to be mean. Or, I don't know, maybe you thought I was hoping to move in on your friends and take your place in the gym by forcing you out. Is that it? Is that why you're angry?"

"You know why," Jessie said through the door, but this time her voice was a lot closer; I could tell she was standing on the other side of the door.

"But that's not why I did it," I said. "I *want* you

in the gym. I *want* to train with you. I *want* to be your friend. And friends can't let friends throw everything away, which is what I was afraid you were doing."

"*Friends*"—the emphasis Jessie put on the word made it sound almost like a curse—"don't go behind their friends' backs and spill all their secrets."

"They do if those secrets are dangerous," I said quietly. "They do if they're worried about their friends."

Tiffany was starting to look interested in this whole exchange, and I gave her a wobbly smile to let her know that everything was good, this was just two gym buddies talking shop. I repeated my plea for Jessie to open the door, and finally it cracked open an inch. I saw a sliver of her bloodshot eyes, and I knew she'd been crying.

"Go away," Jessie said. "We're not friends anymore. I don't know if we ever were."

"But—"

"No. Leave me alone, Britt. I don't have anything more to say to you." And with that, she slammed the door in my face.

Tiffany let out a long breath, as though she'd

been watching an intense reality show and it was finally the commercial break. "Wow, she is *mad*," she said. "What was that all about?"

I tried to remember the lie I'd come up with earlier—something about balance problems. "Jessie's having trouble on the beam," I mumbled. "And she doesn't think I should've gone to the coach about it."

"God, you gymnasts argue about the stupidest stuff." Tiffany started to show me to the door, but I shook my head. I already knew the way.

The worst part was that I couldn't blame Jessie at all. It would have been so much easier if I could've just pretended that she was being unreasonable, that it wasn't worth it to be her friend anyway, and that eventually she'd realize how ridiculous she was being. But when I put myself in her shoes, I knew exactly why she was so mad. I'd be angry and hurt and unforgiving, too.

This was the part that my grandmother hadn't talked about, that Atticus hadn't told Scout. If I were Jessie, I'd have hated me. So then, did empathizing with Jessie mean that I should hate myself? I turned the question over and over in my head, until I felt like my brain might explode. Maybe this was how Boo Radley had become such a recluse—he empathized so much with other people's feelings that he started having trouble sorting out his own. There it had been only a few days of this mess for me, and already I was thinking that holing up somewhere else for a while didn't seem like such a bad idea.

Fifteen

Without Jessie at the gym, I found myself eating snack alone at the table where we'd once sat together. Who was I kidding? Even if she were still at the gym, it wasn't like she would've chosen to sit with me. Nobody sits with Boo Radley.

I'd seen the names of the competitors at the upcoming qualifier, and now it was official: Jessie wasn't in it. Apparently, Mo had left the possibility open that Jessie could still come back and try out, but Jessie's mom thought it best if they focused on her health first. At that rate, Jessie wouldn't have been able to try out for the Elite team until fall.

Christina and Noelle gave me dirty looks as they passed. They were eating their snacks by the pro shop again, where Mrs. Flores was working the desk. Before I could give in to second thoughts, I tossed my apple core into the trash and strode over to where they were sitting.

"Can I talk to both of you?" I asked. The people whose opinions I cared about, in order of importance, were Mom, Mo, and Jessie, my only true friend. I'd already tackled all three of those confrontations, with mixed results; now I was ready to take on Christina and Noelle. Considering that we'd never really been friends in the first place, I didn't have much to lose.

"I know you're both mad at me." I noticed that Mrs. Flores seemed to be watching the whole exchange with interest, and I dropped my voice. "Look, maybe we can go somewhere else?"

Christina gave me a haughty look over her cup of yogurt. "Anything you have to say, you can say right here."

"Okay," I said, although I darted one more glance at Mrs. Flores. God only knew what Christina had told her already. "I just wanted to let you know that I understand, and it's okay."

Noelle looked perplexed. "Understand what?"

"Why you didn't say anything about Jessie earlier," I said. "You're not bad friends at all—you were just too close to see it."

"Gee, thanks," Christina said, her voice dripping with sarcasm. "I can't tell you how much it means to me to have your approval."

I was doing my patented foot-in-mouth thing again, but this time I was able to recognize and try to correct it. "No—that's not what I mean. I just don't think you should feel guilty. Christina, you have a ton of pressure on you with this qualifier coming up, and with—" I almost said, *with your mom*—who I knew could be a bit overbearing—but I stopped myself just in time. Although Mrs. Flores had gone back to sorting incoming mail, I knew she could still hear us.

"And Noelle, your parents own a store, right?" I tried to remember what Jessie had told me about Noelle's home life. "I know they need you to help out a lot. And even though you're not competing at the qualifier, you're the only gymnast in the state who got invited to the Nationals, at the training camp. I mean, wow. I can't imagine how awesome that must be, but I know it must be stressful."

Noelle chewed on her bottom lip, as though she was actually thinking about what I was saying, and I felt encouraged. "All I'm trying to say is that *of course* you guys know each other better than I know you. You've been a team for years. But sometimes it takes a person on the outside to see what's going on, and that's what happened with me and Jessie."

I took a deep breath. The last part would be the hardest. "It's not because I don't care about her, or you guys. If anything, it's the opposite. I care so much about being a part of this team that I would hate to see anything bring it down."

It was totally true. It had only been a few short weeks, but more than anything in the world I wanted to feel as if I truly belonged with these three girls. I wanted to be a Texas Twister, through the good and the bad.

Noelle looked at her hands, pulling at a cuticle as she avoided my gaze. Christina stared at me silently, and for a moment I allowed myself to hope. But then her black eyes turned steely, and I knew my entire speech had been useless, even before she opened her mouth.

"At this point," she said, "the only thing bringing this team down is you."

I wondered why I was the villain in her scenario, when I was at least making an attempt to get into their skins and understand how they were feeling. If Christina had taken even a second to put herself in my position, she wouldn't have bothered being mean to me anymore, because she'd have seen that I was already feeling completely defeated.

I tried to convince my grandmother that she should go easy on the homeschooling, considering that the competition season was starting, but she wasn't having it. "You need to exercise your mind as well as your body," she said.

It felt like all I'd been doing for the past few weeks was exercising my mind—mostly, trying to figure out how to get out of all the messes I had gotten myself into. But to Grandma, that wasn't the same as writing an essay about *To Kill a Mockingbird*, so I guessed that was what I had to do.

I was trying to craft a thesis statement about the meaning of the book's title, but I couldn't concentrate. "Grandma, what if you do what you know is the right thing, but it blows up in your face?"

One thing my grandmother was very good at was knowing when I was just malingering (one of her favorite words to describe me) and when something was seriously going on. She seemed to sense that this question was important to me, because she didn't even try to get me back on task.

"Define 'blows up in your face,'" she said.

"Well, like if you lost a friend over it."

She thought about this for a moment. "Are you positive you did the right thing?"

"Yes."

"Then there are two possibilities," she said. "Your friend will realize that, and come back to you, or else, maybe she's not as good a friend as you thought—if she can't see that you acted in the only way you could've."

Adults always said things like that, about how you were better off, blah-blah-blah. But I missed Jessie. She was the only person who'd made me feel welcome when I came to Texas. And sometimes being right didn't feel quite as good as having your friend back.

Before Grandma was forced to prod me, I went back to writing my essay. The title of *To Kill a Mockingbird*, I wrote, referred to a saying that Atticus used, about how it was a sin to kill a mockingbird, because all they did was provide beautiful

music, without hurting anyone. Was I the mockingbird in this case? But as much as I hated to admit it,
I *had* hurt people—from Christina, when I rubbed
it in her face about the full-in, to Noelle, when I
took Sparky, to Jessie, when I betrayed her trust.

So then, was Jessie the mockingbird? Had it
been a sin to reveal her secret the way I did, when
she'd done nothing to me?

I didn't think so. It might have been cheesy,
what my grandmother had said about true friends
realizing you were acting in their best interests. But
it was true. I'd seen a mockingbird with a broken
wing, and I had to stop it from trying to fly, in case
it got hurt.

A mockingbird couldn't thank me for my help,
of course. And maybe that wasn't the point. Maybe
the only thing that mattered was that the mockingbird was able to fly away someday, healthy and
happy.

Suddenly, analyzing *To Kill a Mockingbird*
seemed a lot less complicated than all the stuff
swirling in my head.

Sixteen

Cheng had the three of us—minus Jessie now—work out on the floor. We would line up at one corner and, at Cheng's signal, flip and tumble our way to the opposite corner. Then we would start the whole process over, going back and forth with our passes until he determined we'd practiced enough.

For me, it felt like one of those classic word problems: a farmer needs to get his chicken, fox, and grain over to the other side of the river, but the fox can never be alone with the chicken, and the chicken can never be alone with the grain. In this case, I was the chicken. If I was left with the fox (Christina), she'd eat me alive. If I was left with the grain (Noelle) . . . Well, it wasn't really like I would eat her. So maybe it was more like I was left with *two* foxes.

Christina landed her double twist and went to take her place in line behind me, nudging my shoulder as she passed. I knew it was on purpose. There was only an entire *gym* full of space for her to walk around me, so there was no reason to come that close. I tried to ignore her, but I couldn't help taking a small step forward to put more space between us. I watched Noelle land her tumbling run (feet perfectly planted on the mat, waist not piked too far down, of course) before preparing to take my turn again.

At least the girls were now just cold and quiet. A few days before, when the incident with Jessie was still fresh, Christina would whisper nasty things if we happened to be standing near each other at the chalk bowl or something. She whispered to me about how it was all my fault, about how much better off the Texas Twisters had been without me, and about how I should go back to Ohio.

I'd be lying if I said it didn't hurt. When I thought back to my first day at the gym, how nervous I'd been, how much I'd wanted these girls to like me, I felt this pain in my chest that was something like the burn I got after eating Grandma's spicy chili, but different. It was deeper. When I'd first moved to Austin, I had thought that these girls were all sticks in the mud who could use some lightening up, and that I was just the girl to help them do it. Now it seemed as if all my attempts at fun had been misguided, and when it came time to deal with something really serious, I'd messed it up.

Before Christina set off on her next tumbling run, Cheng told her to try the tucked full-in she'd been struggling with.

"You'll spot me, right?" she asked, and her voice shook slightly. So the Great Christina was human, after all.

"I'll be right here," Cheng said, but he didn't agree to spot her, exactly. He obviously wanted her to try it without his help, although he'd be there in case she needed him.

Christina's back was to me, so I couldn't see her face, but I could tell by the way she clenched and unclenched her fists at her sides that she was nervous. Even though we were far from being friends, I found myself cheering her on—in my head, of course; I didn't want to get her Glare of Death again.

"Come on, Christina," Noelle said. "You can do this."

"Just on the floor?" Christina asked.

Cheng nodded. "You ready," he said.

Her shoulders moved up and down in an exaggerated motion, as if she were taking a deep breath, and then she stretched her fingers reflexively before straightening her arms at her sides, with one foot flat on the ground and the other pointed in front of her.

Once she took off, it was like everything happened in slow motion. She was running, springing into her round-off back handspring, and then she was in the air, her body flipping and twisting. I knew when she was still in midair that she wasn't going to make it, and in those stretched-out moments it felt almost as if I should *say* something, *do* something to help her. I saw Cheng moving toward her, but everything felt impossibly delayed.

In reality, it was only a millisecond before Christina crashed onto the floor, her feet touching the mat an instant before her head did, her body folding at the waist. The only thing that stopped her from face-planting was Cheng's intervention; he took hold of her arm and pulled her upper body away from the floor.

That was why it could be nerve-racking to do a skill for the first time without a spot. Your trainer might have been there, but you had to be realistic. He was not always going to be able to get there in time to save you.

Noelle and I rushed over to Christina. At that moment, I wasn't thinking about Jessie or the fact that Christina hated me. I just wanted to make sure she was okay.

Mrs. Flores also came running over from the parents' viewing section, and she bent over Christina. I heard her exclaiming over her daughter. As soon as she realized that it had looked scarier than it actually was, her tone changed and she stood up.

"The qualifier is in a week," she hissed at Christina. "If you can't get this, you won't make Elite. Do you want that? To watch everyone leave you behind?"

Whoa. I hadn't transitioned yet from my concern about Christina, but apparently her mother had. Christina was rising to her feet now, and her mom towered over her in her alligator-skin heels, lecturing her about the importance of doing something over and over again until you got it right.

"The new girl can do this move," Christina's mom was saying as she led a stunned Christina off to the side. I didn't know if the dazed look was the aftereffect of the fall, or if it was surprise at her mother's attack. "When are *you* going to?"

I couldn't believe that, at one point, I'd actually been jealous of Christina's relationship with her mother. I'd envied the fact that her mom was always at the gym and seemed to care about her daughter's gymnastics, unlike my mom, who was caught up in her own work. But I realized that my mother didn't really care whether I moved up a level or not, as long as I was happy and I tried my best. I don't know if I could have handled her breathing down my neck all the time.

I turned to Noelle. "Man," I said loudly, "I wish I had half of Christina's grace."

She wrinkled her forehead in confusion. "What?"

"Have you seen her full turn on beam? It's, like, the most beautiful thing I've ever seen. The judges love that kind of stuff, but I suck at it."

"Um . . . okay."

I continued undaunted. "I mean, you can *learn* how to do tumbling passes, you know? Anyone can do a piked full-in after a bit of practice. But if you're not a good dancer, forget it. It's so much harder to work on that."

Noelle glanced over at Mrs. Flores and Christina, who weren't bothering to disguise the fact that they were listening. Finally, she seemed to get it. "Oh, yeah," she said. "Christina's always been awesome at the artistic part of gymnastics."

"So lucky," I said. "She'll get that piked full-in by next week; but me? I don't think I'll ever learn how to do a perfect arabesque."

Mrs. Flores had her hand on Christina's shoulder. She gave it a squeeze. "Let me buy you a Gatorade at the concession," she said. "I'm sure Cheng would understand if you took a five-minute break."

Christina turned to leave with her mom, but she shot me a look over her shoulder. I couldn't tell if she was grateful for my intervention, but it didn't matter. I'd just done what I hoped someone else might do for me—been a friend.

Cheng gave us all a short break, and I headed in to the locker room. I don't know how long I sat on the bench, lost in my own thoughts, before Christina and Noelle came in. Christina was holding her Gatorade, and I watched them approach like those slow zombies in the movies. I knew they were going to tear the flesh from my limbs and snack on my intestines, but I was glued to the spot. I couldn't do anything but stare as they stopped right in front of me.

"We—" Noelle began.

"Listen—" Christina said.

They glanced at each other. "Let me go first," Christina said. "I'm the one who's been such a heinous jerk. Britt, we want to apologize."

"Apologize?" I repeated, like an idiot. Surely I must have heard wrong. *They* wanted to apologize to *me*?

"You were right," Noelle said. "About everything. Jessie's been acting weirder and weirder for a while, and if we had bothered to look closer, we would've seen it wasn't just stress about the qualifier. I don't know if we didn't want to see it—"

"—Or we were just too busy with our own drama," Christina broke in, shaking her head in disgust. "Honestly, I was so wrapped up in my competition with you that I barely noticed Jessie.

If it hadn't been for you, nobody would've ever spoken up."

I wondered if this was a dream, or if there was a way to ask them to repeat all the nice stuff they were saying to me into a tape recorder so that I could play it back whenever I started thinking they hated me.

"Jessie asked me not to tell anyone," I said. "I should've handled it differently—made her tell someone or whatever. I shouldn't have brought it up at your sleepover."

Christina waved her hand. "I was being a brat about that sleepover, anyway," she said. "I'm sorry I didn't invite you."

"You did," I said, "eventually."

"We should have another sleepover soon," Noelle said, "and maybe we should skip Truth or Dare."

I bit my lip. "It won't be the same without Jessie, though."

Noelle drew her eyebrows together. "Why wouldn't we invite Jessie?"

"I just don't think she'll come," I said. "She's really mad at me. I doubt she'll ever forgive me."

It might've been different if Jessie and I had been friends for years, if we'd grown up together and gone through Girl Scouts together and told countless secrets to each other. Maybe then, Jessie would someday have realized I'd been acting out of concern. But what did we have holding our friendship together, really, except for a couple of conversations during our snack break and one homework help session?

Christina and Noelle glanced at each other.

"Let us take care of that," Noelle said.

I shrugged. I doubted there was much they could do, but it was nice of them to want to try. Turning back to my locker, I took out a roll of athletic tape and started wrapping my ankle.

"Are you hurt?" Christina asked. It was going to take a while to get used to hearing her speak without any sarcasm in her voice, but it was definitely a welcome change.

"Nah," I said. "But since we're going back out on the floor, I thought I'd tape up my ankle just in case. For some reason, I've been landing my passes with more weight on this side, and I don't want to put any extra stress on it."

"Don't take this the wrong way," Noelle said. "But you'd better not. Mo and Cheng have very strong feelings about using bandages or tape in practice."

"We're not allowed to use tape?"

"Only if you're hurt," Noelle said. "They think that using it when you're not is just a crutch that weakens your body."

A few weeks earlier, I would've assumed that they were messing with me, making stuff up in order to get me in trouble or make me look stupid. But I believed them now. I started unwinding the tape, wincing as I ripped off a strip around my anklebone. "Thanks," I said.

"Any time," Noelle said. "We're teammates, aren't we?"

Seventeen

Excitement was in the air on the day of the qualifier. I climbed to the top of the bleachers with Noelle, since neither of us was competing. I don't think I'd ever just sat and watched a gymnastics meet before. Even back in Ohio, once when I'd gotten really sick in the middle of a competition, I'd waited out the rest of it in a back room with my head between my knees.

"This is fun, right?" Noelle asked. We were both wearing our new team jackets, which Mo had ordered in a bright red with white stitching across the back advertising our gym. The logo depicted a gymnast with a bunch of swirls around her, as though she were a cyclone.

"Totally," I said. "It's weird, though. Don't you feel like we should be out there, somehow?"

"Yeah." Noelle grew quiet; I was sure she had the same images running through her head that I did: sitting perfectly still while someone spritzed hair spray all over your hair; the premeet pep talk from your coach; the adrenaline rush as you walked out onto the floor for the first time, taking in all the equipment that had been set up and the other teams as they began to stretch.

In order to qualify for Elite competition, Christina had to get a certain all-around score. Noelle said that she'd gotten scores that high before, at a competition last year, but it hadn't been an official qualifier, so it hadn't counted.

"Well, if she's done it before, she can do it again," I said.

Noelle nodded, but she looked a little worried. I guess when you'd seen a friend compete at ten separate meets, the fact that she got such a great score at one of them wasn't a big confidence-booster.

"She's got the full-in now," I pointed out.

Christina had gotten much more consistent at performing that skill in the last week. I liked to think it was because of the advice I'd given her, which she was now finally willing to listen to—but I knew it was probably all Cheng's general awesomeness. He didn't talk much, but my experience working with him over the past couple of weeks had taught me that he didn't have to. He had a way of showing you what you needed to do in the fewest steps possible, so that it seemed almost effortless. One minute you were hitting a brick wall, and the next minute you were flying. It was incredible.

An announcement came over the loudspeaker, asking everyone to stand for the national anthem.

After the anthem, we sat back down. The program said that Christina was in the first group, which started on vault. I knew she would be relieved by drawing Olympic order, which goes: vault, then bars, then beam, and ends with floor. She likes to get vault out of the way early, so that she can focus on the events she says actually interest her.

I saw my mom at the bottom of the bleachers searching for me, and I waved to let her know where we were. She'd dropped Noelle and me off in front and then circled around the parking lot to find a space. It was totally insane how crowded places could get for these things.

"It sucks your mom couldn't be here," I said to Noelle. I realized I'd never met any of Noelle's family.

She shrugged. "It's hard with the store. My older brothers can't run it on their own, so my parents pretty much always have to be there."

"I didn't know you had brothers."

"Four of them." Noelle rolled her eyes. "The twins are eight, and then Radu and Mihai are both in high school. And before you ask, no, they are *not* cute."

Like I'd have been interested. I still thought boys were, for the most part, complete wastes of time. Who wanted to go to the movies with some kid who'd rather tell fart jokes than watch the thing he'd paid eight dollars to see? It was stupid.

"Cute like Scott, you mean?" I teased, waggling my eyebrows.

As expected, Noelle flushed a little.

"What's the deal with you and him, anyway?" I asked.

"There's no *deal*," she said. "I get that he's older

than me, and it could never happen. It's just . . . I like dreaming about it, I guess."

"Has he ever actually spoken to you? I mean, other than—" I didn't want to remind Noelle of the time I'd taken her stuffed animal. Not when we were finally getting along. "Other than a little bit here and there?"

"Not yet," she said, lowering her voice as my mom reached our row. "But someday."

"Hi, girls." My mom smiled at us, unaware of our topic of discussion—which was a good thing, because I didn't even want to think about the way she would have squealed with delight if she'd thought I was talking about *boys*.

I knew it wasn't easy for her to spend her whole Saturday here when she still had a lot to do to get the day care ready. But she was making an effort, and so was I. I told her that I'd be happy to spend the next day going through kids' toys with her in exchange for her coming to the meet.

"Hi, Mrs. Morgan," Noelle said. Sometimes I still felt a little jealous of my mother's obvious affection for Noelle, but I knew my mother cared about me. And honestly, it was hard not to be completely charmed by Noelle. She was good at everything, but she didn't have a big head about it.

And then it was Christina's turn at vault, and we all grew quiet. She ran down the runway, did a round-off onto the springboard, and then flipped backward to push off the vaulting table into a full twist. It wasn't at quite the level of difficulty of some of the other girls' vaults, but she landed fairly solidly.

I didn't pretend to care about the other competitors. I was really only there to watch Christina. So, while some short, mousy-looking girl got set up for her vault, I turned to Noelle.

"I can't wait for the Classic. I really want to get back out there on the floor. It feels like I haven't competed in forever."

Noelle sighed. "I know. I'm not competing at the Classic, although there's Nationals later this summer. I want to go so badly I can taste it, but . . ."

I waited a few seconds for her to finish her sentence; when she didn't, I prompted her: "But what?"

"It costs a lot of money," she said. "They're in Philadelphia, so there's the flight, and the hotel, and the new leotards. . . ."

"You've gotta go," I said. "If you don't, who's going to be my competition?"

I hadn't meant to make it sound like I didn't think Christina would qualify—because I totally did—or like I didn't consider her competition. Even though, if I had been honest, I really saw Noelle as my biggest rival . . . at least, gymnasticswise. Obviously, she was the best, since she'd been hand-selected to compete at Nationals. Christina—if she qualified—and I would have to score big at the upcoming Classic for that privilege.

Noelle smiled distractedly.

Then a girl took a particularly nasty fall on the bars, and we both winced.

"I wouldn't want to be feeling like her in an hour or so," I said. "One time I belly-flopped on the mat like that, and I didn't think it hurt so much at the time, but by the time I got home, my muscles were all stiff and sore."

Noelle and I traded gymnastics war stories while we waited for Christina to rotate to her next event. Neither one of us had ever been seriously injured. The worst I'd ever had was a sprained ankle; Noelle had broken a few fingers and pulled a muscle in her leg.

Then Christina was on the bars, and we watched as she swung gracefully back and forth, switching between the low and high bars with ease. She really did have the most beautiful lines. I wondered what her secret was—metal rods implanted in her legs, to keep them so perfectly straight?

She stuck her dismount, and I finally let myself breathe. I knew Noelle was doing the same.

"Next is beam," she said. "That's one of Christina's best events. So far, she's doing awesome."

I couldn't wait to get out on the competition floor again. That was when I really came alive. There was just something about the atmosphere, the pressure, the other girls in the background competing for the same thing . . . It always revved me up.

Okay, so I'd been known to get *too* revved up and totally choke in a crunch. But I was getting better. And it's better to have too much energy than too little, right?

My mom must have been thinking the same thing, because she leaned over and said, "Do you remember the time you fell off the beam three times in one competition, and the last time, you actually slapped the beam, you were so frustrated?"

"Mom!" I didn't need for Noelle to hear a high-light reel of my greatest misses.

"What? You were only seven years old. It was cute."

"Losing is not *cute,* Mom." Out of the corner of my eye, I saw Noelle smirk. Note to self: whenever I do get to meet the Onestis, ask them to regale me with embarrassing stories about Noelle.

When Christina finally got to the beam, I could see what Noelle meant. Sometimes you hear commentators for gymnastics meets say that a gymnast "works the beam like it's floor." (Actually, you hear it all the time, because apparently, gymnastics commentators are like those old Barbie dolls you pull a string on and hear the same stupid phrase over and over.) Well, that's exactly what I thought of when I saw Christina. She danced from one end of the beam to the other as though she had no idea that it was only four inches wide or that she had a long way to fall. She might not have felt so fearless, but I could see she had more courage than she gave herself credit for.

The audience applauded when she landed her series of flip-flops into a front aerial linked to an immediate sheep jump; this meant that they were watching her and not the other girl who was performing on floor at the same time. Every now and then, the other girl's floor music was perfectly matched up to Christina's movements, so that it looked almost as if Christina was leaping and twirling to the beat. For a moment, I felt as though there were something magical in the building.

"She's going to qualify," I said. "She has to. She's having the best competition of her life."

But Noelle was more cautious. "She's doing great, but floor is next. She loves all the dancing parts, but that one tumbling pass is still not a sure thing."

"Then why throw it in there at all? Why risk a mistake?"

"Christina had to improve either her vault difficulty or her floor difficulty to be competitive," Noelle explained. "Cheng decided it was easier to upgrade her first tumbling pass to a full-in than to try the new vault, since that's the event that scares her the most."

It felt like forever before the girls rotated to their last events. Christina was competing toward the middle of the pack, which wasn't a terrible position to be in. Usually, girls competing toward the beginning of the rotation get scored lower, because the judges want to give themselves room to raise scores as the competition progresses. You don't want to give an almost perfect score to the first girl and then have the next one hit her routine out of the park, because then all the scores get inflated. So it was better for the competitors to go toward the end, but middle wasn't all that bad; in this case, it meant that Christina wouldn't have to wait around as long, with all that time for her muscles to get cold and for her to psych herself out.

I was on the edge of my seat as the girl before Christina took her place on the floor, performing a decent routine to some classical music I'd never heard before. Somebody, punch me in the face if I ever do a routine to boring dead people playing harps and stuff.

The girl finished her routine with a flourish, and I felt my heart jump into my throat. This was it. The big moment. I was surprised at how badly I wanted Christina to qualify, even though she'd been my archnemesis just a few days ago.

There was a rustling next to me. I glanced over, annoyed at whoever was choosing *this* moment to get up and go grab a hot dog and a bag of chips. But then I forgot about hot dogs, about Christina, and about the competition.

"Jessie?"

"You didn't think I'd miss it, did you?" She smiled brightly at Noelle and me.

My mother raised her eyebrows at me over the top of Jessie's head. I'd ended up telling her everything that was going on and had expressed my confusion over why Jessie's mom had chosen to pull her out of the gym right before what would have been the biggest competition of her life. My mom had said that someday, when I had children of my own, I'd understand. Gymnastics might have been our dream, but making sure we were healthy and happy was our parents' dream, and it had to come first. I pretended to gag when she said stuff like that, but deep down, I liked to hear it.

"You're just in time," Noelle said. She didn't look nearly as surprised as I was. Maybe she'd just known that Jessie would show up to support her teammate, no matter what. "Christina's about to go on."

Right on cue, Christina's music started, a swirling Latin beat that wasn't too fast but still managed to sound cool. Christina was in her starting pose, one arm crooked behind her back and the other held high in a gesture that almost screamed, *Watch what I'm about to do.*

The big tumbling pass was right at the beginning. It would have made more impact if it had been the last pass, but by the end of the routine you were usually totally out of breath, so sometimes it made sense to play it safe then. Cheng had said that if Christina got more comfortable with the move, they might change it, but for now it was in the first ten seconds, so that she could concentrate all her energy and focus on landing that skill.

She danced into the corner, placing her feet with the heels just inside the white line. I saw her shoulders rise and fall, and then she was off.

Her back handspring was much better. I knew as soon as she hit it that she would have enough power to fling herself backward into the double flip with a single twist. The question was whether she would stick it. . . . I held my breath as I watched her body flip through the air.

The sound of her feet hitting the springboard-loaded mat could be heard throughout the building. It wasn't until she threw both of her arms up in a triumphant salute that it fully registered.

"She did it!" I cried. "She did it! She did it!"

But Noelle was biting her lip. "No. She stepped out of bounds," she said. "That's going to cost her a couple of tenths. And if it throws her off her game, it might cost her even more."

I'd been so focused on the fact that Christina was up and on her feet that I hadn't even noticed where she'd landed. But sure enough, her back leg was way over the white line.

I did some quick calculations: Christina needed a 9.5 or better on this routine to secure her Elite status. It was totally possible, but depending on how much they decided to deduct for the out-of-bounds step, it might not happen.

Christina kept a brave face on, getting through the rest of her routine with only minor shakiness on one of her leaps and finishing with a relatively conservative double twist. That 9.5 was looking a little further out of reach.

"They can't take more than one-tenth for that step, right?" I asked as we waited for her score. "That would be totally unfair."

My gaze caught Jessie's at that moment, and I quickly looked away. She was probably the last person who wanted to weigh in on what was fair, considering that this was supposed to be her competition, too. I wished I could've detected any forgiveness in those eyes, but I was too afraid of the alternative to look really closely.

They flashed her score, and we all cheered. Apparently, they'd seen her grace and beauty and knew that she deserved the 9.5.

Noelle and I grinned at each other, and I automatically smiled at Jessie before reality hit again with a thud. Christina was an Elite now, which meant that all of us were officially on the Elite team . . . except for Jessie. She would still train with us, but she was a Level Ten. There would always be two different competitions: one with the three of us, and one with just her.

"Jessie . . ."

But she shook her head, as if she didn't want to hear it. Even though it was awesome that Christina and Noelle and I were cool now, I realized how much I missed having Jessie as my best friend in the group. Christina and Noelle were clearly tight—they were always going over to each other's houses and giggling about something that had happened in school, since they were in the same grade. I had hoped that Jessie and I could've also been like that, but now it was too late.

"Can I talk to you?" she asked me in a low voice. "Outside?"

I nodded, trying not to get my hopes up. It was possible that Jessie wanted to have an I-will-always-hate-you-so-please-don't-even-look-at-me kind of conversation, but as I excused myself from Noelle and my mom and followed Jessie down the bleachers, I tried to feel encouraged. At least she wanted to talk.

Eighteen

May in Texas was really hot, although there was a little breeze sometimes that shook some of the trees and provided relief. Jessie and I sat on a bench under one of those trees. I waited for her to speak.

"Noelle and Christina said you feel really guilty about what happened," Jessie said.

So, they had talked to her. I'd wondered what they'd meant by "taking care of it." One thing was for sure—I was glad they were on my side now.

"A part of me says that you should be," Jessie

continued. "I told you a lot of stuff I usually keep to myself, about my true feelings about the way I look and how inferior I feel to the rest of you guys in gymnastics. You all make it look so easy. Even though Christina has some trouble with the harder moves, she just looks so *beautiful* up there that of course the judges are going to give her high scores for her long lines."

I tried to imagine how I would have felt if I had spilled all my secret fears—that I wouldn't fit in anywhere, that I'd put my foot in my mouth so much that my only option was to become a mute, that my mother would see some adorable little three-year-old orphan at her day care and think, *Hey, this one's cuter than the one I've got at home, and better behaved, too.* If I'd told that to Jessie and she'd blabbed about it during a game of Truth or Dare, I'd probably have been pretty mad, too.

"I really trusted you," Jessie said. "And I feel like you betrayed that."

If anyone had tried to stand between me and my gymnastics by going behind my back and talking to my coaches, I'd have been livid. I would've thrown a huge tantrum in the middle of the gym and accused everyone of conspiring against me. I definitely wouldn't have quietly packed my stuff and left, the way Jessie did.

I would have hoped that I had friends who cared enough about me to stand up and say something if they thought I was hurting myself. I wanted to say that in my defense, but I sensed that Jessie wasn't finished yet.

"I just wish maybe at the very least you'd talked to me about the whole thing," she said, "instead of talking to other people."

She was right. I could see that now. But at the time, it had seemed as if Jessie was in such denial about herself that I couldn't trust her to actually listen to anything I said. Still, I realized that I should've given her the chance, so that when I did go to Mo and the other girls, at least I'd allowed her to handle it herself.

"You said a *part* of you thinks I should feel guilty," I said, my voice almost a whisper. I couldn't look Jessie in the eyes as I traced the diamond-wire pattern of the bench with my finger. "What about the other part?"

"The other part of me knows you did the right thing."

I did look at Jessie then, and I felt like I was

seeing my old friend. She gave me a small smile. "I still don't think I have anorexia or something, like this woman my parents are taking me to seems to think. She's a psychologist, and I have to talk to her once a week now, to make sure I'm not falling back into my pattern of 'irrational thoughts.'"

She noticed my confused look and laughed. "That's what they call it when you think you're really fat but you're not, and you think everyone's judging you but they're not. She thinks I'm my own worst enemy."

Sometimes, I thought, we were all our own worst enemies. That sounds superdeep, I know, but it's true. Christina lets her own fear stand in her way, Noelle worries about everything, Jessie feels insecure, and I . . . well, I'm insecure, too, I guess. I think that people won't like me, so I decide to do outrageous things that will *make* them notice me, even though I know as I'm doing them that I'm only making it worse.

Wow. It was like I was having a minibreakthrough, and I wasn't even paying anyone to tell me this kind of stuff.

"Anyway," Jessie went on, "I know things got out of control. Somehow, I just told myself, if you lose all this weight by the qualifier, you'll win. And then that number started getting bigger and bigger."

"I'm sorry that I messed up the qualifier for you," I said. "Now you'll have to wait for the next one."

Jessie shrugged. "I wasn't ready. If I had competed today and lost, I would've crawled into a hole. It's better that I take some extra time for myself before I have to worry about something so huge."

"You are coming back to practice, though, right? We've missed you."

"Wild horses couldn't stop me," she said.

"So, what are you doing this summer?" I asked. "School gets out soon, huh?"

"What do you think I'm doing?" Jessie grinned at me. "Gym, gym, and more gym. But we always make some time to have fun, too. Once a summer, Mrs. Flores usually takes us all to the beach. And there's a carnival that comes to town."

"That sounds fun." I thought wistfully of the carnival back home in Ohio, where the Ferris wheel was so old that it just had those little benches with a single metal rod to hold you in place. I used to love to go on it with Dionne and shake the bench, just to mess with her. But then one time she threw up all over me, so I guess I learned my lesson.

"And my mom was so happy you helped me with my algebra homework, you're welcome over anytime." Jessie looked down at her hands. Her fingers were entwined with the diamond cutouts, although I noticed that she didn't go past the first knuckle. That was a good thing. I'd gotten my fingers stuck in those holes before. "We're still—"

The door opened, and Noelle and Christina walked cautiously toward us, as though making sure that we weren't about to gouge each other's eyes out or something, with them caught in the middle. Christina had her gym bag slung over her shoulder and was wearing her nylon jacket and pants over her leotard.

"What's up?" she asked.

"What's up?" Jessie repeated incredulously. "What's *up*? You're an Elite gymnast now, that's what's up!"

Christina flushed. "I didn't want to say anything, but . . ." She let out a big whoop, pumping her fist in the air like she was that boxer Rocky, who always seemed like he was down but then always came through in the end.

"We're walking over to the awards now," Noelle said. "You guys want to come?" She glanced from Jessie to me, as if trying to gauge what had gone down between us.

I smiled at Jessie to show that we were cool, and she put her arm around me. "We're down," she said. "As long as it's not one of those where they give ribbons out to, like, sixteenth place."

"It's not," Christina promised.

"And if it is, you won't have to stick around that long," Noelle pointed out. "We'll just grab Christina's gold medal and head out to lunch!"

"Gold? That's awesome!" I knew Christina had scored high enough to qualify for Elite, but I hadn't known she'd gotten the all-around gold, too.

We walked to the building where they were holding the awards ceremony, which I knew would be all decked out in balloons and crepe paper. You'd think they'd figure out a way to decorate these things other than like a birthday party, but whatever.

"I was telling Britt about our summer plans," Jessie said. "The beach, and the carnival . . ."

"Oh, God, the carnival!" Christina laughed. "Don't eat the Elephant Ears. Seriously, they're so greasy they'll make your stomach hurt for days."

"Is the Ferris wheel one of those old kinds, with the benches?" I asked.

Noelle frowned. "I can't remember. Why?"

"Oh, no reason . . ." I said. I probably wouldn't play that trick on them, because I felt like I knew better now than to do that. I was able to put myself in their shoes and to realize that sometimes being scared wasn't fun. Before, I would've just assumed that everyone liked to be teased. But now I knew that part of being friends was knowing the limits, and knowing when to be serious and when to let loose.

As we walked side by side, feeling the breeze on our faces and knowing that we had an afternoon of celebratory lunch and postcompetition high to enjoy before starting another week of bone-pounding practice, we were definitely more than just teammates.

We were friends.

★ GO-for-GOLD ★
GYMNASTS

Book Two
Balancing Act

To my mother and dearly departed father. As Romanians starting a new life in America, your courage and resolve planted the seed in my heart to become a champion. For this and countless other reasons, I will always be grateful to you.
—D.M.

For my mother, who always supported me
—A.T.

One

E ver since Mr. Van Buren had used the term *muscle memory* in science class, I'd been obsessed with the idea. The concept wasn't new to me, but now I had a name for it. I'd been doing gymnastics practically since I could walk, so it was easy to believe that there were memories buried deep in the muscles of my legs and feet that were way older than the memory of the first time I ate watermelon, or saw the ocean.

Now, standing at the very corner of the floor mat on my tiptoes, ready to launch into a tumbling pass, it wasn't like I had time to consider all of the philosophical implications of this idea. But that was the whole point of muscle memory—I didn't *have* to think. It was just there, in the flex of my ankles, the texture of the mat under the balls of my feet as I sprang into a run across the floor, the stretch of my calves as I kick-started the momentum that would carry me flipping from one end of the mat to the other. When I landed my double pike, my feet planted firmly and my hips square with my shoulders, it was like déjà vu. My body had been in this exact position so many times that I lay in bed at night and re-created it, until it was almost like I fell asleep flipping.

Cheng nodded his head and twirled his finger, his signal for *again*. With Cheng, you learned that this was all you were going to get. He was not the most vocal of coaches, and would never be the one to sweep you up in a bear hug on national television and scream, "You did it! You did it!" but he showed his satisfaction in other ways. Mostly, it was by telling you to keep working.

"Man," Britt said, rubbing chalk on the bottoms of her feet as she joined me at the corner of the floor. "Hasn't he heard of the Thirteenth Amendment? I'm pretty sure it abolished slavery."

I smiled just enough to let Britt know I'd heard

her, but not so much that it might have looked like I was participating in the conversation. Britt was the newest gymnast at Texas Twisters, and when she first got there, she had made a lot of waves because of how outspoken she was. She worked harder than she let on, and she was more determined now than she used to be, but sometimes she still joked around. It could be fun, but pretty much the only thing that scared me more than spiders was getting into trouble, so I tried not to give the coaches any reason to call me out.

Christina had been stretching on the side, but came over to line up behind Britt. "It can't be slavery if you're paying to be here," she said, rolling her eyes.

I preferred to avoid thinking about the dollars adding up and multiplying for every day that I trained at Texas Twisters. My parents never talked about how much it cost, exactly, but I knew being an Elite gymnast was not cheap.

"Noelle," Christina said, jabbing me in the shoulder, "are you going to go, or what?"

I blinked, realizing that somehow I'd allowed myself to get distracted, when that was the last thing I should have been doing as the competitive season started. Squaring myself up on a corner of the blue mat, I took another deep breath and allowed muscle memory to take over.

When we'd finished stretching at the end of practice, our coach Mo called all of us together. Adrenaline made my heart race; I knew what this would be about. The U.S. Junior National Championships were coming up in a few months—so close it was like reaching out to grab the high bar after a big release skill. I only hoped I could catch it.

Mo surveyed the four of us: me, Christina, Britt, and Jessie, who'd returned full-time to practice but wasn't planning on trying for Nationals. She'd taken some time off to cope with her eating disorder, and was still dealing with it. We had all been walking on eggshells, afraid of saying the wrong thing, but she mostly didn't talk about it.

Christina was examining her brand-new manicure as though this meeting didn't have anything to do with the most important event in her career so far. She'd just qualified for Elite competition two weeks ago, and there was no guarantee that she'd be eligible to participate in the qualifying event this early, much less in the Nationals. I could tell she was trying to act like she didn't care, but how could she not? This was *the* competition of the year, the one that determined whether or not you made the National team and got to compete internationally. They featured new up-and-comers from that competition in the biggest gymnastics magazines in the world. It was huge.

Even Britt wasn't pretending it was all a joke, the way she sometimes did. Her blue eyes were sparkling, and she was clenching and unclenching her fists at her side as though she could actually reach out and touch that National Championship gold medal. I felt a spurt of competitiveness. Nothing against Britt, but I'd be more than happy for her to take home the silver and leave the gold for me.

"You know this is important time," Mo said. Mo wasn't a talker, either, but compared to Cheng, she might as well have been Oprah. Maybe that was why Cheng was happy to spot us on the floor and help us with vault timers while Mo handled the business side of things.

"U.S. Classic is in one month," Mo continued, referring to the event that would determine whether Britt and Christina would go to Nationals. I'd already qualified earlier in the year, through a training camp. "Here, you are not against each other. You are together. Understand?"

Britt and Christina exchanged a look, but both nodded. It had been a little tense the past few months, until we decided that Britt could be just as much a friend as a threat, and I knew that Mo didn't want us to be distracted by that kind of drama as we started training for the Classic.

Only a handful of gymnasts qualified for Nationals through a training camp, and it was a relief to be one of them, since it meant that I could focus completely on that goal without worrying about the Classic. Every year, Coach Piserchia held these training camps where he invited gymnasts from all over the country to participate. This year, I'd been the only representative from Texas Twisters, and it was one of the most nerve-racking experiences of my life. Coach Piserchia was officially retired from individual coaching, but he still played a huge role in deciding who would represent our country at World Championships and at the Olympics, so impressing him was majorly important.

Now, Mo handed each of us a thick envelope. "Make sure parents get this," she said. "They need to come to meeting at gym, too."

It was irrational, since everyone had gotten an envelope, and surely *everyone* couldn't be in trouble, but like I said, I get paranoid. I hated the thought of people being mad at me, so as I looked down at the sealed envelope filled with papers intended for my parents' eyes only, all kinds of scenarios started whirling through my head. Maybe it was an assessment of my abilities up to this point, and Mo wanted to break it to them gently that any chance of my making the Olympics someday was very, very slim. Or maybe Cheng had noticed my distraction earlier that day and added it to a list of times when I'd been off my game. I mean, I thought I worked hard and did my best, but I got tired and restless just like anyone else.

"Mo?" I asked, once the other girls had moved toward the lockers.

She looked at me, not blinking as I tried to figure out how to word my question without sounding too insane. *What is in the envelope?!?!?*

"I'll probably have to read some of this stuff to my parents, since their English isn't so good," I said, and immediately felt guilty. It was true that my parents had defected from Romania before I was born; but they'd taught themselves English by watching daytime television and reading newspapers, and they were proud of the way they'd made a life for themselves here. Sometimes there were still things I needed to explain or help them with, but if it weren't for their accents they could have passed for having been born in this country.

"Okay," Mo said. "You can read to them."

"So it's not . . . secret or anything?"

"No, Noelle. It's not bad." One corner of her mouth pulled up, and I blushed. Of course she would know exactly what I was trying to get at. "It's just information about competition—boring, grown-up information, like flight to Philadelphia and leotards and money and itinerary. You don't need to worry."

The weight in my chest lifted, but only for a second, as Mo walked away, and then it settled in deeper than before. At least if I had been in trouble, I could have done something to fix it, like work harder, or apologize. But this was something I couldn't fix. Mo's words echoed in my brain—*flights, leotards, money*—and suddenly, my dream of the National Championships seemed impossible.

To go to that training camp with Coach Piserchia, my parents had had to take out a second mortgage on the building that housed both our home and our family's business. They'd made such an investment already I didn't know if I could ask them to make another one so soon. Then again, everything we'd put into gymnastics so far wouldn't have been worth much if I didn't take it all the way.

I tried to take a deep breath and visualize myself grabbing for that high bar that represented my dreams, feeling the smooth wood as I wrapped my fingers securely around the bar. But for some reason, whenever I got to that part, I could only imagine brushing it with my fingertips, close enough to leave marks in the chalk, but not close enough to stop myself from falling.

Two

As soon as I set foot in my parents' store, I knew the envelope would have to wait. There was a line of customers all the way back to the shelves with the zacuscă spread (made with eggplant or cooked beans, and one of the many things that I get weird looks for when I unpack my lunch bag), and I saw only my brother Radu working the counter.

"Where's Mihai?" I asked, tying an apron around my jeans and T-shirt. I was still wearing my leotard under that, which meant that I was now technically wearing three layers of clothes. In Texas. In June. In a store that had only a few overhead fans rattling weakly to disperse the heat.

Radu shrugged. "He was supposed to be here right after school, but I guess something came up."

"Something *always* comes up," I muttered, but pinned a smile on my face for the next customer in line. "How can I help you?"

Although we always referred to it simply as "the store," it was also a deli and bakery where we made our own dishes from scratch. We had a few regulars, mostly fellow Romanian immigrants who missed the food from their home country. Half of our usual customers were even related to us in some distant way, whether it was an aunt or an uncle or someone who had lived down the street from my parents back in Bârlad. But the woman who approached the counter was not someone I knew. She had dark, frizzy hair that looked like something out of those daytime shows my parents watched over ten years ago, and she wore more eyeliner than anyone I'd ever seen in my life.

"Oh!" she said as she approached, placing a basket of groceries on the counter. "You're so tiny I didn't even see you!"

I smiled wider, even though I get this a lot. No, I'm not quite five feet tall. Yes, I need a ladder to reach some things in the store. No, I don't need any help—I can do fifty press-to-handstand exercises straight without breaking a sweat, so I think I can manage to grab a can of pickled olives.

"Y'all are busy!" she observed, picking up one of our flyers and fanning herself with it. I was proud of those flyers. I'd made them myself with a photo editing program Mihai had illegally downloaded onto the computer, and then I'd helped my father drop them off at other local businesses and apartment complexes. *If people only knew we were here,* my father always said, *they'd come running. There's nothing like good Romanian food.*

The flyers were meant for people to take and hopefully pass along, not for someone to crinkle up in her talon fingernails as she carelessly flapped it near her face. I was glad when I finally finished ringing the woman up and was able to get through the next few customers, including a cousin and another family member whose connection I'd never been able to fully grasp.

Once the store had cleared out, I allowed myself to lean against the counter and take a breath. We had been busy, but it was temporary, I knew. We often got a small surge of people around dusk who were picking up a few things after work, but it wasn't uncommon for the store to remain completely empty for the rest of the evening. Still, we stayed open until nine o'clock every night, with my father usually wolfing down his dinner sitting on a stepladder in the storage closet, then going back to stocking shelves even as he finished chewing his last bite.

That's where I found him: in the storage closet. Mama hated it when he shut himself in there. *Let one of the boys do it,* she always said. *Their backs are younger.* But the truth was that my father was the shyest person I knew, even shyer than me, and he still got so tongue-tied dealing with customers that he preferred someone else to handle the front during the rush.

"Hey, Tata," I said, as he leaned down to press a kiss to my forehead. "Is Mama upstairs?"

"Mihai was supposed to be here so Radu could watch the twins," he said gruffly. "But he didn't show."

Mihai was the oldest, and was just finishing tenth grade; Radu was in ninth grade, and the twins, Cristian and Costel, were four. It seemed like we used to be one big happy family, with Mama and

Tata working in the store and my brothers helping, but lately Mihai had been flaking out, and Radu was starting to get resentful about working while Mihai got to do whatever he wanted. And then my younger brothers were getting to be a handful, always running around underfoot, and there I was, stuck in the middle of the whole thing. I felt guilty when I was at the gym, because I knew I could have been helping at home, and I felt trapped and restless at home, because I wanted to be at the gym.

I loved my oldest brother—he'd always been able to make me laugh, from the time I was born. My mom said I had awarded my first smile to Mihai at only two months old, when he tickled my feet. But at times like this, when I saw the lines etched in my father's face, I just wanted to shake Mihai and tell him to stop being so selfish.

"How was gym?" Tata asked. It was hard to tell if he was smiling or not underneath his bushy mustache, but I knew he was, from the crinkling around his eyes. He loved hearing about my gymnastics, even though he never really understood it. Mama had been an Elite gymnast back in Romania, so her questions were deeper, more probing, but Tata just wanted to know if I enjoyed myself and if

I still followed the same dream I had had since I was three years old.

I thought of that thick envelope, slid neatly in between my warm-up clothes and my water bottle at the bottom of my gym bag. It seemed impossible that my dream could be contained in that envelope, written on slips of paper, disguised as flight numbers and hotel arrangements.

"Oh, you know," I said, "when I was doing my giant swings on the uneven bars, I felt like I was flying!"

This was the kind of thing my father loved to hear. To him, gymnastics was an exhilarating experience, like bungee-jumping or skydiving. He'd seen the calluses on my hands and the blisters on my toes, but he prefered to pretend they didn't exist. In his mind, my feet never touched the ground.

The stillness in our upstairs apartment told me that the twins were already in bed. If they were awake, they would've immediately rushed me at the door, each vying for my attention until my mother appeared behind them, reminding them gently to take turns. Even though it was nice to have peace and quiet, I missed the usual routine.

"Mama?" I called out. I thought she was probably watching television in the room she shared with my father and the twins. After all those years of watching daytime soap operas, my mother's one true addiction was television. Lately, she'd been watching all of these embarrassing reality shows about rich kids hooking up, going to parties, and getting into trouble. It was weird to hear my mother talk about the same program all the kids at school were watching, too.

I knocked softly before pushing her door open, expecting to find her sitting in the rocking chair, folding laundry while she watched the latest episode. She'd always look up from the clothes when something got really juicy or good, which meant that she only made it through one basket per show, and she'd make this clicking sound with her tongue whenever a character did something she disapproved of. Which, of course, was often.

But she wasn't sitting in her chair. Instead, I found her sprawled out on the bed, still wearing her glasses, a pile of papers strewn next to her. There was a thin line of drool hanging from one corner of her mouth, and she was snoring.

Her favorite show was playing softly in the

background; I switched it off. Those kids who went out all night and did whatever they liked would probably have been mortified to find a parent looking like this—clothes rumpled, no makeup on. Even without all those cameras, even if no one else in the world would ever have had to see, they'd probably have been disgusted that their parents could show any sign that they weren't perfect.

But it just made me sad. There was a pile of envelopes next to my sleeping mother, including one from the gas company, with a red outline around the dollar amount that let us know our payment was late again, and one from the insurance company, on pink paper that told us our rates were going up. And I thought about my own envelope from gym, and wondered how I could ever think it contained my dream. All it contained was another bill.

The last couple of weeks of school were always crazy, and most teachers didn't even bother trying to teach anything. But Mr. Van Buren had to be different, and so he was talking about muscle fatigue and pretending to ignore everyone passing notes and giggling in the back of the class.

I never passed notes. Yet another symptom of

being the girl who stays out of trouble, but also . . . it wasn't like I had anyone to pass them to. My only real friends at school were Christina and Jessie, and I saw them at lunch, and that was it. I had nothing against my classmates, but when you spend most of your waking time outside of school at the gym, it makes it hard to bond with girls over sleepovers or trips to the mall.

"What is muscle fatigue?" Mr. Van Buren asked the class expectantly. He had just gone over the definition half an hour ago, and so it should have been an easy one. But it's like that riddle he'd told us once: if a teacher talks during the last week of school, does he still make a sound? Nobody was paying attention.

Tentatively, I raised my hand, and Mr. Van Buren beamed at me. "Yes, Noelle."

"Muscle fatigue is when you can't perform normal movements, or when it requires more effort than it should to perform normal movements."

"Exactly, Noelle!" One thing I would miss about Mr. Van Buren was that he always acted like you'd just said something brilliant, even when you were only parroting something he'd said earlier in the class. I felt myself flush, and I only got redder as I listened to the whispering behind me.

"Like *she* ever has muscle fatigue," one girl said.

"Oh, I know. Have you seen her arms? She looks like a comic-book character."

"And *not* in a good way," the first girl added.

Self-consciously, I tried to hide my upper arms with my hands, feeling the familiar ripple of muscle underneath my T-shirt. Normally, I was proud of my strength and what I could do with it. But sometimes, like when I was forced to wear a junior bridesmaid's dress with spaghetti straps for my cousin's wedding, I felt like a big freak. All of the other girls had looked like little princesses, whereas I looked . . . well, like I was about to run down the vault runway and attack it wearing pink tulle.

I was relieved when the bell finally rang and I could go meet Christina and Jessie at lunch. Britt was homeschooled, which was too bad, because she was really smart, and it would've been nice to have a friendly face in my advanced science class.

If I felt out of place during my classes, it all changed when I sat with Christina and Jessie. Maybe it was because we'd been so worried about Jessie lately that it made my problems seem petty by comparison. Or maybe it was because Christina was so beautiful and confident, and some of that rubbed off on me when I was sitting next to her. If Christina had heard those girls whispering about *her*, she probably would've turned around and flexed her bicep and then said something about using it to punch their lights out, or something cutting about how they *wished* they looked like Wonder Woman.

"Can you believe Ms. Rizzi passed out bags of candy, like we were in kindergarten?" Christina was saying when I sat down. "How lame."

I saw the moment when Christina actually reflected on the words coming out of her mouth. Her face got a pinched look, and she glanced nervously at Jessie. "I mean, candy is cool and all—" she started to say, but Jessie held up her hand to cut her off.

"How many times do I have to tell you? It's okay to talk about food. You're supposed to talk about food! Look, I brought a healthy lunch, and I plan on eating it. Okay?"

Christina was still a little pale as she bit into her chicken salad, and it occurred to me that even she wasn't completely immune to self-doubt. But then she flipped her hair and gave a flirtatious smile to a guy at another table, and I figured I must've imagined any chink in her armor.

"I am *so* excited about the end-of-year dance," she said. "Do you think Logan will ask me?"

Jessie shrugged, but there was a glint in her eye. "I heard that Kelly was asking about you."

"No! Really?" Christina made a face. "He's so *gross*. And hello, Kelly is a girl's name. Didn't anyone give his mom a baby-name book?"

"Kelly can be a boy's name," I pointed out. "I think it's cool that someone likes you. I don't think anyone's ever liked me."

Christina rolled her eyes. "Whatever. You're so cute, you're like a little doll, with your brown hair and your big brown eyes. Who are you going to go to the dance with?"

I took a loud, crunchy bite of a carrot stick to avoid answering the question, but when I was done chewing, both Jessie and Christina were still staring at me, obviously expecting me to answer. "I didn't think we were allowed to go," I said finally.

"What do you mean, *allowed*?" Christina asked.

I glanced back and forth between the two of them in disbelief. "Competition season is starting! Once school is out, we're going to be training eight hours a day. There's no time for dances."

Jessie sighed. "I probably wasn't going to go, anyway," she said. "It's not like I've been asked."

"No, we're going." Christina slammed the palm of her hand against the table with such force that some of my lite ranch dressing splattered onto my shirt. "Forget the boys, we're going together. And forget gym! We can have our full practice on Friday, still have time for frozen yogurt afterward, and show up at the dance fashionably late."

Christina saw the look on my face. "Don't worry, Cinderella, we'll get you home before you turn into a pumpkin. And the experience will leave you energized, ready to take on Nationals!"

Nationals, the dance . . . these were the last things I wanted to think about at this point. Trying to figure out what to do about one led to worrying about the other, and it was too much. I reached for a napkin and started dabbing at the spots on my shirt while Jessie and Christina talked about dresses and hairstyles. At least ranch dressing was something I could clean up . . . unlike the rest of my life.

Three

I t was true that I was worried about the dance being off limits. After all, there was a reason Christina wasn't asking Mo about it. It was also true that I didn't have a dress, couldn't afford a dress, and looked like a stupid munchkin in dresses anyway. But there was one thing I hadn't shared with Christina and Jessie, another reason I wasn't looking forward to the dance, and that reason was standing over by the pommel horse.

Scott Pattison. With his dark, curly hair and blue eyes, he'd have been reason enough to come to the gym, even if I didn't care about someday winning an Olympic gold medal. So what if he was eighteen and about to start college and had barely said five words to me except for the time he'd tried to help find my stuffed animal (it was a good-luck charm, but still, embarrassing). So what that he already drove a car and probably had a girlfriend who was taller than a midget, but not so tall she'd tower over him? And I bet she wasn't a gymnast, which meant she could actually have a body that looked good in prom dresses. Whenever I was in the gym, I couldn't help sneaking little looks at him as he flipped across the floor or wiped his brow with a towel.

And let's face it: it would have been ridiculous for a twelve-year-old girl to ask a guy like that to a school dance, much less for him to say yes. Even if he did come, he'd probably be doing it for community service hours for college. *Chaperoned middle-school dance. Made some girl's dream come true.*

Britt caught me staring. I blinked quickly. "Chalk in my eye," I said.

"Uh-huh."

It occurred to me that Britt might actually be the perfect person to talk to, given that she didn't go to our school. "It's just that—" I began, waiting for Jessie to pass by before continuing, "there's this dance at our school in a week."

"And you want to go with *Scott*?" Britt blurted out. "He's, like, ancient. You'd be slow-dancing and you'd hear his bones creak."

Now I remembered why it was a bad idea to tell Britt anything. It wasn't so much that she was terrible at keeping secrets as that she had no concept that you might not want everything shouted across the gym through a megaphone (which was about the volume of her everyday speaking voice).

"I didn't say anything about Scott," I snapped. "I was just thinking about this dance, that's all. Christina and Jessie really want to go, but I'm not sure. . . . Don't you think it'll interfere with training?"

"Probably."

It was the honest answer I was expecting, so there was no explanation for the fact that I suddenly felt deflated. "Of course it will," I said. "I'll be off all through practice, because I'll be thinking about it, and then I'll be tired the next day, because I'll have been out too late. Plus, I haven't even mentioned it to my parents, and who knows what Mo would say?"

Britt clapped her hands together, sending the freshly applied chalk flying into the air. Now I really did have chalk in my eye.

"So, don't ask permission," Britt said. "Better to ask forgiveness, right?"

That was my anti-motto. I always asked permission, and I hated the uncertainty of asking someone to forgive me for something I'd already done.

"Are you saying I should go, or not?" At that point, I really just wanted a concrete answer; it was like Britt was the devil or the angel on my shoulder, and I would have to do whatever she said.

Britt turned to me. "Yes, it might cause a blip in your training routine. But yes, you should go. How many times do you get to do something fun like that? Some of us don't even have school dances to go to."

Now I felt bad. I hadn't even considered that Britt might be jealous, or feel left out. "You could probably come," I said. "Nobody would have to—"

"Don't worry about it," Britt cut in. "I'll just spend another rip-roaring evening at home with my grandmother, learning about the Battle of 1812 or whatever other random thing she wants to talk about at the dinner table, as though I didn't just hear about it *all day*. That's where you're really lucky to be in public school: your parents probably don't quiz you on multiplication tables on weekends just because they're around and can't think of anything else to do."

That was true. My parents rarely asked me about school—both because I'd always gotten good grades and because they were too busy to really think about it. Just like how, lately, they'd been too preoccupied to do anything about the fact that Mihai was out with his friends more than he was at home, and just last week I accidentally put one of his shirts in my load of laundry and noticed it smelled like smoke.

"So . . . you're giving a thumbs-up to the dance?" I said. I knew I was being neurotic, but like I said, I'm a worrier. I needed someone's absolute conviction to persuade me, and even then I knew that I'd go home and second-guess myself.

Britt sighed. She was familiar enough with my flaws by now to know exactly what I was doing. "You know that song by the Clash?" she said, without bothering to look at me. I shook my head. Another of my flaws: I was hopeless with pop culture. "'Should I Stay or Should I Go?' The answer, Noelle, is *always* go."

I wrinkled my forehead. "Why's that?" I could think of lots of times it might have been better to stay home. Like if my family was taking another trip to the circus, which had been our big present one Christmas but which I had hated every second of. The clowns were scary, the animals were sad, and the whole place smelled weird.

"Isn't it obvious? Wherever you could go, it's probably better than where you are. And between staying home on a Friday night and going out with your friends . . . well, that's a no-brainer."

Mo walked by, her gaze sharp as she looked at us. "Enough chalk," she said. "Britt, work on your giants reps on the strap bar. Noelle, you go with Cheng to work on your release."

"Sorry," I muttered, my head down.

Britt's apology was chirpier, almost cheerful. Then she leaned in toward me. "See? If we had asked permission for that conversation, Mo would've said no, and we never would've had it. But now, we got to chat, we said we were sorry, and we're about to continue our workout. No harm, no foul."

I remembered the way Mo's face had looked in that instant, her mouth tight with disapproval, and I wondered how Britt could say that. Even if I was the recipient of that look for only five seconds, I would dwell on it for the next five days. At least, if

I asked permission, I didn't have that sinking feeling in my gut.

One thing people may not realize about gymnastics: even when you land on mats, it still stings a bit. Not as much as it would if we were practicing on hard wooden floors, like they did in the olden days, but think about your body being propelled through the air and then stopping suddenly as your feet smack onto a mat that's designed to be soft, but firm. Sometimes we practice new or risky skills into a pit filled with foam, and that's a blast, but when we're just landing dismounts onto the regular mats in practice, it can start taking its toll on the ankles.

I had landed my sixth double tuck in a row when Mo approached me. Immediately, I worried that I'd been cowboying my legs too much—which meant not keeping my knees together—or that I was piking down as I hit the mat, which would cost me valuable tenths of a point in competition if I had to take a step on the landing to keep my balance. I waited for Mo to say something about my form or technique, but instead she just pursed her lips and looked at me as though sizing me up.

"Yes," she said, even though I hadn't spoken. "You need to add full twist to dismount. Only way to be competitive."

I'd been wanting to add a full-twisting double back to my routine for forever. But I wasn't like Britt, who could just toss out a new move and have faith that her coach would let her do what she wanted. I thought about each new skill for a while, visualized myself successfully completing it, and then hoped that my coaches could read my mind and would let me increase my difficulty level.

"Okay," I said. "I mean, great. I'm ready."

Mo nodded. "With full twist, you make National team."

Even though Mo was more talkative than Cheng, she didn't say any more than she needed to, and she didn't often give praise. Encouragement, maybe, but not outright praise. This was even better—Mo was telling me straight up that I would make the National team. Not that I would do my best, or that I would try, but that I would definitely make it.

I wanted to jump up on the beam and throw a high, tight, full-twisting double-tuck dismount of Guinness World Records proportions, but I knew I had to be patient and wait. It was just so hard when I felt as if I could already fly.

"Your parents will be able to be at meeting next Friday night, yes?" Mo asked.

My stomach plummeted with the same force as those dismounts I'd been landing earlier. There was already reason to dread the meeting with the huge dollar sign attached to it, but next Friday was also the night of the dance. How would we get away with going to a dance when our parents would all be at the gym that very same night, listening to speeches about how focused we needed to be right now?

I thought of that song that Britt had mentioned, but I knew that the differences between me and Britt were greater than just our knowledge of music. While she wouldn't have thought twice about hounding the coaches until they let her compete a new skill, I figured that, when it came to my skills, they knew best, and I held my tongue until they thought I was ready. While her motto might have been always to choose *go*, I pretty much always stayed.

That night, I tried really hard to give the envelope to my mother. I caught her at the best time, when she'd put the twins to bed and before she'd completely shut down for the night.

"Can I help you, Mama?" I asked, reaching for a rag to dry the dishes she was washing and placing in the rack.

"Don't you have homework?"

I shook my head. "It's the last few weeks of school. I think the teachers have given up."

She smiled, handing me a handful of forks and knives she'd just run under the faucet. "How is gym? You know, I've been meaning to come see you, but with watching the boys and running the store . . ."

"I know," I said, and I really did. Of course, I loved it when my family came to see me practice, even when my mother or father came alone or with the twins. And they never missed a competition. But with my parents the only full-time employees of the store, it was hard for them to get away. Half the time, my mother brought the boys downstairs with her and had them count out beans while she worked. It was amazing to me how long she could keep them going on the bean-counting game. Maybe she'd done the same with me when I was little, and that was why I actually understood and liked math.

"I'll be training most of the summer," I said,

"but we still get Sundays off, and a half day on Wednesdays, so I could help around the store if you needed me to."

"You," my mom said, leaning over to kiss my cheek, "are so sweet. But you work too hard as it is, and you know you shouldn't be in the store. You're only twelve."

"I can do everything Radu can," I protested. "Even carrying boxes—I'm stronger than him, you know." This was a sore point between my brother and me, ever since I'd beat him at arm-wrestling last Christmas in front of all our cousins. I could probably have beaten Mihai, too, but he never let himself lose. He always found a way to make a joke of things he wasn't good at, so people thought he was playing around.

"You'd be employee of the year," my mother assured me, "but you're too young. I don't want you spending all of your time in the store when you have school and gymnastics, and besides, there are laws."

My father had worked in my grandfather's store from the age of five, sorting things in the back, and he believed that the only way to teach children a work ethic was to start them young in the family business. But my mother was more cautious. She was very conscious of the fact that we'd come over to this country to pursue opportunities we wouldn't have had in Romania, and she didn't want to do anything to mess that up. She wouldn't even go a mile over the speed limit. If she had known that I'd worked behind the counter the other day, she'd have gotten that worry line between her eyes and told me to not even think about tying an apron on again. Assisting my father in the stockroom was sometimes okay, or organizing shelves when no one was in the store, but interacting with customers was a definite no-no.

"Enough talk about work," my mother said. "What about play? What things have you girls cooked up for the summer? I'm sure Mrs. Flores will take you all to the carnival again. You had so much fun last year."

This was the perfect opportunity to bring up the dance, and then lead in to the competition. I could say, *Actually, there's this big dance at school*, and I knew my mother would be excited and would start planning to sew me a dress to wear. Then I could say, *I'm just worried it will interfere with training. Remember, Mama, that this is the first summer I might be eligible for the Junior National team. And* she'd say, *Oh, no, you have to go to the dance! And don't you worry about Nationals. Your father and I have been saving for it for the past year, and you're going to do so great that you deserve a night off.*

It was all complete fantasy, of course. My mother would offer to sew me a dress for the dance if I wanted, although she'd express a little concern about its distracting me from my training. She liked to see me enjoy myself, but she'd been an Elite gymnast, too, and she knew what even the slightest hiccup in routine could mean for an athlete. And that big red square around the amount due on the gas bill meant that my parents probably hadn't been saving up money to send me to Philadelphia for Nationals. Not that I could blame them—they already spent almost as much on my training as they did on the mortgage for the store.

So I decided to ignore the rest of my mother's questions and just focus on the easy one. "Yeah, I think Christina mentioned something about her mom taking us all to the carnival when it comes to town." That would be in late June, and the Classic wasn't until the end of July, so hopefully it would work out. I kept that part to myself. "I love those Elephant Ears!"

I thought for sure my mother would know something was up then. I mean, Elephant Ears are good and all, but I usually only eat a few bites of one, since it's nothing but fried carbs and sugar . . . not exactly the staples of an athlete's diet. I also cringed when I imagined how I must have sounded. *I love those Elephant Ears*? Was that really the best I could come up with?

But I guess my mother didn't notice my bizarre enthusiasm, because she just smiled. "I used to love the corn dogs," she said. "When we first came to America, we couldn't believe that they even existed. What was a hot dog? And what was this hot dog on a stick with the bread already wrapped around it?"

I laughed weakly. Even though I desperately wanted to mention the envelope and the parents' meeting and just get it all out there, I was also relieved to be talking about something as unthreatening as fried carnival foods.

My mother finished rinsing the last plate and handed it to me to dry, switching the faucet off and wiping her hands on her skirt in a gesture that was very familiar to me. She didn't care what she wore or if she was covered in baby spit-up or flour from baking, so long as the store was running smoothly and her children were happy.

"Well," she said. "You let me know when you go, and I'm sure we can spare twenty dollars for you to make yourself sick on Elephant Ears."

And that's the real reason the envelope stayed in my nightstand drawer upstairs. It wasn't that I was scared of my mother's telling me we didn't have the money for me to go. It was that I was scared to think what she might sacrifice to make sure that I got what I wanted.

Four

That night, I couldn't sleep, so I was still awake at midnight when the front door creaked open. For a few moments, I just lay there, my muscles still and my eyes wide as I stared at the ceiling.

Someone's robbed the store, I thought. Now there's definitely no way we can afford that trip to Philadelphia for Nationals.

I didn't have time to feel guilty about that selfish thought before it occurred to me that I might not even *make* it to Nationals if someone came in and murdered me in my sleep. The newspaper would run a story around the time I would've been going to the competition, about the local girl whose life was cruelly cut short before her potential could be realized. Christina would go to Nationals, and she'd wear a black leotard or some kind of armband as a tribute to her fallen teammate, and she'd tearfully dedicate her gold medal to me (well, maybe not tearfully—even in my fantasy, it was hard to imagine her crying).

Then I thought about my little brothers, lying all sweaty and intertwined in the bed they shared, and my mother and father, sleeping soundly after a hard day's work. As much as I wanted to dive under the bed and hide, I wondered if I could just warn my parents before anything bad happened. I pictured myself saving the day; maybe the police department would give me some kind of reward, which I could use to pay my own way to Philadelphia. It was completely ridiculous, but at least it calmed me down.

I slipped out of bed, wishing I was wearing more than a tank top and shorts that spelled out GYM RAT across my butt. When I stubbed my toe on the corner of my dresser, I bit my lip to stop myself from crying out, and then I edged out of my bedroom, trying to make myself as small as possible. Sometimes there were benefits to being so short.

If I had come across any robbers or would-be killers, I would've distracted them by doing a back walkover and then kicking them in the crotch or something, but it turned out not to be necessary. The only person I surprised was my brother Mihai, and he jumped even higher than I did. He almost stepped into the pot my parents had placed on the ground next to the couch, which had a quarter inch of rainwater in it from where the roof leaked above.

"What are you doing up?" he hissed, once he'd finally stopped huffing and puffing. Now that the danger of a break-in was past, I was enjoying seeing my brother caught off guard.

"What are you doing sneaking in?" I shot back.

He waved his hand towards my parents' closed door. "Keep your voice down," he said. "And mind your own business."

I could do the first thing, but not the second. "Where have you been?"

Mihai ran his hand through his dark hair. "I ran downstairs to get something to eat, okay? Are you satisfied, Snoopy McSnoop?"

Maybe it was just because I hadn't seen him for more than a few minutes here and there in the past couple of weeks, but suddenly he looked taller, and

I noticed that he had a couple of angry red blotches on his chin. It was weird to think of my brother having acne and those strange raised veins in his arms the way older guys did, but there was the evidence, right in front of my face. My brother had changed, and not just physically—gone was the guy who used to make me laugh by pretending to be a Southern belle or a talk-show host, and in his place was this guy who disappeared in the middle of the night and lied about it. I knew he hadn't just gone downstairs— for one thing, we had more than enough food in the kitchen, and for another, we never helped ourselves to stuff from the store without asking my parents. Somehow I knew that even if my brother broke curfew and all kinds of other rules, he would never have broken that one.

I could tell from the way his gaze met mine that his thoughts were running along the same lines. Wherever he was coming back from, it must have been bad if he'd rather have had me think he was taking food from the store without permission.

"Please, tell me," I said. "I won't say anything, I promise."

If there was anyone Mihai could trust, he had to know it was me. When he and Radu broke our great-grandmother's vase, I'd kept my mouth shut. They'd glued it back together and turned it so that the cracked side faced the wall, and I hadn't said a word when Mama was dusting one day and it just fell apart.

Mihai rolled his eyes, but then he admitted, "I hung out with some friends. That's it. Maybe you'd get it if you did anything besides school and gymnastics."

In all the years I'd been doing gymnastics, I don't think I'd ever heard my brothers complain, even though they had to resent certain things. While they had to share a secondhand gaming system, I got a new leotard and some hair ties. They had been dragged to Saturday competitions and forced to sit through endless presentations of awards, though I knew they'd rather have been out with their friends. Once, Mihai had even taped over a BMX event he'd recorded for himself when the Goodwill Games were on TV and I would've missed it otherwise.

So, while I knew Mihai had a point, it still stung to hear him say it so harshly. I wanted to tell him that he *had* a life, and that it used to include us. I wanted to tell him that I didn't think he should be hanging out with his so-called friends if they were the reason his grades were slipping and his breath smelled like an ashtray. But instead I just shrugged, like I didn't care.

"I promised I wouldn't say anything, and I won't," I said. "But you should think twice about this sneaking-around stuff."

"Mama and Tata have no clue," he said. "They're so tired at the end of the day I doubt a hurricane would wake them up." He tousled my hair in a patronizing gesture and disappeared into the bedroom he shared with Radu. It was true that my parents, although they had been concerned about Mihai's behavior lately, would probably have let him get away with it, just because of how busy they were. But that wasn't what I was trying to tell him. I was trying to warn him about thinking only of himself and not anyone else.

Then again, it wasn't like I was one to talk. My first thought, when I'd worried that someone was breaking into the store, had been about Nationals, and though I could tell that my mother had been preoccupied earlier that night, I'd been too wrapped up in my own troubles to concern myself with hers. At this point, I wasn't really sure if I was that much better than my brother.

We were waiting for Christina's mom to pick us up after school when Christina waved her hand in front of my face. "Earth to Noelle," she said. "Aren't you listening?"

I had been dwelling on the run-in last night with my brother, but I didn't want to mention that to Christina, for several reasons. For one thing, it seemed like it was getting into my family's business, and even though Christina was my best friend, I wasn't sure I wanted to tell her about all of the tension and stress at home. For another thing, sometimes I got the impression that Christina thought Mihai was cute, which was just gross.

"Sorry," I said. "I'm paying attention now, I promise."

Normally, in situations like this, Christina would have gotten huffy and refused to continue, making me apologize over and over again and then acting like it was my great privilege to listen to what she had to say. But this time, she must've been overly excited, because she launched right into her topic without even a sigh about having to start over.

"My mom bought me some glittery yellow

eye shadow," she said. "I can't wait to wear it at the dance."

"Is your dress yellow?" I asked. I hadn't even thought Christina had bought a new dress yet. I'd been to her house many times and could vouch for the fact that she had millions of dresses, all hanging up in her closet, on plastic hangers, not wire ones, because Mrs. Flores thought they got misshapen and stretched out the clothes. But this was an occasion, and there was no way Christina wasn't taking advantage of the opportunity to buy a new dress.

"Not exactly," she said. "But if the perfect dress doesn't match the eye shadow, I'll trade it in for a different color. The makeup, I mean. I only picked yellow because I read in a magazine that it was on trend for this year to wear bright colors."

I never paid attention to that kind of stuff, because . . . well, it didn't really matter to me. But sometimes I wondered whether, if I'd been given everything, the way Christina had been, maybe I'd have cared more about clothes and makeup and hair. And then maybe I'd have been more confident and outspoken, like she was, and not so afraid to stand out.

"You can totally borrow it," Christina said.

She studied my face as though she were planning my makeover in her head at that very moment. "Actually, it might be better if I exchanged it for another color, like aqua. That's still bright, and it would look nice against your complexion. Your skin is too light for yellow, I think."

"It's your makeup," I said. "You can get whichever kind you want."

Christina shrugged. "We could always ask my mom if she'd buy both."

I knew that Mrs. Flores got her makeup from one of the most expensive stores in the mall—and not just a counter in a department store, or a kiosk in the center, but an entire store devoted to lip stain and foundation and anything you could think of. She said that her skin was allergic to the cheaper stuff. I also knew that she bought Christina makeup from the same place, even though Christina had perfect skin and had probably never had a pimple in her life.

I felt my usual jealousy rise up in my throat, and it was hard for me to reply. So, instead, I just nodded.

"Your eyes are so pretty," Christina said. "We should definitely make them pop for the dance."

I grimaced. "I don't know that I want them to *pop*."

"Oh, be quiet," Christina said, laughing. "You know what I meant."

I did. And that was one of the reasons it was hard to stay mad at Christina when she brought up buying a hundred dollars' worth of makeup like it was buying a pack of gum at the gas station—she was so generous. Yes, her parents gave her whatever she wanted, but she'd always been willing to share. Over the years, she'd lent or given me countless things, and she'd never demanded them back or made me feel guilty about taking them. She would say things like, "Oh, my mom gave me this dress but I hate it, so if you could take it off my hands, that would be amazing." And I would wonder if she was just being nice or if she knew more than she let on about my family's situation. I was normally careful not to talk a lot about my home life or how the store was doing, but Christina was my best friend. In some ways, she knew me better than I knew myself.

When Mrs. Flores dropped me and Christina off at the gym after school, there was a News Channel 8 van outside. Immediately, Christina flipped down the passenger visor mirror and started smoothing her hair. "How do I look?" she asked, checking her makeup.

Once Mrs. Flores had parked the car, she licked her finger and reached over to wipe a smudge from under Christina's eye.

"Mom!" Christina protested, but she was obviously more worried about looking good on camera than about being embarrassed, so she didn't pull away. I wanted to do something about my appearance, too—after my day at school, there were probably little flyaway hairs coming out of my ponytail, and my face would have been shiny from the heat—but there was no mirror in the backseat. Besides, they'd probably end up interviewing Britt or Christina instead, anyway. Last year I'd had a small article in the paper when I was state beam champion. Britt was so outgoing, though, and Christina was so pretty that they'd made better on-camera interviewees. I'd end up stammering or whispering something stupid about how I wanted to do my best or how I knew my competition would be tough. Which was true, but, you know, hardly a scintillating sound bite.

Christina must've been worried about someone

else beating her to the interview, because she was almost running to open the front door of the gym. I tried not to be annoyed when she let it close almost in my face, and I slipped in right before Mrs. Flores, who was a little slower, because she had heels on. But when we got into the gym, it wasn't Britt they were interviewing, or even Jessie or Mo or Cheng—it was Scott. He was looking cuter than ever in a Conner University T-shirt over his usual workout clothes, and he smiled at the news reporter as she held the microphone in front of his face.

They were standing over by the big sign at the entrance—where, if they moved a little to the left, people would see HOME OF STATE BEAM CHAMPION NOELLE ONESTI underneath the Texas Twisters logo—and we could hear everything.

"It's truly a blessing," he was saying. "To be able to compete for Conner at all is amazing, but to get the scholarship on top of that . . . I know my family has worked really hard to get me where I am today, so it's nice to be able to pay them back by earning my way through school."

I melted a little bit; I couldn't have said it better myself. Clearly, Scott was perfect for me.

The interviewer beamed her approval. It was

a good thing she was, like, forty years old, or I might've been jealous. "Well, I know I speak for all of Austin when I say how proud we are. What's next for you?"

"Just training for the fall," he said. "And maybe going to the National Championships this summer. The qualifier's coming up, so wish me luck."

"Good luck!" the interviewer said, as though Scott needed it, and then did her wrap-up spiel, after which the cameraman gathered his equipment and headed toward the door. She took a moment to shake Scott's hand and say something inaudible before following. I was surprised when Christina reached out to grab the reporter's sleeve.

"Hi!" Christina said, flashing her teeth in her biggest smile. "My name is Christina Flores, and I'm one of the Junior Elite gymnasts here at Texas Twisters. I was just wondering if you wanted to talk to me, maybe, about training here? I hope to go to the Nationals this summer, too."

"Oh, good for you!" the reporter gushed. I recognized her now from television; she was the one who always wore a gold chain around her neck with a ring on it. It was surreal to see that same necklace now, up close and personal. She also wore a lot of makeup, which hadn't been as obvious on TV. With all the lights and cameras and everything, she appeared normal, but when she stood just a few feet away, it was obvious that there was a layer of foundation caked on her skin. Maybe it was better that my mother didn't let me wear makeup, if only to keep me from ever looking like that.

"Well, congratulations, and good luck!" the reporter said to Christina, smiling at me before sliding her sunglasses down over her eyes. And just like that, the reporter and the cameraman were gone.

Christina gaped after them. "I cannot *believe* that," she said. "What universe are we in where a guy gymnast is getting all the press?"

It was true that, generally, women's gymnastics was the really popular sport. Men's gymnastics got shown on TV less, had lower ratings, and didn't bring the sponsorships or publicity that women's gymnastics did. Normally I thought this was pretty unfair, but I admit that I was as stunned as Christina. Obviously, *I* knew that Scott was amazing, but why was he getting all this attention?

Mo walked by, and Christina asked her that very question.

"You don't need interview," Mo said. "You need

practice. Get changed, and get out on floor."

I hadn't really expected any other reaction from Mo, but I still made a sympathetic face at Christina as we headed toward the locker room. "It was just a question," she grumbled, although I knew she wasn't really surprised, either. Whenever the younger gymnasts were over on the floor playing a game or there was some kind of drama up at the front desk, Mo was the one to snap at us to get back to work and mind our own business.

It was a lot like how Mihai had told me to mind my own business last night. Apparently, this was a theme in my life, a huge neon sign telling me that I needed to concentrate and not let so many other things filter through.

That didn't stop me from listening when I heard Jessie explain more about the interview, of course. She'd gotten to the gym before us, and so she filled us in on a little background while we sifted through our bags for everything we needed for the day's practice. It didn't count as breaking my focus, since I hadn't even started training yet.

"The woman called it a 'human interest piece,'" Jessie said, her green eyes intent on a point on the ceiling as though she was trying to remember the reporter's exact words. "It's only because of Scott's scholarship and all that."

"Well, we're *humans*," Christina said. "Isn't Miss News Channel Eight interested in *us*?"

"But Scott found out about the scholarship a couple of months ago," I pointed out. It had been a Friday, to be exact, and he'd come in waving a folded piece of paper and had talked excitedly to Mo, who'd actually given him a hug. Hugs were even rarer than praise in Mo's world. I remembered it had been a Friday, because he'd been wearing his Birchbark High School senior class T-shirt, which is what he always wore on Fridays, to show his school spirit. That was just the kind of guy Scott was.

Jessie shrugged. "I guess he hadn't officially accepted the offer and everything until this week."

Britt came in just in time to catch the end of the conversation; she swung her locker open, and the metal clanged loudly against the locker next to it. I winced. "Are you guys talking about that interview, too?" she said. "It's all they'll talk about at the front desk. Who cares? That woman from Channel Eight is scary. Her eyelashes look like spiders' legs."

If only Britt had seen her in person. The makeup was ten times as intense.

On my way out of the locker room, I saw Scott by the water fountain, and before I could stop myself, I'd turned and was walking in his direction. He was still leaning over to get a drink when I came up behind him; I stared at the darker gray triangle that his sweat had made on the back of his shirt while I waited. If there was a picture definition of *pathetic* in the dictionary, it'd probably have been me at that moment. I mean, his sweat? I must have been crazy.

He almost jabbed me with his elbow as he spun around, wiping his mouth, and then he smiled. "Sorry," he said. There was a drop of water on the tip of his nose where he'd dipped it into the stream, and I knew if I didn't stop staring I'd make it into the thesaurus, too, for all the synonyms of *pathetic*.

"Hey," I said. "I mean, it's okay."

He started to leave, but I cleared my throat. "Cool interview," I said. I tried to make it sound casual, but my voice came out a little squeaky. "About the scholarship. That's so . . . cool."

Now I was repeating myself. I should just fill up my water bottle, I thought, and end this nightmare.

But he smiled wider, and it looked so genuine I couldn't help grinning back. "Thanks," he said.

"I'm really excited. You'll be at Birchbark next year, right?"

I couldn't believe he knew something about me! Well, almost. "The year after that," I said. "I'm only in seventh grade now."

Why had I said it like that? *Only* in seventh grade. I was too young for him, but still, there was no reason to make it so obvious. I should've said it breezily, like, *Oh, I'm going into eighth grade,* or maybe, *I wish! I still have another year of middle school to go. Kids there are* so *immature.*

"Awesome," he said. This was how I knew he was being nice to me, because there was nothing awesome about being in seventh grade.

"So you'll be at Nationals?" I asked. I hoped that I didn't sound as if I'd been listening too closely to his interview, even though I knew I'd probably go home and watch it that night on TV and memorize every word.

He glanced toward the parallel bars. I was probably keeping him from practice. I was keeping *myself* from practice, but this was the longest conversation I'd ever had with Scott, and I didn't want it to end.

"Hopefully," he said. "What about you? What

am I saying?—of course you'll be there. You're like some sort of prodigy."

I blushed even harder, if possible, than I already had been. Scott watched my gymnastics! And he thought I was good—a *prodigy*, even. "Well . . ." I began, wanting to sound humble, but then I couldn't think of anything to say. The word hung in the air for an awkward moment before Scott raised his eyebrows.

"So, I'll see you there," he said. "Have a good practice today."

"You've been to Nationals before, right?" I blurted out. Out of the corner of my eye, I could see the other girls stretching on the floor, and I fumbled for my water bottle. Just a few more seconds, I told myself, and then I'll get back to work.

"Yeah, I went two years ago, but last year . . . You might remember, I pulled a hamstring."

He'd been doing a really cool flare on the pommel horse at the time, and all of a sudden I'd glanced over and he was on the ground, holding his leg. It had taken him a couple of weeks to get back to his full strength, and in the meantime, he'd missed his chance to qualify.

"What's it like?" I asked. "It's just that I've

never been before, and I'm a little nervous."

Did he think I was flirting with him? My voice sounded all weird and breathless to me, and I didn't want him to think I was coming on to him, even though I kind of was. Then again, I thought guys liked it when girls flirted, so maybe it was okay if he thought that was what I was doing. I was feeling lightheaded, and I hadn't even started flying around the uneven bars yet.

"It's fun," he said. "I mean, it's a lot of pressure, but you'll do fine. Just treat it like any other meet. Listen, I have to get back to training, but if you have any other questions about Nationals, just let me know. Okay?"

I nodded and watched him walk away. Had that gone well? I wished I could tell. He'd been in a rush to get away from me, which was not really a good sign. But then again, he'd invited me to talk to him again, so that meant a door had opened at least a little bit to a future interaction. And of course he'd wanted to get back to training—that was what I liked most about him. He was totally dedicated to gymnastics, and he knew what was important.

It only reminded me that, while Scott was showing his true work ethic, I was standing there at the water fountain as my teammates warmed up. I hurried to fill up my bottle, splashing a little in my rush to finish and get out there on the floor.

"What was that all about?" Christina whispered when I finally took my place, but I shook my head, not wanting to get into trouble with Mo for talking. I was just relieved that my face was pressed against my knees as I reached for my toes, and she couldn't see the silly smile that I was finding it hard to suppress.

Five

S unday was the only day in the week we got off practice, unless it was Christmas or some other major holiday, and those Sundays were supposed to help make up for all the "family time" we missed out on throughout the week. Usually, I spent my family time working in the store, which I guess counted.

We stayed open most Sunday mornings in case a customer came by, but it was generally slow until lunchtime. So, when the door to the store swung open, my mother and I both looked up, surprised. My mother greeted the newcomer with a smile.

"Good morning," she said.

"Mrs. Onesti?" the man replied; something about the way he said it made my eyes dart to my mother. He didn't look like a threatening person—he was on the short side, wearing khakis and a wrinkled button-down shirt. Maybe he had just heard how great our food was and wanted to compliment the chef. But then, why was my mother now gripping the counter so hard her knuckles turned white?

"Yes?" she said.

"Andrea Onesti? I'm here to serve you with a complaint. Can you sign here to accept service?"

I had no idea what the man was talking about. Everyone raved about our food, and our facilities were clean, so I couldn't think what someone would be complaining about. But when I glanced back at my mother, she seemed unsurprised.

"What is this in regards to?" she asked stiffly, but I could tell by the way she tilted her chin that she already knew.

"I'm just a process server, ma'am," the guy said. "But it looks like a complaint for foreclosure against you and"—he turned the paper in front of him around to read the name—"Dimitru Onesti?"

The way he butchered my father's name would

have been laughable if it weren't so obvious that something was very, very wrong. I'd heard the word *foreclosure* on the news a lot, and not in those human interest stories they like to show. The last program I'd seen had been about this neighborhood just outside of Austin that was almost completely deserted because the bank had had to take people's houses away.

My mother signed the paper the man presented to her, a bloom of red high on her cheekbones. He thanked her before he left, but she didn't reply. She stood at the counter, staring down at the stack of papers in front of her.

"Mama—" I began, but just then the phone rang. Could it be the bank?

My mother's voice was tight as she answered the phone. "It's for you," she said. "It's Christina."

"Hello?" It occurred to me that, even though I'd been to Christina's house several times, Christina had only been to the store on a handful of occasions, and she'd never been invited upstairs to see where we lived.

Maybe she'd never get to see the apartment now.

"What are you up to?" she asked, cutting to the chase with her usual forcefulness.

"Not much," I said automatically. Out of the corner of my eye, I could see my mother moving on to the onions I hadn't finished chopping for the traditional Romanian stew. "Uh, but I do need to get going."

I could hear the impatience in Christina's voice. "You need to get back to the nothing much that you're doing?" When Christina took that tone there was no stopping her. She probably *had* to tell me about a new leotard her mom had bought for her or something, and I would have to listen for five minutes before I could hang up. I loved Christina, but at times like this I wondered why it was always about her. Shouldn't a true friend have been able to sense my mood and ask how *I* was doing?

"What's up?" I asked finally.

"Okay," Christina said breathlessly, her annoyance replaced by excitement. "So, I told my mom about the dance, and she thought it was a great idea for us to go. I mean, you know how she is. She wants me to do extra sets of crunches at home to make sure I don't miss out on any training, but she loves the idea of us all getting dressed up and having a night out. She even offered to take us shopping for dresses and then out for coffee when we were finished. I'm going to invite Jessie and Britt, too, even though Britt doesn't need a dress. What do you say?"

"That sounds like . . . fun. But I really can't go. Sorry."

"Why not?" Christina demanded. "Ask your mom. Is she there? I want to hear you ask her. I bet she'd let you go."

Mama *would* probably have let me go. She was always saying I worked too hard with my homework and gymnastics, and that I should take some time to play, too. But it was almost impossible to think about fun when everything around me seemed like it was falling apart.

"She had to take the twins somewhere," I lied.

Christina's huffy sigh into the phone was so loud I held the receiver away from my ear. "All right, loser. Well, my mom and I are leaving for the mall in half an hour. If you change your mind, give me a call."

And then all I heard was a dial tone. I knew Christina didn't really mean it when she called me a loser—that was just the way she was. She'd probably called me that a million times, from the time I'd been too scared to jump off the high dive two summers ago to the time I'd said I didn't get the big deal with the latest teen heartthrob on the cover of one of her favorite magazines.

Still, it stung a little bit. Joking or not, that was probably how the other girls saw me, too. Good, dependable Noelle, who never gets in trouble and never does anything fun. What a loser.

"What did she want?" my mother asked. She'd efficiently chopped all of the onions and was now slicing up tomatoes. I knew that she wanted to have this stew simmering on the stove soon, so that it would have time to sit before lunchtime, the only really busy part of Sunday.

"Nothing." I motioned for the knife, intending to finish the vegetables, but my mother held it out of my reach.

"What did you say you couldn't go to?"

"Oh, just the mall," I said, making a face as though I hated the idea. "Christina, Jessie, and Britt are going shopping." I refrained from mentioning the dance.

My mother smiled, although it didn't quite reach her eyes. "That sounds like fun," she said. "Of course you should go!"

"You need me here."

"I can manage," she said, but she didn't look at me as she said it. Instead, she was already searching in her pockets, pulling out a crumpled five-dollar bill and a few singles. "I have eight dollars—that's enough to get some costume jewelry, right? You can bring something with you to eat, or else you can use your money to get something at the Food Court."

The necklace I'd admired at the mall before cost thirty dollars. There was no way I could ever spend that much money on something so frivolous.

"Christina's mom is going to take us out to lunch," I said, then realized I'd basically given in. I should've felt guiltier about it, but the truth was that I was happy to get away from this tense environment and spend the day with my friends. Then, of course, *that* made me feel guilty, so it was like I came full circle.

"Perfect!" she said, pressing the money into my hands. "Go call Christina. Her mom can pick you up, right?"

"Yeah." There was definitely no way I could ride my bike all the way to the mall and back, especially in the Texas summer heat. "Thanks, Mama."

"Have fun," she said, planting a wet kiss on my

forehead. Her hands still smelled like onions, which must've explained why my eyes watered a bit.

"Oh, my God, you *have* to try this one on." Christina thrust a strapless purple dress at me, and I automatically reached out to take it, less because I wanted it and more because I was afraid she'd stab me in the eye with the hanger if I didn't block her.

"It's not really my style," I said. And this was before I'd looked at the price tag: eighty dollars, which was *really* not my style. It was a good thing I thought that wearing anything strapless before you had any boobs was a huge mistake. I hung it back on the rack when Christina wasn't looking.

"I want to find something in green," Jessie was saying, sliding clothes from one side of the rack to the other as she scrutinized each one. "It's my favorite color."

"Plus, you can wear it on St. Patrick's Day and avoid getting pinched," Britt said. She was standing off to one side, smacking some gum that, knowing her, was four pieces of sugar-free watermelon flavor all mashed together. I almost envied her. She wasn't going to the dance, so no one expected her to buy anything.

Christina glared at Britt. "Green would look nice with your eyes," she said. "But you're not talking lime green, right? That would be totally bizarre."

Jessie flushed. "No, of course not," she said, but in a way that made me think maybe that had been her idea all along.

Christina surveyed the entire wall of dresses and wrinkled her nose. "I swear, all of these are meant for a fifth grade square dance or something. Let's go to the Taverna. You know they'll have a better selection there."

The selection would also be twice as expensive. I'd never been to the Taverna, but I'd heard about it from girls at my school. Once, this girl in my history class had been wearing a plain white T-shirt (short-sleeved, with a round neckline, nothing fancy) that she said had cost her fifty dollars at that store. The weird part was that she'd said it like it was something to be proud of. My mother bought me a pack of three of the same kind of shirt in the boys' underwear section at Walmart.

Jessie immediately agreed to move our shopping to another store, and Britt made a snarky comment about the *a* at the end of the Taverna's name but otherwise didn't object. There was no need for either of them to object—they'd probably been given sizable allowances to buy whatever they wanted. I even saw Mrs. Flores hand Christina her credit card before telling us to meet up with her at the coffee shop later.

The dresses at the Taverna *were* nicer, but a glance at their price tags confirmed my fears. Two hundred dollars for a minidress with spaghetti straps? You'd think there'd have been a price cut for all the material they'd skimped on. Christina saw me looking at the dress and must have misinterpreted my expression of disgust as something else, because she started rifling through the hangers looking for my size.

"You have the right idea," she said. "Shorter skirts make your legs look longer—good for us. But this pink is a little garish. Let's see if they have it in another color."

And that was how I found myself being pushed into the fitting rooms, clutching a deep blue, silky dress that would probably make me look like a little girl playing dress-up. I could hear the chattering of the other girls outside the dressing room as I slipped it over my head, leaving my jean shorts on underneath. I'd try it on, to humor Christina, but

I saw no reason to go all out when there was no way I'd buy it anyway.

Considering I had no curves to speak of, I fully expected the dress to hang in all the places it was supposed to cling, and for the waist to hit me somewhere halfway down my leg. But when I looked in the mirror, it was like I was a completely different person. The deep blue color made my skin luminous and my brown eyes huge, and my shoulders looked smooth and strong under the spaghetti straps, rather than bulky, which was what I'd feared. The dress was short, with a swirling skirt. I wriggled out of my jeans, and that made the dress fit a lot better on the bottom, but I would still have to wear a pair of my tighter gym shorts underneath or else be self-conscious all through the dance.

There was a pounding on the door, and I heard Jessie's voice. "Come on, Noelle," she called from the other side of the door. "We want to see."

I could've answered that the dress didn't fit, or that I didn't like it. But a stupid, vain part of me really wanted my friends to assure me that I actually looked . . . pretty.

When I opened the fitting-room door, there was no faking the looks on my friends' faces. I knew it looked great before they even said anything.

"Wow," Britt said. "What a dress."

I stood a little taller. "You think so?"

"Yeah," Jessie said. "You look amazing. You *have* to wear that to the dance."

My smile faltered as I remembered that I was about a hundred and ninety-two dollars away from being able to afford the dress. Not including tax.

"Most definitely," Christina agreed. "You're so lucky—you found the perfect dress right away. I've been looking all through the store, and I still can't decide."

I retreated back into the fitting room, only half listening to the conversation outside, as it went from Jessie's preference for an A-line skirt to Christina's opinions on what constituted too much bling for a middle-school dance. "If it was prom," I heard her say, "sure, I'd get something with sequins on the top *and* jeweled trim on the bottom. But that's totally tacky for this kind of dance, don't you think?"

Her words washed over me as I stared at my reflection in the mirror. If Scott could see me in this dress, maybe he wouldn't think I was such a kid. He might even think I was beautiful, something special. I had a vision of him escorting me to the dance, offering his arm as he smiled down at me with those perfect white teeth, his tie a dark blue to match my dress. He'd have called the night before to make sure he knew what color I was wearing, and also to find out if I preferred roses for my corsage or something else. *Surprise me*, I'd say breezily, and then he would give me an even better flower, one that he'd picked because it matched my eyes. . . .

I frowned at the reflection of my chocolate-colored eyes in the mirror. They might match a dried-up carnation, which would be a more likely possibility for a corsage. My daydream hadn't accounted for the fact that the dance was being held in the school gym and would be decorated with crepe paper, or the fact that I wasn't going to walk in there in this beautiful blue dress I couldn't afford. Or that there was no way Scott would ever escort me to a middle-school dance.

I heard a sharp rap at the door. "Are you finished?" Jessie asked. "Christina's trying on something now, and she wants all of our opinions."

I shimmied out of the dress, leaving it hanging in the fitting room. I mumbled something about wanting to look at other dresses before I made up my mind. It was a flimsy response, but before anyone could question me, I launched into enthusiastic feedback on the coral dress Christina had chosen. It was true that the color looked amazing with her smooth, tanned skin, so I felt only moderately guilty about gushing over it. Yes, I was trying to distract everyone from me, but I also sincerely meant the compliments.

Without the need for too much persuasion, Christina headed over to the front counter, happily extracted her mother's credit card from her purse, and charged the dress and a dangling crystal necklace to go with it. The bill came out to three hundred dollars, but she didn't even blink. I tried to think of all the things you could buy with that kind of money—my parents could have paid the electric bill, I could have gotten three custom-made leotards or a practice beam for my room, so I could work on my dance elements and basic acrobatic skills. Three hundred dollars was as much profit as my family's store pulled in some days. But when I closed my eyes, all I could see was a dress the color of the ocean.

We met up with Mrs. Flores at the coffee shop, although she sat at another table and played a game on her smartphone after Christina rolled her eyes when she tried to join us. I stirred my soy decaf slushee, which had sounded so good just a few minutes before but now seemed like a complete extravagance. The coffee slush was already melting a bit and settling toward the bottom of the cup.

Christina was still talking about her dress—saying that it wasn't what she had envisioned but that she thought that with the right accessories it could come pretty close—when Britt cut in. "You guys don't even know how lucky you are," she said. "I've never been to a school dance. Ever."

"They're really not all they're cracked up to be," Jessie said. "It's not like in the movies, where some awesome band plays and the boy you like finally confesses his feelings. You dress up, and then you wish that you were at home in sweatpants watching TV instead. Or at least, that's how the Valentine's Day dance was last year."

I hadn't gone to the Valentine's Day dance, and this year they had canceled it because of some inappropriate behavior on the part of the eighth grade boys. I'd never found out exactly what had happened, but it had had something to do with the assistant principal's golf cart.

"Still," Britt said. "It'd be nice to have something like that to look forward to. What am I going to do, dance around the living room with my grand-mother?"

There were days when I wished I was home-schooled. It seemed like it would be so much easier—not having to worry about other kids' comments, where to sit at lunch, whether your teacher liked you or whether she thought you used gymnastics as an excuse to get out of work. I was so paranoid about that last one that I made it a point never to turn in an assignment late, even when I had a huge competition and it meant that I had to spend all of my free time typing up a report about the Battle of the Alamo when all I really wanted to do was nap.

"I told you that we could get you in," Christina said. "It's not like there's a velvet rope at these things."

Britt shrugged with one shoulder.

Jessie idly tapped a finger on the cup of her lemonade–iced tea. "It's probably for the best that all I have to worry about this summer is qualifying for Elite," she said.

It was a random thing to say, but we waited her out to see where she was going to go with it.

Of the four of us, Jessie was the only one who was not eligible for Elite-level competition, which meant that there was no way she'd be competing at Junior Nationals with the rest of us—assuming that Christina and Britt made the cut at the U.S. Classic, and assuming that I could scrounge up the nerve to ask my parents about going.

"That's not *all* you have to worry about," Christina pointed out. I caught Britt's wide-eyed look as we both thought the same thing. I really hoped this wasn't Christina's insensitive way of referring to Jessie's eating disorder. Because she could be thoughtless sometimes, but that would just have been too much.

But Christina continued without skipping a beat. "I mean, you've got to worry about whether you'll find a hot guy to dance with on Friday."

I let out a nervous laugh that sounded more like a yelp. "Yeah, right," I said, hoping that no one had caught that weird little sound. "Like there's a boy in the entire school who could be classified as 'hot.'"

One corner of Christina's mouth lifted in acknowledgment of this sad truth. "There are some moderately cute ones, though," she said. "Like Justin . . . even though he's going out with that ditz Tessa. Or Zac, if you ignore his narcissistic personality. Or . . ."

"David Schaeffer," Jessie whispered.

Christina wrinkled her nose. "He's okay," she said. "But he's always got his face jammed in a book. Don't get me wrong, reading is awesome and blah-blah-blah, like Mrs. Bishop is always going on about, but he walked right into me the other day. I was at my locker and he could've knocked me over. He didn't even look up."

"No, I mean David Schaeffer is *coming over here*," Jessie said.

Christina looked stricken for just a moment, as though she was afraid he might've overheard her, but then she pasted a smile on her face. "David, hey!" she said as he approached our table.

David had been in some of my classes since sixth grade, and this year he was in my English class and my P.E. period. Since I sat in the very front row in English, I was barely aware of his sitting two rows back. And I had P.E. every morning, but got to skip it for gymnastics practice and have that count toward my physical education requirement. Luckily, the school recognized that when you could press into a one-armed handstand and support that position for ten seconds, it seemed kind of redundant to make you walk laps around the track to get a stupid stamp on your hand.

In fact, the only time I'd ever really talked to David was the one day I'd been forced to go to P.E. Morning practice had been unexpectedly cut short because of a power outage at the gym, and so I'd ridden my bike to school just in time for the second half of P.E. All of the other kids were in the middle of a baseball game, and the coach was so surprised to see me that she let me sit on the bleachers to watch. David had been sitting there, too, reading a book, as usual.

I'd caught a glimpse of the front cover and seen that he was reading the seventh book in the Harry Potter series. It was one of my favorites, and I'd read each of the books at least eight times. I considered asking him what he thought about the books versus the movies, but starting conversations has never been my strong suit. So instead I just sat there until he glanced up.

"I forgot my uniform," he said. It was one of those stupid rules that made me glad I got to skip P.E.: if you didn't have the ugly orange T-shirt with your name written on it in black Sharpie and the ugly navy shorts that hit you at the most awkward part of the thigh, then you weren't allowed to participate. And if you missed too many days, you could fail P.E., which would have been completely lame.

But David didn't seem to care, because a few minutes later he confessed, "Actually, my uniform is in my locker. I just didn't bother to put it on, because I'm on the second-to-last chapter and I'd rather finish this book than wait thirty minutes for my turn to run around the bases."

Using that as a conversation starter, I finally got up the nerve to ask him about Harry Potter, and we ended up spending the next twenty minutes discussing how we liked Daniel Radcliffe in the early movies but found him a little annoying later on, and how we hated people who spoiled major plot points before you had a chance to read the books yourself.

Even though I hadn't really talked to David since then, it still felt natural to smile and wave at him when I saw him now. He grinned back, and for the first time, I noticed that he had a very nice smile. He had a way of making you feel like he was thrilled to see you, even when you weren't close friends.

"Hi, Noelle," he said. "Christina, Jessie. And . . ." He looked inquiringly at Britt, who extended her hand and introduced herself.

"Where's your book?" Christina asked, and inwardly I cringed a little. She could be so abrasive sometimes. But David didn't seem to take offense.

"I'm in between right now," he said with a laugh. "Any suggestions?"

"You mean, to read for *pleasure*? Hardly." Christina wasn't exactly the biggest reader in the world. Not that she did poorly in school—she got decent grades. You had to, if you wanted to stay on the Elite team at Texas Twisters. It was one of Mo's rules. But Christina didn't believe in reading a book when you could get the story from a movie or on TV.

"What about you?" he asked, turning to me.

I knew that David would pick up just about any book, but I also knew from observation that he seemed to like fantasy series. I named a few off the top of my head, and he appeared to take each suggestion seriously, mulling it over and asking questions about why I would recommend it.

"So, you've read all of those?" he asked.

I flushed a little. "Well, no," I said. "Not all. It's

hard to find the time. Summer is when all the big competitions are, so I'm training a lot."

I wondered if I shouldn't have mentioned gymnastics. Obviously, David knew that I was a serious athlete—the whole school knew, thanks to an embarrassing congratulatory announcement they'd made on the morning show after I won the gold on beam in last year's state championships. But it seemed to me like people always got awkward when it came up, as though it was a reminder of how little I resembled a real human being.

"That's cool," David said, and he didn't seem weirded out, although he could just have been hiding it well. "Are you too busy to go to the dance on Friday?"

"We're definitely going," Christina broke in, glancing at me with this strange, shiny-eyed look, then turning back to David. "What about you?"

"I was thinking about it," he said, still looking at me. "I'm not really good at dancing."

"What's there to it?" Britt said. "You just hold on to someone and sway back and forth. And for the fast stuff, you just let go of the person and move faster. It's a no-brainer."

It looked as though Christina nudged Jessie,

but I couldn't think why. Jessie's elbows *were* encroaching a bit on Christina's side of the table, so maybe that was it. "Plus," Christina added, "Jessie or I would be happy to hold your book for you if you wanted to take a spin on the dance floor. Right, Jessie?"

"Of course," Jessie said brightly.

David laughed. "Okay, thanks. I'll keep that in mind. I've got to get going, though. My mom's waiting for me. I'll see you guys around?"

"Definitely," Jessie and Christina said in unison.

"See you, Noelle," he said, touching my shoulder briefly. It was a grazing touch, but it was so unexpected that it caught me off guard. It felt weird—not bad, just . . . interesting.

"'Bye," I said.

Christina craned her neck until she saw David disappear around the corner, and then she turned to me. "Oh. My. God."

"What?"

She shook her head. "You can't be serious," she said.

I was totally lost now. "Why?" I asked, glancing at Jessie and Britt. It was Britt who finally answered.

"That guy *likes* you," she said. "Duh."

"No, he doesn't," I protested automatically. "He can't."

"Like, it's against the law?" Britt ticked off her points on her fingers. "He clearly was asking if *you* were going to the dance, and he asked *you* about books you'd read."

"So? We're friends." It made sense to me. If I ran into David and his friends at the mall, of course I'd talk mostly to David, since he'd be the one I knew the best. It didn't mean anything.

"For now," Jessie said. "But wait until the dance."

I still didn't know if I was even going to go to the dance, but I knew better than to open that can of worms. I tried to replay in my head the conversation we'd just had with David, searching for any clue that the other girls were right, but I couldn't imagine that they were. The very idea made me want to run as far as I could away from the dance on Friday.

I mean, I didn't like David—I couldn't. When I gazed into Scott's bright blue eyes, my heart beat as quickly as if I'd just completed back-to-back tumbling passes. When I looked into David's eyes behind his glasses (they were an unusual amber brown color, I'd noticed today), my heart beat at the same pace it would have if I'd been watching one of my teammates flip across the floor. And while I could barely get a word out without stuttering when I talked to Scott, I found talking to David surprisingly easy. Even that day in the bleachers, twenty minutes had flown by as we moved from subject to subject.

Mrs. Flores signaled to us that it was time to go, and we gathered up our trash. I realized I'd barely touched my drink. It was only later, watching the shadowy patterns of the trees through the window as Mrs. Flores drove me home, that it dawned on me that I also hadn't thought about Junior Nationals much since arriving at the mall. My mind had been too much on the dance and the dress and David. I reminded myself that I couldn't afford to lose focus, but then I remembered—I might not have anything to focus on, if I wasn't going to go to Junior Nationals in the first place. If that was the case, then I could obsess about anything I wanted to.

That idea wasn't as comforting as I'd once thought it would be.

Six

I spent the next few days awkwardly avoiding David in English, and dodging Mo after practice in case she asked me about the parents' meeting. When there were only three sets of parents invited, I guess it was pretty obvious if you didn't get an RSVP from one of them.

Although I usually felt proud of the level of trust Mo had in me, this time I only felt guilty. She could've called my house directly, instead of asking me whether my parents were planning to attend. But I was sure she couldn't have conceived of a scenario where I hid the information packet in the drawer of my bedside table, and only took it out late at night when everyone else was asleep. She couldn't have imagined how many times I'd closed my eyes and tried to envision myself boarding a plane to Philadelphia and sharing a hotel room with Christina and Britt, every nerve end in my body buzzing with anticipation of the biggest competition of my life. She couldn't have fathomed how many times I'd imagined winning the all-around gold—or sometimes, in my grandest dreams, sweeping every single event.

To Mo, it was a cut-and-dried decision. I had a chance to go to a competition that could define the rest of my career, so of course I would do everything in my power to go. Of course I would ask my parents and let them figure out how to make my dream come true, probably in the same way they'd managed to eke out the payments for my training every month.

And maybe it should've been that simple. But at this point, every day that passed where my parents didn't know about the upcoming competition was another day during which we lost the opportunity to try to earn the money for me to go. I felt the delay like a tightening vise, but I still found myself responding to my parents' questions about gym with monosyllabic answers.

"So, your parents come tomorrow?" Mo asked at the end of Thursday's practice. "I don't hear from them."

"They can't." It was amazing how quickly the lie fell off my tongue. "There's a big event at the store, and they can't get away."

Mo's eyes were an inky black—not dark brown, but black—and they were completely unreadable as she looked at me. I thought for sure she could see right through me, and I opened my mouth, ready to add to my story, when she shook her head.

"They read packet, yes?" she asked. "Make sure they know to register for hotel early. Athletes have rooms reserved, but other rooms fill up quick."

I hadn't even thought about the fact that they would have to pay not only half the cost of the room I would share with a teammate, but also for another room, for the family. "Okay, thanks," I said, not wanting to compound my lie any further.

I tried to make my escape, but Mo touched my arm. "Noelle," she said. "I know you worry. You do not need to."

Did she suspect something? I'd never been a good liar. My mother always said that even when I was little, she had known immediately when I'd snuck a treat. If she asked me directly about it, I'd shake my head, but my hands would go immediately to my bottom, as though I was anticipating a spanking. My mother said she rarely needed to actually punish me—my fear of punishment was enough.

So it was possible that, though I thought I was cooking up a totally believable story, my face gave me away. Mo had her fingers in every aspect of this gym's operation, including admissions and billing, as well as coaching and recruitment.

Or maybe Mo knew about our plans to go to the dance, and disapproved. It was happening tomorrow, after all.

"You are making good progress," Mo said, and for a second I couldn't figure out what she was referring to. Progress on telling my parents about Nationals? Because I wasn't making any progress on that front at all. I'd had multiple opportunities to bring it up—I'd even tried to steer conversations in that direction, but I always chickened out at the last minute. Progress on the dance? Because I still didn't have my dress, even though Christina had offered multiple times to buy the blue one for me if I really wanted it.

Mo must've seen the confusion on my face,

because she clarified her meaning. "On your dismount," she said. "You are making good progress. I know you will have it by Nationals, and you have very good chance at winning medal."

Mo was not exactly the kind of person I imagined playing the lottery, so I knew if she said she thought I could win a medal, she wasn't just taking a gamble. It made me feel proud and confident. And it made me feel suddenly angry that I might not get my opportunity, when there were other gymnasts who weren't as good but who weren't held back by financial problems. It also made me feel guiltier than I'd ever thought possible.

"Thanks," I said, hoping my smile didn't show any of these emotions. I thought about how appalled I'd been only a week earlier, when Christina had suggested not telling Mo about the dance, in case she objected to our going. And now I was not only withholding information—I was actively lying. I was doing it to avoid conflict, but I knew that the eventual fallout would be way worse. Still, that didn't stop me from feeling relieved that I could bury my head in the sand for at least another day, and pretend everything was fine.

* * *

If my life were one of those feel-good ABC Family shows, I would've found a way to earn the money for that perfect dress I'd tried on in the Taverna. Or maybe I'd have a quirky friend who would sew me a copy of the dress; it wouldn't be the same, but somehow it would be even better, because she'd made it with love.

Although my script could have included Christina's buying the dress for me, that seemed uncomfortably close to a miniseries called *Noelle Onesti: Charity Case*, so I shrugged her off whenever she offered.

Instead, I found myself getting ready for the dance by changing into the same black dress I'd worn to Papu's funeral the year before. Rather than spaghetti straps, it had cap sleeves and a rounded collar. And instead of a flirty skirt that twirled around my legs, it had a straight, knee-length skirt that was more appropriate for a secretary than a girl at a school dance.

I had a couple of other dresses, including a flowered one I'd worn to the Easter service at St. Mary Magdalene, but these seemed so babyish when I tried them on. The black dress might have been dull, but at least it made me feel somewhat sophisticated.

Both Christina's and Britt's parents were at the meeting at the gym, so Jessie's mother was driving us all to the dance. I'd told my parents about the dance but still hadn't mentioned the meeting, so I said a quick good-bye on my way out the door and hoped they wouldn't come out to talk to Jessie's mom. It would have been too easy for her to ask them why they hadn't been at the meeting, and then the entire story would blow up in my face.

Christina couldn't hide her look of horror when I climbed into the backseat with her. "*That's* what you're wearing?" she asked. "It looks like you're going to a funeral."

Which had been the original purpose of the dress, of course, but I didn't say that. "It seemed stupid to make such a big deal about a middle-school dance. As you said, it's not like it's prom."

Christina self-consciously patted her hair, which was coiled in an intricate updo that I knew she'd probably gone to a salon to get.

"*You* look beautiful," I said, because she did. I didn't want her to think I was making a pointed dig about her trying too hard, when really I just wanted to get the focus off my boring dress.

I had put on a little mascara and some lip gloss

for the occasion, which made me feel very grown-up (I'd tried on some of Christina's eye shadow before, but didn't like the crusty way it felt on my eyelids with all that glitter). I usually wore makeup only for big competitions, but that was different. Those cosmetics were designed to stay on my face for hours while I sweated and blew chalk everywhere, and were also made to be seen by the judges and up in the stands. They really bore more resemblance to Halloween makeup than to anything else.

I didn't see Jessie's dress until we all got out of the car, since she had been sitting up front. It was the color of the grass on a golf course, which I knew was exactly what she'd wanted. The fabric had a slight sheen to it and caught the light as we walked up to the door of the gym, where teachers were checking student IDs.

"See, I don't think Britt could've come after all," Jessie said.

Christina waved her hand. "There's always a way. What do they care if some extra kids are sipping off the watered-down punch?"

As much as I'd resisted coming to the dance, if it hadn't even been an option for me to go I would've felt bummed out. I made a mental note to be extra nice to Britt when we were back in the gym tomorrow, to try to make up for the fact that she was probably sitting at home tonight watching a marathon of *America's Next Top Model* while we had fun at the dance. Although right now, with the butterflies fluttering in my stomach, *Top Model* kind of seemed like more fun.

I tried to picture Scott in this environment, but I couldn't. As I'd expected, the decorations consisted of orange and blue crepe paper hanging from the ceiling and a couple of hand-markered banners wishing all the eighth graders good luck. Scott might not have been much taller than many of the boys— according to his USA Gymnastics profile online (as part of the Junior National men's team), he was five foot six—but he had more muscle and more maturity. He probably wouldn't have pulled any pranks with a golf cart or thrown wet toilet paper at the ceilings of the bathrooms until the school took all of the toilet paper out and made us carry rolls from our classroom stash as our "hall passes." There were boys on the dance floor doing the robot or awkwardly jabbing their arms in the air in time to the hip-hop beat; I imagined what Scott would look like dancing.

It was difficult to see anyone *not* dancing like an idiot to this kind of music, so instead I tried to picture him swaying slowly to a John Mayer song. But for some reason, I could only see him as if from a distance, looking down into some girl's eyes, though I could never imagine myself as that girl, in that moment. I squeezed my eyes shut to concentrate.

"I'm already bored," Jessie said.

Christina toyed with the beaded strap of her tiny purse. "We just got here. Chill out."

"Noelle's fallen asleep."

I opened my eyes. "I'm not asleep," I protested. I *had* been daydreaming, but I wasn't about to bring that up.

Christina suggested that we get some punch, as something to do, and so, minutes later, we were back, standing in the same corner, only this time with fruit punch that was so diluted it was more pink than red. It didn't take long before we were discussing gymnastics. The gym pro shop sold T-shirts that said things like GYMNASTICS IS LIFE— THE REST IS JUST DETAILS, and it was pretty much true. When you spent more of your life in the gym than anywhere else, it was hard to find other things to talk about.

"I'm going away for a week," Jessie said. "But it shouldn't interfere too much with training, since I'll be gone while you guys are at Nationals. Mo and Cheng won't even be here, anyway, so you know I'd just be doing repetitive stuff with one of the assistant coaches."

Even a week away from practice was a lot, though. It was like cramming for an exam and then having spring break before you actually took the test. You could never expect to remember everything that you knew before the vacation. A week away from practice meant that your muscle memory might've had the chance to atrophy in much the same way.

I didn't want to ask Jessie why she was taking a week off, since the last time she'd done that had been when she began treatment for her eating disorder just last month. But she provided the answer without being prompted, saying, "I get to stay with my dad. He's going to take me camping and everything."

Jessie's parents were divorced, and she lived with her mom and her stepdad. In all of the years I'd known Jessie, I'd never met her father, and I'd only heard about him a few times. I knew that he was an anchor on a television station that broadcast out of Houston, and that Jessie recorded his segments. I also knew that she was supposed to spend some Christmases and occasional weekends with him, but that it never worked out.

But if she was talking about it this time, that must have meant there was a more definite plan. "That's cool," I said. "My dad used to take us camping; we'd make s'mores and try to find constellations, even though we always ended up making up new ones."

I realized that it had been years since we'd last been camping, or on any vacation, for that matter. The last time had been when I was eight, and we'd gone to Galveston Island for a weekend. Of course, then I'd just been a Level Seven gymnast, competing at meets held at rival gyms, with chairs set up for the parents to sit in and watch. That was back in the days when they'd given a ribbon to every single girl who participated, even if it meant you got the pink ribbon for coming in in eleventh place in the Level Seven, age 8–10 category.

It was yet another sacrifice my family had made for my gymnastics. With the money that Junior Nationals would cost them, my parents could have afforded to fly my older brothers to Romania stay with relatives, or take the whole family to Florida or something. It hardly seemed fair.

"It's going to be awesome," Jessie said, snapping me back into the present. "And it'll be just me and my dad—the stepmonster's not even going to come."

I'd heard a little bit more about Jessie's stepmother than I had about her father, which had never struck me as odd until now. I knew that she didn't work, and that she spent her time on ridiculous things like spreading all her hats on the bed to organize them. "Who has that many hats?" Jessie had said. "And who needs to organize them that often?"

"I can't afford to miss much practice," Christina said. "I know I'm already behind, since I just qualified for Elite. Britt's been Elite for a while, and Noelle's earned her place at Nationals. And now my mother wants me to meet with a publicity coach, so that's one more thing to worry about."

Jessie and I exchanged a look, and Christina caught it and rushed to explain. "I know I haven't won anything yet," she said, tripping over her words a little. "But I guess once my mother saw Scott's interview, she got it into her head that I should start practicing being comfortable in front of the media."

I remembered how upset Christina had been that the news crew wasn't there to interview her, and I wondered if she'd had more to do with the hiring of this publicity coach than she was letting on. It was the kind of thing that Mrs. Flores would totally have done, but it was also the kind of thing that Christina would eat up.

It was good that Christina hadn't mentioned this in front of Britt, because Britt would've laughed in her face. Christina was the most intimidating person I knew in some ways, but Britt was the most fearless. She'd make some crack about how stupid it was to pay someone five thousand dollars to basically tell you to smile a lot and appear humble. Then again, if there was anyone who needed that kind of lesson, it was probably Britt or Christina.

Christina turned to me. "You should think about doing the same thing," she said. "Let's be honest; you have the best chance of any of us of winning a medal."

I laughed, trying to turn it into a joke. "I hope not," I said. "I want to win, of course, but do you know how many Junior National champions went on to win Olympic gold? Let's just say I'd rather peak later in my career."

It was something I told myself, to help prepare for the disappointment of losing a competition. I always reminded myself that the Olympics were the ultimate goal, and no one cared how many medals you'd won at the Junior level if you couldn't make your mark at the Olympics. Deep down, of course, I wanted it all. I wanted to sweep the gold medals at every competition I went to, and then continue on to be the greatest Olympic champion that the world had ever known.

But I was starting to realize that champions were, at least to some extent, bought rather than made. The girls who could afford to travel to the Pan American Games or who could afford private choreographers and specialist coaches to perfect individual routines were always going to have an edge over girls like me, who were already financially maxed out. I was lucky to train at what was probably the best gymnastics facility in the southwest, and one of the top five in the country.

As excessive as I thought a publicity coach sounded, it must be nice to have the option. And yet it was the kind of thing that Christina took for granted, like the custom leotards she got every year for Christmas or the mini training area her parents had built for her in their basement. I hated myself for the uncharitable thought, considering that Christina had been more than willing to help me out with money on many occasions, but there it was.

Just then, a slow song came on, and the dance floor cleared except for the couples, who started to gently sway to the music. It was surprising how uncomfortable some people looked as they shuffled from side to side. I tried not to let it affect my perfect vision of dancing with Scott, but it interfered anyway. Now I could only picture us from a distance, taking hesitant steps that barely masqueraded as rhythm.

"This is kind of lame," Jessie said. "I know the boys in our school are savages, but you'd think at least one of them would've asked us to dance by now."

"Speaking of . . ." Christina muttered. Jessie and I turned to see David Schaeffer heading toward us.

I hadn't expected him to clean up so well. He was wearing a blazer over his usual black T-shirt and jeans, and his hair was gelled into spikes. I also noticed he was short, for a guy, but kind of a perfect height for me, since I was so short myself. When he saw me, he smiled, and I nervously looked away.

"Enjoying yourselves?" he asked as he joined our group.

"I was saying how boring this is so far," Jessie said. "I mean, if we wanted to stand around and talk about gymnastics, we could hang out after practice."

"But then you wouldn't have this delicious punch," David said wryly, holding up his glass in a mock salute.

Christina and Jessie giggled, but I could barely manage a smile. I felt all wound up for some reason, like I was a coil stretched to its breaking point. I told myself it was because it was so hot inside the gym, and I tried to take some deep breaths. I was focusing so much on the act of inhaling and exhaling that it took me a few seconds to register that David was talking to me.

"Sorry?" I said.

He flushed, and I wondered if he also thought it was too warm. "If you don't want to, that's cool," he said. "I just thought that this song wasn't as heinously awful as the rest of the music they've been playing."

Now I was more confused than before. I tried to listen to what song was playing, but it was like the notes were all out of order—I couldn't even process the melody. "What?"

Christina gave me a shove. "She'd love to dance with you," she said.

Now it was my turn to blush as I let David lead me to the dance floor, his hand letting go of mine only when he rested both palms on my waist and I instinctively wrapped my arms around his neck. I tried to imagine what we must look like to my friends, and whether they were laughing at us as we became yet another cringeworthy couple performing a mime of a slow dance. But for some reason it was almost like I had the opposite problem from the one I'd had with my daydream about Scott: I couldn't remove myself from the situation enough to picture us as an outsider might. I could only look up at David and glance away when his eyes met mine.

"So . . ." I searched for something to say. "Read any good books lately?"

He listed a couple of titles, but I wasn't listening. I was thinking about how, even though David was nice and smelled really good, I couldn't help comparing him to Scott. And while I did like David, Scott was so perfect that it was hard for anyone to measure up, even someone as fun to talk to as David.

I had just reached the conclusion that I definitely did *not* like David as more than just a friend when it hit me that he might feel differently. I'd denied it to my friends at the mall, but it became kind of obvious when his face started to come closer. I turned my cheek just in time, and his lips only brushed the corner of mine.

"What are you doing?" I squeaked.

His face was as pink as the lukewarm punch they were serving. "Kissing you?" he said, his voice rising on the last syllable in what was more a question than a statement.

"You could've warned me first!" If he had said something to indicate that he was about to kiss me, I would've stopped it. Right?

We had stopped swaying and were now just standing in the corner of the dance floor, his hands still at my waist. I wanted to glance behind me and see if my friends were watching, but I knew they must be, and I felt even more mortified.

"I don't know. In movies and stuff they always just, you know, *kiss*. I thought it would be more romantic than telling you that I liked you."

"But we were talking about books we'd read," I said. "What's romantic about that?"

If possible, David only got more flustered. "I wasn't thinking about it," he said. "I didn't even know we were talking about books. I mean, of course I *knew*, because you asked me about what I'd read and I was telling you about why I hated it when they turned good books into movies because they always messed up absolutely key details, but I was also thinking about how to tell you that I liked you, and I thought . . . I guess I thought kissing you was a good idea."

Suddenly, all I could focus on was the fact that David Schaeffer had *kissed* me. My first kiss. The first kiss that I'd been saving for Scott, who was supposed to give it to me in the park, after he'd pushed me on a swing, or at a romantic picnic, or even under the mistletoe at the Texas Twisters Christmas party. It wasn't supposed to be an awkward brush of the lips at a middle-school dance, wearing the wrong dress and being kissed by the wrong guy.

"I have to go," I said.

And then I was running off the dance floor, past Jessie and Christina, who were both staring after me with their mouths open. This was why things would have been much easier if I just went to school, gym, and home. I knew how to handle a problem like not getting enough rotation on an Arabian double front, but put me in a situation like this . . . and I was just hopeless.

Seven

The last time Mihai had come into my room, I was nine years old and had convinced him to play Barbies with me. At a yard sale, Mama had bought me a special Barbie doll that had flexible joints, and I used to play with her for hours, pretending that she was a gymnast competing at the biggest meet of her life. I made up whole routines consisting of my favorite moves from all of my gymnastics idols' routines and crafted medals out of bits of tinfoil and ribbon. Mihai would make fun of me, but he could usually be persuaded to play one of the judges or a rival gymnast if I let him take some liberties with my story line. This usually consisted of the judge's doubling as a BMX star, or the rival gymnast's being the first ever to execute a quadruple-twisting, quadruple-flipping vault.

So when Mihai showed up now, I was a little surprised. It had been a few days since the dance, and even though I'd had some time to calm down and reflect on the whole weird situation with David Schaeffer, I was still spending most of my time outside of the gym shut up in my bedroom, staring at the ceiling.

"What's up?" he asked, leaning against the doorframe.

It had to be obvious that *nothing* was, but I sat up in bed to face him. "Just thinking," I said.

"As exciting as that sounds," Mihai said, "why don't you come on a walk with me, instead?"

We told Radu where we were going on our way out. He didn't look happy to be the only one of us working in the store, but I was too intrigued by this rare opportunity to hang out with Mihai to really care. Was he going to ask me to cover for him while he escaped for the night? It was hard for me to imagine refusing my favorite brother (nothing against Radu or the twins, but the twins pulled my hair and screamed too much, and Radu liked to tease me), but I couldn't imagine going against my parents, either.

There were some trees and overgrown bushes behind the store, and Mihai led me to the chain-link gate at the end of the street, which kept trespassers from entering.

"It's locked," I pointed out.

He raised his eyebrow. "So? I thought you were a vault champion."

He set one fake-Converse-clad foot in one of the diamond-shaped spaces and swung his other leg over in a fluid motion. Then he wiped his hands on his jeans and gave me a daring grin. "Well?"

When signs said things like NO TRESPASSING in huge red letters, I tended to take them pretty seriously. But it was not like I'd ever seen cops out there in the entire time we'd lived above the store, and nobody was using this land for anything. I just hoped nobody cared if they saw two kids walking around there. Unless Mihai had some other mischief planned besides just hanging out, which, knowing him, was totally possible.

I hesitated for another second before following him up and over the fence. Maybe it was because I was nervous, but my movements weren't nearly as agile as his, and he had to help me over. I let out a shaky breath once my feet hit the ground.

"I consider myself more of a beam champion," I said.

"Come on," he said, taking my hand. "I want to show you something."

We stepped over some tree roots and dead leaves as we wound our way deeper into the woods, until eventually we came to a clearing. The sun shone through the trees as if in a painting, as if there was a heavenly spotlight on this secret hideaway. It was beautiful, but I couldn't figure out what it was that Mihai wanted me to see.

"Is this it?" I asked.

"*Shhh*," he said.

"What *is* it?" I asked.

"*Shhh.*"

When I was younger, Mihai used to love to play this game on car trips where he would exclaim over something outside the window. I would press my nose to the glass or turn completely around in my seat, trying to see what it was that he had seen, and finally I'd ask him about it. It always turned out to be nothing, every time. And yet I fell for it again and again, thinking that Mihai had spotted something amazing through the window that I wouldn't have wanted to miss out on.

I wondered if he remembered that game as well as I did, and if that was the game he was playing right now.

"Tell me what I should be looking at," I said.

Mihai squeezed my hand before letting it go.

"Breathe, Noelle."

And so I did. I closed my eyes and felt my chest rise and fall as I inhaled the smell of birch trees and exhaled deep, even breaths. For those endless moments, I let go of some of the stresses in my life. It was easy to pretend that everything was going to be okay while standing in the middle of this clearing, feeling the shade of the trees at my back and the warmth of the setting sun on my face.

"Better?" Mihai asked, his eyes on me.

I nodded. I didn't need to ask now what he'd wanted me to see. "How did you know?" I asked.

"Are you kidding? You've been a stress-ball for the past two weeks. I may not be around much, but I'm not blind."

"Mama and Tata seem to be," I said without thinking, then wondered where that had come from. This whole time, I'd been totally focused on hiding things from them, but was that just a cover? Did I really want them to force the issue, by letting them see that I was distracted?

"I come here to think," Mihai said, "when I just need to get away from everything. I thought you might be able to use a little of that relaxation."

"Is this where you disappear to?" I asked hesitantly. I didn't want to ruin the tentative truce Mihai and I had reached in this magical place that seemed so removed from the rest of the world, but I also really wanted to know.

"Sometimes," he said vaguely. "Listen, I'm sorry about the other night. I didn't mean what I said, about you having no life."

I shrugged. It was kind of true. And mostly, I really didn't mind. I was happy to spend eight hours a day at the gym. I loved the feeling of mastering a difficult skill that I'd been working on for a while. I loved the smell of foam mats and chalk and sweat. I loved the sound of the springs in the beam as I landed a jump. I might not have had much of a life outside the gym, but when gymnastics meant everything, who needed anything else?

And then, before I could stop myself, the whole sorry saga started pouring out. I told Mihai about the guy who had come to the store tossing around words like *foreclosure*; about Junior Nationals and how much they would cost; and then I threw humility to the wind and revealed how confident I was that I could come away with at least one medal, if only I could go in the first place. I left out the whole part about Scott and David, because who wants to discuss boys with their *brother*, but otherwise I let the words trip over each other and fill the silence of the clearing while Mihai listened.

When he was finally able to get a comment in, it was one I'd expected but hoped not to hear. "You have to tell Mama and Tata," he said. "You know that, right?"

"I can't," I said. "I know we don't have the money."

"How much are we talking?"

I did some mental calculations as to the cost of the hotel, the flight, and the custom red leotard that Mo had been reminding me about all week, and named an amount that made Mihai whistle. Of course, I'd known it was an impossible sum, but his reaction still made my heart fall into my stomach.

"So, what do you see as your options?" he asked. "Because missing Nationals isn't exactly one of them."

The thought of staying home while Christina and Britt went on to compete made me want to throw up. And I felt that helpless anger rise up in my throat, the familiar burn that kept coming back no matter how I tried to ignore it. Out of the whole Elite team at Texas Twisters, *I* was the only one who'd already qualified for Nationals. I'd shown Coach Piserchia everything I had back in training camp, and he'd chosen me as one of only three gymnasts who were good enough to skip the U.S. Classic and go right to Nationals. Britt and Christina hadn't even qualified yet, and their parents were already attending meetings and booking hotel rooms and making plans to go to Philadelphia. It didn't seem fair.

I knew Mihai was right. Missing out on the biggest competition of my life so far was *not* an option. But it was impossible for me to consider the alternative. It wasn't like my parents had that kind of money in savings—if they had, I'm sure we wouldn't have had a leak in our roof, or been in danger of the bank's taking the house and store. I couldn't ask them to shell out all that money for what was essentially one weekend for me, when we'd had to put pots out every time it rained for over a year. We could lose everything.

"Promise me you won't tell them," I said.

His brown eyes held mine. "Promise me that you will."

"Mihai." My voice was low and insistent. *"Promise."*

He gave me the Boy Scout's salute, even though he'd never been a Boy Scout. "Okay, I promise," he said. "But you really have to tell them, Noelle. Soon. The longer you wait, it's only going to make it harder for them to come up with that money."

"I know."

We stood there for a few moments, watching a sparrow that hopped from one tree branch to another in the fading light. It was getting to be dusk, and I knew that Tata would have retreated into the storeroom just in time for the after-work crowd. We couldn't leave Radu to handle the rush alone.

Mihai was obviously thinking the same thing, because he started back the way we had come. As he helped me over the fence one more time, I thought how nice it was to have my brother back. I also thought about the promise he'd made me, and wondered if he realized that I had never made any in return.

* * *

A week had passed since the dance, and Christina and I were stretching on the floor, waiting for Jessie and Britt to emerge from the bathroom and join us. Christina kept looking at me weirdly, and after I'd already run a self-conscious tongue over my teeth, worried I might have had something stuck there, I finally asked her what was up.

"Why didn't you let me buy you that blue dress?" she asked.

It took me so by surprise that I stuttered as I tried to respond. "I told you," I said, "I was still looking around."

"And you decided that the ugly black thing you wore was *better*?" That was Christina—always blunt.

"Look, not everyone has hundreds of dollars to spend for one stupid outfit," I snapped.

Christina's eyes turned blacker than usual, and for a second I thought she was going to strike back. Christina is not exactly known for keeping her temper. But instead, her voice went soft. "Look, Noelle—" She stopped, as though unsure how to phrase it. "I mean, I know that your family doesn't have as much money as mine. And my mom likes shopping. She likes to buy things. You've come over to my house so much you're like a second daughter, only you're not as bratty as I am. So it's really not a big deal if you need help . . . with anything."

It was a struggle for me to match her quiet tone, when all I wanted to do was scream. "Maybe we all don't live in mansions," I whispered hotly, "but that doesn't mean that we're charity cases, either."

Christina shook her head. "Sorry, that came out wrong. I'm just saying, I know you haven't gotten your custom leo yet. And I know my mom wouldn't mind—"

Luckily, I was spared the rest of this humiliating discussion when Jessie and Britt plopped themselves down on the floor next to us. "What are you guys talking about?" Britt asked.

"Nothing," I said, while Christina, at the same time replied, "The dance."

Jessie's face brightened in a way I shouldn't have trusted. "I know you don't want to talk about it," she said to me. "But *come on*. You're the first one of us to have a boy actually *kiss* you. Don't leave us in suspense."

"I've been kissed before," Christina put in. Her gaze was studiously trained away from me. She was holding her left elbow behind her with her right hand, working on her shoulder flexibility before we moved over to the uneven bars.

Jessie was momentarily distracted. "When?" she asked. "You never told me about this."

Christina rolled her eyes. "I don't tell you *everything*," she said. "And it was last year, at Lindsay Barnes's birthday party. Carter kissed me during Spin the Bottle. It wasn't a big deal."

"That is so gross," Britt said. "I thought people only played that game in the movies."

"Maybe you're just not going to the right parties," Christina muttered. Even though she and Britt were on much better terms than they'd been when Britt first moved to Austin, Christina still got a little testy when she thought Britt was making fun of her. To be fair, Britt usually *was* making fun of her.

Jessie looked up from her piked position on the floor. "Focus, please!" she said. "Noelle, what is the story with you and David Schaeffer?"

I glanced at Scott, who was doing dips on the parallel bars at the other end of the gym. Even though there was no way he could hear our conversation from all the way over there, I still found myself lowering my voice. "I told you, there's

351

nothing to tell. He just . . . thought we had a moment, I guess."

"I think it's kind of romantic," Jessie said.

"We were talking about books!" I blurted out. "How is that romantic?"

Christina and Jessie looked surprised by my outburst, but Britt just gave me an exasperated roll of the eyes. "Obviously, that was the only way he could connect with you," she said. "So, 'Do you agree that the movie version of *Bridge to Terabithia* ruined the spirit of the book?' is his way of saying, 'Hi, I think you're cute.'"

It wasn't the first time Britt's goofy sarcasm had left me completely unprepared for the truth of her words. This whole time, I'd been so caught up in how easy it was to talk to David that it hadn't occurred to me that maybe he had been choosing his words carefully to try to get closer to me. Now that I looked back on our conversations, it made some sense. And then I felt kind of bad, like maybe I'd led him to believe that I liked him back, when the whole time I'd simply been having a straightforward discussion with him about books.

Mo walked by. I put my head down and pretended like I was superintent on stretching. The last thing I wanted to do was get in trouble, especially since I'd gotten the feeling in the last week that Mo might have known more about our going to that dance than she was letting on, and that she might not be pleased about it. It was the kind of thing that she would never confront us about—technically, we were allowed to do what we wanted after we left the gym—but her disapproval could still be felt. We were allowed to go to dances, but as Elite gymnasts, we just weren't supposed to *want* to.

When warm-up time was over, we went to grab bars equipment from our gym bags. I looked up to see Scott approaching us.

"Hey," he said; I tried to figure out if his smile was directed at me personally or at the whole group. I wanted to pretend that it had been aimed in my direction, but there was nothing in his blue eyes to show that he was singling me out. And the other girls, the traitors, just giggled and smiled back at him. I hated to think how silly Scott must have found us.

"Hi, Noelle," he said, making my heart flutter. He *did* notice me! He hadn't said a special greeting to anyone else, and this time, he was definitely flashing his smile at me.

"Hi," I said, my voice squeaking, as I heard Britt stifle a laugh. I resisted the urge to nudge her in the ribs. "What's up?"

"I was thinking about you the other day," he said, and I felt my heart drop. "You said you had some questions about Junior Nationals, and I remembered one bit of advice I wanted to give you. I would definitely recommend flying in a day early, so you can get some rest and adjust to the time zone change. It also helps to have that extra time to get used to the equipment."

"Wow, thanks." True, it wasn't like he was confessing his undying love for me, but he had to know that Britt and Christina would probably qualify and would have questions, too, and yet he was directing his advice to me, not them. Maybe like how David had used books to try to connect with me, Scott was using this ruse of Junior Nationals. I got a thrill thinking that Scott, the same guy who'd effortlessly answered a reporter's questions with the kind of smooth, confident sound bites that ended up on television, might be nervous about starting up a conversation with *me*.

Scott wiped the sweat from the back of his neck with a towel. "No problem," he said. "Mo mentioned that your parents couldn't make the meeting last Friday, so she suggested that I might be able to help answer any questions."

If my heart had been flying somewhere above my head only a few moments before, it now crashed down to the ground. *Mo* was behind this? Scott hadn't chosen to talk to me at all. The reason he'd ignored Christina and Britt and addressed me specifically was because I was the only person whose parents hadn't attended the meeting.

"Oh, yeah," Christina said, turning her back on Scott. "My mom said that she'd like to arrange some kind of group dinner for when we're all in Philadelphia. You know, like where we all meet up at a nice restaurant."

Even if Scott had been put up to talking to me, I'd still wanted to prolong the encounter. But as soon as Christina closed him out of the conversation, he walked away. She hadn't really done anything wrong, but it made me suddenly furious at her.

I had only a few opportunities to show Scott how mature and interesting I could be, and she'd just ruined one of them. And didn't she get by now that her mother's idea of a "nice restaurant" was much different than my parents'? Her mother didn't work and devoted her entire life to shopping and monitoring Christina's gymnastics. Christina was her only child, and so of course she spared no expense—even hiring that stupid publicity coach so that Christina could give better interviews than the rest of us. My parents had five children and used to take us to the drive-in movie once a month as our only treat. They couldn't afford surf 'n' turf to celebrate, any more than they could afford to fly me to Philadelphia and have me stay extra days in the hotel just to get some rest.

Christina's smile was uncharacteristically gentle. "We could pay for you," she said. "Not a problem. My mom just wanted everyone to be able to celebrate after the competition."

"That's a little premature, don't you think?" I muttered. At first, she didn't respond, and so I thought she hadn't heard me, but then I looked up and she was staring at me, any tenderness gone.

"Excuse me?" she said. I'd heard Christina utter those words a thousand times, usually in a snide way, with the emphasis on the second syllable (ex*cuse* me?). But this time she sounded truly befuddled.

"You haven't even qualified to *go* to Junior Nationals yet," I said, "much less earned any reason to celebrate with a nice dinner. Don't you think you should just chill out?"

Now Britt and Jessie were staring at me, too. I knew that I was being horrible, and normally, I would've immediately apologized. *Normally,* I would've never said such hateful things in the first place. But I still felt that white-hot anger burning inside me, and, looking at their astonished faces, I suddenly didn't care that I had been mean.

"What?" I demanded.

But nobody answered me. Instead, Christina turned to Britt and said, "Well. I guess we should get to work if we want to actually make it to the competition."

"Yeah," Britt agreed. "We need a lot of practice if we're going to have that celebratory dinner."

Christina stalked over to the uneven bars, with Britt at her heels. I remembered that it wasn't too long ago that Christina and I were inseparable and Britt was the outsider. Not that I wanted it to be like that still, but I felt a pang as I watched them walk away.

Jessie put her hand on my shoulder, her green eyes dark with concern. "Noelle," she said tentatively, "is everything okay?"

In a different mood, I could've almost laughed. No, everything was *not* okay. I had a problem that had no real solution—either I told my parents about Junior Nationals and let them pay for me to go, even if it meant that we lost our house and the store and everything my parents had worked for, or I kept my mouth shut and risked being left behind.

Jessie was still waiting for an answer; I resisted the urge to shrug her hand away. "Everything's fine," I said. "I'm just tired, that's all."

She gave my shoulder a squeeze. "I know you get stressed about big competitions," she said. "But if anyone can do it, you can. You're good, Noelle. You know you're going to rock it."

If I had allowed myself to be completely honest, with no false humility, I would have admitted that Jessie was right. I had complete faith in my abilities. It was everything else that I had a hard time believing in. I used to buy in to all that stuff about how the most important thing was to do your best, but there were some situations where that just wasn't enough.

I didn't know what I was supposed to do.

Eight

By the time I got home that night, my words to Jessie weren't just an excuse. I really was tired, and cranky, and all I wanted to do was throw myself onto my bed and lie there on my stomach until I fell asleep. Even taking off my clothes first seemed like too much to deal with by that point.

But when I walked through the front door of our apartment upstairs, Radu was sitting on the couch, and he shook his head at me.

"What?" I asked. The serious expression on his face scared me. I couldn't remember the last time I'd seen it—maybe not since Papu's stroke. My first thought was that the bank was there to take everything away.

He put his finger to his lips and gestured to me to come join him on the couch. "Mihai's in big trouble," he whispered.

And then I heard it—the walls of the apartment weren't that thick, and Mama's voice cut right through them.

"How could you?" she was saying, at a decibel level usually reserved for when the twins were trying to play with electrical sockets. "We trusted you! We may not have been happy about you skipping out on your shifts at the store, but we figured it was just a phase, that you'd come back around when you were ready."

There was a pause, and then her voice came again, only louder this time. "It *is* a big deal!" she yelled. "You could've gone to jail. Do you realize that?"

I raised my eyebrows. "What did he do?" I whispered to Radu. Had he been busted for trespassing on that empty lot behind the store? It made me shudder to think that I could've been caught for the very same thing only a few days before, but it also seemed like a relatively minor offense. Of course it wasn't our property, but it wasn't like any-one else ever used it, and Mihai went there to reflect on things sometimes. Where was the harm in that?

"He got brought home by a cop for trying to buy cigarettes with a fake ID," Radu whispered back. "Now, be quiet; I'm trying to hear Tata."

Then it was worse than I had thought. I'd kind of known that Mihai was smoking, from the stale smell on his clothes, but it was still jarring to get such clear confirmation. I didn't get what would make him take up such a disgusting habit. I remembered that back in elementary school, a traveling troupe had done a show in our gym about the dangers of drugs and alcohol. I'd only been in second grade, but Mihai and Radu had been old enough to go to the performance. They'd both signed a pledge right there and then, promising not to make bad choices. I wondered if Radu remembered that. It appeared that Mihai didn't.

There was a lower-pitched rumbling through the wall that was obviously Tata's voice, but I couldn't make out the words. He seldom raised his voice; he didn't need to. With a disappointed look or a shake of the head, he could make you feel ten times worse than Mama could, even after all her yelling.

I bit my lip, torn between feeling there was something wrong with listening in on one of my brother's worst moments and not wanting to miss a single word. Then Mama started in on him again. I stayed frozen.

"You're grounded, do you understand me? You'll go to summer school, come home, work in the store, and spend time with the family. That's *it*."

Our parents almost never grounded us, so this was yet another sign of just how much trouble Mihai was really in. It wasn't that Mama and Tata were so lenient; it was more that we never usually gave them any cause to take such drastic measures. The last time any of us had been punished to that extent, it was Radu, when he left to go swimming in the lake with his friend and didn't tell anyone. That time, I was pretty sure my parents grounded him not only to teach him a lesson, but because they didn't know how to handle how scared they felt. Maybe now with Mihai, it was a similar situation.

As if Mama had read my mind, she said, "You know I hate that it comes to this, but you leave me no choice. I'm not going to search your room for stashed cigarettes, but I'm trusting you when you say you don't have any. If I find out that you're still smoking, I'll look in every drawer and under your bed. Got it?"

My parents never invaded our privacy. Christina used to write in a diary, and her mom always "happened" to find it while she was putting Christina's laundry away. I had pointed out to her that maybe she should start doing her own laundry, but instead she'd just stopped keeping a journal. She said that there wasn't a lot in there, anyway—mostly just embarrassing stuff about what boy she liked. The biggest thing that had gotten her in trouble was complaints about her mother. Apparently she'd once written something about hating her mother's empanadas that Mrs. Flores read and took really personally.

The door to my parents' bedroom opened, making Radu and me both jump. Tata didn't even look at us as he crossed the living room and headed back downstairs to the store. It was closed, so I knew Tata was going down there to get a little space. Sometimes, when he needed to think, he would shut himself in the office and "go over the books." That was how you knew he had something on his mind, because Mama *always* took care of the accounting for the store, and she complained bitterly if Tata tried to touch it. She said she spent more time undoing his mistakes than balancing the accounts in the first place.

The next person out of the bedroom was Mama, who gave Radu and me a disapproving look as she went to the kitchen. But that was nothing compared to Mihai's scowl as he finally emerged from the room.

"Don't you have anything better to do?" he asked Radu.

Radu just smirked. "Not really, no. And it sounds like you won't have much else to do, either. Enjoy house arrest."

Mihai reached over to slap the side of Radu's head, but he was grinning. That was the thing about the two of them—they fought all the time, but they also made up quickly. Since they were only a year apart, Mihai and Radu had always shared a special closeness. They had each other, Mama had Tata, and the twins would no doubt grow up in their own little world. Sometimes I felt like the only one without a partner.

As if on cue, Mihai finally acknowledged my presence. "Hey, isn't it past your bedtime?" he asked.

It was true that most nights when I had late

practice, I came home, ate a little dinner, and then pretty much collapsed into bed. In fact, that had been my plan earlier. But for some reason, I didn't like the reminder. It emphasized the fact that I really didn't have a life outside of gymnastics.

"I was just leaving," I muttered, pushing up from the couch.

Mihai ran his fingers through his hair. "Hey," he said. "Noelle, come on."

He called after me again as I headed for my room, but I pretended not to hear. Instead I closed my door and fell onto my bed on my stomach. My face was mashed into the covers, and I could feel the wetness of my own breath on my cheeks and nose, but I didn't care.

Gymnastics *was* my whole life, which meant that if I didn't go to Nationals . . . I'd have nothing. I still didn't want to have to ask my parents for the money, but there had to be *some* way to make it happen.

It wasn't even two days after Mama and Tata's big talk with Mihai that he skipped out on his first Saturday shift at the store. As soon as I got home from a half day of practice, I had put on some disposable latex gloves and joined Tata in packaging soups and salads for sale.

"He's probably just hanging out with his friends," I said, stealing a glance at Tata's tight face. Radu had said that Tata had been livid when he'd found Mihai gone that morning, although his was a simmering anger. Mama's bad moods usually manifested themselves in her slamming things and muttering to herself, but when Tata got mad he got really quiet, as though he couldn't trust himself to say anything at all. In some ways, his were worse.

Now, Tata only grunted. I realized that he probably placed some of the blame for Mihai's behavior on those faceless friends who were terrible influences. "He might be studying for his geometry summer school class," I said. "I heard it was really hard."

"Don't make excuses for him," Tata said, so low I almost didn't catch it. "I don't know my son. He can look us in the face and say one thing and then do another."

That day when Mihai and I had talked in the clearing, I had wished I'd thought to ask him what was going on with *him*. I'd been so focused on my own problems that I hadn't even checked to see if everything was okay in his life. It was one thing to sneak out and start smoking, but to disobey our parents so blatantly after they'd talked to him was unlike my brother. We'd always been brought up to have more respect than that.

Tata wiped his hands on a dish towel before rumpling my hair. "You don't need to concern yourself with this," he said. "You've always been the easy one, the one your mother and I didn't have to worry about."

I wanted to tell him that he didn't need to worry about Mihai, either, that everything would turn out all right. But I wasn't sure anymore myself. Instead, I smiled, reaching for the aubergines to peel for our specialty salad. Their purple skin was soft from boiling, and I enjoyed the familiar feel of it underneath my fingernails.

"How is gymnastics?" he asked. "It's been a while since you've told me what's new."

"Oh." I wanted to tell him about my new dismount on beam, but if I did, there was a chance that he'd ask why we were adding it, and then I would have to lie outright about the National Championships. "Not much. Practice, practice, practice. You know."

"You still having fun?" he asked sternly, as

though there would be punishment if I said I wasn't.

I nodded and smiled, although I didn't look up from peeling the aubergines. I reached for the special wooden knife to cut them up. Mama had taught me that using a metal knife would give the eggplant a weird flavor, and she always said it was attention to detail that made things go from good to great.

That was a lesson that I'd carried with me my whole life, from school to gymnastics. It was why I always pointed my toes, fanned out my fingers, and kept my knees together. Any one of those things might have meant only a tenth of a point here or there, but when you put them together, they made your whole presentation crisp and beautiful.

"We're so proud of you for qualifying for Nationals," Tata said. "Aren't they soon?"

I froze. How could I answer that question without lying? Or revealing more than I wanted to?

"Um . . ." I began, but then Radu popped his head in the doorway.

"Hey, Noelle," he said. "Your boyfriend's here asking about you."

Tata shot me a startled look, and I felt heat crawl up from my neck to the tips of my ears. "Scott?" I asked, my voice shaking. "He's not my boyfriend."

I tried to say it casually, as though it had never occurred to me even to *want* Scott as my boyfriend. But it was hard to stop my hands from trembling. What could Scott be doing here? Did this mean that maybe he did think of me, at least a little bit?

"Scott?" Radu repeated. "He said his name was David. How many boyfriends do you have?"

"Just one," I said, then hastily corrected myself. "I mean, none. I don't have a boyfriend. David's a boy, and he's my friend, but . . ."

Tata and Radu were both staring at me now as I peeled off my latex gloves. "I'll see what he wants," I muttered.

David was standing out front drumming his fingers on the counter. He straightened when he saw me approach.

"Hey, Noelle," he said. "Wow, you look . . . great."

Considering that I was wearing cutoff jean shorts and an old shirt that Mihai had tie-dyed back when he was eight years old (yeah, and it still fit me now—the joys of being small), I knew David must be lying. I tugged self-consciously at the hem of my shorts.

"Uh, thanks."

Radu and Tata had joined us out front and

were sorting random items at the other end of the counter in the most obvious way possible. I grimaced at Radu, but he just wiggled his eyebrows back at me.

"Let's go outside," I said, the words coming out more clipped than I had intended.

It was a dry, hot day, and the sun overhead was unrelenting. I led David to a shady spot under a tree, but even then I could feel the heat seep through my shirt, as if we were in a sauna.

"What are you doing here?" I asked.

"I'm sorry," he said. "I can't seem to get anything right. I came here to apologize for the other night, but I guess I should've called first."

Maybe it was the heat, but I felt some of my tension melt away hearing that. As awkward as David's kiss had been, part of me didn't want him apologizing for it. I couldn't explain why, but there it was. "It's okay," I said. "I'm sorry I ran out like that."

"No, I shouldn't have . . ." David's face went red, and it wasn't from the sun. "You know. . . . Sorry."

I leaned back against the tree, but I couldn't meet his gaze. "It's okay," I repeated.

And then suddenly, David was talking quickly,

his words tripping over one another. "I've liked you for a while. But you probably knew that—it was so obvious. You're amazing, the way you're so smart and pretty and easy to talk to, and I think it's really cool that you're a gymnast. I'm the most uncoordinated person in the world, so I can't even imagine doing what you do."

"Sometimes *I* can't imagine doing what I do," I said ruefully.

David kicked at a tree root, loosening some dirt from the bark with the toe of his sneaker. "So . . . what do you think? Would you go out with me? We could go to the movies, or to the carnival. Whatever you feel like."

It all seemed too surreal. I couldn't believe I was standing there, my hair pulled back in a sloppy ponytail that probably left hundreds of flyaways around my face, wearing this stupid shirt, and a boy was asking me out. For some reason, it was a scenario that I had never pictured actually happening to me.

Or maybe I had, and it was just the wrong boy.

"I don't know," I said. I hated the way David's smile faltered. It wasn't that I wanted to hurt him, and I tried to think of an excuse that would make him understand. "Like you said, I'm a gymnast. And unfortunately, this is the big competitive season right now. I can't afford to lose focus."

He was still looking at me as though I'd kicked his puppy. "Oh."

"It's nothing against you," I said. "But Junior National Championships are coming up, and I have to concentrate on that."

I wondered what David would think if the competition rolled around and I wasn't there, but then I told myself to stop being so paranoid. He probably would've forgotten all about me by then, and there was no way he was going to follow a gymnastics competition just because he'd once liked a girl who might be competing in it.

Besides, I would find a way to be there. I had to.

Then again, David seemed to have other ideas. "But after that," he said, "when school starts back up . . . You might have a different answer?"

By then, I hoped that maybe Scott and I would have had a chance to get closer. After all, we had the whole rest of the summer to train together, and even if Scott *was* put up to talking to me by the coach, at least that was something.

But of course, I couldn't say any of this to David.

It wasn't that I wanted to lead him on; I just couldn't stand to see him crushed.

"Maybe," I said.

He grinned, and this time it reached his amber-colored eyes. "I'll take it," he said. "So here's where I guess I wish you good luck in your competition?"

I thought I'd been handling this the smoothest way possible, but suddenly I wondered if I'd only made a complicated situation even more so. "I guess," I said.

"Good luck," he said. "Not that you need it."

At this point, I didn't know what I needed, although a time machine might have come in handy. Then I could have rewound to the day that Mo handed me that envelope about the championships, and this time I might tell my parents about it right away. I could have rewound back to before the man came about the foreclosure and figured out a way to prevent that from happening. I could have rewound back to when I was a five-year-old who just loved gymnastics and had nothing to worry about except whether I'd ever get the momentum to kick my legs over my head and execute a perfect back walkover, a move I could do now in my sleep.

Nine

I did end up going to the carnival, just not with David. The next Sunday we had off, Mrs. Flores dropped us all at the gates with instructions to call if we needed anything. Mama had given me a twenty-dollar bill that morning, which I'd tried to refuse.

"Take it," she'd said. "I know it will only buy you a couple of rides and a corn dog. I wish I could give you more, but we have to put in our supply orders today."

"But the house—" I started to say, but Mama's lips tightened.

"You let me worry about that," she said. "If I

can't spare a little money for my daughter to have fun, well . . ." I waited for the end of that sentence, but it didn't come.

I was so tired of feeling guilty, so sick of this pattern, that I just took the money. Sometimes I hated the fact that I was a huge drain on the family, what with the expense of my gymnastics training and all of the stuff that went with it, and then other times I felt like I was the only one of the kids who cared about our family's situation. Radu would've taken the twenty and whined for more. The twins would've cried until they got what they wanted. At the rate Mihai was going, he probably would've stolen the twenty from Mama's purse.

Maybe that wasn't fair. But even after Mihai had gotten yelled at—*again*—for slacking off on his responsibilities at the store and not coming home by curfew, he seemed only to sink further into his own juvenile-delinquent world. I had begun to wonder if I'd imagined that conversation we'd had in the woods behind the store.

Britt insisted that we head to the Ferris wheel first. I'd always been kind of a wimp about the Ferris wheel. I hated the uncertainty of that moment when the momentum stopped, suspending you in midair while more people boarded the ride. It always seemed like I got stuck at the very top when that happened. I could fly off a bar eight feet in the air and trust that I was going to catch it again, but I felt all fluttery about sitting in a totally encased and completely safe box with my three closest friends. Another example of one of those weird personality conundrums you faced as a gymnast.

I swallowed my doubts and climbed into the Ferris wheel car with Christina, Britt, and Jessie. The ride operator closed the door behind us, and I felt a lurch in my stomach as the wheel swayed into motion.

Jessie had been rambling on about her father, and she didn't skip a beat as we started our ascent. "We'll go camping the weekend that you guys are at Nationals," she said. "Since it's not like I'm eligible to compete anyway, it's perfect timing."

"Yeah," I said. "The timing of everything just couldn't be better."

It wasn't surprising that no one seemed to get the irony in my tone, since I was almost never sarcastic, but it was annoying. I turned to stare out of the Ferris wheel car, pressing my lips together before I could say anything else. I'd been in a bad mood since that morning, and I knew if I didn't clear my head the entire day would be ruined.

Of course, the best way to clear my head was possibly *not* to look down and realize just how high up we were. From this vantage point, I could look out over the entire carnival, from the Tilt-a-Whirl to the concession stands, surrounded by crowded picnic tables. Almost directly below us, I saw a toddler holding a stuffed panda bear that was bigger than she was.

I tried to look away, but my eyes kept seeking confirmation of how high off the ground we were, as though I needed to be reminded. I turned to glance at the ground behind me, and that was when I saw them.

Scott was at the carnival. With a girl. She had dark, curly hair, and even from this distance I could see that she was smiling. He was buying her pink cotton candy from a vendor, presenting it to her with an exaggerated flourish.

My completely irrational fear of the Ferris wheel had been that there'd be some horrific accident, while my more reasonable worry had been that I would get one glimpse of the ground a hundred feet below me and pass out. Now I was more concerned that I would throw up. If Scott leaned in for a kiss with his mystery girl, this was a very distinct possibility.

"So, Christina," Britt said, pointing an invisible microphone in Christina's direction. "Your public is dying to know—what is your favorite ride?"

Once Britt had found out about Christina's media coach, she'd teased her every chance she got by pretending to interview her. It was getting kind of old, but Christina seemed to relish any opportunity to practice what she'd say, even if it was because Britt was making fun of her.

Christina flipped her long, dark hair behind her shoulder and pretended to think about the question. "That's tough," she said. "Each ride is fun in its own way. I don't think I could pick just one."

Jessie frowned. "But I thought you liked the carousel."

I craned my neck to try to find Scott and his date, but they had disappeared. The funhouse was right next to the cotton-candy stand, and I imagined them stumbling toward a dark corner where they could be alone.

Britt continued with her fake interview. "We know you're very busy, but one more question before you go. What's your take on the carnival? Is it a ridiculous waste of time and money, or good clean fun?"

Christina gave Britt a wide smile that showed off her beautiful white teeth. Maybe I was imagining it, but it seemed as if Mrs. Flores might also have sprung for some whitening strips when she paid for the publicity coach. "The carnival is what you make of it," she said in an overly bright voice. "Me, I choose to make it a positive experience to enjoy with my friends."

Jessie wrinkled her nose. "What kind of response is *that*?"

"A noncommittal one," Christina said. I could tell by the way she enunciated *noncommittal* that it was a direct quote from her publicity coach. "The trick is to answer every question in a vague, middle-of-the-road way that makes you look good and doesn't give them any sound bites they could take out of context."

Britt dropped her fake reporter act. "It kind of makes you sound like you're just an idiot who didn't understand the question."

"No, you don't get it." Christina sighed, as though this were the thousandth time she'd explained this, when really it was the first any of us was hearing about it. "Say a reporter asks you if you're going to Nationals. How would you respond?"

"I'd say I hoped to qualify for Elite later this summer," Jessie said, "but that I wouldn't be Elite in time to go to Nationals."

"And that's the wrong way to handle it."

Jessie furrowed her brow. "Why? It's the truth."

"Because it only reminds everyone that you're not Elite yet," Christina explained. "You should be crossing your fingers that that little tidbit of information wouldn't come up at all in the interview. You definitely shouldn't bring it up yourself. Instead, you say something about how this year you'll be rooting for your teammates, and you can't wait to join them on the floor next year."

The Ferris wheel had stopped to let on new riders, and just my luck, we were stuck at the top. *Someone* had to be in the car that stopped toward the bottom, or halfway up, but for whatever reason, it was like the carnival gods knew that I dreaded this moment, and now they were cackling away as they froze my car at the highest point.

To make matters worse, Britt had started to rock back and forth next to me in her seat. I closed my eyes, the car swaying with each movement.

"That's stupid," Britt said, as though she hadn't been in the middle of giving me a panic attack. "What you said is basically the same as Jessie's answer."

"That's the beauty of it," Christina said. "It's not. Jessie admitted that she wasn't a member of the Elite team yet, and then she said she *hoped* to be there next year, both of which make her seem insecure."

"Better than being cocky," Jessie muttered, in a tone that made it clear she thought Christina was acting a little full of herself.

"That's why I *said* you have to go middle of the road," Christina shot back. I opened my eyes just in time to see her throw her hands up in the air. The Ferris wheel car was still rocking. "Obviously, none of us knows for sure if we'll make it to Junior Nationals or not, or how well we'll do."

Britt had one hand on the pole that connected the bottom of the car to the roof, and there was a sharp squeal from an un-oiled joint somewhere as she continued to use the force of her body to move the car. I reached over to still her, but the sound of my hand slapping her bare knee was a lot louder in the confined space than I'd expected.

"Stop," I said, my voice low.

Normally, Britt would have continued to push it, but something must've told her I was serious, because she raised her eyebrows, but immediately quit moving. "Okaaay," she said, drawing the word out to make it sound like I was the unreasonable one.

"God, Noelle, don't be so touchy," Christina said. "As you so kindly pointed out, *you* don't need to worry. You could tell a reporter you've earned an invitation to the Nationals without even being arrogant. And everyone knows you'd have to break a leg not to earn a medal."

"Thank you," I said, and this time there was no hiding my snarky tone. "I can't tell you how privileged it makes me feel to benefit from your wisdom. Who needs a publicity coach when they have friends who know everything?"

Christina gaped at me. Britt made a show of rubbing her knee where I'd slapped it, and Jessie carefully turned her eyes toward the view outside the car, as though she'd rather have been reminded of the huge distance we had between us and the ground than meet my gaze.

I just closed my eyes again as I felt the ride

lurch back into motion, hoping that next time, we'd be getting off.

The rest of the day at the carnival, I kept my eyes peeled for Scott and his girlfriend, but as much as I dreaded running into them, I wasn't prepared for the person I saw instead.

The first thing Christina said to me after the tension on the Ferris wheel was "Hey, isn't that your brother?"

I glanced over in the direction she was pointing in, and sure enough, it was Mihai. He was wearing a white collared shirt with a picture of a red tent on the back that looked like it belonged at the circus instead of the carnival. He was breaking down boxes and shoving them into a Dumpster. As we watched, he stopped to wipe sweat off his forehead, surveying the piles of boxes he had left.

"Mihai?"

He spun around at the sound of my voice, his eyes shadowed with some unknown emotion for a second before he scowled at me. "What are *you* doing here?"

I glanced meaningfully at the row of booths set up with various games—toss a ball into a cup of water to win a goldfish, hit a balloon with a dart and win an airbrushed picture of a wolf howling at the moon with a castle in the background. "Obviously, I'm here with my friends. Having fun. You know, a totally normal thing to be doing at a carnival."

Mihai waved halfheartedly at my friends. "Hey, guys."

"Do you work here?" Christina asked, even though it said so right across the front of his shirt.

I didn't give him a moment to answer before cutting in. "Do Mama and Tata know about this?"

Mihai grabbed me by the upper arm and led me away from my group. Unfortunately, that also meant that we were standing closer to the Dumpster. I wrinkled my nose at the stench of rotting concession food.

"No, they don't," he hissed. "And they *can't.*"

"But you're missing your shifts at the store," I sputtered. "You're breaking curfew. Mama and Tata are already mad, and what about your grades in summer school? You failed geometry once; are you really going to fail it again because you're skipping class to pick up trash?"

"You let me worry about that," he said. "This is just temporary, okay? I know it's grunt work, but for the month the carnival is in town, they're paying me pretty well to do it. Please . . . don't tell Mama and Tata."

I bit my lip. "You're not using the money to buy cigarettes, are you? Or to do anything else that's bad?"

"Believe me," he said. "That is not what this is about. I quit smoking, not that I really did it that much in the first place—I just started it to impress some friends. It was stupid."

My gaze flicked back to Jessie, Britt, and Christina, who made no attempt to hide the fact that they'd been watching the whole exchange. Britt raised her eyebrows and gestured as if to say, *Well?*

I turned back to Mihai. "Okay," I said. "I won't tell. But promise me that you've got a good reason for lying to them."

He looked me in the eyes. "Do you have a good reason for lying about Junior Nationals?"

I wanted to protest that I wasn't *lying* so much as not telling, but he had a point. "I thought I did," I said.

"Then so do I," he said. "Now, I have to get back to work. You go enjoy the carnival with your friends."

The girls said their good-byes to my brother, and as we walked away, Christina and Jessie were all atwitter about running into him. Britt just wanted to know what we were going to do next, but Christina couldn't believe I hadn't known about Mihai's job.

"He's my older brother, not my confidant," I said irritably.

"I just thought that your family was, like . . . tight. You all work in the store, and whenever there's a birthday or a third cousin graduates, there's a huge party."

I'd been friends with Christina for five years, and she'd always had her insensitive moments. She didn't mean to, but she spoke her mind, and sometimes what came out of her mouth sounded harsh. But couldn't she see that she was *not* helping? Maybe my family had been close once, but now . . . who knew? I was lying to my parents (by omission, mostly, but still), Mihai was lying to my parents, I was lying to my parents for Mihai. It was all such a mess.

Maybe, I thought, I could get a job at the carnival, and pay for my competition that way. But there was no way I'd earn enough in time, and then it would just mean more lies and more secrets.

I felt a familiar heat rising in my body. It was like the sensation I had when I was out on the competition floor, sprinting toward the vaulting horse and about to launch myself ten feet in the air—the adrenaline, the pent-up aggression. Only this time, there was nothing to channel it into. It was just there, this swirl of hot anger running through me like a current.

"How about bumper cars?" I suggested.

Ten

For the next week, things were a little tense in the gym. Part of it was due to the upcoming competitions—which was totally natural—but it wasn't just that. Jessie was still irritated with Britt, because Britt had repeatedly banged her bumper car into Jessie's at the carnival. "It's not called 'gently touching cars,'" Britt had pointed out when Jessie yelled at her. It was a stupid argument, but Jessie was so wound up about the upcoming camping trip with her father that she seemed extra sensitive.

Then there was Christina, who was holding a grudge against me. A month earlier, I probably would've just apologized for any hurtful comments and moved on. But now, I was determined that I wouldn't be the one to budge. I'd only spoken the truth, after all. Christina *was* getting ahead of herself, talking about what she'd say to a reporter about Nationals and making assumptions about who was going and who wasn't. It wasn't fair that she was allowed to say whatever she wanted, but I didn't have the same privilege. It wasn't all about her.

And that was why I was upset: Christina was so busy worrying about herself that she didn't even seem to notice that her supposed best friend was dealing with her own insecurities.

So when Parents' Day at the gym rolled around, the four of us were hardly feeling like a cohesive team. Parents' Day was held every year and was a chance for all the gymnasts—from those in the toddler tumbling class to the members of the Elite squad—to showcase what we were working on. We would all preview parts of our competitive routines for the parents, but the highlight would be the group exhibition, where we performed a synchronized dance with the younger girls and took turns tumbling across the floor. It was practically the same every year, but people always got a kick out of seeing one of us unfurl a double twist only to be followed by a four-year-old attempting a cartwheel.

The younger classes were showing off their skills while we were in the locker room, having just changed into our Parents' Day exhibition leotards, with sequins in the shape of a *V* across the chest. They wouldn't have seemed so tacky if it weren't for the fact that we all had to wear them. There was some strange phenomenon that made it okay for our outfits to match when it came to competing at the World Championships or something, but kind of cheesy when it was only for your parents.

"Why doesn't Mo just put a ruffled collar around our necks and make us dance around on our hind legs?" Britt muttered, pulling the shiny purple fabric of her leotard away from her stomach.

"We *are* dancing on our hind legs," Jessie said. "What other legs do we have?"

Britt rolled her eyes. "Obviously, I'm making a reference to those dogs at the circus, not that I would expect you to get it. And technically, we don't have *hind* legs, we just have legs."

"Well, why not say we have to jump through

hoops, then?" Jessie snapped. "Wouldn't that be a better joke?"

"Because jumping through hoops is kind of cool," Britt said. "But have you ever seen dogs dancing on their back legs? It's sad. It's worse than sad—it's abuse, like this exhibition dance."

Christina broke in with a guttural sound of frustration. "For the love of Mary Lou Retton, would you shut up? This is the stupidest argument I've ever heard in my life."

I couldn't have agreed more, but I wasn't about to admit that to Christina, given that I was still mad at her. Instead, I stepped out into the hallway and peeked around the wall. The Level Fives were standing in rows on the floor mat, their feet on the lines where pieces of the blue carpet joined. They were executing slow, deliberate back walkovers, trying to stay straight.

My eyes skipped to the wooden bleachers against one wall. Mrs. Flores was there, sitting in the very bottom row, chatting with other gym mothers, including Jessie's mom. Britt's mom wasn't there yet, but she'd promised Britt she was on her way and would arrive by the time we took the floor. Britt's mom owned a day care center, and so she was often running late, because of some spit-up emergency or parent meeting or whatever else.

Tata was still back at the store, but Mama was sitting two rows up from Mrs. Flores and Jessie's mom, at the very top of the bleachers. She'd brought the twins with her, and Cristian was squirming to get off her lap while Costel rhythmically banged his favorite Matchbox car against the padded seat. She looked a little harried, as she often did when she was out with the twins, but she was smiling at the gymnasts on the floor.

I only hoped that she would be too distracted by the twins to get a chance to really talk to Mo. Mama had asked me about Nationals just a few days before, but luckily she'd had so much other stuff going on that it had been pretty easy to change the subject and get her thinking about something else. My go-to subject to ask about was what was going to happen about the house and the store, which brought that closed-off look to Mama's eyes and made me feel like a complete jerk for bringing it up, but it was also the only subject guaranteed to make Mama forget about gymnastics.

Mama had been a gymnast back in Romania, until a back injury had stopped her from getting much further than the level I was at now. On the internet, I'd been able to find a very grainy version of her beam routine from the European Championships held in the 1980s. I used to watch it ten times a day. I even sent a message to the person who'd posted it, asking if she had any other footage from the Romanian team during those years, but I'd never heard back. When I showed the clip to Mama, she'd watched it silently with shining eyes. Whether she was crying from nostalgia or regret, I didn't know.

You'd think that all of this would have meant that Mama would be the typical sports parent, trying to live her dreams through her kid, but it really wasn't like that. Mama understood all the work gymnastics took, and she wanted me to learn the discipline of the sport, but she also wanted to make sure I was having fun. She'd admitted to me once that it wasn't always fun back in Romania, where they took gymnastics very seriously and where there were girls lined up to take your place if you stopped working hard enough or if you got hurt. Sometimes I wondered if Mama would rather I be one of the Level Five girls, whose biggest aspirations were a blue ribbon at a gym-hosted invitational.

She stood up, finally letting the squirming Cristian out of her arms, and waved to someone. I turned to follow her gaze and saw Mihai and Radu come in through the entrance.

The Level Five girls finished their part of the exhibition, and I retreated back into the locker room before my family saw me. There was no way to keep Parents' Day a secret from my mother, since she had gone every year, so my only concern was keeping my mother away from Mo and the other parents. Considering that Mo always made it a point to tell our parents how well we were doing, this seemed almost impossible. Short of pulling the fire alarm, I couldn't think of any way to do it.

My eyes went to the tempting red square on the wall that said PULL DOWN in big letters. If Britt had been in my position, she would totally have done it, without a second thought. I wasn't Britt, but I was starting to wish I'd shared my problems with the other girls so I could have gotten their insights right now.

"I've seen you do the Electric Slide," Britt was saying to Jessie, making an exaggerated step to her right, complete with sarcastic jazz hands.

Maybe I could fake having hurt my wrist or

something. Not enough to have to miss practice, but just enough to have to stay off it today and go home immediately afterward. But then Mo would definitely talk to my mother, to make sure I was icing it and wrapping it and all that.

The Level Five girls filed into the locker room, which was our cue to take our places on the floor. Jessie stuck her tongue out one last time at Britt, who didn't have time to respond before Christina shoved her toward the door.

"Come on, guys," Christina said. "Let's just get this over with. We'll do our little dance and routines, the parents can coo over the tots doing their thing, and then we can go back to being competitive Elite gymnasts."

Since she was the shortest, Britt led us out, to the sound of our parents' applause; then I went, followed by Jessie and Christina. The toddlers in the tumbling class were waiting for us in their starting positions on the floor, which were supposed to be straddle splits. Instead, it just looked like they were sitting with their legs a little wider open than usual. I had been faking a smile up until that point, but I couldn't help biting back a grin at the image. I remembered the days when I'd been that proud to show off my split to my parents, when I wasn't even able to get all the way down on the floor yet.

I sought out my family in the bleachers, and my mother picked up Cristian's hand and waved it at me. Radu made a goofy face, and Mihai smiled, although I could tell even from this distance that his eyes were serious. I knew he was probably thinking about his job and my competition and all the other secrets that we had between us at that point. At least, those were the things I was thinking about.

And it was right then that I let go. It was too late for me to compete at Nationals now; the competition was in just under two months, and the deadline to register at the special rate for one of the hotel rooms was coming up sooner than that.

The music started—some horrible medley that included a dance remix of a popular pop-country ballad about reaching for your dreams—and I took the arm of one of the toddlers to help her to a standing position. After that, the Elite girls were each supposed to do a back handspring while the little girls did backward somersaults, but my toddler's was more sideways, and so I had to break out of formation to lead her back to the group.

That was pretty much how it went for the rest

of the routine. I spent more time chasing after one of the toddlers than I did on the actual choreographed dance, but that was the point of the whole ordeal, anyway. Parents didn't come to watch a perfect performance from the Elite girls; they came to marvel at tiny, adorable children with hair in pigtails who didn't know a cartwheel from a round-off.

The CD being piped over the loudspeakers played the last strident note of the mix as we hit our last pose with a flourish. Or at least, the Elite girls did. The tumbling toddlers mostly staggered into a position closely resembling ours, beaming up at their proud parents in the audience and waving even when they weren't supposed to. I caught Christina's eye, and I knew in that moment that we were all united: we were just glad the humiliation was over.

I looked back at the bleachers again; I was half expecting to see my mother chatting with Mrs. Flores and Jessie's mom, comparing notes. But when my gaze reached the top row, she was gone. Only Mihai remained, his hands in his pockets. I broke away from the other girls, ignoring the music that had started up to signify the final showcase event. I was supposed to be out there on the floor for that.

We all were, even Scott, although his parents weren't there, since he was eighteen and almost in college and didn't need his parents to come to things like this. He'd smiled at me earlier, but I hadn't been able to look at him without thinking about him buying cotton candy for his mystery girl.

I climbed the bleachers, searching Mihai's face for any clues. Had Mama found out about my big lie? I wasn't stupid. If she'd had to hear about the biggest competition of my career from someone else's mom or my coach, she'd have felt like an idiot. She'd be hurt. She'd be angry.

"What's going on?" I asked. I didn't need to spell it out; Mihai knew what I meant.

"Mama had to leave," he said. "Costel said that he had to use the bathroom, and Radu said he'd take him, but then Costel said it was like the time we went to the zoo, and you know what that means, so . . ."

"Ugh, TMI," I said.

Mihai grinned. "Nothing like a little diarrhea to really break up a party, huh?"

"Don't even say that word," I said. "I am totally grossed out right now."

"And totally relieved?"

Of course, he would know that Mama's leaving early meant that she hadn't had a chance to talk to the other parents or to Mo, who was over by the beam helping Level Fours show off some of their skills for the grand finale. Cheng was nowhere to be found, but then, he usually avoided these kind of events. With Cheng, it was like he only had twenty words to say on any given day; he didn't like to waste them on small talk with parents. Instead, he used them up in saying things like, "Again!" or "Tighter! Higher!"

"Yeah," I said. "And relieved."

Mihai gestured toward the floor. "Are you supposed to be participating in this?"

"Technically. But I'm really not feeling it."

"Good," he said. "Neither am I. Let's go grab some fries at the concession stand—sorry, apple slices for you or whatever else you gymnasts eat—and we'll wait out the explosive diarrhea outbreak."

"*Mihai!* Seriously, you're going to make me sick."

We headed down through the bleachers and around the floor mat to the exit. I caught Mo's frown, but I knew that there was nothing she could do to stop me as long as she was spotting the Level

Fours. My rebellion wasn't quite the same as pulling the fire alarm, but it felt good. It was like letting some of the air out of that angry balloon of energy that had been sitting in the pit of my stomach for what felt like a long time.

But it didn't make it go away completely. I realized that it was true, what I'd told Mihai. Obviously I *was* relieved to have my secret still intact. And yet, as much as I'd dreaded her reaction, a part of me *wanted* Mama to know the truth. The weight of this whole deception was still on me, and until it lifted, there could be no relief.

Eleven

Y ou're not setting up," Mo said after my tenth rep of my beam dismount. "You need more power in back handspring."

Of course, Mo was right. I wasn't getting enough momentum with my round-off to back handspring on the beam, which meant that I wasn't setting up the full-twisting double back dismount properly. Because I wasn't getting the height on the move, my landings were piked, my body bent at the waist, throwing my balance off. Every single time, I was forced to take a small step forward.

"Try again," she said. "This time, do like you on floor."

Beam was usually my best event, and I prided myself on being able to flip on the four-inch-wide surface as though I was frolicking on the floor mat. But for some reason, today it wasn't coming together.

I climbed back up on the beam, taking my position at the very end. I always touched one pointed foot to the back of the beam, just to be sure that I was as far as I could go and wouldn't run out of room as I flipped down the beam toward my dismount. At this point, I didn't really need the assurance. I knew every single centimeter of that beam. But it was like a superstition: before I got on the beam, I always measured out an arm's length from one end and made a chalk mark to tell myself where my punch front should start, and before I dismounted I always touched the end of the beam with one foot.

Mo was waiting, arms crossed over her chest. I took a deep breath, feeling the area between my ribcage hollow and expand. I could do this. I *would* do this, not for National Championships or for Mo but for myself.

I launched into my round-off, and from the moment my hands touched the beam, I knew this time would be the same as all the others. My shoulders weren't angled toward the beam just right, and so I wasn't able to get the push I needed, which slowed everything else down. Because I didn't have the power going into my round-off, I also didn't have the momentum in my back handspring, so my feet felt like lead as I opened up into my full-twisting double back.

I saw the mat coming toward me only a split second before my feet hit, but it felt like I wasn't done flipping. My body was propelled forward, and I reached out a hand to touch the ground, one knee dropping to the blue foam as I landed. In a competition, that would have been considered a fall, and would have cost me the hope of any medal at all, much less gold.

A cloud of chalk puffed into the air as I slammed my fist against the mat. Mo shook her head. "Focus," she said. "You are not yourself today."

I felt like I hadn't been myself in a long time. Even the other girls were giving me darting sidelong glances, as though they were waiting for me to start growing and bust out of my leotard like the Incredible Hulk. I looked over in Scott's direction, hoping that he hadn't been witness to my utter failure.

Scott was talking to Cheng, who was making some motion with his hands that seemed to indicate that Scott's body position should be straighter. Scott nodded, his eyes never leaving Cheng's. I was relieved he hadn't been watching me mess up, but I was also a little disappointed. I felt like I kept tabs on most of his movements, whereas he could go an entire day without glancing in my direction at all.

I wanted to catch his attention, and I'd had an idea the other night that might turn out to be a way to do it. "Mo," I said. "About my beam mount. I was wondering . . ."

She looked at me expectantly. I took a deep breath. I'd never really tried to personalize my routine before. I always figured that Mo and Cheng were the experts, and so I would just do whatever they told me.

"I was watching a routine of my mom's on the internet," I said, "and she used to do this really cool mount. It was like a Silivas, only she rotated more times and . . ."

Mo nodded. "I've seen," she said. "She would get it named for her if she do at world competition, but she did not have chance."

The Silivas mount was named after a superfamous Romanian gymnast from the 1980s. Instead of my current boring beam mount, I would jump on a springboard and into a neckstand on the beam (like a headstand except that my head would be in front of the beam, my arms gripping it from behind). I would straddle my legs, then make them straight again as I turned to face the other way, then straddle again, then back to straight as I turned one more time. When my mom had done it, it had looked cool and interesting and beautiful.

"So, do you think I could change my mount?" I asked.

This new mount looked deceptively simple, but I knew that it would be a challenge to learn. For one thing, it would put pressure on my shoulders, and would require a ton of upper-body strength.

Mo considered this idea for a moment, as though she had had the same thought and was gauging whether or not I could do it. I was already working on a new dismount, so I knew this was a lot to take on.

"We could work on it," Mo said. "Now, practice almost over, so we will start tomorrow."

I glanced at Scott again, but he was still working with Cheng over by the rings and didn't look in my direction at all. He would, though, once I showed off my new mount. And my mom would be so proud of me. I couldn't wait.

Mo called us all to attention before we rotated to our next apparatus. "News crew is coming to talk to you," she announced.

There was an eruption of excited whispering from Christina, Jessie, and Britt. I didn't say a word. I was already scared to death of any kind of public speaking, and now was the worst possible time to be asked to do this. I was having a hard enough time saying things to my family and friends, much less a stranger or 20,000 viewers at home.

"Settle down," Mo said. "This reporter wants to ask you questions about the National Championships. You be polite, humble, answer a few questions, and then get to work on your tumbling passes with Cheng. She will tape that, too. Understand?"

"Do we have time to touch up our makeup?" Christina asked. I shot her a quick glance. I hadn't even known she wore makeup to practice, although I guess there was no way she could have been born with eyelashes that long and perfectly separated.

Mo didn't dignify Christina's question with a response, but the tightening of her mouth answered it well enough. "I introduce you to reporter, and you have ten minutes. Okay? Let's go."

It wasn't the same woman who'd interviewed

Scott a few weeks before. This woman wore a teal suit and had dyed-blond hair that looked as dry as tumbleweeds. With all that hair spray, it'd probably have ignited if you held a match next to it. I'd never seen her on TV, but I saw from the sticker on her microphone that she was from a rival news station to the one my parents usually watched. They didn't like the weatherman on her station, who'd once treated an incoming hurricane like it was a monster-truck event instead of a serious catastrophe.

"She's from my dad's station!" Jessie hissed to us as we approached. "But why would she want to talk to me? I'm not even technically an Elite yet."

Apparently, Mo was listening, because she gave Jessie a sharp look. "You are part of this team," she said. "You can be part of this, too."

The woman gave us a huge, red-lipstick smile. "Hi, y'all," she said in the heaviest Texas drawl I'd ever heard. I bet it was fake. "Y'all must be the talented girls I've been hearing all about. Sorry to interrupt your practice like this, but I just wanted to ask a few questions."

"Girls, this is Lyla Quin, from Channel Thirteen," Mo said. "Ms. Quin, you know the girls, yes?"

How did she know us? Had she been watching

us, or was she familiar with our gymnastics? The idea that I might actually have been on someone's radar as a gymnast to watch was kind of exciting, even if it added a bit of pressure.

"Please," Lyla said, "is there a place I can do the interviews?"

Mo led us into the pit room, where we usually went to practice our big skills into a huge pit filled with foam. Lyla fussed at her cameraman for a few minutes, directing him to move various equipment to get the best shot possible. In the end, she had us sit on top of a tall stack of mats, lined up in front of a huge banner that advertised an invitational event that had been held at Texas Twisters a couple of years ago.

I tried surreptitiously to smooth my hair, wishing I had a mirror so I could check to see if I had any flyaways. Considering that I *always* had a halo around my head of tiny baby hairs that escaped from my ponytail, I'm sure I did.

But Lyla Quin was a professional. She handed Christina a tissue to blot her face, saying it was shiny (Christina's smile slipped a little bit at that), told Britt to sit up straighter, and tapped me, telling me to cross my legs at the ankles instead of at the knees. Then she spent a minute talking to the cameraman in weird code about wide-angle shots and making sure everything was "in frame," before sliding her tongue over her teeth and turning to face the camera.

"Ready?" she asked, but it was more like a statement than a question, because she didn't wait for anyone to respond. The cameraman counted down from three, and Lyla started talking.

"We're here with four very talented young ladies," she said in that twang, "who are on their way to gymnastics greatness at the Junior National Championships coming up in Philadelphia. They took time from their very busy schedules to chat with us and tell us what it's like to follow your dreams."

And then, suddenly, the microphone was on me. I felt like a deer in the headlights, and I only hoped I didn't look like one.

"Noelle, you already qualified for the competition through a training camp earlier this year. What was that experience like?"

Didn't they tell you the questions they were going to ask before they put you on the spot? Or was that only for when Drew Barrymore went on Letterman or something? "Um," I said, "it was great."

Lyla Quin's smile got wider, but I swear she was thinking, What an idiot. How could she not? *It was great?* Christina said it was best to be vague, but this had to be taking it too far.

"It's a relief," I added, trying to think of something more interesting to say, "knowing I definitely have a spot."

Did that fit in with what Christina had said about not appearing too arrogant, but also not seeming like you were unsure of yourself? What did it matter? It was true that I'd had a perfect opportunity after the training camp, but it was also true that I'd completely blown it by now.

Lyla Quin moved on to Jessie then, asking about when she was going to qualify for the Elite team. I had to hand it to this woman; she'd done her homework. Jessie stumbled through her answer; I could tell she was thinking of what Christina had said, too, and trying to remember what the ideal answer was supposed to be.

Then Christina fielded a question about how long she'd been doing gymnastics (since she was five), and finally, Lyla Quin asked Britt what it was like to be homeschooled. She must have really gotten some background on each of us from Mo.

It made me a little nervous about what she'd ask me next.

"Actually, it sucks," Britt said. "I get left out of everything. And it's not even like I have less homework, because my grandmother is like a Nazi about education."

I saw Christina roll her eyes. It was obvious that Britt hadn't listened to any of her advice, but then, Britt marched to her own beat. I tensed up as Lyla Quin pushed the microphone into my face again.

"Gymnastics is mostly an individual sport," she said. "How do you balance that with being on a team like Texas Twisters?"

"Oh," I said, and then I meant to follow it up with something, but my mind went blank. There were times when gymnastics did feel very isolating; even when you were competing on a team, it was always just you up there on that apparatus, hoping to land your skills and stick your dismount. Mostly, I really loved having other girls to talk to, friends who were going through the same stuff that I was going through and could relate. But lately, I wasn't feeling so connected. It kind of seemed like I was up on that beam alone, struggling to keep my balance, but no one was spotting me.

Christina broke in, giving a flip of her hair that seemed practiced. Because it totally was—I remembered her doing it during Britt's fake interview of her on the Ferris wheel. "Being a gymnast might be like walking a tightrope, but your teammates are your net. So of course we love being part of a team."

I frowned. That made it sound like Christina was the main gymnast, and we were all just there to support *her*. I mean, who wanted to be the net when you could be the acrobat? I wondered if that was another technique her publicity coach had made her practice—Christina could still be arrogant, but she seemed to be getting better at making it more subtle.

Lyla Quin asked us a few more questions before gesturing to the cameraman to stop rolling tape. He lowered the camera from his shoulder—it looked heavy—and Lyla Quin fluffed her already gigantic hair.

"Thanks, y'all!" Her voice dripped with syrupy sweetness. "That was fabulous. Now, Pete and I are going to get some footage of y'all training, okay? Don't be self-conscious around the camera; just pretend it's not there and do what you do."

I had already probably made a fool of myself in the interview. Knowing my luck, I'd mess up on floor, too. It was a good thing Lyla Quin hadn't gotten any footage of beam practice. I started to head out of the pit room back to the main area, but the other girls were hanging back. I paused in the doorway to listen.

"You can cut out the part where I called my grandmother a Nazi, right?" Britt was saying. "I didn't mean she was actually a *fascist*, you know, I was just trying to say that she really gets on me about my homework."

"Did my face still look shiny on camera?" Christina asked. "If you give me a few minutes, I could touch up and give you another interview. We could talk about whatever you wanted. I bet a lot of your viewers don't know what a day in the life of a gymnast is like."

It was actually quite tedious. Training, school, training, and then home to sleep. Don't get me wrong, I usually felt most myself in the gym, but to an outsider it was probably just as interesting as watching a golf game on TV was for me.

Lyla Quin did a good job of deflecting all the questions, but she stopped to consider Jessie's, which was about Jessie's dad.

"Mark Ivy," Jessie said. "He's one of the anchors on your channel. Do you know him?"

It seemed like a strange thing to ask. Of course Lyla Quin knew Mark Ivy. They worked for the same station.

But from the sudden downturn of the corners of Lyla Quin's mouth, it seemed that maybe Mr. Ivy wasn't well liked at the station. She hid her feelings quickly behind her toothpaste smile; I wondered if Jessie even saw it.

"Oh, Mark," she gushed. "Right, yes. He's such a dynamic anchor. He really has a presence."

"He's going to take me camping soon," Jessie said. "Since I'm not going to Nationals. He was supposed to take me over Christmas break, but it didn't work out."

"Well, great," Lyla Quin said. "That's just great, sweetie. Now, I promised your coach I'd have you back at practice soon, so let's get on out there, and we can get the rest of our footage and be out of your hair."

At this, the other girls reluctantly made their way toward the door, but this time it was I who hung back to talk to Lyla Quin.

"Uh, Ms. Quin?" It was weird to call her that, but I didn't feel comfortable calling an adult by her first name. On television, she was always Lyla

Quin, but it also felt weird to use her full name in person.

"Yes, honey?" She pushed some of her hairsprayed bangs out of her eyes.

"What made you come here today?" I asked. "I mean, why did you do these interviews?"

She chuckled, but it was a kind laugh. "I heard that four of our country's best gymnasts were right here in Austin, Texas," she said, "and that the competition of their lives was just around the corner. Now, that's too good a story to pass up."

And then she leaned in closer, so only I could hear. "And you know what? I was told that there was a little powerhouse named Noelle Onesti, and that she was the one to keep my eye on. So I'll be watching you, little girl. Do Austin proud."

Somehow I managed a weak smile. At this point, I couldn't imagine making anyone proud, much less the entire state capital.

When I arrived at the store that evening, covered in a sheen of sweat from the workout and the bike ride home in the Texas summer heat, Tata was behind the counter. The rush was over, and he had the television muted behind him as he usually did when things were slow. I saw that it was tuned to News Channel 8, and I was glad that my parents hated that weatherman on Channel 13, although I was curious to see the feature myself. In other circumstances, I would have been totally excited for my parents to see it. They'd have wanted to tape it and send copies to my relatives in Romania. Or Mama would bug Radu to help her figure out "that YouTube thing" until she could post it.

"Hi, Tata," I said, sliding onto a stool next to him.

"How was gym?" he asked, just like he always did.

Usually, I tried to find the best, most exciting thing to tell my father—whether I'd learned a new skill or gotten praise for my execution or finally mastered a difficult dance move. But the only good part had been getting the go-ahead to work on Mama's old beam mount, and something told me to keep that a secret for now. Plus, I felt drained of energy, and it was difficult to muster excitement about much of anything. My conversation with Lyla had reminded me of how serious my family's situation was right now.

"Hard," I said. "And tiring. I can't seem to get my new beam dismount."

"You'll get it," he said.

I leaned my elbows on the counter, resting my chin in my hands. "I don't know," I said. "I might not. Everyone has a limit to their abilities, I guess."

"What is this dismount?"

Even though my father wasn't as knowledgeable about gymnastics as my mother was, he still knew some of the lingo. It was impossible not to pick it up after living with me and Mama.

"It's the same as my old one, a tucked double back, but now I'm adding a full twist to the first flip. I can't seem to get enough height to complete all the rotations without messing up the landing."

"You will," he said. "You need to believe in yourself."

Of course, that was what a parent would say, and I appreciated it. But it also wasn't that easy. "It's like, if you told me I could fly if I believed hard enough, that doesn't mean that I actually would. I could jump off the top of a building and believe all I wanted, and I'd fall flat on my face."

Tata looked at me then, his brown eyes serious. I'd never realized how much Mihai looked like my dad, but they had the same eyes, deep-set, with the ability to level you in an instant.

"When you're in that gym, what do you think you are doing?" he said. "You are defying gravity. You are doing things that most people would call impossible. And do you know how you do it?"

"How?"

"Faith," he said. "Faith makes you fly."

Twelve

Christina and Britt left at the end of the month for the U.S. Classic, and Mo went with them. I wished them the best of luck, and I meant it—I really hoped that someone from our gym would be able to go to the National Championships, and they deserved it.

There were sixteen spots open, which meant that the top fourteen girls at the U.S. Classic would go on to compete at Nationals. Christina and Britt could nab two of those spots easily. Christina's routines weren't as difficult as Britt's, but she had the artistry and elegance that Britt sometimes forgot about in her quest to pull off the biggest tricks.

At one point, I thought I had the complete package. Ballet training from when I was younger made me more conscious of my body's movements and helped me with the required dance elements, and I tried to be meticulous about all of the little details. I wasn't as fearless as Britt, as muscular as Jessie, or as graceful as Christina, but I worked hard.

Maybe that was just what Christina's ridiculous publicity coach was always telling her, about how you were setting yourself up for failure if you were too arrogant. I'd focused so much on making my gymnastics perfect and believed so deeply that I really was one of the best that I'd been blind to other things. Like how hard it was to think about medals when everything else was falling apart.

The U.S. Classic wasn't being broadcast on television, but I'd promised Britt and Christina that I would watch the streaming webcast of it online. Since Jessie wasn't at the Classic, either, because she was preparing for her Elite qualifier coming up, she invited me over to her house to watch it. It would definitely beat trying to convince Radu to get off his World of Warcraft game and let me use the computer for a couple of hours, and then trying to listen to the commentary through only one speaker, while the twins screamed in the background. I agreed right away.

So that was how I found myself with a Saturday off for a change—or at least a half day, since we had trained with Cheng that morning. But by that afternoon, we were at Jessie's house, setting out chips and dip in the kitchen in anticipation of the webcast's starting. Jessie's stepdad had even figured out a way to use the Wii to show it on their big-screen TV.

"There's no way we're going to be able to eat all of these," I said, lining up the bags of salt-and-vinegar; sour-cream-and-onion; cheddar cheese; regular; and ridged chips, not to mention the pretzels and tortilla chips with salsa.

"I know," Jessie said. "But when my mom found out I was having friends over, much less for a party with *food*, she went a little nuts. My stepbrother and stepsister will polish off what we don't eat, believe me."

The first thing I focused on was Jessie's emphasis on the word *food*, which reminded me that she was still going through treatment for her eating disorder, even though none of us ever talked about it. I hoped she hadn't thought I was being insensitive in my comment. It was easy to think that she was all better now, but of course I knew that it wasn't that simple.

But then I realized that she'd used the plural, and I had to ask. "Friends?" I said. "Who else are you expecting?"

She gave me a sheepish look. "I kind of told some other people from the gym that they could come over and watch the competition at my house." Just then, the doorbell rang, and she brightened. "That could be them now."

"Wait, who?"

We heard the heavy footsteps of Jessie's stepbrother pounding down the stairs as he raced to get the front door, and Jessie sprinted to get there first. "I've got it!" she yelled up. Then, to me, she said, "Felicia, Carolina, Jacob, and Scott."

She was opening the door and greeting her new guests, but I was reeling. *Scott*? She'd invited Scott over? I glanced down at myself. I was wearing a stretched-out old T-shirt from a competition I'd gone to five years ago and my cutoff jean shorts that I wore when I was just hanging out. They were house clothes, or spending-the-day-with-a-close-friend-who-doesn't-care clothes. They were *not* crush clothes.

But Scott was coming through the door, smiling at something Jacob was saying. His eyes flickered over me for a moment while he said hello, and then he was making his way toward the chips in the kitchen, arguing with Jacob about whether salt-and-vinegar chips were gross or delicious. (I said "delicious," but Scott seemed to think they were disgusting. I made a mental note not to touch the salt-and-vinegar chips.)

Felicia and Carolina followed the boys in, but I barely paid them any attention as I tried to decide on the coolest way to approach Scott. Maybe, I thought, I should ask him if his ankle was feeling better—I'd seen him roll it in practice a few days ago, but he seemed to be putting his full weight on it again. Then again, I didn't want to come off as a stalker.

I reached for a handful of pretzels at the same time as Scott did, figuring that our hands would brush against each other and it would be the perfect opportunity to strike up a conversation.

He drew his hand back. "Sorry," he said. "You look like a girl on a mission for pretzels."

Great. Now he thought I was some rude pig who'd practically shoved him out of the way for a stupid snack. I compensated by taking a single pretzel. "I just, um, wanted to try one," I said. Then I added, "I've never had a pretzel before."

Scott knitted his brows together. "Really?" he said. "I didn't think there was anyone on the planet who'd never had a pretzel. They're awesome."

I was going to ask him why he wasn't at the U.S. Classic, even though I knew that the men's qualifier didn't happen at the Classic, but then Jessie called into the kitchen, "Come on, guys, it's on!"

We all filed into the living room. I tried to stay a step behind Scott so I could find a seat next to him, but he chose an armchair, leaving me standing stupidly in the middle of the room while the girls piled onto the couch and Jacob sat cross-legged on the floor.

Jessie moved over a fraction of an inch. "There's room for you, Noelle," she said. "Sometimes our stunted growth pays off, right?"

Everyone shifted, but I still had to squeeze myself between Jessie and the arm of the couch. It was not very comfortable.

"Look!" Felicia said, pointing at the screen. Felicia was fourteen, but only a Level Seven gymnast. I'd always felt kind of weird around gymnasts who were close to my age but at a lower level. It wasn't that I was trying to be snobbish or cliqueish . . . but when you trained six days a week for up to eight hours a day with the same three people, it was easy to pretend that the other gymnasts didn't exist. I was surprised Jessie had invited them at all, even though I knew it was the nice thing to do.

The picture on the TV was a little pixilated—a full-screen webcast through a Wii on a big-screen television did have some limitations, after all—but we could see a list of the competing athletes' names scrolling down. On that list, in big letters, it said: CHRISTINA FLORES, and then, BRITTANY MORGAN. We let out a little cheer.

We watched a few routines from other gymnasts, including an almost flawless bars set from Peyton Clarke, who was probably one of my biggest rivals (not personally—I'd barely spoken to her—but on the gymnastics floor). She was really good, and the only reason she hadn't been chosen at the training camp was because she'd had tendinitis in her elbow and had been forced to sit it out. But now she was back, healthy again and apparently better than ever. I knew she'd be a threat at Nationals. I'd have loved to challenge her right then and there, but I had to settle for the hope the other girls could do the job for me.

And then Britt was up on the balance beam. It was strange to see her on TV, her blond hair back in her usual ponytail, that familiar steely look in her eye as she waited for the signal to mount the apparatus. And yet there was something slightly different about her. . . .

"Oh, my god," I said. "Is Britt wearing *makeup*?"

Jessie laughed. "It's a competition, Noelle. You know you have to wear it to look good for the judges. Otherwise, all they see out there is your pasty, washed-out face."

I did, in fact, know that. Maybe it was because Britt was such a tomboy and this was the first time I'd actually seen her at a competition, but for some reason the sight of her face all covered in foundation and her lips unnaturally glossy totally threw me for a loop.

"Even Scott wears makeup for big meets," Jacob said. Scott made a fist, pretending he was about to throw a punch. The men's gymnastics program wasn't very big at Texas Twisters, and at sixteen, Jacob was the oldest boy in the class, which consisted of seven-year-olds on up. It must have been frustrating to have to practice with all different levels, but we didn't have the equipment or the resources to field competitive teams at each age level. Scott was eighteen, and technically not part of the Texas Twisters team. He received some private training from Cheng, and then, once the fall semester started, he'd be at Conner University with the collegiate team.

I turned back to the television just in time to see Britt mount the beam with her powerful punch-front move. She launched into her first acrobatic series right off the bat, but when she landed her back layout, one of her feet shot out from underneath her. Her leg went up and she bent at the waist, but she managed to regain her balance and avoid the fall.

Still, it was not a good start.

I bit my lip. "Come on, Britt," I whispered.

Britt managed to finish her routine with no other major incident, but her face showed her frustration. I saw Mo put her arm around her shoulders and talk to her in that calm way she had. I could just hear what she'd be saying: *Don't worry about it; there are other events.*

"She'll be fine," Jessie said. "She only needs to make top fourteen here. She'll do it."

Christina started on vault, which was her least favorite event, but at least it meant that she got to end on floor, which was her specialty. She executed a clean Yurchenko with a full twist, but the relatively low level of difficulty meant that her score was only enough to put her in tenth place.

Scott clapped his hands. "It's okay, she'll get it."

I didn't know what would have been better: being there with Scott, or being cheered on by Scott. Even though I knew he'd root for any gymnast from Texas Twisters, there'd have been something so romantic about him watching *my* routines and wanting me to do well.

They didn't show Britt on floor, which was a shame, because she ended her routine with an awesomely high double back into a punch front. They did post her score, however, which I happened to know was a personal best for her. With that number, Britt moved into seventh place. She'd have been higher if not for that mishap on the beam, but at that point it didn't matter. Obviously, you always wanted to win a medal, but the most important thing at this competition was breaking the top fourteen.

Christina's routine on the uneven bars shifted her into sixth place, and then Britt executed two phenomenal vaults to move into fourth. They didn't show Christina's beam routine, even though that was always one of her best events, and today was no different. She posted a score high enough to move into fifth place, just behind Britt. It was proof that, in the current scoring system, big gymnastics often paid off more than stunning artistry. Christina had the long lines and grace, but her difficulty level was low compared to Britt's, so she trailed her, even though Britt had had a mistake on her first routine.

They didn't show Britt's uneven bars routine, either, but it must've been relatively clean, because it was enough to keep her steady at fourth place, but not amazing enough to advance her any higher. Still, fourth place meant that Britt was definitely going to the Junior Nationals, and we all shouted and high-fived each other.

It came down to Christina on the floor, but we weren't worried. Unless she had a disastrously awful routine, there was no way she'd miss making the cut. And although she ended up stepping out of bounds on her first pass, a tucked full-in that was relatively new for her, she easily scored high enough to keep herself in the running, even though she did drop one place in the standings.

The entire webcast took two hours; by the end of it, I felt as drained as if I'd actually competed. I also felt . . . depressed. Watching Christina and Britt out there, getting guidance from Mo and smiling as they saluted the judges, hearing the cheers from the crowd when the girls landed big skills, all made me ache to go to Junior Nationals. I wanted it so badly I almost didn't care anymore about my parents, or about the store, or about how much debt they'd have had to go into to send me. At that moment, I just wanted to compete in Philadelphia, more than anything else in the whole world.

"Well, thanks, Jessie," Scott was saying, picking up his paper plate from the coffee table. A boy who wasn't a complete slob like my brothers! I fell for him all over again. I wondered if I would ever work up the courage to talk to him.

"Thanks, Mrs. Ivy," Scott said to Jessie's mom, who was wiping down the kitchen counter.

Even though I knew that wasn't her name— Jessie's last name was Ivy, but her mom had remarried—she didn't correct Scott. "No problem," she said.

"My laptop is a million years old," Scott said. "I doubt it would've been able to stream this. Watching it on the big screen was pretty cool."

He and Jacob were walking toward the front door, as though they were already leaving. "Are you going to get a new laptop before college?" Jacob was asking. "I've heard that they're just a little important when you have all those term papers or whatever else to write."

And I remembered why it was so hard to talk to Scott: we were in completely different worlds. He was in the world of frat parties and late-night cram sessions, and I was still such a kid. He had goals and was working toward them—going to Nationals, then to college. I didn't know what I was working toward anymore, but at least I didn't feel as powerless as I had just a few weeks ago. I might not have been brave enough yet to talk to Scott, but I was sure that would change soon, too.

Thirteen

It seemed like I'd experienced this moment a thousand times over, every single night as I lay in bed and tried to visualize landing my full-twisting double-back dismount on beam. But nothing prepared me for how good it felt to actually do it, to feel the beam beneath my feet as I pushed off and launched myself high above the mat, my body already twisting, until I landed with my feet firmly planted. I didn't have to windmill my arms at all to keep my balance. I drilled it.

I was smiling so wide that I almost didn't hear Mo's praise. Landing it once in practice didn't mean that I'd nail it like that every time, but from now on it was all about muscle memory. My body had done it once, and so my body could be trained to do it again and again.

On top of that, I was really starting to get my new mount, and I couldn't wait to unveil it. Nationals would've been the perfect place, but now . . . Well, I guessed I would have to see what happened.

Christina and Britt had gotten back from the U.S. Classic all aglow from their competition experiences and pumped up for the Nationals. At that point, I'd completely resigned myself to the fact that I wasn't going. There would be other competitions, other opportunities. There was no point in dwelling on this one.

The deadline to register for a hotel room with the block reserved for our team had already passed, so there was no way around it. My only fear was admitting to Mo that I wasn't competing. She'd been so focused on getting Britt and Christina through the Classic that she hadn't paid as much attention to me, but I knew she thought it was a foregone conclusion that I'd be there representing the gym. I hated to let her down.

My plan had been to to approach Mo after practice, but on my way out of the locker room I spotted Mihai across the floor. He was talking to Christina, waving his arms and gesturing. I headed over to join them, wondering what he could possibly have to say to Christina. It had better not be anything embarrassing about me, like a story about the time he caught me dancing around my bedroom to "I Ran" by Flock of Seagulls. Tata had gotten really into some eighties music when he first came to this country, and sometimes I listened to his old CDs.

Mihai stopped talking when he saw me coming. This seemed very suspicious. I glanced from his face to Christina's, trying to figure out what was going on. "Hey," I said. "What are you doing here?"

Mihai shrugged. "Haven't you heard? Mama and Tata basically put me under house arrest. They're really serious about me not going anywhere but summer school and working at the store. The only way I could get them to let me out of the house was if I promised to ride my bike over here so you'd have some company on the ride home."

"Okay, but I have to talk to Mo first."

For some reason, that made Mihai dart a quick look at Christina. I studied both of them again. Christina had been my friend for a while, but she didn't come over a lot. If we were going to hang out outside of gym, we mostly met up at the mall, or sometimes I would go to her house, where they had cable. So it wasn't like Mihai and Christina had had a lot of opportunity to notice each other. From the phone calls I'd had to field at the house, I knew girls inexplicably seemed to think my brother was cute, and Christina had batted her eyelashes at him a couple of times, although I'd thought she was just being silly. I hoped that wasn't what this was about, because if Christina and my brother liked each other . . . Gross.

"I don't think we have time for that," Mihai said. "If I don't get you home in the next fifteen minutes, Mama's going to think I ran away and send out a search party."

"It's kind of important—" I said, but Christina cut me off.

"I need to talk to Mo, too," she said, "and I was here first."

I was a little taken aback. Hadn't she just been wasting time talking to my brother? Obviously her issue couldn't be *that* important. But when I pointed this out, she waved her hand.

"It's something to do with the Classic," she said. "You understand."

So, basically, because I hadn't competed, I was somehow less important. It was a nice preview of how things would be after the Nationals.

"Come on, Noelle," Mihai said. "Let's get going."

Once outside, Mihai and I unchained our bikes and headed for home. He signaled to me that he wanted to race, and suddenly it was like we were both five years younger, sailing down the streets at breakneck speed, weaving expertly around fire hydrants and other obstacles until we coasted onto the busier street where the store was located. That had always been our unspoken finish line, and as usual, Mihai broke it first.

"You'd think with that workout you do, you'd beat me for once."

"You have longer legs than I do," I pointed out. "And your bike is bigger. You have an unfair advantage."

Mihai laughed as we dumped our bikes in the storage shed behind the store. "Do your coaches listen to those excuses?"

No, they didn't. And I wasn't the type to make excuses, either, even when I had a legitimate one. One time I'd competed through an entire meet with a broken finger, because I didn't want Mo to think I was weak. After the competition, when she saw how purple and swollen my finger was, she told me I should've said something if I was in pain. But when you're a gymnast, some pain is acceptable. It's expected, even. So I'd fought through it.

Now, in this situation with Junior Nationals, I wondered if my parents would feel the same way. They'd been shelling out money for my gymnastics for years. There were the general expenses, like the monthly fees for my training, the equipment, and new leotards. We got some secondhand from other girls in the gym, but there were still times when I needed a new one for a competition. And then there were all the hidden expenses that you might not think about: the Ace bandages, heating pads, ice packs, medical visits, makeup and hair accessories for meets, and gas for travel.

Maybe, to my parents, needing to shell out thousands of dollars for one competition was the equivalent of competing with a broken finger. Sure, it hurt. But it was something you had to deal with, something you just had to find a way to get through, because you knew quitting wasn't an option.

When I rationalized it that way, I wanted to

race through the back door of that store and grab my father and let him make everything right. But the difference was that this time, it wasn't me with the broken finger. It was my parents, and instead of just a finger, it was like their whole hand was hurt. The entire body of our family was breaking down.

"I've really messed things up, haven't I?"

Mihai paused at the door to the storage shed. He'd been fastening the padlock, which we always kept locked even though most of what was in there was just old yard equipment and our bikes.

"Nah," he said. "Nothing that can't be fixed, anyway."

I kicked at the dirt, watching it speckle the toe of my sneaker. "Today was the deadline to register for the hotel," I said. "Which I obviously missed. And I know Mo submitted my name as one of her athletes competing. People are going to be asking where I am, and she's going to have to make excuses for me."

As Mihai had so accurately pointed out, Mo hated excuses, whether she was listening to them or making them herself. She said that excuses were the enemy of the truth.

"Don't worry about it," Mihai said. "It'll all work out."

Of course, Mihai could be nonchalant about everything. That was the way he'd always been. Even now, when he was in more trouble with our parents than ever before, he was still acting like it was no big deal.

"What about you?" I asked. "Did Mama and Tata find out about your job?"

He shot me a sharp look. "No—and I plan to keep it that way. Look, the carnival is only in town for another two weeks. I really need this, so don't blow it, okay?"

I'd never broken a promise in my life, so I was irritated that Mihai would doubt me now. "I said I wouldn't tell, and I won't. But don't you think that it would be better for them to know you're blowing off the store for another job than to think you're just doing it to hang out with your friends?"

"Are you going to tell them about Junior Nationals?"

Why did Mihai always make this comparison? My not telling our parents about the competition was to protect them, especially given all that was happening with the store and our house. The competition just wasn't going to happen, so there was no point in dwelling on it. Mihai's not telling about his job was . . . I didn't know.

I sighed. "You know I'm not," I said. "Anyway, it's too late now."

"Then don't worry about me." Mihai turned to face me as we reached the back entrance of the store, grabbing the handle and pushing against the door with his hip to open it.

"Trust me," he said.

And I did. I had no choice. Throughout my life, whenever there'd been times I felt like I couldn't trust myself, it had always been Mihai I'd put my trust in instead.

During the summer, we got an hour break for lunch in the middle of our training days. Sometimes, I biked home to eat a fresh sandwich from the store and hang out with Tata, but most days, I brought something to the gym and ate it there. At first, the other girls had teased me about my "weird" food, but they'd stopped once they tried some. No one could resist Mama's cooking.

Today, Mama had sent me to gym with a traditional Romanian casserole, Musaca de vinete, in the basket on the front of my bike. I knew that she could tell there was something going on with me, since she usually cooked big meals only for family occasions. Between our family and the store, she already had enough food preparation to worry about. But this morning, she'd wrapped clear cellophane tightly over the top and helped me load it onto my bike, telling me to share it with the other girls and to be sure to tell Mrs. Flores that she said hi.

So, when I saw Britt, Jessie, and Christina already sitting together in the concession area of the gym, I approached their table with the casserole, hoping to catch them before they'd already dug in to their own food. They were leaning over a notebook, where Christina was jotting down notes in between gesturing with her hands. As I came closer, Jessie said something to Christina out of the corner of her mouth, and the notebook disappeared.

"Hey, guys," I said, glancing at Britt, who'd moved the notebook to her lap. "What's up?"

"Nothing," Jessie said, while Britt said, "Oh, the usual."

My eyes darted among the three of them, trying to figure out why they were acting so strangely. "Okay . . . Well, my mother made Musaca de vinete, and I was wondering if you would want to share it." Self-doubt made my voice rise on the last few syllables.

"That sounds awesome," Britt said.

Christina shook her head. "We can't."

"It's mostly vegetables," I said. "And low-fat cheese. So, it's healthy."

"Sorry, Noelle," Jessie said. "We're just, um, kind of busy. Sorry."

The fact that she apologized twice made me very suspicious, along with the fact that I couldn't think of anything that the three of them would need to discuss or do without me. It couldn't be a high school thing, because Britt was there, and she was homeschooled and only going into the eighth grade. It couldn't be a U.S. Classic or Nationals thing, because Jessie was there, and she hadn't qualified for Elite competition yet. My birthday was on Christmas, so it couldn't be planning a surprise party or anything like that.

"Actually, we were just leaving," Christina said. "But your food looks yummy—you should totally enjoy it. We'll see you later, okay?"

Why would I want to eat lunch all by myself? But I just watched as they packed up their stuff, including the mysterious notebook, and I pretended I was totally cool with sitting alone, this giant casserole in front of me as a glaring reminder of my loser status.

I watched them leave, feeling rejected and dejected and depressed. A month ago, I'd been part of a team. I'd had friends who shopped for dresses together. Now, it seemed like I had nothing.

Using one of the plastic sporks I'd grabbed from the concession stand, I dug into the casserole, not bothering to cut off a slice. What was the point? I'd eat a little bit of it, then throw the rest away. I hated to be wasteful, but I wasn't going to let my mother know that my friends had abandoned me.

"Mind if I join you?"

I almost choked when I saw Scott standing over me, gesturing toward an empty chair. I wanted to shout that *of course* it was okay, but my mouth was full, and I wasn't about to gross him out with a vision of my mashed-up food. So I tried to tell him with a closemouthed smile, while continuing to chew, that he was more than welcome to sit down.

He raised his eyebrows, and I finally swallowed my bite.

"Yes," I said, "I mean, no, I don't mind."

He smiled at me. "That looks good. What's in it?"

I listed some of the key ingredients, which led to a discussion of what chard was, exactly, and before I knew it, Scott had a plastic spork of his own and was attacking the opposite side of the casserole. For the moment, the other girls were forgotten; I couldn't believe my luck. Scott Pattison was sitting with *me*! He was eating my mother's casserole! It was practically like we were married.

"So," I said. "You leave tomorrow for your qualifier, right?"

Luckily, he didn't ask why I seemed to know so much. It was common for gymnasts to keep track of each other, so it wasn't completely bizarre for me to know his schedule. Now, if he knew that I could name every single skill he competed in at each event, to the point where I could probably calculate his difficulty levels myself, that might come off a little stalkerish.

"Yeah," he said. "God, I hope I make it. I'm not really worried, though. I've been practicing like crazy all year—first to get that scholarship, then to prepare for the college team, and now for Nationals."

Scott didn't even need Christina's publicity

coach. He obviously knew the art of being confident without appearing cocky. If you worked hard and you earned something, there was no reason not to own it. I realized that that was the position I would've been in had I actually been going to the competition. I'd worked really hard, and I would have expected myself to do well. I guess I didn't expect to give myself the chance.

"Hey." He jabbed at the air with his spork, as though just remembering something. "Didn't you say you had some questions for me about the big meet? 'Cause if you do, shoot. I know the men's competition is a little different, but I'll do what I can to help."

It might've been a good idea to prepare some questions for this situation earlier, considering that I had pestered him twice now to give me this guidance. But first of all, I knew I wasn't going to Nationals, and second of all, I'd never imagined Scott would actually take the time to talk to me.

"Do you have a girlfriend?" I blurted out instead. I could've died.

He blinked but recovered quickly. "Uh . . . no, I don't."

I was itching to ask about the dark-haired mystery girl at the carnival, but again: stalkerish.

I feared I was sprinting down the runway toward Scott's thinking I was totally psychotic, and I tried to think of how to tie this conversation back to gymnastics.

Luckily, Scott did it for me. "Is that what this is about?" he asked. "Do you like someone? Is it messing up your head before the competition?"

"There is someone," I admitted truthfully.

"Well, I can tell you: don't let that boy come between you and your training. This is an important time, and you can't get it back. Don't let a crush make you lose sight of that." He glanced around the gym, craning his neck to look at the group of guys hanging out in the corner by the still rings. "Is it someone here? Is it Jacob?"

I looked over just in time to see Jacob shove his fist underneath his armpit, pumping his arm to make a farting noise that had the other guys slapping their thighs and laughing. Gross. "No, it's not Jacob," I said, and then I took a deep breath. "But it is someone at this gym."

Scott nodded. "In that case, he should understand your commitment as a fellow athlete. It's fine to flirt a little, but you really don't have time to date, not with the biggest competition of your life coming up." As if I needed to be reminded of that. "Is he going to Nationals?"

"He hopes to," I said.

There was a flash of something in Scott's eyes that I couldn't bear to look at, so I stared down at my white fingers gripping the plastic cutlery. "I'm sure that whoever it is," he said slowly, "is very flattered. And I'm also sure that whoever it is cares about you a lot . . . but sees you more as a younger sister."

"Who said he was older?" I said, just to save face. I could feel mine burning up.

"Nobody," Scott admitted with a rueful smile. "You're an amazing athlete, Noelle Onesti, and a very special person. Good luck at Nationals . . . Not that you'll need it."

And then he was getting up and walking away, before I even had time to register the fact that he'd pronounced my last name correctly. My casserole was completely cold, but inside I felt even colder. I guess if I had been honest with myself, I'd always known that there was no way Scott would ever *really* be with me. If there was one thing I'd learned in the past couple of months, it was that there was a big difference between having a pipe dream and having no dream at all.

Fourteen

Usually, I almost dreaded our Sundays off from gym. Don't get me wrong— the rest was welcome after a bone-crunching, muscle-straining, body-pounding week. Once, I'd seen this thing on *60 Minutes* about a football player who was exempt from Monday and Tuesday workouts because he literally couldn't get out of bed after Sunday's game. They showed him covered with ice packs, and then they showed the way he dragged himself around his house, as though walking upright took every last breath. They showed footage of him on Sundays, running full speed into grown men each weighing two hundred and fifty pounds, as though his only goal in life was to crush them.

Most weeks, I could relate. Sure, I was tired and I ached all over from my workouts, but it was all worth it for the adrenaline of sticking that dismount or nailing a release skill on bars. Being away from that environment made me feel somewhat empty. It was as though I was never as much myself as when I was in the gym, and every Monday I breathed in the familiar smell of chalk and sweat as though it were my first time.

But this Sunday, I found myself wishing I never had to go back. First, I had sabotaged my own gymnastics career. Then, my friends had completely deserted me, and although I wanted to play the victim and say I couldn't understand why, I thought I had a good idea. I just wasn't fun anymore. Ever since Mo had handed me that envelope, I'd become a neurotic mess, a tangle of nerves and anxieties that prevented me from enjoying hanging out, or enjoying the carnival or gymnastics. I couldn't blame them for not wanting to be around me—*I* didn't particularly want to be around me.

And then there was that mortifying incident with Scott.

I buried my face in my bedspread, as though the moment were replaying right there in my bedroom and I couldn't stand to see it. Although I'd been awake for hours, I'd been just lying there, my thoughts traveling a pessimistic circle from gymnastics to Scott to my family and my friends and back to gymnastics. And every time I got to the memory of the look on Scott's face when he realized that *he* was the guy I had a crush on . . .

I purposely shoved that from my mind. I had too much else to worry about for the upcoming week. Today, I got to relax, but tomorrow, I had a plan that could change my family's future.

There was a rap on my door before Mihai burst in.

"Don't you knock?"

"I did," he said, which was technically true, although common courtesy usually dictates waiting for a response before barging in. "Get up. Get dressed. There's something you have to see."

I had been looking forward to a day when I didn't change out of my white tank top and my blue shorts with the word TUMBLE across the butt. The plan was to stay in bed until noon, get up for food, bring my lunch back into my room, and then maybe take a postmeal nap until dinnertime or until the twins woke me up, whichever came first. My plan definitely did *not* include leaving the house.

I told Mihai that, but he just ripped the quilt off my bed, leaving me exposed to the cold air. Desperately, I tried to reach for the cover, but he dumped it on the floor.

"Come on," he said. "We're already late."

"Late for what?" I was still annoyed, but I realized I wasn't going to win this battle. Plus, I was actually starting to get a little curious.

"Don't worry about it," he said. "Just hurry up!"

With that, Mihai left, slamming the door behind him. I lay in bed for a few seconds, still debating trying to continue my plan of relaxation, but the window for that had already passed. It was like when you woke up and wanted to hold on to the last lingering remnants of a dream, but it was too late. So I scrambled up and stood in front of my closet, wondering what you wore to such a mysterious event.

In the end, I threw on a pair of shorts and a T-shirt. Mihai wasn't in the apartment; when I went downstairs, he wasn't in the store, either. The whole place was oddly quiet, and I wondered if Mama and Tata had taken the twins to the park or something.

Since the store was open only a half day on Sunday, they usually tried to do something fun like that, to make up for the amount of time the twins spent cooped up in that small apartment during the week.

I found Mihai outside, unchaining our bikes. "Are you going to tell me what this is all about?"

"Nope," he said without a moment's hesitation, and then he was off on his bike, trusting me to follow.

I wondered if Mama and Tata were okay with wherever he was taking me and whatever we were doing. The carnival had left town, which meant that he was back to hanging around the store a lot and sticking closer to home. It seemed to have mollified them a bit, but they still watched him warily, as though at any moment he might go back to sneaking out. For the time being, I guess they just breathed a sigh of relief to see him working at the store, his geometry textbook propped up on the counter for when it was slow and he could cram in some summer-school homework.

He was peddling faster than I'd ever seen him, his feet like whirlwinds as he wended his way down the streets. Even though we hadn't officially announced a race, I was fighting to keep up, flying toward a finish line I couldn't see. It wasn't until we came to a familiar intersection that I guessed our destination.

"The gym?" I asked while we waited for the light to let us cross. "Really? On a Sunday? Mihai, this is really the last place—"

"Trust me," he said, and I had only a second to reflect on the fact that he'd been asking me to do that a lot lately when we got the green light and were off again.

I rarely saw the gym on a Sunday. A few times, when I'd been in the lower levels, we'd had Sunday competitions and would all meet up in the parking lot to carpool to San Antonio or Houston or Fort Worth. Then, the parking lot had been mostly empty, except for a couple of parents' vans or SUVs, the coolers and other supplies spread out over the asphalt as everyone figured out the logistics of who was riding in what car.

Now, there were a ton of cars in the parking lot. They were lined up out into the street, and Mihai and I had to navigate a maze of large vehicles trying to wedge themselves into compact spaces. Finally, we reached the front door of the gym.

"What is this?" I asked. Across the lot, Christina,

Jessie, and Britt were hard at work washing cars. It looked like they were having a fair amount of fun, too. As I watched, Britt took her sponge and demonstrated a "Wax On, Wax Off" move on one of the cars for Jessie, who pretended to karate-chop Britt's outstretched arm.

So this was what they'd been whispering about that day. They'd been planning this car wash, and for whatever reason, they hadn't wanted me to know. I didn't get it. I was a hard worker. I could have washed cars with the best of them. Even though I'd been a bit of a downer lately, I could still have fun. But they hadn't thought to include me.

Mihai hopped off his bike, letting it fall to the sidewalk, but I stayed seated on mine, with one foot on the ground for support. "Great," I muttered. "I don't know how you found out about this, but thanks for showing me. It's just what I needed."

He glanced at me, his brown eyes searching mine. "Don't you get it, Noelle? This is all for you."

And then I looked around me. I mean, *really* looked. I saw the hand-lettered signs: SEND NOELLE TO NATIONALS! I saw Christina directing cars, tearing sheets of paper from a yellow pad to make impromptu receipts. I saw Scott and Jacob and Felicia and others from the gym tackling cars with sudsy water and soft rags (Scott looked adorable in his wet T-shirt and swimming trunks, I couldn't help noticing). I saw Mo standing to one side, smiling in a way I never saw her do in practice. And then I turned around, and I saw my parents.

"I—" I started to say, but couldn't get the words out. This car wash was for *me*?

Mama hugged me fiercely, pressing my face into her shirt. "Why couldn't you tell us?" she asked. "You know we would've done anything to make sure you could follow your dream."

That was exactly what I'd been afraid of, but it all seemed so silly now. "I know," I said. "I'm sorry. . . . I just got tired of holding our family back just because of my dream."

Tata gave my shoulder an affectionate squeeze. "*Our* dream is to see you happy," he said. As always, he didn't have a lot of words, but he had the right ones.

"But the house—" I said. "There has to be a way to get some kind of extension, or break, or something."

"Actually," Mama said, her gaze darting to Tata, as though checking to make sure it was okay to share the news with me, "we've already spoken with the bank, and we were able to work something out."

"We're not going to lose the house? Or the store?"

Mama shook her head. "No," she said. "We're all going to have to live on an even tighter budget, but we can make it work. The bank has agreed to take lower payments for a couple of years, and hopefully the economy will get better in the meantime and things will pick up."

Mama gestured to a group of kids, including the twins, who were jumping through the water from a sprinkler in the grass next to the gym. Mrs. Morgan, Britt's mom, waved to us from where she was watching them.

"And Pam has offered to watch the twins part-time during the day at her daycare, so that will free up more time for me to work in the store," Mama said. "They seem to already love playing with some of her other kids."

"Wow," I said. "That offer might not last, once she sees how crazy they are. I'd use that extra time to go get your nails done or something."

Mostly, I needed to lighten up the situation before I totally broke down. I could feel the tightness in the back of my throat from the flood of emotions I was feeling just then—relief, gratitude, awe. My mother must have sensed it, because she gently pushed me toward the action.

"Go on," she said. "Get in there and get your hands dirty."

First I turned to Mihai. "This was you, wasn't it? You did this."

"Not exactly," he said. "I made you a promise I wouldn't tell Mama and Tata about Junior Nationals, and I didn't. But I did tell Christina, who put this car wash together to raise some money for you to go, and *she* told Mama, so technically, I didn't break my promise."

Mihai dug in his back pocket, pulling out a folded piece of paper. "Also, I went ahead and used my carnie money to buy you a round-trip ticket to Philadelphia. Good thing they gave me extra hours, or else it would've been one way."

I unfolded the paper. It was a confirmation e-mail from an airline, with my name listed as the passenger. I'd never flown on a plane for a competition before, and I couldn't believe I was going to get to now.

I enveloped Mihai in a huge hug, making him stagger back a bit. I could tell he was taken aback by my show of affection, but then he wrapped his arms around me, too.

"You're the best brother ever," I whispered.

He laughed. "You have three other brothers who might have something to say about that. Now, enough of this mushy stuff—you can't let everyone else do the dirty work for your own fund-raiser. Go wash some cars!"

It was almost noon, and the sun was high in the sky. Normally, I found the Texas summer heat oppressive, but today it seemed like the perfect weather to be outside in, hosing down cars and gulping down Gatorade. Jessie and Britt saw me coming toward them and smiled.

"Sorry," Jessie said. "I know we were acting kind of weird before. I hope you get that it was nothing personal. We were trying to keep this on the down low."

I picked up a sponge and wrung it out, adding more water to the puddles that were already gathering under a shiny red truck. "How could I be mad? This is totally awesome. If anything, I'm sorry. I haven't been the best friend lately. I guess I was distracted with all of this stuff."

"It's okay."

Maybe, but that didn't make it right. It occurred

to me that I wasn't the only person who had been going through some stuff this summer, though I'd been so caught up in my own drama that I really hadn't paid much attention to anyone else's.

"When do you leave for your camping trip?" I asked. I remembered that Jessie had been looking forward to the chance to see her dad. It couldn't have been the mosquitos or having to use leaves as toilet paper that had gotten her all excited. Personally, I didn't see the point in roughing it.

Jessie's eyes clouded over, and I immediately wished I could take the question back. "Oh . . . it didn't work out."

It was common knowledge that Jessie's dad flaked out on her a lot, so I wasn't going to bother with any follow-up questions, since I figured that was what had happened. But then Britt cut in, trying to prevent anything that might make Jessie feel worse.

"It's all good, right, Jess?" Britt flicked water from her wet fingers in my direction, and I made a show of wiping the droplets off my arm, although I was smiling. "Now you get to come to Junior Nationals instead and watch us totally rock everyone else off the beam."

Even though Britt was new at the gym, she'd

already become protective of Jessie. Meanwhile, I'd been friends with Christina for years, but rather than tell her what was going on with me, I had shut down and shut her out. And yet, she'd arranged all of this, because she knew I needed help.

I tried to catch Christina's gaze, but she was on the other side of the parking lot talking to a woman with big hair whom I didn't recognize. Then Britt nudged me, gesturing toward someone getting out of a dark blue hatchback.

"Hey," she said. "Isn't that David?"

He was scanning the parking lot, clearly looking for someone, and a couple of weeks earlier, I would've ducked out of sight. But now, for some reason, I felt my heart lift a little at seeing him. The sun was glinting off his glasses in a dorkier version of the classic slow-motion shot of an action star walking in the light, and he was wearing a *Star Wars* shirt and jeans with a hole in one knee.

"He might be here for an encore of his performance at the dance," Britt said, wiggling her eyebrows. "Want me to be bounce him? I could be, like, your security."

"No," I said absently. Whoever was driving the car he'd come in had pulled around to the line of cars waiting for a wash, and David was standing in the middle of it all now, his hands in his pockets. I handed my sponge to Britt without looking to see if she had a grip on it, accidentally soaking the front of her shirt more than it already was.

"Guess not," she said, but I was already walking off toward David. He finally spotted me and met me halfway.

"Hi," he said.

"Hi."

And then there was awkward silence for a moment, until I said, "Look, I'm sorry— "

"This is really—" he started to say at the same time; he laughed. "Go ahead."

"Okay." I took a deep breath. "I'm sorry I kind of blew you off before. It's just that I'm not used to this sort of thing, and—"

"And you don't like me that way," he finished for me. "It's okay, Noelle. I get it. You have a lot going on right now. I think you're really cool and smart and sweet, and I wanted to let you know that I'm willing to settle for being your friend. I saw on the news that your friends were doing this fund-raiser, and I thought, I want to be her friend, too. I want to do anything I can to help you get to Nationals."

This was a lot to process, but one thing he'd said especially stuck out, and I felt the need to address that first. "The news?" I said. "What are you talking about?"

"Channel Thirteen." Seeing my blank expression, he explained, "They advertised this car wash last night, telling people to come out and support a local gymnast. It was a follow-up to that interview you guys did. You were great in that, by the way."

I still hadn't had a chance to view that piece, although I knew that Jessie had recorded it on her DVR, and Britt had probably uploaded it to the internet already. I wasn't sure I ever wanted to see it. The idea of having to watch myself, hear my own voice, made me shudder.

Glancing over at Christina, I realized now who she was standing with. It was Lyla Quin, the reporter who'd done that interview with us. I wanted to go over there and thank them both for everything, but first there was something else I had to do.

Before I could second-guess myself (because if I'd waited even a second, I definitely would've chickened out), I stood on my tiptoes and gave David a quick kiss on the cheek.

He immediately turned as red as the Camaro

behind him, raising his a hand to the spot where my lips had been. "What was that for?" he said, a goofy smile on his face.

I didn't want to look over at Scott, in case David followed my gaze and got the wrong idea. But I could picture him—his perfect teeth, blue eyes, the way his hair curled a little bit at the nape of his neck if he hadn't had a haircut in a while. And I realized that that was all Scott had ever been to me—a picture in my head. It was beautiful, but it wasn't real. I knew all this trivia about Scott Pattison, like what ankle he'd sprained before and what movie he'd seen three times in the theater, but I didn't really know *him*.

I didn't know David, either, but I wanted to.

"I still can't do this right now," I said, which had to be the most awkward thing anyone could possibly say after kissing, but I hoped he understood. I'd needed to make the gesture.

"That's cool," he said. "Can we talk when you get back from Nationals?"

I nodded, not trusting myself to say anything else.

"Awesome," he said. "That way, I'll be able to say I'm hanging out with a national champion."

I lightly slapped his stomach, and even though I mostly got his shirt and barely tapped him, I still felt a small thrill. This was flirting! I was doing it! "Don't jinx me," I said.

"Impossible," he said, and I realized that even though David's teeth weren't as straight or white as Scott's, he had a very nice smile. Better, even, in some ways. When Scott looked at me, I thought about what an amazing person he was, but when David looked at me, it was like he was telling me how amazing *I* was. Maybe it was self-centered of me, but it felt good to be reminded of that once in a while.

I tried several times to connect with Christina, but it seemed like she was always busy collecting donations from people or showing them where to go. Finally, she came over to me. She had Lyla Quin with her.

"You remember Lyla, right?" Christina asked. I couldn't believe how casually she said the reporter's name, like they were bosom buddies.

"Of course," I said. "The interview you did was great." I figured this was not the time to mention that I hadn't seen it yet.

"I just want to do a follow-up," Lyla said, her

bright red lips stretching into a smile as she held out her hand. I shook it, feeling very grown-up.

"Thanks to Lyla, this fund-raiser's been a huge success," Christina said. "So far, we have more than enough to pay registration fees and the cost of your team leotard, warm-up suit, and duffel bag."

Lyla was smoothing her hair, although it didn't look any less poufy than when she'd first walked up. "Your friend is very enterprising."

Christina shrugged. "My publicity coach actually helped a lot," she said to me. "I asked her how I could get a good turnout for something like this, and she set up the thing with Channel Thirteen where they would advertise the event. Lyla said the station got a ton of e-mails from people wishing us all luck after her first interview, so people were eager to help you get to Nationals."

Lyla was gesturing now to her cameraman, the same guy who'd come out with her on her earlier visit to the gym. "I hate to rush y'all, but can I have you two move here? I want to get all the cars in the background, so we should get this shot while it's as busy as it is."

Christina and I moved to face the gym, the car wash at our backs. I realized I hadn't yet gotten to talk to Christina personally, which is what I really wanted to do, but Christina was already getting ready for the camera with her biggest smile and a toss of her hair.

Lyla nodded at the cameraman to begin rolling. "Well, y'all, we're back with our favorite local gymnasts." It was weird how she sounded the same, and yet different. It was like she took her normal voice but put this television spin on it that made it a little louder, her words enunciated more precisely. "Today we're at the Texas Twisters gym, where there's a car wash being held to raise money to send one promising gymnast to the Junior Nationals in a couple of weeks."

And even though I'd been expecting it, I still felt thrown off when Lyla actually turned to me. "Noelle, this fund-raiser is all for you. How does it feel to know you have so much community support?"

I tried to think about Christina's publicity coach, and the advice she might have given me on how to answer this question, but it all just flew out of my head. And I realized that I didn't need it. I knew exactly how to respond.

"It's awesome," I said. "I was having a hard time

believing in myself, and knowing that so many people believe in me . . . It really inspires me. You interviewed me before and asked me about gymnastics being such an individual sport, even though we may compete for our gym or our country. But I think this shows how team-oriented it is."

I was trying not to cry, because I didn't want to be a baby on television, but I had to clear my throat before I turned to Christina. "You're my best friend in the whole world," I said. "I can't thank you enough for all of this."

And then Christina was crying and hugging me, and I could feel the wetness in my own eyes, but I no longer cared about what anyone else might think. I was going to Junior Nationals, where I was going to do my absolute best to show everyone that their faith in me wasn't misplaced. I was going to travel to Philadelphia with the most incredible friends a girl could possibly ask for, and we were going to have the time of our lives. I'd woken up that morning feeling empty, and now my heart felt so full it could have burst.

Fifteen

Junior Nationals didn't go the way any of had expected. Britt rolled her ankle on her floor routine on the first night of all-around competition and couldn't finish, which meant that she didn't qualify for event finals on one of her best events. Even though she taped up the ankle and was able to finish that night and the next, she wasn't in top form.

Christina fared a little better, placing ninth all around and qualifying for event finals on floor and bars. Finishing in the top ten meant that she had a chance to go to a camp that would help determine the final team of girls who'd compete in international competitions for the United States.

I'd be going with her to that camp, because I finished fifth all-around. Since the World team would consist of six members, as long as I proved myself to Coach Piserchia at the camp, I had a pretty good shot at making that team. I was still disappointed that I'd placed outside of the medals, but as David had pointed out in a congratulatory text message, it was pretty awesome to be one of the top five gymnasts in the country.

I really wished I had my own cell phone, so I wouldn't have to explain to my mother who it was that I kept texting back and forth. She'd teased me about it all through the team dinner we'd had the night before, which had turned out to be superdelicious Philly cheese steak sandwiches. Of course, Britt and Christina and I had eaten the meat and cheese without any bread, but they'd been tasty and not that expensive. Tomorrow, after the pressure of the competition was over, we were going to tour the historical parts of the city—where they had signed the Declaration of Independence and where Benjamin Franklin had lived, all for free or for a small donation. It was going to be so much fun.

* * *

Now it was the night of event finals. Britt had earned a silver on vault; Christina won a bronze on bars. It was my turn to go up on the beam.

I waited for the signal from the judges. Once the head judge lifted the green flag, I raised both my arms in a salute and forced myself to smile. Normally, I stayed pretty cool in competitions, but this time I knew the stakes were high and couldn't convince my body otherwise. This was the biggest competition of my life; I'd been through a lot to get here, and this was my last chance at a medal. My nerves were buzzing like a downed electrical wire.

I jumped into the first neckstand of my new mount, feeling my muscles stretch as I straddled my legs. Using my shoulders, I spun to face in the opposite direction, repeating the skill until it was like I was twirling around the beam, my legs scissoring straight and then straddling. I could hear a hush come over the audience, and I knew that this mount was something special. I wondered about my mother, sitting up in the stands and supporting me, and I hoped she knew that this mount was my way of saying I loved her. Every time I spun around that beam, the same way she'd done so many years ago, I was saying, *Thank you.*

I lowered myself to the beam and got to my feet, ready to launch right into my acrobatic series. The crucial part of the whole thing was making sure I connected the skills. I would earn bonus points on my score for starting my tumbling immediately after my feet came down from the handstand. Usually, it wasn't a problem; I'd been doing handstands on the beam since I was six years old, and keeping my balance was second nature. But on a stage this huge, you just never knew. Anything could happen.

But not this time. It was just like in practice. The balls of my feet touched down on the beam, and I barely felt my heels skim the surface as I threw my body backward into my first element: four layout-step-outs in a row, my feet coming down together squarely on the beam, one slightly in front of the other. Now this part was over, but I still had a little more than a minute left to go. When you're up there on that four-inch-wide beam, with the judges and thousands of spectators all watching you, a minute can feel like an eternity.

I had to get through a few dance elements and leaps before my next big skill, which included the mandatory full turn. Lifting one leg up until it was parallel to the beam, my toes pointed and my knee perfectly straight, I spun 360 degrees on the other foot. My heel came down hard on the beam as I stopped my momentum, but I didn't wobble. I allowed myself to let out a breath I hadn't even known I was holding.

Moves like that are sometimes more difficult than the really flashy ones. When you go to do something major on the beam, you prepare yourself for it. You slow down for just a second, square your shoulders, and imagine feeling your hands grabbing that beam the instant before it actually happens. If you make it, you feel energized. If you don't, you're disappointed in yourself, but at least you fall on something impressive.

But a full turn can be deceptive. It's relatively simple; it's something you've been doing since your compulsory routines in the lower levels. It's easy to rush through it, because you're already thinking ahead to the punch front with the blind landing you're about to do, or the illusion that's been giving you trouble in practice, where you keep kicking one leg up but can't get the complete circle you're supposed to get without touching your hand to the ground. If you make the full turn, you don't care.

Of course, you think. But if you don't make it, you suddenly find yourself standing on the mat with no idea how you got there. For the rest of the night, you think, *how could I have done that?*

The only big skill I had left before my dismount was a punch front, where I tucked my body into a front flip, the landing totally blind. I executed it cleanly, dancing my way to the end of the beam for my dismount.

This was it. I knew I'd had a good routine, and although I tried not to let myself think about the other gymnasts or the standings or the score, I couldn't help feeling hope blossom inside me while I stood there. My hands were rigid at my sides, my fingers pointed in toward my thighs as I touched my foot to the back of the beam, everything so familiar, even in this strange setting. And then I was launching myself into my round-off, and I knew I had the momentum. My back handspring was powerful, and I felt weightless as my feet left the beam for good. At that point, muscle memory took over, and I was spinning in the air, completing a full twist as my body spun in the first of two flips. And then my feet hit the mat.

It was a stuck landing. I threw my arms over my head in a salute, and this time I didn't have to force a smile. I knew it was one of the best routines I'd ever done.

Mo was waiting for me as I stepped down from the podium; she pressed me to her in a quick hug. It only lasted a second or two, but Mo rarely gave hugs, so I enjoyed the feeling of her hands squeezing my back, telling me before she even said the words that she was proud of me. "Good job," she said. "Good job."

Britt and Christina came to congratulate me, both wearing their warm-ups over their leotards. It was cold in the arena, and normally I would've put on my jacket immediately after finishing my routine, but my adrenaline was so high that I felt warm all over. Britt gave me a fist bump, and Christina wrapped one arm around me.

"You rocked it!" she said, and I put my arm around her waist to draw her closer.

"I couldn't have done it without you guys," I said, pulling Britt into a group hug.

And then came the hardest part: the waiting. Even though I'd had the routine of my life, there was a little voice inside telling me not to be too confident, that you never knew what the judges would do. It was possible they'd seen some minor bend of a knee here, or slight balance check there. Or maybe I hadn't connected two skills as fluidly as I needed to in order to get my bonus. Anything could happen.

Without having to search too hard, I found my family in the stands. I'd avoided glancing up at them too often during the competition, since I was worried that even a small wave from my brother or a smile from my mom would distract me. But now that it was all over, I allowed myself to look.

Only Mama and Mihai had been able to make the trip; it had been difficult enough to afford two extra tickets, much less the six that would have been needed to fly the whole family out.

I saw Mama standing up, clutching Mihai's hand in a tight grip, and I knew from the way her face looked all soft and shimmery that she was crying. Not in a sad way—more how she looked when the twins made her Mother's Day cards, or when Radu kissed her cheek in front of his friends. Mihai gave me a sheepish look like, *Sorry, you can't take her anywhere*, but he seemed different, too, as if he might explode from the force of his smile.

In that moment, I knew, even before they

flashed my score of 9.8. I knew it from the expressions on Mama's and Mihai's faces and the cheers of my teammates next to me. I'd won the gold medal. I was officially the best beam worker in the entire country, but even if I'd fallen, even if I'd gone home empty-handed, I knew that I still would've been the luckiest girl in the world.

Gymnastics glossary

acrobatic series: On the balance beam, at least three connected acrobatic or tumbling elements in a row from one end of the beam to the other.

aerial: A cartwheel done without the use of hands for support on the floor.

all-around competition: The part of a competition where gymnasts compete in all four events, and in which their combined scores are used to determine who is the best all-around athlete.

arabesque: A dance element in which one leg is on the floor and one leg lifted backward toward the ceiling to form an extended line.

Arabian: A skill where the gymnast jumps backward, as though to perform a backflip, then does a half twist in the air to execute a front flip, and lands facing forward. A *double Arabian* is a skill that involves two flips in the air instead of one.

beam: A horizontal, raised apparatus that is four inches wide, sixteen feet in length, and approximately four feet off the floor; on this, gymnasts perform a series of dance moves and acrobatic skills.

blind landing: A landing in which the gymnast ends up facing forward, sometimes away from the apparatus, and she cannot see the floor before landing.

dance elements: Required dance sections of the routine that are done on the balance beam and used to connect acrobatic skills and leaps.

difficulty level: A way of measuring what a skill is worth in the gymnastics code of points, or how hard a skill is to execute.

event finals: The part of a competition during which the gymnasts with the highest preliminary scores on an apparatus compete to determine the best gymnast in each event.

floor: A carpeted surface measuring forty feet square, over springs and wooden boards. Also the term for the only event in which a gymnast performs a routine set to music; the routine is ninety seconds in length, and composed of dance and acrobatic elements.

full-in: Two flips in the air with the first flip featuring a 360-degree twist.

full turn: A 360-degree turn on one leg, performed on floor and beam.

grips: Strips of leather placed on a gymnast's hand to prevent calluses and allow for a better grip on the uneven bars.

handspring: A move in which a gymnast starts on both feet, jumps to a position supporting her body with just her two hands on the floor, and then pushes off to land on her feet again. This can be done forward or backward, and is typically used to start or connect an acrobatic series.

illusion: A turn requiring a lot of flexibility, starting with one leg high in the air; the gymnast swings her lifted leg in a circle, keeping her body in a straight position and creating the appearance of a front flip.

Junior Elite: The level before Senior Elite, as designated by regulations of the governing body of gymnastics. Junior Elite gymnasts are not allowed to compete in the Olympics.

layout: A maneuver completed in the air with hands held against the body and a pencil-straight overall position; flipping can be forward or backward, and the move ends with the gymnast standing on both feet again.

parallel bars: One of six apparatuses in men's artistic gymnastics. The parallel bars are much like the women's uneven bars in that there are two bars, but instead of one being high and one being low, they are at the same height and closer together.

pike: A position in which the body is bent double at the hips, with legs straight and toes pointed.

pommel horse: One of six apparatuses in men's artistic gymnastics. The pommel horse is a padded, nearly cylindrical apparatus similar to the old-fashioned vaulting horse, which has two graspable pommels on top. The gymnast performs a series of balancing, swinging, and rotating maneuvers to earn his score.

press handstand: A move beginning on the floor with legs in a straddle position and all of the weight on the hands. The entire body is raised over the head and moves from a straddle position into a straight-body handstand.

punch front: A jump from a position on both feet into a forward-flipping somersault in which the gymnast lands again on both feet, still facing forward.

release skill: Any skill performed on the uneven bars that requires the gymnast's hands to leave the bar before returning to it, usually after a twisting or flipping skill has been executed.

round-off: A move that begins like a cartwheel, but in which the legs swing together overhead, and the gymnast finishes facing in the opposite direction.

scale: A position in which one leg is raised high into the air while the other leg is firmly planted on the ground. Ideally, this position ends in a 180-degree vertical split.

Senior Elite: The level after Junior Elite, as designated by regulations of the governing body of gymnasts. In women's artistic gymnastics, a gymnast must be turning sixteen years of age within the calendar year during which the competition takes place to become a Senior Elite.

sheep jump: A move in which the gymnast jumps into the air, throws her head back until it touches her feet for a split second, and then returns to a straight-body position to land on both feet.

split: A position in which one leg is stretched in front of the body and the other behind.

standing full twist: A move that begins in a stationary position on both feet, followed by a jump into a flip with a 360-degree twist in the air (usually in a tucked position with legs bent at a 90-degree angle) before a landing on both feet. Typically, this move is completed on floor or beam.

still rings: One of the six apparatuses in men's artistic gymnastics. Two rings are suspended from cables, and the gymnast must use them to perform a series of strength maneuvers, holding himself high off the ground, while controlling the movement of the rings, which are meant to remain as still as possible.

straddle: A position in which the right leg is stretched out to the right side of the body and the left leg is stretched out to the left, as the gymnast faces forward.

stuck dismount: A move in which a gymnast executes a landing with both feet firmly planted on the ground and no wobbling occurs.

tuck: A position in which the knees are folded in toward the chest at a ninety-degree angle, with the waist bent, creating the shape of a ball.

tumbling passes: A series of connected acrobatic moves required in a floor-exercise routine.

twist: A rotation of the body around the horizontal and vertical axes. Twisting is completed when a gymnast is flipping simultaneously, performing both actions at the same time in the same element. Twisting elements are typically named for the number of rotations completed (e.g., a half twist is 180 degrees, or half a rotation; a full twist is 360 degrees, or a full rotation; and a double twist is 720 degrees, or two complete rotations).

uneven bars (often, just "bars"): One of four apparatuses in women's artistic gymnastics. Bars features the apparatus on which women perform mostly using their upper-body strength. This event consists of two rails placed at an uneven level; one bar acts as the high bar and the other as the low bar. Both bars are flexible, helping the gymnast to connect skills from one to the other.

vault: A runway of approximately eighty feet in length, leading to the springboard and a padded table at one end. The gymnast runs full speed toward the table, using the springboard to launch herself onto it; she then pushes off with her hands, moving into a series of flips and/or twists before landing on the mat behind the table.

walkover: A basic gymnastics skill where the gymnast either arches backward (for a back walkover) or leans forward (for a front walkover), places her hands on the mat to lift herself into a handstand, and holds a split position before "walking" each foot back to the ground.

Yurchenko vault: A vaulting move that begins with a round-off onto the springboard, followed by a back handspring onto the table; the gymnast then pushes off into a series of flips and/or twists before landing on the mat. This style of vault was named after Soviet gymnast Natalia Yurchenko.

Don't miss the rest of the

★ GO-for-GOLD ★ GYMNASTS series!

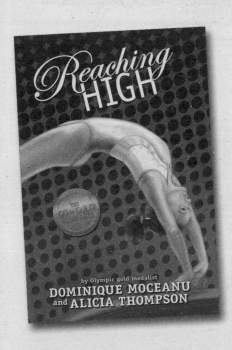